MEET THE AUTHOR

TEASERS,
TRAILERS & MORE...

Also by Sandra A. Miller

Trove: A Woman's Search for Truth and Buried Treasure

WEDNESDAYS AT
ONE

SANDRA A. MILLER

Zibby Books
New York

Zibby Books, colophon and associated logos are trademarks and/or registered trademarks of Zibby Books LLC

This book is a work of fiction. Names, characters, places, historical events, and incidents are the product of the author's imagination or are used fictitiously. Any resemblance to actual persons, living or dead, events or locales is entirely coincidental.

Library of Congress Control Number: 2022942885
ISBN: 979-8-9852828-6-3
eBook ISBN: 979-8-9862418-8-3

Book design by Ursula Damm
Cover design by Emily Mahon
www.zibbybooks.com

Printed in the United States of America
10 9 8 7 6 5 4 3 2 1

For Phineas and Adeline

What if you slept
And what if
In your sleep
You dreamed
And what if
In your dream
You went to heaven
And there plucked a strange and beautiful flower
And what if
When you awoke
You had that flower in your hand
Ah, what then?

—Samuel Taylor Coleridge

1

Gregory's garage exuded a comforting reek of bone meal, rusty tools, and the waft of gasoline from his father's old red lawn mower. As he inhaled the familiar cocktail, his shoulders unlocked, his breathing slowed. The cool dark atmosphere answered to an ache inside him. He was more relaxed here in this dilapidated carriage house at the base of the long, sloped driveway than anywhere in the imposing Victorian up the hill. Originally his wife's childhood home, the house on Ashford Street in Cambridge, Massachusetts, had never, not once in the past decade of actually living in it, felt like home to him.

After seeing eight clients in as many hours, the smells in the garage calmed him. So did his routine of sitting on the rickety bench to put on his worn work boots, surrounded by a hodge-podge of terra-cotta pots, swathes of bird netting, and a bouquet of shovel blades and rake tines rising out of a whiskey barrel. The garage, which he refused to call a carriage house, always soothed him but never more so than on an early summer evening like this one, when a broad shaft of light poured through the west-facing window and cast a rosy glow across the concrete floor.

Although he was eager to start digging a new strawberry bed, Gregory stayed seated for another moment to make his daily appeal: *Forgive me. Please, forgive me.*

He didn't even know if it was possible anymore or whether he would recognize the feeling of his guilt lifting, if only for a few fleeting seconds. But he never stopped praying for it.

As Gregory opened his eyes, he saw someone peering at him through the dusty glass of the window. He stumbled backward, catching himself on the coarse edge of the barrel. Those eyes with their penetrating gaze. Did he know them?

"Hello?"

But the eyes were gone. No doubt he'd simply seen his own reflected in the glass. He put his hand over his racing heart and exhaled in relief. Then he grabbed the nearest shovel and bolted outside.

Gregory walked briskly across the paved driveway that divided the gracious, circular lawn into two green hemispheres. Behind him, on the west side, a grove of old pines formed a shady path from the back door of his garage up to the house. On the east side of the driveway, Gregory's perennial gardens created a bright border around the much-coveted property—a rare, sunny double lot across the river from Boston and not a mile from Harvard Square. In the middle of the lawn, he had planted a sizable vegetable garden surrounded by marigolds. He couldn't be sure the flowers served their purpose of repelling critters, but he still loved the bright orange frame of blooms and their deep spicy scent.

Gregory stood at the spot where he planned to extend the bed and lifted his shovel. He soon fell into a rhythmic digging, piercing the earth hard with the blade. He rarely wore the canvas gloves Liv kept buying and leaving for him on the garage's cracked granite entry step. It was a small protest against what he felt was a passive-aggressive gesture. Liv cared more about his dirty fingernails than what was going on in his head. And when was the last time she'd actually held his hand? "Your nails are a mess!" she chided at least once a week in the summer months, usually as they were heading to the club for their regular Saturday night dinner. But Gregory liked the musty smell of loam seeping into his palms, the dirt lodged under his nails, his blistered hands breaking through the dullness of their overly scrubbed life.

As he made progress on the strawberry bed, he began to feel better. The sky was that vivid June blue, the color moments before the gold shot of sunset, and it charged him with energy. He even felt a bit horny; not an immediate, teenage horniness but an ache for something he and Liv had lost long ago, an unapologetic lust he once believed was inexhaustible. Gregory thought of his wife's legs, muscled from tennis and swimming, and the sweet softness between them. In the beginning, their lovemaking was constant. They would fall into bed and press themselves together. It was an escape for him, both an answer to a question about his own moral worth and a respite from the darkness that lurked in his memory. Those early years with Liv felt so far away now, as unrecoverable as the idea that he could be a present, loving husband to her and a dedicated father to Carrie and Petey. A happy family of four in that moss-green Victorian with scalloped shingles and cheerful coral trim.

He hadn't been sleeping well and had been devoting his evenings to working in the garden, tending the established beds or building new ones. Meanwhile, Liv spent most of her free time playing tennis at the club, Carrie was always at some friend's house, and Petey was glued to his video games. Under that precariously steep mansard roof, inside the maze of twelve white rooms, they were all living separate lives.

Gregory released the shovel and got down on his knees to work. He pulled at the loosened sod with his torn-up hands, stopping to bite a leaf of garlic mustard and let the bitterness fill his mouth.

"Bye, Dad!" said Carrie, phone in hand, strolling down the driveway. She was dressed in ripped jean shorts that squeezed her thighs and a yellow T-shirt, practically see-through. But he was not allowed to comment, let alone advise. Carrie was short like Liv, but not petite, and had none of her mother's finely cast features. Those went to her little brother—blond, thirteen-year-old Petey. Carrie's physical legacy was Gregory's: strong nose, brown eyes, and thick dark hair, which she had twisted loosely in a bun on top of her head. She was almost seventeen but looked younger, no matter what she wore.

"Where are you headed, honey?" he called out.

Carrie approached steadily, her thumbs frantically texting. "I'm getting bubble tea with a friend," she said. She smiled at something she'd read on her phone and passed him without a glance.

"Which friend?"

This question stopped her; she had to think.

"Someone from school. You don't know her."

Gregory hoped that bubble tea was the only thing she would be drinking that night.

"What time are you coming home?"

"Dunno! I start work tomorrow, so this is, like, my last night of freedom all summer."

He got to his feet and opened his arms. Too late. She was already walking toward the street again.

"Wait, don't I get a hug goodbye?"

"Huh?" She looked back and seemed surprised. "Oh. I'm kind of in a hurry."

"Then I'm going to give *you* a hug."

Gregory took a few giant steps toward her, awkwardly put an arm around his daughter's sturdy shoulders, and pulled her close.

He felt her resistance before she briefly relaxed into the embrace. He was trying, he told himself. Wasn't that what Liv wanted? For him to make more of an effort?

"Have fun," he said and released her.

"Thanks, Dad."

"Hey, Carrie?"

She paused, her head cocked with impatience. "What's up?"

"Were you looking in the garage window a while ago? I mean, did you happen to glance in?"

"Why would I do that?" she said. "You ask the weirdest questions."

"That's my job," he said, but she didn't laugh.

As Carrie headed out past the spruce stands bracketing their property, a woman in a bright sundress appeared on the far side of the street. Not unusual in this neighborhood, where people liked to walk on summer evenings. But there was something different about her, the way she hesitated for a moment and seemed to throw him a brief glance. Although he couldn't distinguish her features from such a distance, Gregory thought again of the eyes in the garage window. Could they have been this woman's? He shook off the idea and tried to peer more closely through the fading light.

At first, he thought he knew her, or maybe she was looking for Liv. His wife was acquainted with the families in every home for blocks. But this wasn't a Liv person. Liv people moved with purpose, while this woman had a slow, modulated grace not typical of either evening power walkers or commuters rushing home from the nearby bus stop.

He wondered if he should wave, but then she disappeared. She was probably just admiring the purple hydrangeas that had recently begun to bloom.

On the way back to his garden, Gregory spied Liv's latest offering: gray suede gloves with rubbery green accents on the fingers and thumbs. Some kind of green thumb joke?

Whatever the message, Gregory put them on. He couldn't pick up that shovel again without some protection for his torn skin, and he was determined to finish digging the strawberry bed. He needed to be able to fall asleep and stay that way until morning. And if Liv happened to look out the window, it wouldn't hurt for her to witness him accepting one of her kindnesses, because he would not be going back into that house before dark.

2

The following day, just before one o'clock, Gregory opened his office door and ushered out his noon client. Fifty minutes every Wednesday with Eleanor S. and her narcissistic personality disorder left him depleted. Worse, he had once again slept poorly last night.

He decided he had earned a walk to Chinatown for dumplings, but there was a woman sitting in the waiting room. He couldn't remember scheduling a new client. Was she in the wrong office?

She was hunched over a copy of *The New Yorker*, so engaged with the text that she hadn't looked up when his office door opened. Her magenta scarf had slipped down, revealing the strap of a sleeveless orange dress. Only after Eleanor S. had closed the waiting room door behind her and Gregory remained standing, hands by his side, did she lift her head.

Her eyes were chocolate brown, and her easy smile seemed genuine, suggesting a friend delighted by the arrival of her lunch date.

"Hello," she said, her voice so warm that Gregory half expected her to stand and hug him.

"I …" he started. "Are you here for Dr. Bodkin? I'm afraid he's not in today." Phillip Bodkin, his mentor and friend who had the lease on the suite, was never in on summer Wednesdays, but perhaps he'd made an exception to his weekly round of golf at the club.

The woman stood as if cued, ignoring his question. The magenta scarf drifted down her arms, revealing the rest of the dress, a summer shift that suggested curves without clinging to them. She approached him unencumbered, no purse, no phone, nothing left on the table except the copy of *The New Yorker*. Everything about her was vibrant; against the beige backdrop of the waiting room, she seemed to emit a radiant glow.

"Dr. Weber?" She extended her hand. "I'm Mira. Thank you for making time for me."

When they shook, gripping longer than was customary, he felt like he was tacitly agreeing to something, but he didn't know what. He noticed a pale scar running from her nose to the corner of her lip.

He wanted to tap open his calendar to see if he had scheduled this Mira months ago and overlooked the appointment. He typically tried not to book anything in his one free hour in the middle of the workweek, but he had made some scheduling mistakes recently, an issue he attributed to his problems with Liv and sleep deprivation. But to completely forget an appointment with someone new? This was a first.

Perhaps she was the mother of one of his young adult clients, and they had planned this meeting to discuss the child's progress. He didn't think so. Those mothers approached with a mix of pleading and terror, a desperate hope that this particular mental health expert, with a PhD and twenty years of clinical experience, could extricate their child from a vortex of angst or anxiety, often both. This Mira seemed untroubled. Agelessly beautiful, in that range between twenty-five and forty, she was possibly the most composed person who had entered his office in years.

"Come in, Mira," he said, stepping aside. When she passed, he got a faint scent of her—mint and maybe a whiff of smoke.

Instead of waiting for him to indicate a seat, Mira settled herself in his black ergonomic chair and leaned back. The chair was spun away from Gregory's mahogany desk, which was pushed against the wall. The positioning allowed him to face his clients without an imposing piece of furniture separating them. But now Mira was the one facing him.

He wanted to ask her to switch chairs, but instead he half perched on the armrest of one of the two dark green wing chairs and considered how to proceed. That's when he realized that in addition to his not even knowing her last name or how she ended up in his office, she hadn't brought in the seven forms he emailed to every new person before their first session. She must have forgotten them. Or had he forgotten to send the email?

"Mira," he said, trying to steady his voice. "I'd like to have you start by filling out a few intake forms. And please remind me who referred you?"

She focused her gaze on him. "You did. You asked me to come see you."

Gregory pinched his lips together and drew back. Had he really? Because he didn't remember. But he wasn't going to tell her that. "Right. So let's get you started on those forms," he said. "If you'll excuse me." He tried to indicate with a nod that he needed access to his desk, but Mira had already lowered her head.

"Perhaps I can fill them out after our session?" she said. "This is a big step for me, and I'm eager to dive in."

He knew he should ask her to move, but the combination of his bewilderment and her beauty made him ignore protocol, at least for another few minutes. He had already forgotten that she was coming in, and he didn't want to do anything else that would make her feel unwelcome or uncomfortable or—possibly worse—reveal his confusion. He tried to keep his face neutral, tranquil, his body language inviting her to stay, although in truth she showed no actual signs of wanting to leave, which was a relief.

"After our session is fine," he said, "but—"

"Thank you, Greg. I appreciate that," Mira said. "Is it okay if I call you Greg?" Her voice was soft and musical. A slight rasp sanded the corners of her words.

"I... I suppose." He couldn't remember when anyone except his family had called him Greg, probably not since graduate school, and he shifted at the memory of a nearly forgotten self. He cleared his throat. "Now tell me how you're doing."

"Oh, I'm fine." She shuddered lightly and pulled the scarf tight to her shoulders. "I love summer, but I'm not a fan of air-conditioning. My parents grew up in New Delhi and never let us get one."

"Yes. Isn't that why we live in New England, because we like interesting weather?" he said. "Unfortunately, most of my clients expect air-conditioning." He rose off the armrest. "Let me turn it down. The temperature control is just in the waiting room." While he was out there, he figured he could type *Mira* into his contacts to see if she was there. But she waved the offer away.

"I have my wrap. Let's not waste any more time. I've waited so long to see you."

He dropped into the wing chair. *How* long?

He must have scheduled her months ago. Unless there was another Dr. Gregory Weber in the Boston area and she was at the wrong address. Unlikely, but not impossible.

Mira slowly crossed one long leg over the other. As she rested her left hand on her knee, Gregory noticed she wasn't wearing a wedding ring, just three thin silver bracelets that jangled like chimes when she moved.

"Were you not expecting me?" Mira said. She had a playful look in her eyes that unnerved him even more.

"Oh, no," he said, feeling his face flush, despite the cold room. "I'm just recalibrating after a busy morning."

Recalibrating? What is wrong with me? Gregory wondered. He had treated dozens of attractive women over the years, including a famous Hollywood actress and a female model who regularly appeared on the covers of glossy magazines in the grocery store checkout line, but none that threw him off his game like this Mira. He had a substantial client list, filled his calendar with referrals, and was known to have an impeccable reputation as a clinician. So why was he feeling this out of control? It wasn't only her beauty but her poise and unapologetic certainty that she belonged there. Her intensity left no room for him to gather his thoughts. He ran through various possibilities for who, if not a client, she might be. A teacher from the kids' school? A new member at the club? A neighbor? One of Liv's walking buddies?

He felt an inner jolt.

There was that woman staring at the house last night. It had been nearly sunset, and he couldn't see her well. Was that Mira?

He dismissed the idea. He was grasping now. But he could not shed a different feeling—an eerie sense of déjà vu.

Gregory glanced around his office, which Liv had helped him decorate. The walls were pale green, with artwork meant to be soothing. To the right of the desk hung an oil painting of a meadow in spring. On top of the bookshelf, chockablock with therapy tomes, he'd placed a simple black-and-white photo of a row of birch trees against a moody sky. The large picture window offered a pleasing enough view of Downtown Crossing, a bustling pedestrian neighborhood with a mix of historic buildings, department stores, and some predictable retail chains.

He adjusted himself in the wing chair again but wasn't able to settle in. He either had to sit on the edge or sink in deep, and he couldn't commit to that. He felt exhausted and shaky with hunger and wished he could eat the granola bar stashed in his briefcase. When he glanced at it on the floor next to his desk, he was distracted by Mira's brown leather sandals and pink toenails, the same color as the scarf.

"Are you always this nervous?" Mira asked.

His gaze jumped from her feet to her eyes. "I'm not, actually. Not nervous."

"Well, you're making me nervous!" She laughed shyly while staring right at him.

"Please don't be," Gregory said, trying to steady his voice. "I want you to be comfortable, so we can figure out how to best work together."

"In that case," Mira said, "may I ask you a few questions?"

Gregory's shoulders, high and tight, dropped with relief. "Of course," he said, hoping a routine preliminary conversation about the therapeutic process would put him back into his comfort zone. "It's fine to ask me some questions in our first session. Please do."

"I appreciate that." Eyes averted, Mira twirled the stiff bracelets around her wrist.

Gregory sat forward, grateful to feel the dynamic shifting back toward him. He anticipated the typical inquiries regarding his education and training as well as his theoretical approach. He would be able to give his well-honed speech about how cognitive behavioral therapy creates personal coping strategies for unhelpful thoughts and behaviors and also learn a little about what brought her to his office. This he could handle. This would ground him.

Mira looked up at him and asked, "So, how have you been doing, Greg?"

He almost choked. "How have I been doing?"

"Yes," she said. "Doesn't anyone ever ask how *you* are?"

"No. I mean, yes. They do. I'm fine, thank you."

Why was she this interested in him? Most of the people he saw were so broken, all they cared about regarding his state of mind was that he was well enough to treat them, which was how it was supposed to work. It was one of the reasons he chose this career. The questions went one way. Beyond the perfunctory greeting—*How are you? Good, thanks*—he didn't want anyone probing him, even on the most mundane level. It was upsetting and unprofessional, but he found that he wanted Mira to keep probing. Her presence was starting to have an analgesic effect, dulling the noise of his life so it was just the two of them, speaking openly in this room. He'd never considered crossing professional boundaries with a client, but watching her—backlit and glowing in his chair—he felt he already had.

"I think we should keep this focused on you," Gregory said.

Mira's face went dull. Her eyes, so animated a moment ago, dropped.

"If that's okay?" he added.

"I'm not interested in talking to a blank slate," she said, stroking her scarf as if she were petting a cat. "I'm looking for a real connection. If I'm going to open up, I need to be able to trust you."

So she was looking for a connection. Being worthy of trust was the work of his entire adult life. "You can trust me," he said.

When she met his eyes again, he felt so exposed he had to let go of her gaze. Did she know something? He quickly dismissed the thought. He read intensity, not accusation, in her eyes. She was also the wrong age. But that was how he had lived his life, always wondering who might have some piece of damning information about his past. When the telephone rang unexpectedly, was it the police? The statute of limitations had long since passed, but he knew that if his family ever found out what he'd done, they'd never speak to him again.

"I would like there to be humanity in our exchange," she continued. "I'm not interested in rote therapist statements coming from behind a professional mask."

He strained to find something—anything—familiar about her. Maybe they had met before, but it seemed impossible that he would forget someone so striking. If they didn't know each other, why her casual tone?

He felt a flicker of longing, a feeling he had become expert at extinguishing. He thought of the things he never shared with anyone. Not with his sister. Not with Liv. Not even with Phil, his suitemate and mentor, a seen-it-all psychiatrist who could handle the complexities of any situation. Sitting across from this gorgeous woman, so full of curiosity and kindness, he realized how alone he was.

"Okay." Gregory took a deep breath, then emptied his lungs completely, just as he taught his clients to do. He was beginning to think that she'd been to therapy before. It was her voice, both calm and reassuring, modeled after some previous doctor, he guessed. Maybe if he opened up to her a little, she would reveal what had brought her there. That would allow him to get to know her a bit and resolve his confusion without his having to admit it. "I'd be happy to tell you a few things about myself," he said, with renewed confidence.

As Mira smiled with approval, he felt relieved—and less undermined. His calloused hands, which he had been gripping in his lap, released and fell open, palms up. As he drew another breath, the tension drained from his body. Just sitting opposite her, saying nothing, breathing rhythmically, he suddenly understood why some of his clients, many chronically sleep-deprived from the constant siege of punishing thoughts, almost fell asleep in that chair. Watched over by a vigilant doctor, they were released for fifty minutes from life lived on high alert. He'd never been in therapy as an actual patient, only as a student in classroom simulations, but relaxing into the low chair, he surrendered to Mira's attention.

"Okay, let's see," he said, searching for a few ordinary details from his life. "My daughter will be going into her junior year in high school this fall. Today she started work at our"—he paused, trying to sound less entitled—"our local club." He cleared his throat. "This Saturday we're taking my son to his camp in New Hampshire, a tradition he loves." Gregory felt awkward saying "we," as if he were trying to send a message that he was married and committed. Which he was. But he didn't want that to deter her.

He glanced up. Mira's dark eyes were narrowed at him. He recognized the look from all the times he had studied his clients in that same manner, searching for the real story that had to be mined from the protective layer of superficial chatter.

"Your children's summer activities sound lovely. Now tell me how *you* are."

Gregory shook his head slightly. Even Liv didn't talk to him like this anymore. Of course, she was solicitous about his health, urging him to get more sleep and cut back on sugar. But after twenty-one years of marriage, she had stopped trying to pry into the source of his brooding and his habitual bouts of distraction. Liv seemed more interested in keeping him functioning. *We need you!* she would prompt whenever she found him zoned out at his desk, alone and disconnected. But even if he was the one who paid for the majority of expenses incurred by an affluent family living in an upscale neighborhood, it was not like she *really* needed him. Liv's salary from the publishing house, plus the substantial trust fund from her parents, would allow her to continue living well without his financial contribution.

Mira laughed. "It's not that strange a question, is it? I would just like to know how things have been going for you. That way I'll feel more comfortable sharing my story."

"Fine," he said, trying to be strategic but also inviting. "I'll tell you one or two things, then I'd like to get back to what brought you here."

Mira nodded. "Perfect."

"Well," Gregory said, without overthinking it, "my wife likes to be at our club all summer, but I'm not much for golf or tennis. Then there's the whole social scene."

Mira smiled. "Not your cup of tea?"

"I guess that's it. It seems so..." Not sure how he wanted to finish that thought, he let his head fall back against the chair and closed his eyes. He could feel a tightening in his cheeks and a slight welling behind his eyes. He couldn't remember when he had last cried in front of someone.

"What is it?" Mira asked. Her voice left an opening.

"I don't know." He touched his hand to his chest. He half expected the bones and muscle to give, crack like the hollow chocolate bunnies he and his sister, Margaret, used to get in their baskets on Easter morning. Gregory opened his eyes. "Who are you?"

Mira smiled gently. He wanted to know her history and why she was there—and whether it was possible to keep seeing her. She brought so much life to his bland office, and the air between them seemed to vibrate with energy. Did she feel it, too? The attraction?

"What was your life like growing up, Greg?" she asked, as if she hadn't heard him. "Tell me about that."

Gregory stiffened. He wasn't going to tell this unusual woman about his mundane childhood woes. His father, an insurance underwriter with rigid expectations. His cowed mother, not allowed to have a job or spend money on anything except groceries and sanctioned household essentials. Dinner was to be on the table at six o'clock sharp, and every day there was a list of chores for his mother to do. When she didn't complete her assigned tasks to her husband's exacting standards, he shouted his frustration or—as Gregory once witnessed—hit her.

"It was fine," he said. "Normal."

"Normal?" She loosened her grip on her scarf and let it fall from her shoulders.

"I was a middle-class kid. We had a split-level ranch in the Hartford suburbs. I went to Catholic school, was an altar boy at church, played Little League in the spring. Pretty typical," he said, eager to shut this whole thing down and learn more about her.

"Anything else?" She leaned back, just as he did with his clients, leaving room for expansion and honesty.

What was she after? Did she guess that the hundreds of photos stored in a shoebox in the back of a closet documented a happy childhood that never existed? In those shots he was a skinny kid in a baseball cap, mugging for the camera with his arms around Patrick Callahan and Joey Didowski. But he also remembered his mother's stricken expression behind the point-and-shoot, betraying her fear that by trying to capture this trio of smiling boys, she would invite interrogation: *How much did it cost to have those developed? Did Gregory go out to play without finishing his chores?*

Joey Didowski. Did he say the name out loud?

Gregory was uncertain how much time had passed, but he was hesitant to check his watch, not wanting to suggest impatience. He had an inexplicable sense of time having stopped, as if he were suspended in what a New Agey client once described as *the timeless now.* The direct sunlight was nearly gone, dashed out by a new building that chipped away at his view, closing him in even tighter. Had he been sleeping, and was this woman Mira, who was watching over him and tugging on hidden strands of his life, a part of his dream?

Did it matter? She had already seen more than he had meant to show her, not judging by the expression on her face—still open and inviting—but by how he felt unburdened, like he had handed her something heavy. He stretched his fingers and drew a deep breath, feeling an even stronger pull toward her.

Mira smiled. "It's time to go."

"You're going?" Gregory asked, a little panicked. He glanced at his vintage Rolex, a gift from Liv on their wedding day, a watch as difficult to read as the marriage itself. Looking at the two gold hands, he saw it was only one thirty. Paul C., who was trying to process losing his tenure at Brandeis after a colleague reported his pattern of lecherous predation, wouldn't be here for another half hour. He liked working with Paul C., who made Gregory feel slightly less loathsome, but he only needed the usual ten minutes to take a quick break before their session.

Mira stood and smoothed her orange dress.

When he started to stand, too, she waved him back down. "I'll let myself out."

"Wait!" Gregory said. "Do you want to make another appointment?"

Mira tilted her head in thought. "Is next Wednesday at one good for you?"

"Yes. I think that's available." He paused. "Actually, I know it is."

She nodded and slipped through the door.

Gregory waited until he heard the click of the outside door. Only then did he stand and walk to the chair where Mira's magenta scarf remained, a bright bloom of cloth flowing over the seat. He took it in his hands and buried his face in the softness, desperate to absorb some lingering scent of her. He smelled mint and smoke again—maybe from a bonfire—and something resinous he couldn't identify. Feeling hot, almost feverish, he wanted to open the window and let in fresh air, but more than that, he wished everything could stay exactly as it was in that moment.

3

Under the strong blast of hot water from the shower, Gregory sighed with relief. In one evening, he had planted the strawberry roots, fertilized and mulched the bed, and weeded the perennial borders, all while replaying the afternoon encounter with Mira in his head, trying to recall every minute of their session before a night's sleep could dull the memory. He wasn't sure whether he had actually told her those things about his family or just felt as if he had. If it weren't for the scarf, now locked in the bottom drawer of his desk, along with a small cache of tranquilizers he kept in a Ziploc, he would have thought he'd imagined their meeting. He knew nothing about her, and the fact that he felt okay with that was maybe the most disconcerting part of all. He'd let her take over the session and then spent most of their time babbling about himself, desperate to impress her and make sure she came back the following week. What was wrong with him?

In the shower, still processing the weirdness, his head started to hurt. While he didn't want to stop thinking about Mira, he was starting to feel like he was losing his mind. If he popped even half an Ativan, he was afraid she would cease to exist altogether, even in his memory.

He needed to calm down and decided to try one of the techniques he recommended to clients who were overwhelmed by obsessive thoughts: he had them sing in a way they wouldn't normally sing—in a funny voice or repeating one line over and over to jolt the brain out of the fixation. He put his face in the shower spray and belted out "The Star-Spangled Banner" in a vigorous bass, but at the end of the first verse, he had no idea how the second one started, so he went back to the beginning—"O say, can you see"—when the bathroom door opened, sucking out a whoosh of steam.

"Nice!" Liv called out. "I feel like I'm at the Super Bowl."

Gregory stopped singing and swiftly rinsed the remaining lather from his body. He shut off the valve and shoved aside the white cloth curtain. With his feet braced apart in the already high, claw-foot tub, he towered above his five-foot-three wife. He slicked back his hair and whisked the water from his face, feeling the scratch of his five o'clock shadow. Even though he was in decent shape for forty-six—lean with only the beginnings of a belly—he was usually embarrassed by his dripping wet nakedness. Not tonight, though. He felt uncharacteristically playful, especially after his meeting with Mira, who had reignited his desire. Instead of hurrying to reach for a towel, he placed his hands on his hips. "If you don't like that song," he said, still using the same deep voice, "I'm taking requests."

Liv glanced at him, her eyebrows raised. He wanted her to laugh and lift her face for a kiss, the way she once would have. He wanted to believe that he still might be appealing to her, that they weren't lost to each other in this way—something that seemed inevitable, until today when Mira walked into his office and reminded him that he was still a physical, sentient being whose life mattered; that he was deserving of attention, and maybe even love. He wanted to make a last-ditch effort at intimacy with Liv, but she went straight past him to the toiletry cabinet.

"You sing whatever you want," she said and dangled a pearly white bottle of polish in front of him like she was ringing a bell. "Maybe I'll catch a few bars while I'm touching up my nails."

She tucked a strand of shoulder-length blond hair behind her ears and reached into the jar of cotton balls. He wasn't sure what mysterious process she used to keep the gray away, only that she was meticulous about it. With the shower steam softening her lightly tanned face, she looked less like a woman of forty-four and more like a co-ed preparing for a date. She still had the frame of her college body, thin torso and small, firm breasts. The only noticeable change, wrought by motherhood and age, was the rounding out of her once boyish hips, a transformation that she struggled to embrace. She carried that part of herself apologetically, like ill-fitting clothes. "Just tell me I don't look fat," she'd say as she zipped herself into a dress before an evening out, running her hands over her broadened hips, trying to disappear what her perfectionism despised but he found soft and lovely.

"Wait!" Gregory said, just as Liv was about to leave the bathroom. He suddenly wanted to be close to her and tell her that a strange thing had happened at work and he didn't know if he was crazy or hallucinatory or—worse. He thought of his client Brandon G. S., who was so convinced he was being tracked by government spies that he asked Gregory each session if there were microphones hidden in his office.

Gregory didn't think he was that detached from reality, plus he wasn't sure how Liv would interpret the story. He wanted to say that whatever transpired with that woman in his office filled him with longing for something he had been too scared to ask for, so scared he couldn't even name it. But Liv might think he was interested in Mira.

And he was—but it wasn't as simple as sex or female attention. What was it that he wanted? To be heard? To be seen? To be touched in a way that didn't feel perfunctory?

Instead of disclosing any of that to Liv, he said, "Would you hand me a towel?"

"Feeling lazy?" she said, eyeing a plush white one on a hook next to the shower. Gregory had only to extend his hand.

What was he thinking? It was clear she was keeping things light. And she would excoriate him if he told her what he'd done. As the spouse of a therapist for two decades, Liv knew the difference between professional gaffes and wholesale irresponsibility. This was the latter.

Rather than risking her anger or capsizing the conversation, he aimed to meet her levity. "I thought you might help dry me off."

Liv's head turned toward him. She didn't respond right away, but he could read her curiosity about his suggestion of sex, an offer that came so seldom these days from either one of them—maybe every other month after a night out with wine when they remembered their original magnetic pull. That first year together, especially, held the pleasure of discovery, not just in sex but in all of the wonders Liv introduced him to. Nasturtiums tumbling from Italian vases in the courtyard at the Isabella Stewart Gardner Museum. The Mapparium at the Christian Science Center where he whispered "I love you" on one side of the globe-shaped room and she heard it with clarity on the other, then whispered the words back.

Almost twenty-four years later she stood in front of him in their steamy black-and-white-tiled bathroom, and it seemed like he knew her less than he did when they were young and open to each other.

Liv casually held out the towel and grinned slyly, which was promising, but then she said, "I'm going to let you dry off. I'll take a rain check, though."

"Do you have a work deadline?" he asked. He needed to keep her with him. Maybe if he started a conversation, something between them would shift and open. He hated how he had failed her, but he couldn't tell her the truth.

"I just finished the Bartley project, and I'm taking some time to clear my head." As a senior editor at Beacon Hill Press, Liv worked on art and design books. She had bred-in-the-bone knowledge in the field from her now-deceased mother, a renowned art historian who advised curatorial teams at the world's most venerable museums on multimillion-dollar acquisitions.

Before the kids were born, Liv had tried to write a novel, but there were always distractions, and a few years later, when she got pregnant with Carrie, she shelved her manuscript for good. These days, Liv created coffee table books about home décor, a job that suited—rather than excited—her. She found much more joy in her avocation: tutoring Boston schoolchildren with learning disabilities. She called them her "kiddos" and would return home from an afternoon in the city animated with stories of the day's events, sometimes pondering the idea of going back to school to become a reading specialist.

Liv gave him a last rueful smile and left the bathroom. He could hear the pad of her bare feet on the hardwood floor, then the click of the television. She'd most likely spend the next hour watching one of those Netflix shows that everyone at the club discussed, saying, *Hey, Gregory, have you seen such and such? You'd love it.* And he'd have to feign interest in the tribulations of a random cast of characters that inevitably included a fucked-up shrink sleeping with a patient. No, thank you.

Gregory stepped out of the tub and swiped his hand across the steamed-up mirror. The clear streak of glass revealed his broad forehead, high cheekbones, almond-shaped brown eyes set in a web of fine wrinkles. He moved closer, realizing he spent much of his day studying people's eyes for clues to their well-being but almost never considered his own this way—each iris like a tiny orbed mirror. Bloodshot and glazed, his eyes showed no signs of well-being.

Liv used to tell him he had flirtatious eyes, which was maybe her way of getting him to flirt with her more. Or she would take his face in her hands and say, *Do you even know how handsome you are?* Then she'd kiss him on the tip of his nose or eyelids.

Gregory smiled at the memory. He peered into the mirror again and hardly recognized himself—it was like a stranger was staring back. He turned away and locked the door.

As he stood there, he thought about quietly escaping. He took his limp penis in his hand and tried to summon the feeling of excitement from a few moments before. But it was gone. Until he started thinking about Mira. Her deep brown eyes, the curves of her body through that dress. He quickly became aroused, but he couldn't keep masturbating, not with Liv on the other side of the door.

He had to tell her about Mira.

He pulled on his boxers and threw open the door to their spacious white bedroom that now had the acrid chemical smell of nail polish. Liv, with her white cotton nightgown pulled around her thighs, sat on the end of their king-size bed, one foot resting on an upholstered bench. Rigid with concentration, she dabbed at her toes. On the TV, a chirpy comedian was telling jokes about her ex-husband's inadequacies.

Gregory picked up the remote and paused the show. "Do you have a minute to talk?"

"Sure." Liv's face tightened with concern. "Is everything all right?"

"Yeah, fine." Gregory sat uneasily on the side of the bed, legs apart, his hands folded as he hunched over. "I just wanted to run something by you."

"Okay." She loosely capped the polish and set it on the bench. "Go ahead."

"It's this new client, I guess. I saw her for the first time today, and, well, she acted, I don't know, strange."

"Strange how?"

Gregory hesitated, already regretting saying anything. Liv was always eager to hear his thoughts about work, though he had mostly stopped sharing them. On the rare occasion that he still did, she would often speculate about a diagnosis or hypothesize about something in the client's past. She could be insightful, and there were times that he even incorporated her suggestions into his therapy. But his session with Mira was hard to describe without sounding like he was the one who should be in treatment.

"So how was she strange?" Liv repeated. "Inappropriate?"

"No. That's not it."

"Paranoid?"

He could feel the spell shattering, the way a mirror cracked but still held its shape. Mira was his, and if Gregory couldn't understand what happened during her session, he certainly wouldn't be able to explain it to his wife.

He waved his hand at the air. "Actually, it's no big deal. I shouldn't have bothered you. I know you want to relax with your show." He handed the remote back. Liv set it down on the bed.

"It's not a bother. You know I love hearing about your work."

She was looking at him expectantly, but he knew it was foolish to give her even the smallest piece of information about Mira. His wife was not stupid.

Gregory shook his head. "It's okay. I'll figure it out."

Liv picked up the remote and jabbed at it. Instantly the audience was howling at the divorced woman's jokes, masking Liv's words.

"What's that?" Gregory asked.

She hit the remote again, freezing the screen. "I said, 'I'm sure you will figure it out.'" She screwed the top on the nail polish bottle tight and looked at him. "It seems like you're always just about to tell me something when you stop and withdraw. And I'm left wondering what I did wrong."

"But, Liv."

"What are you trying to tell me? Please just finish your thought for once. I'm your wife, Gregory. It's okay to share things."

She was always asking for details about his gardening or long runs or occasional solo hiking trips—things he did to forget himself. A few years ago, Liv pressured him into going to some insufferable couples' workshop in the Berkshires. When the group leaders—a married gray-haired couple with dubious academic degrees and matching crystal necklaces—instructed them to whisper something to their partner that they'd never said out loud to anyone, Gregory felt the blood drain from his face. He couldn't remember what made-up thing he told Liv, but he could still feel his wife's warm mouth against his ear as she whispered, "I never feel like I'm enough."

Liv knew better than to ever sign them up for another workshop, but that didn't stop her from offering him her own relationship advice: *Try a little harder with our friends at the club. Spend more time with the family.* They were more like admonitions than suggestions. But she was right. He had been retreating from her and the kids, especially Carrie, who would soon be seventeen, the age when he, an immature high school graduate, young for his grade and always trying to play catch-up, messed up his life. To be near his daughter felt like a jinx, so he'd been keeping his distance, working even longer hours.

In truth, *he* never felt like he was enough. Yet at least he'd done one good thing for his family by building a thriving therapy practice. His robust salary meant they would never have the financial worries he had experienced growing up. And for fifty-minute sessions, eight times a day, he could hear about everyone else's screw-ups instead of dwelling on his own. In some way, helping other people with their problematic lives felt like the closest he'd ever get to atoning for his.

Gregory glanced around the room. It was almost blindingly white. White fluffy comforter, white silk curtains, white armchair, white throw pillows piled on the bed. Even the original woodwork, brown when her mother died, was now all painted white, as if Liv had tried to exorcise her mother's darkness.

He wasn't the only one with wounds.

"I'm sorry," Gregory said.

"I know," Liv said. "You're always sorry. That's one of the few things you will tell me. But I'd like you to do something about it. Be my husband. Reach out in some way."

"I tried," he said, his chin sheepishly drawn in, "in the shower."

Liv shook her head. "I need more than that. I need actual communication."

Gregory turned to face her. He put a hand on her forearm and used his thumb to stroke her warm skin. God, how he missed the way things used to be between them. She was smart and thoughtful. She would do anything for their family, for him. He knew he'd been slowly killing their marriage for years, but he couldn't seem to stop.

The problem was he didn't love—or even like—himself. And then Mira had unleashed something in him and in one short session introduced him to another path. What would happen if he took her hand and followed where she seemed to be leading him?

Liv put a hand over his. "Why can't you tell me about your new client? You had something to say, and then you stopped."

Gregory made himself maintain eye contact. If he turned away, she'd know. "I'm starting to think she's unspecified bipolar," he lied. "I should probably check in with Phil. But I'll definitely keep you posted."

Liv nodded and slipped her hand out from under his. "How about you go in and talk to Carrie? She's been up in her room since she came home. And I'm taking Petey to camp on Saturday, so I'm sure he'll want to spend some time with you."

"You're taking him?"

"Remember we talked about this? I'm going up with Jeanine and her son because she doesn't want to do the drive alone. We're going to need every bit of space in the car."

Gregory looked back at his wife, her face strained and sad. He couldn't feel even a fraction of the light she used to beam at him. For years she had shined it unconditionally; now he feared she unconsciously mirrored his darkness.

Liv squeezed his hand and released it. She unpaused her show, signaling the end of their conversation. In an hour or so, they would crawl into their enormous bed and fall asleep, back-to-back, several feet apart.

4

Out in the hallway, a strip of light beamed from under Carrie's door. Gregory stood back, listening for sounds. When he heard nothing, he knocked softly. "You up, sweetie?"

There was shuffling and shifting about.

"What?" Carrie said, her tone unwelcoming.

"I just wanted to say goodnight."

"Goodnight."

"Can I come in?"

"I'm on the phone."

"Please let me in, just for a second."

There was another moment of rustling before Carrie unlocked the door and opened it a few inches. She had turned off the light, and for a moment, Gregory wasn't even sure it was his daughter. Her round face was coated in makeup, and thick black circles rimmed her eyes. Her mouth looked large and unnaturally red, like she had just tried, and mostly failed, to rub off lipstick.

"Goodnight," she said, lowering her head so he could kiss the top of it, which he did.

"Are you okay?" he asked.

"I'm fine."

"How was your first day of work?"

"Fine! But I told you, I'm on the phone."

She started to shut the door again, and he had to pull his face back. Before she could shut it completely, he said, "I love you."

The door stayed open an inch. "What?" Carrie said.

"I said, 'I love you.'"

"Oh. Love you too."

Gregory heard her turn the lock.

Across the hallway, Petey's room was dark, but he could hear him in there tapping away at his video game. Gregory didn't have the energy to compete with *Minecraft* for his son's attention, but he made himself knock anyway.

"Door's open!" Petey shouted.

The lingering note of boyhood in his son's deepening voice made Gregory wistful about the awkwardness of that in-between stage of life. He cautiously entered the room, a shrine to the sports Petey loved. Chelsea F.C. posters covered the interior wall, and a large aerial photo of Fenway Park hung above his double bed. Gregory winced at the reminder of that summer night and quickly turned to face his son.

Petey, who was fixated on the computer, paused his game and spun his chair toward Gregory. "What's up, Dad?" His blond hair flopped across his forehead, and while he was as lanky as Gregory had been at that age, he seemed comfortable in his body in a way Gregory hadn't until after college. Until Liv.

"Not much. I thought you might want to watch a show, or we could make milkshakes and play cribbage."

Petey's eyes shifted to his monitor, then back to Gregory. "I'm kind of in the middle of a game. But could we do it later? Or tomorrow? Would that be okay?"

Gregory stuffed his hands in his pockets and smiled. All he'd wanted as a boy was to spend time with his father doing something other than chores. All his son wanted was to build virtual worlds in which avatars—not actual people—interacted, each "win" another level of excitement and challenge. How could he compete with that? "Tomorrow sounds good."

"You sure, Dad? Because if you really want to hang out now—"

"It's fine. Enjoy your game."

Gregory walked downstairs and out the front door. He stood on the steps and sighed into the growing darkness. One of the longest nights of the year, the sky was still a rich mauve at almost nine o'clock. He thought about sitting on the side patio, but the cushioned chairs were damp from an evening rain shower. He was about to head back into the house when a text came in from Phil Bodkin: *Still up? Dropping something off in 5.*

Gregory texted back: *See you outside.*

Phil and Gregory had met at the club, through Liv, who was friends with Phil's first wife, Kathy. A few years later, Gregory felt like he'd been knighted when Phil suggested he join him in his three-office suite after the previous occupant—Gregory suspected Phil had been sleeping with her—suddenly moved to Vermont. *I think there's real efficacy in your cognitive behavioral approach*, Phil had told Gregory when he made the offer over burgers at the clubhouse. Old-school trained, as most Boston area psychiatrists were, Phil was equally adept at psychopharmacology and psycho-analysis. But he liked the idea of Gregory working with his patients who needed something beyond medication and a deep dive into their intrapsychic conflicts. People whose maladaptive behaviors—cutting, isolating, gambling, drugging—got them into serious trouble. *We could be good for each other*, Phil had told him. *A nice balance.*

Apart from paying rent, most of the good flowed from Phil to Gregory. Phil had shown him how to run a successful therapy practice and fed him dozens of patients over the years. Gregory referred people to Phil, too, mostly for medication consults. Phil, renowned in psychiatric circles, never wanted for patients, even with a price tag of a thousand bucks an hour. Despite his messy personal matters, including an affair with a Boston Symphony Orchestra cellist that ultimately ended his first marriage, Phil had a thriving career.

Gregory was checking on the strawberry bed when Phil arrived on his old maroon mountain bike, standing on the pedals to pump it up the hill.

"Evening!" Phil called. He dismounted a few feet from the garden and let the bike drop on the grass, the lights still blinking. He slung off his backpack and pulled out a white bag that he handed to Gregory. "Beth's been at it again. If you saw all the bowls of dough fermenting in our kitchen right now, you'd have a diagnosis for her."

Gregory laughed and patted the bag of bread. It was still warm. "And you're the delivery boy?"

Phil raised his wire-frame glasses and blinked the sweat from his eyes. "It was her ruse to get me out exercising. I told her I'd bring yours to the office tomorrow in the car, but she wasn't having it."

Phil was sixty-three, a bear of a man, always a bit disheveled. His T-shirt was half tucked into his black bike shorts, and strands of thinning, gray hair shot out from under his helmet that sat askew on his large head. Phil's lack of vanity only made him more revered, and he was a regular on *Boston Magazine*'s list of best doctors, known within professional circles as the "mood disorder whisperer"—the shrink who could craft the right medication cocktail to lift an intractable depression or decrease a hypomanic episode without causing the patient to feel flattened. Phil had sixteen years on Gregory, and his exalted position in the medical community added a shine to Gregory's practice.

"Everything good with you?" Phil asked, studying Gregory in the fading light. "You don't look like you've got your cool summer vibe on yet."

Gregory gazed down at the grass but knew he couldn't hide from Phil's laser vision. He saw things that anyone else would overlook or ignore. Liv joked that he had supernatural powers and could divine information. "I'm good," Gregory said. "Just working through a few things."

"Like?"

He was reluctant to start talking about Mira because he worried what Phil would think of him, but if he didn't give Phil something, he'd keep pushing. He drew a sharp breath and tucked his hands into his pockets. "Did you ever have someone take over a session so it felt like you were the patient?"

"Narcissist or run-of-the-mill resistance?"

"Not sure yet."

"Male or female?"

Gregory hesitated. "Male." He immediately regretted the lie. He needed Phil's advice. Now it was too late.

"He couldn't be worse than that bipolar attorney we shared," Phil said. "The one who acted like he was prosecuting us."

"Jason P. Benedict, *Esquire*. That guy was a nightmare."

"And you handled him like a pro. Better than I did. So what's got you bothered with this guy?"

Gregory shrugged, trying to appear casual. "It's not a big deal. Just caught me off-guard."

Phil studied him for another few seconds, and Gregory was terrified he was going to keep digging. But Phil reached for his bike and threw a burly leg over it. "Keep me posted," he said. He settled onto the seat and started rolling back down the driveway.

"Will do," Gregory called after him. "Tell Beth thanks for the bread. It smells delicious."

Past the garage, Phil was about to turn into the street when he braked. Still straddling the bike, he turned back toward Gregory, peering at him through the darkness.

Gregory waved, "I'm good. No worries. See you tomorrow at the office." He watched as Phil cycled away.

But Gregory wasn't good. He had now made Mira a secret, one that he couldn't even share with his wife or closest professional confidant. And secrets never worked out well for Gregory.

Instead of heading back inside, he strolled down the driveway into the garage, unfolded the beige-and-white-striped aluminum beach chair that was leaning against the back wall, and lowered himself into the seat. He reached into the bag and broke off a ragged chunk of bread.

Chewing on the warm sourdough, he thought of his honeymoon in Paris. One afternoon, he and Liv sat by the Seine drinking wine from the bottle and tearing off pieces from a fresh baguette. They laughed at the cliché—to be so in love in the City of Love. Buzzed and horny, they later headed back to their hotel room in Saint-Germain but somehow got lost and ended up at the Zoological Park, which amused Liv, who for all her trips to Paris never even knew it had a zoo. They stopped to marvel at the lions, Gregory's favorite animal, and afterward lay down on the grassy lawn and fell asleep until a guard ordered them to leave, which they did hastily, Liv apologizing in halting French.

Gregory loved those long days of strolling hand in hand with Liv around the city, an ocean away from everything that vexed him. Even the jet lag gave him a sense of having escaped his life, as if he had left his past in a different time zone and a happy marriage could insulate him from what had come before.

Not long after they returned, Liv surprised him with a kitten, an orange tabby they named Leo, after the African lion that had captivated him in the Paris zoo. Growing up, Gregory's father had never allowed them to have a pet, and he was astonished at how much he grew to love that sweet, lazy cat. When Leo was stretched out next to him on the couch, looking for nothing more than to have his back stroked, Gregory could almost forget who he was. Sometimes Liv would sit down next to them and say, "Can you rub my back, too?"

Gregory brought the bread to his mouth but hesitated to take another bite. What could he have whispered in Liv's ear at that god-awful couples' workshop in the Berkshires? What should he have told her?

I miss us. But even "us" was a lie, as long as he kept his past a secret.

I can't love you the way I want to until I forgive myself. That seemed more honest.

I'll never be able to forgive myself. That was the sad truth, to which he might add what he really felt in that moment: *I'm not worthy of you.*

He took a bite of the bread, tearing hard at the crust, wondering why it felt impossible to tell his wife about Mira. Was he not being honest with himself? He chewed slowly, tears welling in his eyes for the second time that day.

5

As soon as Eleanor S. left his office at 12:52, Gregory tidied his desk and cleared out the trash, lest the room smell like yesterday's turkey sandwich. He had hardly eaten that day, but the gnawing in his stomach seemed more like nerves than real hunger, and he didn't have an appetite anyway. Once the office was in order, he took his travel kit from his top drawer and went to the bathroom down the hall to brush his teeth. While he was in there, he combed down his thick hair but decided it looked silly, so he ruffled it up the way Petey sometimes wore his, like it was leaping off his head. But he wasn't a teenager, so he patted it down again. At his next haircut, he'd ask his barber to give it some edge, so he'd look a little younger. He returned to his office, left the door ajar, and sat in his chair.

Gregory had spent the past six days obsessing over what was going to happen when Mira returned. On Saturday, while Liv was taking Petey to camp, Gregory had wandered aimlessly from the garden to his garage then back to the house, unable to focus on any single task. At lunchtime, he walked to Pemby's for an empanada. While he was there, he bought some ginger cookies and overpriced organic chocolate bars and put together a care package for Petey that he mailed at the post office on his way home. His son hadn't been gone a day and already Gregory missed him. In that missing, he longed for connection and found his thoughts turning to Mira.

A moment before one o'clock, Gregory heard the waiting room door open and let out a breath he didn't know he was holding. Before standing, he counted to three and walked toward the office door. Mira was sitting in the same chair, this time wearing blue jeans and a blouse with rich swirls of color. Her lips were crimson, punctuating the red in her shirt. Her dark hair cascaded over her narrow shoulders. He couldn't help his smile.

"Hello," he said, aiming for the right balance of professional formality and warmth. "It's nice to see you again."

"Same," Mira said, laughing lightly.

He had been worried all week that he had misread something in their encounter, but that laugh reassured him that she was happy to be there—with him.

"Come on in." This time, Gregory stayed in the doorway, ready to head directly to his own chair while she followed behind him. Although darting ahead felt rude, it would leave her no opportunity to usurp his seat. On one of the wingbacks, he had left the seven intake forms for her to fill out, which meant he'd finally have the appropriate information to proceed with their therapy.

Gregory entered his office with Mira a few steps behind. But as he was hastily crossing the room, his phone buzzed in his pocket. It had to be Liv, who often checked in on Wednesdays at one—what used to be his free hour. He reached in his pocket, grabbed his phone, and hit the message: *Can I call you later?*

He barely noticed Mira slip by and take his seat.

Gregory stood there for a few awkward seconds before realizing how foolish he looked. So he sat down as quickly as possible, crushing the intake papers.

Just like that, she had the upper hand again.

Mira crossed her legs and settled in. "Is this okay?" she asked.

Gregory nodded and said, "Sure, make yourself at home." He grimaced at how idiotic that sounded; this was an office for doing therapy and not a house where he was entertaining a guest. His kids and Liv were always pointing out his blunders or rolling their eyes at him. If Liv could see him now, she would call him out for his behavior. You didn't need a PhD in psychology to know he was being inappropriate, knowingly allowing an attractive client to take over the session in order to keep her there with him.

But it seemed clear so far that nothing fazed Mira or provoked scorn.

As Gregory yanked the forms out from under his butt and dropped them on the floor, he realized he couldn't just give in to the absurdity. Anything he asked Mira would sound ridiculous when they still hadn't dealt with the formalities, like what her last name was and why they were having these weekly appointments. He had worked too hard to let himself be dominated by one hyperassertive client. Hadn't Phil reminded him that he could handle these situations? No matter how much she disarmed him, he had to conjure the professional wherewithal to structure the session, and he had to do it immediately.

"So, Mira," Gregory said, his voice seeming to come from outside of himself, "how have you been this week?"

Mira looked past him out the window. "Honestly, Greg," she said, "I'm doing fine." But after a few seconds, she turned her gaze on him again, causing Gregory to grip the upholstered arms of the chair. "It's just that I've been thinking about you and some of the things you told me last Wednesday," she continued. "I'd like to follow up on that. I mean, I'd *love* to hear more about your family." She said the word "love" as if ordering dessert in a café—*I'd love a piece of chocolate cake!*

Gregory carefully released his hold on the chair and folded his hands in his lap. He nodded thoughtfully, just as he would with any client who brought up a topic that required reflection. After a moment, he drew a breath and said, "Mira, my job is to help you with whatever issue has brought you to my office, and I am eager to do that. Which is why I can't let things stay focused on me. I told you a lot last Wednesday instead of letting you talk, and that's fully on me. So now it's up to me to back up, turn this around, and set things right. I hope that makes sense."

Unable to meet her eyes, Gregory reached for the forms scattered on the floor and gathered them haphazardly in his lap. When he looked at Mira again, her mouth was twisted, her brow wrinkled.

"Right?" she asked, so he couldn't tell if she was challenging him or honestly seeking clarification. "What do you mean by *right*?"

For the first time, he considered that she might have a personality disorder, although his professional instincts told him no. After two decades as a therapist, he could sense those disorders when they walked into his office. Borderline felt electric, like summer air after a crack of lightning. It made the hair on the back of his neck stand up. Narcissism looked strong, like an oak towering above the other trees around it, but his trained eye could see that the trunk was hollowed with rot. Mira brought neither of those energies to the room.

Gregory studied her, fearing a trap of semantics, the kind he often got caught in with Liv, both of them arguing their own interpretation of a barbed comment. (*Just what did you mean by "strident"?*) His wife, the wordsmith, usually emerged victorious. Since that couldn't happen here, he needed to be completely clear.

"Right," Gregory said, his voice flat in his effort to maintain control, "means me being an experienced clinician who sits in my chair, which is that one—the one you're in—directing the therapeutic relationship. That means asking appropriate questions, starting with your full name and whether you have insurance coverage for our sessions."

This is good, he thought. Professional but not pushy. He didn't want to risk upsetting her for fear she might leave. There was a fine line to walk.

"*Right* is me creating a safe space for clients here in my office that I've set up for that purpose," he went on. "And *right* is doing what I'm trained to do, something that I believe I do very well." It felt good to reclaim his power from this Mira, who might be charming but also seemed to be playing some game with him. He paused, feeling the engine of his annoyance spur him to the next, essential declaration. "*Right*," he continued, "is that you tell me who you are and what's going on from your perspective, but first we switch chairs, so I can sit at my desk as I've always done. I'd like to start there, and we can proceed in a way that feels professional and helpful to you."

Galvanized, Gregory put his hands on his thighs, rose to his feet, and waited for Mira to do the same.

But Mira didn't get up. She didn't even seem to be considering the idea, and Gregory was left standing there in front of her, while she sat with one leg curled under her in his, Gregory's—that was his name, not Greg—$2,500 ergonomic chair that he had bought to help with back pain caused by poor posture. Finally, after what felt like five minutes but was probably fifteen seconds, Mira looked up at him and blinked.

"I'm sorry, Greg," she said, with such low-register directness that he would be terrified of her if it weren't for the softness around her eyes. "I get that you want our session to be 'right,' but I'm a little confused."

"Yes, that's one reason people come to see me, for help with their confusion."

She looked at him, her gaze unwavering. "Okay, so you want to help me. But are you well enough for that?"

"Excuse me?"

"With the burden that you carry, can you really help anyone?"

Gregory shook his head. "My twenty-year career as a clinical psychologist has been all about helping people. By all measures available, I've been quite successful at that."

Mira nodded. "I understand. But I wonder if maybe your patients actually help you as much as you help them? Is it possible that their improvements relieve some of the guilt that obviously weighs on you?"

Gregory's nails dug into his palms, and his wrists stiffened. How was he supposed to respond to that? More important, was it a lucky guess, or did she somehow know more about him than his own family?

Mira exhaled audibly, waited a few beats, and asked, "Do you want me to be fully honest with you?"

He knew there was only one correct answer if he wanted to keep seeing her. "Of course."

"I thought so," Mira said, "yet I'm wondering when was the last time you communicated honestly? How do you expect your patients to be truthful with the people in their lives when you don't hold yourself to the same standard?"

"You have no basis for that assertion," Gregory said. But he had to turn away to try and regain his composure. The scent of marigolds wafted around him and yet there were none in the office.

"Don't I?" Mira asked.

After a long silence he said firmly, "You have to tell me who you are."

"I'm here to work through something," she said, her voice suddenly tender. "But how can I do that when you're in this condition? I can't, unless you let me help you first."

"Who referred you?"

"I told you. You reached out to me."

He shook his head. "No, I didn't."

Gregory crossed his arms over his chest, trying to keep from trembling. He looked out the window at the new buildings and the ongoing construction. Every year, his world grew smaller, more claustrophobic. He thought about his marriage and family. His and Liv's disconnection at home, their unfulfilling weekends at the club. Carrie, who barely acknowledged him, unless she needed money to go out with friends. Even Petey, once his buddy for building elaborate Lego structures or forts in the yard, now just wanted time in his room playing *Call of* fucking *Duty*. And there was Gregory, alone in his garage, longing to connect with someone, anyone who would recognize the aching in his heart. All of those years spent carrying a burden that he thought he could never set down. Mira seemed to recognize his pain right away. Maybe he could crawl into her arms and find peace, if only for a short while.

Gregory stood motionless by the window, afraid that if he moved, his legs would give out and he'd sink to the floor.

How many times had Liv begged him to see a therapist? "You need help," she'd say, her voice pleading. He was masterful at giving her excuses without revealing the true reason he would never do it. Talk therapy provided insight, but he didn't need insight; he needed forgiveness, and there was no one to offer him that. The real secret he should have whispered in Liv's ear at that couples' workshop: *If you knew what I did, you'd never forgive me.*

A minute ticked by, then another. Gregory slid his hands into his pockets and fingered the two coins he found there, wishing for the courage to tell Mira to stay. If she didn't, then what would he have to face alone? Thirty, forty empty years? Most likely a divorce when Liv decided she could no longer abide his sullenness and distance? Interminable loneliness, until his final years in a nursing home like his father, slumped in a wheelchair, unable to remember his own children's names?

He wasn't sure how much time had passed when Mira shifted behind him in her chair—his chair—and said, "I can go, Greg. It's fine. Just give me back my scarf, and I'll leave."

He was surprised at the mention of the scarf. So she did know that she had left it.

Of course, she did. The magenta scarf was practically fused to her last week. She had to have missed it. But did she know he took it out of his drawer twice every day, first thing in the morning when he got to work, to check that it was still there, and last thing before leaving the office, in case it disappeared in the night? Did she know that he held it to his nose, inhaling the smell of mint and smoke and anything else that might reveal who she was? Did she know that last Thursday morning, the day after he met her, he pressed the soft cloth against his cheek like a compress to a wound?

If he gave it back to her and sent her away, there would be nothing left to remember her by. And maybe he'd never feel this again: truly seen.

Maybe if he was honest with her, she would accept him.

Gregory turned from the window and looked at Mira. Her eyes were less scolding, and he could practically read her understanding of him. He drew a breath and held it in as he walked toward the wingback and sat down. His head fell back, and he exhaled loudly. He took another deep breath and tried to ground himself in what had always been his professional domain, at least before this therapeutic mutiny.

He looked at Mira for a long time, then slowly shut his eyes on her concentrated gaze. "Fine," he whispered, his voice automated. "Help me."

After a minute of silence, Mira said, "Tell me about the night you met your wife."

Gregory's eyes widened in panic, then slowly closed again. *You have to do this*, he said to himself. *You don't want her to shut you out, too.* He needed Mira. Her scent, her long dark hair, the way she leaned back in his chair like it belonged to her. She was the balm he'd been craving.

"Tell me," Mira whispered. "How did Liv save you?"

6

"I was ready to give it up," Gregory quietly told Mira. Behind closed eyes, he could see his life, just as it played out in 1995, when he was a young graduate student at Boston University. "I wanted to forget the PhD because nothing seemed to matter after a situation that happened with a friend of mine. But if I didn't finish my doctorate, I'd have to pay back my scholarship, and that wasn't an option. I was doing a teaching assistantship, in abnormal psychology." He smiled at the memory. "Ninety-two undergraduates in a dreary, midsize lecture hall, and there she was."

How could he not notice Liv, so alert and polished in a way that made her shine among the other students, most of whom looked like they had just woken up, tossed on a pair of ripped jeans and a sweatshirt before stumbling to class, clutching a cup of coffee? There was something pure and old-fashioned about the girl in a white sweater with dirty-blond hair brushing her shoulders as if she steered clear of life's dark side. When she bent over her notes, a piece of blunt-cut hair fell across her face, and he almost rushed over to tuck it behind her ear. Was there a word for it? The feeling of recognizing a stranger as someone you are supposed to meet?

It wasn't *Who are you?* More like *Oh, there you are.*

Gregory scanned the roster, feeling like he'd recognize her name if he saw it. In their dating years, he and Liv would sometimes laugh about it, how he penciled in a tiny question mark by *Olivia J. Stimson; Yr: Junior; Major: English Literature.* And how at the very same moment that Gregory identified her, he looked up, only to catch her looking back at him through her wide blue eyes. It felt less like coincidence and more like confirmation.

They had their first date almost three months later. It wasn't that he didn't want to ask her out sooner, but as one of the TAs, he couldn't cross that line, risk doing anything that the college prohibited. Instead, in a subtle attempt to engage, he made a reading suggestion in his comments on her blue-book midterm: *Based on your answer to question 3a, I think you'd appreciate Freud's* The Interpretation of Dreams. When she approached him cautiously after class that Wednesday to say that Freud's seminal work was one of the reasons she had taken the course, he was quietly thrilled. They proceeded to talk Freud and Jung, extending their conversation into the hallway and eventually outside where they stood together, each separately huddled against the brutal March wind ripping down Commonwealth Avenue. He learned that Liv had grown up on the other side of the Charles River in Cambridge and planned to become a writer. In fact, she had to present a short story in her fiction seminar that afternoon and was feeling apprehensive about it. "Maybe it's too personal," she admitted.

After reassuring her it would go well, he told her he was pursuing a doctorate in psychology. Up until that moment, he had been ready to abandon the program. Chatting with Liv reinvigorated his drive.

After that first meeting, Liv would always find a reason to speak with him after class, once even casually mentioning that she was heading off to grab lunch, in what seemed to be an invitation. Although he could sense her disappointment when he didn't ask to join her, Gregory adhered to his decision.

Finally, on an early May evening, not ten minutes after submitting his students' final grades, Gregory found Liv's number, called her up, and invited her "to do something."

"Something?" she asked with a coyness he wasn't used to. His family did stern and modest. They did not do teasing.

"I just want to see you," he said. "The *what* doesn't matter."

"I'll be out in front of my apartment in thirty minutes. One-forty-five Beacon."

As Gregory approached the narrow brownstone, he spotted Liv leaning against the wrought iron railing, her head turning to track every car that passed. He couldn't remember the last time he'd felt this hopeful.

She slid into the passenger seat of the used black Toyota Supra that he'd bought when he graduated high school and looked at him expectantly. "Where to, Gregory?"

He smiled, choosing not to correct her, happy to have this take-charge woman christen him into a different person. He grew up learning from his father that things like one's name and position in life were intractable. You were who you were, no matter how uncomfortable that felt. *Know your place*, his father used to say. *God resists the proud and gives grace to the humble.* But humility wasn't Gregory's problem.

At Liv's suggestion, they headed up Storrow Drive, a cross-town parkway that flanked the Charles. The river shimmered like a black mirror on that spring night and Gregory remembered how beautiful the city could be, something he'd lost touch with long ago.

Halfway across the Harvard Bridge, Liv pointed out the window to the low steel railing. "A kid I knew from high school jumped off right over there."

Gregory immediately thought of Joey and tried to draw a breath. But the air wouldn't go in. His foot started drifting off the gas pedal, until the driver behind him laid on the horn. "Sorry. Sorry," Gregory muttered into the rearview. When he hit the gas again, the car jerked forward, and Liv had to brace her palm on the dash.

"Did he live? The kid who jumped?" Gregory asked.

"Yes. He was fine. It's only twenty-five feet or so. He did it as a dare."

Gregory nodded. The wheel felt slick under his grip.

"Oh," Liv said, after a moment, her voice low with apology, "did you think I meant that he—"

"No," Gregory cut her off. He didn't want her to say the words. "I just, I didn't know."

They wound into Harvard Square, where Gregory—he would never again introduce himself as Greg—almost magically found a parking spot in front of Cardullo's and dashed in for a bottle of wine and a corkscrew. Once inside, he realized he didn't know if she preferred white or red, but he felt too foolish to run out to the car to ask. Red always seemed fancier, so he settled on a Merlot, five dollars more than he could afford on his stipend.

When he returned, Liv was flipping through the pages of one of his textbooks. "Anything interesting?" he asked.

"It's all interesting."

"Did you ever think about majoring in psychology? You're really good at it."

She smiled at him and returned the book to the back seat. "I did think about it. A lot actually. But as much as I loved our psych class, it made me focus too much on my own issues, and that was kind of distressing. I don't know if that makes sense?"

Gregory nodded and started the car. He wanted to tell her that he chose psychology precisely because of his issues, his need for atonement. But that wasn't a first date conversation. Even though this didn't feel like a first date—having talked after class for months, their being together seemed inevitable, maybe even predestined—he knew enough not to dump his trauma on someone ten minutes into a night out.

"So where should we go with our wine?" Liv asked.

Gregory glanced at her as he considered something. What if he did tell her what he'd done, back in high school? Then he would no longer be alone with his secret. If he didn't tell her now, he might never, and everything going forward would be colored by that lie.

That's when he knew he had to say something, before he got too scared.

"Any ideas?" she prompted.

He needed a place that was quiet and private. "We could sit in Harvard Yard, over by the Widener Library."

She laughed. "I'd be okay with staying away from libraries tonight."

"Good point," he said. "We could walk down to the Charles?"

"How about Mount Auburn Cemetery?" Liv said with a trace of mischief in her voice. "I know a spot we can sneak in. My friends and I used to do it all the time in high school."

Gregory turned away quickly. He sat there, unmoving, staring through the windshield rimmed in a film of yellow pollen. He knew Liv was still talking, but he couldn't take it in, whatever she was saying. He gazed out the window at the life teeming around him in Harvard Square. The neighborhood surrounding the university bustled that Thursday evening with students celebrating their first breaths of freedom at the semester's end.

"What's going on?" Liv asked. She touched her fingers to his forearm, and an electric jolt ran through him.

He made himself turn to face her. She was looking at him with such kindness. "Sorry," he said. "I'm just thinking."

"We don't have to go to Mount Auburn." Liv withdrew her hand. "I get that not everyone likes cemeteries—"

"No," Gregory said, cutting her off. "That's a great idea. Let's go."

Liv showed Gregory where to park on a side street and led him to the place where the chain-link fence had been cut along the steel post. She peeled back the secret gate, ducked in, and held it open. After squeezing through, Gregory stood slowly and tried to calm down enough to absorb the spectral beauty. Gnarled, old-growth trees lined the paths, along with flowers—bluebells, peonies, Solomon's seals. In the distance he detected the silhouette of an elaborate stone chapel. Closer to them, weathered gravestones and statuary—weeping angels, thick marble crosses—were faintly dusted in moonlight.

"Do you smell that?" he said and breathed in deeply through his nose. "Crab apple, I think. It flowers this time of year."

Liv closed her eyes and inhaled. As she exhaled slowly, her face softened. With her pale, smooth skin and parted lips, she looked like a sculpture at the Museum of Fine Arts—*Olivia in Ecstasy*. She opened her eyes and turned to Gregory. He reached for her hand.

Walking in silence, they headed to a tower on top of a hill, past a flowering dogwood, a row of flaming red azaleas, and a dozen other plants Gregory could have named but didn't. He was busy running through the possibilities for what to say. He didn't even know what the words would sound like, because he'd never spoken them out loud. He didn't tell his father, because Bob Weber would have driven Gregory right down to the police station to turn himself in. In the years since, Gregory had tried several times to open up to his mother but always failed to follow through. Jittery under the best of circumstances, she would have been even more of a wreck, beset with constant worry that her son might be caught.

"And, voilà!" Liv said, extending her arm to present the view. They'd arrived at the top of the hill, from which they could see Boston twinkling in the distance, a jewel box that had been opened to him by this golden girl who seemed to have a skeleton key to the world. They stood for a moment, marveling at the skyline, their bodies close and charged with desire. After another moment, Liv led him down a different path, pausing at a tree, heavy with spring blooms.

"It's a magnolia," Gregory said, plucking off one of the milky white flowers and handing it to her.

"How do you know so much about trees?"

"My dad was a gardener," Gregory said, remembering how he would wander around the neighborhood with his father's well-worn *Field Guide to Trees and Shrubs*. There was another smaller book just for flowers. "I tried to impress him by learning the names of every plant I could. I'm not sure it worked, but I learned a lot."

"Well, *I'm* impressed." Liv sniffed deeply at the magnolia. She tucked it behind her ear.

"You're so beautiful," he whispered, taking in her eyes, hyacinth blue. "I would stare at you across the lecture hall and completely forget what I was supposed to be doing."

She smiled shyly. "Me too. I would sit there wondering if you actually liked me, or if you were just being polite when I'd ask you all those questions after class."

"I was definitely *not* just being polite."

She let out a small laugh and cocked her head at him.

He wanted to kiss her but didn't dare. Not until he'd told her.

"Shall we sit down?" he asked, surprised at the formality in his voice, and walked toward a young weeping willow with a small patch of grass beneath it. Gregory sat cross-legged and patted the ground. Liv positioned herself next to him, her movements gracefully efficient.

He took the wine from the bag, and they both laughed as he fumbled with the floppy silver corkscrew. "I don't get much practice," he said, relieved when he managed to pry out the cork in one piece.

"More of a beer guy?"

"Something like that. I forgot to get glasses," Gregory said, apologetically holding up the open bottle.

"Oh, please!" Liv took the wine from his hands. "I'm not as proper as I look." She winked and lifted the bottle to her mouth. She sipped carefully, then giggled as she wiped an errant red droplet from her chin.

She handed the bottle back to Gregory, who gripped the neck, trying to decide what to tell her. He gazed down the hill at the expanse of gravestones. Beneath each one was a casket. And in each casket lay the decaying body of a person who likely once had a secret or two. Gregory assumed that his secret would die with him, and cemeteries reminded him of just how long he would have to lug around the weight of his burden. Six years now and counting. It already felt like a lifetime. He could sense Liv studying him in the spare moonlight. "Are you sure cemeteries don't freak you out?" she asked. She shivered and inched her body toward his.

Gregory shook his head and fixed his eyes on a frowning marble cherub. "Sorry. No. I'm just a little distracted. End-of-semester stuff."

After another moment, Liv reached for the bottle and carefully tugged it out of his hand. She took one more sip, recorked it, and laid it on the grass. She slid the magnolia from behind her ear and shook her head until her hair fell loosely around her face. "Listen, Gregory," she said, twirling the flower stem between her fingers like a small white pinwheel. "I haven't waited months for this night only to have you turn morose on me. Is it really school stuff, or is something else going on?"

He closed his eyes and breathed in sharply. She had been waiting, too. He wasn't imagining it.

"You don't"—she hesitated before raising her eyes at him—"you don't have a girlfriend, do you?"

"No! God, no!"

She blew out an exaggerated breath of relief and returned her gaze to the flower. She brought it to her nose again and sniffed, shutting her eyes as she searched for the faint fragrance. Just looking at her made Gregory's chest ache.

Tell her.

"I, um," he started, but when Liv's eyes shot open, he paused. She lowered the flower to her lap. "What is it?"

Gregory thought of all the times in college that he'd gone to St. Thomas on a Saturday evening, kneeled in the confession booth, as dark and narrow as an upright coffin, and tried to force the words out. But he would become light-headed and fabricate some venial sin that he whispered through the dark screen—*I fought with my parents, swore at my sister.* Then he'd duck out from behind the purple velvet curtain and exit the church, not bothering with the prayers of penance the priest had assigned.

Or how many times he had almost told his sister, Margaret, but stopped himself, unsure if he could trust her. What if she got drunk with her friends from high school and just happened to let slip, *You remember Joey Didowski, that kid who killed himself?*

But Liv was different, not at all like his sister. Margaret was impulsive and strong-willed—just like him, just like their father—whereas Liv was thoughtful and understanding. If she really did like him as much as she seemed to, it would probably turn out okay.

She was looking at him, her eyes gentle with encouragement. Gregory licked his lips and swallowed. "I had a best friend named Joey, and, um …" He grabbed the wine from the ground. His hands were shaky, but he managed to work the cork out. He took a long chug, drew the sleeve of his sweater across his mouth, and lowered the bottle between his crossed legs. "Joey killed himself two years ago."

"Oh, Gregory!" Liv shuttled her body closer until she was positioned in front of him, their knees almost touching. "I'm so sorry."

Gregory nodded.

"That must have been terrible. For so many people. Do you know why he did it?"

Gregory looked up at her. Their faces were close. Close enough that he would only have to lean forward to kiss her and put an end to all of this.

"He did something. Something disgraceful that he never forgave himself for."

Liv waited. "Disgraceful? That's a hefty word. Like a crime?"

"Yeah."

"How bad?"

"Pretty bad."

"Did anyone get hurt?"

Gregory drew a breath and said it before he could stop himself. "It was a hit-and-run."

Liv put her hand over her chest. Her eyes grew wide. "Did the person"—she hesitated—"die?"

"Maybe."

"He didn't tell you?"

"I don't think he knew for sure what happened. We didn't talk about it very much. He didn't want to."

Liv drew back, and Gregory felt the air grow cooler.

"I see," she said.

What an idiot. He had almost told her everything. And then what? She probably wouldn't even let him drive her home, let alone ever go out with him again.

"I'm still sorry. No one should die by suicide," Liv said, hesitantly. "But if I did something like that—and then fled—I don't know if I could live with myself, either." She looked up at him. "Could you?"

Gregory shook his head. His mouth was so dry he could barely speak. "Probably not."

"You must miss him. Your friend. Even if, in the end, he wasn't, well, I don't know, okay."

Gregory's gaze dropped to the magnolia in Liv's fingers. One of the delicate, tear-shaped petals was already bruised. "Yeah. I do. I miss him."

Liv set the flower on the grass near her feet and reached for Gregory's hands. "Friends can help with that, you know?"

Gregory shrugged. "I guess."

"And," Liv's voice lightened, "I've heard there are some good therapists out there. Or there are about to be."

He pressed his lips together and nodded.

"Or maybe," she paused, "I can help you." She slid her hands up to his shoulders and kneaded them until his neck began to relax. "I'm right here," she said. "In case you hadn't noticed."

When their lips finally touched, he felt such relief he almost collapsed on top of her. To keep from falling, he pulled her down into the grass beside him and hugged her so tight she squealed. Then she laughed, and they kept kissing.

Her lips tasted like the tannins in the wine, and as he held her against him, learning the surprising strength of her arms and muscled back, he felt grateful that he hadn't told her the truth about his role in the accident. How could he expect Liv—or anyone—to understand?

When they paused for a moment, Liv pulled away so they could look at each other. "I really like you, Gregory," she said. "You're a good person."

He cringed a little and wanted to argue, but instead he smiled.

Greg had never told anyone what happened that night, and Gregory wouldn't either. Instead, he was going to make Liv fall in love with him the way he was already falling in love with her. He would finish his studies, become a clinical psychologist, marry Olivia J. Stimson in a church filled with white magnolia blossoms, and build a life with her. A house. Some kids. A career helping people.

It would all be okay. He would make it okay—for both of them.

"Hey there," Liv said, gently calling his gaze back. "Don't go away again."

"I won't," he said, looking her in the eyes. "I promise."

He leaned through the darkness and paused before kissing her again. It felt like a pact under the weeping willow, more powerful to him than the marriage vows they would take.

Gregory looked up at Mira. She smiled warmly as he sat there in the client chair. If he kept this up, he could ruin his career. And what if he did? Wasn't everything already lost? At this point, he was willing to risk his practice and his marriage to keep talking to her. Did it really matter that he tried to prevent this person from drinking or that person from starving herself? Did those things justify his pathetic existence? Mira's red lips were parted slightly, and he wondered whom she kissed. He hadn't kissed anyone except Liv since he was twenty-three.

"What was it that you kept from Olivia?" Mira asked.

"What?"

"You held something back that night, just like you're holding something back right now."

Gregory's chest tightened. How did she know? Or was she operating on the same kind of instinct he applied when a situation felt incomplete with a client, and he tossed out a line to see if anything caught? Either way, he had learned how to handle moments like this: he said nothing and kept his face inscrutable.

Mira waited him out a bit. Then she drew a small breath and said, "A wise person once told me that we can never heal as long as we repress. I've certainly found that to be true."

"Have you been in therapy before?"

She nodded carefully. "I have. And you?"

Gregory squirmed and sat up straighter. He needed to shift the focus away from himself and gain back some professional decorum. "Are there things you haven't wanted to look at in your past? Is that why you're here now?"

She gave a knowing smile. She had seen right through his attempt to change their dynamic. "I've certainly tried to both forget and move beyond my past, so perhaps we are similar that way."

He tried not to flinch.

"I'm sure we'll talk about that in time," she said, "but for now, perhaps you can share some of those dark corners you never reveal."

Gregory felt two parts of his psyche pulling for dominance. His desire to fully unburden himself vied with his belief that opening up to Mira would cost him everything he valued.

But how did she know him so well? Maybe she had done her research, found every scrap of information about him online. Maybe she'd been watching him, or, like some of his clients, she was an expert at reading people and manipulating them. She'd been deflecting his questions, redirecting the focus back to him. But none of that really mattered. When she pressed her lips together and studied his face with such open curiosity, he couldn't focus on his clinical assessments.

After a moment in which neither of them said a word, Gregory's subconscious revealed an answer, a safe compromise. "There is something I've never told anyone," he said hesitantly. "Words I've never spoken out loud."

Mira waited.

Gregory shook his head as if clearing his thoughts. "Sometimes I think that marrying Liv is one of the worst things I've ever done to anyone."

"Getting married was the worst thing?"

Gregory looked at her, afraid to ask her things, but desperate to know them. "Are you married?"

Mira shook her head. "Not even in love, but I was once."

"What happened?"

"We hurt each other very badly."

Gregory nodded, not sure how much to push. He needed her to keep talking. He felt such relief at sharing his pain with her. "I feel like I hurt Liv every day."

"So why don't you change that?" She raised her arm to tuck back a piece of hair.

Gregory drew a deep breath and tipped his head back. What was she implying? That he leave his wife? Tell Liv what he'd done and risk losing his family? Of course, he'd already considered these possibilities, and now that she'd opened the door on them, he wondered if she was offering him an escape. A way out. Should he ask her to clarify?

"Well," Mira said in her decisive way. "That's something to think about. But our time is up."

Gregory watched her stand, saying nothing as she shook out her legs and smoothed down her blouse. Looking at her again, he wished he could kiss her. Except he knew that it was too soon. He didn't want to scare her off. Instead he wished she would hug him, lean over and wrap her arms around him reassuringly, pressing her shoulders to his, their chests touching, so he could inhale her scent and feel the heat from her body.

As if she could hear his thoughts, she paused as she passed his chair and gently touched his shoulder. When she did, he felt a light shock of static electricity from the carpet.

"Goodbye, Mira," he said, waiting for her to say, *See you next week*. He needed that confirmation.

When she opened the door into his waiting room, her silver bracelets jangled like chimes.

"Mira."

She halted. "Yes?"

"Next Wednesday at one?"

"Of course."

Gregory sat and listened for the outside door to shut with that annoying bang. When he didn't hear it, he stood and opened his door into the waiting room. Mira was still there. With her hand on the door of the third, unused office, she turned to him, her face twisted with confusion. "It's locked. I can't get out."

"Wrong door," he said, surprised to see her so disoriented. He pointed to the exit.

She shook her head and hurried across the room.

7

Lifting the cooler off the kitchen floor, Gregory was surprised by the heft. Inside, he discovered that Liv had packed steak tips, green salad, and pasta salad with tuna, his dad's favorite. She'd also added cans of seltzer and two bottles of prosecco. Gregory's idea had been to buy a carrot cake and keep the birthday visit short, but Liv said why go all that way unless they were going to have lunch together. So, she had coordinated with his sister, Margaret, and her wife, Jas, to make it a party.

At Liv's emphatic prompting, Carrie dragged herself downstairs, shuffled into the kitchen, and opened the fridge. She stood there, staring at the shelves crammed with the usual staples as well as takeout containers, rarely used condiments, and the many provisions of a family that would never have to worry about the exorbitant cost of groceries.

"There's nothing to eat," she said.

"Look in the produce drawer," Liv said. "It's full of fruit."

"Fruit isn't morning food. It doesn't even fill me up." Carrie shut the fridge door and checked her phone before tucking it in her back pocket. "Why do I have to go if Petey doesn't? I love Grandpa and everything, but I don't want to spend my day off at a fucking nursing home potluck."

"Language, please, Carolyn Weber!" Liv said. "We don't know how many more birthdays your grandfather will have. If Petey weren't at camp, he'd be going, too. You know that." Liv returned her attention to fixing her coffee for the road. "And if you want breakfast, get up earlier and make yourself an egg sandwich."

"Eggs are gross." Carrie unwound her earbuds and headed out of the house.

Gregory waited for the door to slam. "If Carrie doesn't want to go," he said in a low voice, "I'm fine with it. It won't matter to Dad." He picked up the bouquet of delphiniums and foxgloves he had snipped from his garden that morning and set it on the cooler.

"Seriously?" Liv asked, pausing to study him. Gregory thought she looked tired. Even the start of a summer tan couldn't conceal the dark circles under her eyes. "That's the lesson you want to give our kids? That it doesn't matter if we show up for family?"

"Of course not. But it's her day off, and my dad is so checked out. The way things are with Carrie and me right now, I'm not sure it's worth the fight."

Liv looked at him with a closed-mouth smile, and he thought she might capitulate. She had certainly had her own issues when her mother was sick. Helen's Parkinson's had led to a fall and a fatal blood clot, but Liv had rallied daily to get to her bedside, never flagging on those daughterly responsibilities.

"Carrie should go, because that's what family does," Liv said. "And I think we need to be aligned on that point."

Carrie was curled up in the back seat with her earbuds. Gregory guessed she would be aggressively withdrawn all day, and his real hope in suggesting she stay behind was to have a few hours alone in the car with Liv. He still didn't want to divulge the Mira situation—not yet—but he wanted to talk to his wife, in a real way, about their strained marriage. He knew that if he and Liv started discussing things openly in front of Carrie, she would tune into the conversation. She had Gregory's highly sensitive antenna when it came to reading expressions, even in a rearview mirror.

He started the BMW. It had been Liv's choice for him, a good, safe car.

"Can I drive?" Carrie asked.

Gregory gripped the wheel, sucked in his breath, and tried to collect himself. Liv knew he was terrified of their phone-addicted teenage daughter getting behind the wheel, but she had no idea of the extent of it. "Not today, honey," he said. "It's a long way."

"How am I going to get my license if you never let me drive?"

"I'll take you out after work this week," Liv said. She turned to Gregory. "Remember to stop at Pemby's for the cake."

Carrie pulled out an earbud. "Can you get me an iced mocha and a muffin, or something?"

When Liv didn't answer, Carrie said, "Hello?"

"You had time to eat at home."

"Fine." Carrie put her earbud back in and crossed her arms over her chest. "On top of spending Sunday with a bunch of old people, I'll also be starving. Petey has no idea how lucky he is to be at camp all summer."

"We offered you the same opportunity," Liv reminded her. "And you passed."

"Whatever," Carrie said.

A few minutes later when they were stopped at a light, Gregory turned to Liv. "I'm okay if she wants to get a coffee and a muffin." Takeout food usually mollified Carrie, at least for the short time that she was enjoying it.

"She doesn't want a coffee," Liv said. "She wants what is essentially a milkshake. Those drinks are pure sugar. We have a fridge full of healthy food, so I'm not sure why she needs to eat dessert at this hour."

With both earbuds in, Carrie said, "Sorry, Mom, but I'm not the one that's weird about food."

"That's enough!" Gregory said to Carrie. He seldom had the strength to challenge her teenage hostility; she had anger enough to outlast almost anyone, definitely him. But he always took a stand when she charged at Liv's weak spot.

Liv turned sharply to Gregory. "Pull over, please."

"Do you want me to handle this?"

"Just pull over."

"As soon as I find a safe place."

It was possible Liv would get out and walk the half mile back home. And then what? Maybe a car ride to Connecticut with Carrie, just the two of them, would be the best solution. When Carrie was little, they often went on father-daughter adventures, and whenever she asked for a treat, he indulged her, mostly because he had spent his childhood in a state of longing for the things he wasn't allowed to have.

But when Gregory pulled into a free space on Mass Ave. Liv didn't even unbuckle her seat belt. She rotated her torso enough to look at Carrie, whose gaze was fixed out the window. "I am not in the mood today for this attitude. I'll buy you a coffee, but next time, you can make yourself breakfast at home or ask me, and I'll happily make something for you. Is that clear?"

"Yep." Carrie flopped back against the leather.

Liv turned around and nodded. Gregory checked his mirrors twice and pulled out.

"I would really like us all to have a nice day," Liv said. "It's important for you to have a relationship with your grandfather."

"Grandpa is totally off-line," Carrie said.

"You can stop right now," Gregory told Carrie, even though it was true and kind of funny.

When Liv dashed into Pemby's for the cake, Gregory turned to Carrie. "Listening to anything good?"

Carrie shut her eyes and started humming.

A few minutes later, Liv came out balancing a large white box in the crook of her arm. In the other hand, she gripped an iced mocha and a bakery bag. She handed Carrie the drink and the bag, then carefully set the cake on the floor.

"Thanks, Mom!" Carrie said, swinging from contemptuous teenager to sweet kid. "I really appreciate it."

"You're welcome."

"I'm sorry I said that about the way you eat."

In the rearview, Gregory watched Carrie tear the paper off the straw with her teeth.

Liv inhaled sharply. She shut her door harder than necessary and snapped on her seat belt. Before they were even on the highway, she had pulled her tablet from her bag and was curled against the door lost in a book.

"What are you reading?" Gregory said.

Liv looked up. "Oh, one of those self-help things. It's called *How to Manage the Mother Load*."

"Good?"

"It's all right. My therapist recommended it, for dealing with—" She glimpsed back at Carrie, still lost in her music. "It's about how to be a good mother when the one you had couldn't mother you."

"Do you think about her a lot?" Gregory asked. "Your mom?"

"All the time. I'm still trying to please her."

"She'd be proud of you."

Liv lowered the tablet to her lap. "I don't know about that."

"She would be. She really did love you."

Liv sighed heavily. "After growing up in a family that used love as a reward for accomplishments, I always thought my love for my own family would mean something. Because it came without conditions."

"Your love means everything, Liv." It was true. Everything he had was because of her love. His career. Petey and Carrie. His life. Even his need for Mira, in a sick way. He didn't want to lose all of that.

Liv reached for her travel mug of coffee in the cup holder and took a long sip. "Sometimes I think the kiddos I tutor love me more than—" She hitched her neck at the back seat and stopped herself. "I'm just feeling lost these days."

"Lost?"

"I don't know. I guess rudderless is more like it."

"Is it time to put in those grad school applications?"

"Probably. But I'm not sure a master's degree will cure what ails me."

"Which is?"

She hesitated. "Loneliness, I think. I don't know anymore. But I did sign up for a memoir class. I'm at a dead end with my therapist, so maybe if I write what I'm feeling, I'll make sense of things. It's something anyway."

Gregory held tight to the wheel. It was time to tell her what he'd been hiding for so long. He couldn't give her everything she needed, but he had to start somewhere. He owed her that much, even as his thoughts swam with Mira, her dark hair sweeping across her face. "Maybe we should go away for a few days. Just the two of us."

Liv looked at him with a surprised smile. "Really?"

His stomach tightened. "Yeah."

"How about the weekend of Visiting Day at Petey's camp? I could book a place on the other side of Sebago Lake."

"Sure." He rolled down the window to get some air. "Let's do that."

Liv reached across the center console and put a hand on his knee. The car felt hot and he began to sweat. He rolled up the window and blasted the air conditioner. He wondered how he would ever manage this. Confess to her, after all these years?

After a while of driving in silence, he realized something, and it calmed him. Maybe Mira could help him figure it out.

8

As soon as the desk attendant buzzed them through the lobby door, the odor hit him: urine, bleach, and the plastic of IV bags and bedpans. Pleasant Springs was one of the most expensive nursing homes in Connecticut, but they all smelled the same. Gregory checked Carrie's expression. It was carefully blank—the mocha mood still in effect.

With Gregory carrying the cooler, Liv the cake, and Carrie the flowers, they made their way toward room 109, passing two old men in wheelchairs staring at their knees and a nearly bald woman in a loose housedress inching her walker down the corridor. Liv offered a friendly hello to everyone—the staff at the desk, the residents, other visitors—while Carrie and Gregory followed in her wake, smiling awkwardly. In room 109, Gregory's father was hidden behind a curtain in the bed farthest from the door, while his roommate, Frank, slept, mouth open, snoring.

"Hello, Dad!" Gregory called out loudly. "It's your son, Greg. And Liv and Carrie. Petey's not here, but he sends his love."

"Hi, Bob!" Liv said.

Carrie held the bouquet of flowers in one hand while scrolling through her phone with the other. "Please put that away," Liv whispered as she nudged Carrie forward.

"Happy birthday, Grandpa!" Carrie slipped the phone in her back pocket.

"Good morning, Bob's family," a cheery voice called from behind the curtain. "I'm getting Mr. Bob ready for his big day. Isn't that right? You are Birthday Boy Bob today!"

"Oh, hey there, Fitz," Gregory said. "Need help with anything?" He fervently hoped he didn't.

"No, thank you, sir. We are just finishing up." Fitz drew back the privacy curtain with a flourish and smiled broadly at the three of them lingering in the room. Fitz was lanky and buff in his blue scrubs. Gregory's father, propped in his wheelchair, with a spare comb-over of gray strands and a bewildered, slack-mouthed expression on his face, looked like an apparition next to him.

"Look at your beautiful family, Bob! They came to celebrate your birthday." Fitz glanced down at Gregory's father. "How old are you today, Bob? Do you remember?"

Bob smiled weakly. He adored Fitz. A few years ago, he would have spent their whole visit muttering about Fitz's dreadlocks and ponytail, scoffing under his breath to Gregory's mother, *What kind of self-respecting man?* But his dementia had removed his judgmental reflexes and Fitz was now, with a God-given patience that Gregory could only marvel at, Bob's favorite person to spend time with. On a quiet afternoon, they might play a game of gin rummy together, even if Bob couldn't remember the rules, or Fitz would read him an article about the Red Sox from *Sports Illustrated.* Fitz was why Gregory gave the staff at Pleasant Springs a bounteous holiday tip each year.

"I don't know," Bob said, hardly moving his mouth when he spoke. "Am I sixty-two?"

"You're eighty-five, Bob!" Fitz said, clapping him lightly on one shoulder. "But you look sixty-two, so that's a good guess.

And today I want you to party like a young man." Fitz smiled at Carrie, who smiled back. Then he left the room, acknowledging the box in Liv's hand. "I hope that's cake."

"It is," Liv answered brightly. "We'll save you a piece!"

"Make it a big one," Fitz said as he greeted another resident in the hallway.

Gregory, Liv, and Carrie made their way past Frank's bed over to Bob's side of the long, rectangular room, where Margaret had taped several of her watercolors to the wall around the double windows.

Liv leaned down and gave her father-in-law a peck while Carrie set the flowers on the windowsill. When Liv and Carrie cleared out of the tight space between the wheelchair and bed, Gregory hunched over and offered his father a half-committed hug, trying to feel something more than sadness at the chalky touch of his cheek.

"Ready for your party today, Dad?" Gregory asked.

Bob looked at him. "Where's Fitz?"

"It's your birthday," Liv said. "We brought lunch and a cake." She held up the box. "Carrot cake, your favorite."

"There's a cake in there?" Bob asked. "What kind of cake?"

"Carrot cake," Liv said again, this time loudly.

"Not chocolate?"

"Next year!" She turned to Gregory, switching to her normal voice. "I think Carrie and I are going to go set up lunch on the patio. That way you can spend some time with your dad."

"Sounds like a plan." Gregory waited for Carrie to follow Liv out before settling into the chair next to his father, the exact place where he spent the better part of two Sundays each month, watching the seasons move slowly through the stand of oaks behind Pleasant Springs, where there was no actual spring. Margaret came the other two weekends and—God bless her—several times during the week. She only lived twenty minutes away and worked from home doing freelance graphic design as well as her own art on the side. Gregory didn't know if it ever felt like penance for her, too, but he tried to turn the tedious hours into a meditation of sorts, accepting the in and out of his own breath as he and his father sat together saying next to nothing, the minutes passing with anemic slowness. Gregory liked it best when they watched a movie or when Fitz came in and broke up the time with small talk. Even when his dad couldn't put a proper sentence together, Fitz, with his booming laugh, filled the silence, making it feel like they were having an actual conversation, real and robust.

On the rare occasion when Margaret and Gregory were there together, Margaret kept busy, cheerfully puttering around the room, neatening the closet or restocking Bob's supply of non-choking candy in the bottom dresser drawer. Each day, Bob was allowed one small piece—a Reese's Peanut Butter Cup or a Hershey's bar—from the value bags Margaret bought with coupons at Rite Aid. Sometimes it was the only thing in his routine that Bob remembered to ask for. *Did I get my candy bar today?* Or Margaret would bring him a container of split pea or chicken noodle soup from Rein's Deli and spoon-feed him while they watched *I Love Lucy.* "What's this show?" he'd ask every now and then and open his mouth for another spoonful, broth dribbling down his chin. Once last year, when Margaret and Gregory were there together for a meeting with the nursing staff, the siblings returned to the room to find Bob asleep in bed, his hands clasped over his chest. Without a word, Margaret pulled a pencil and battered sketch pad from her bag, dropped into the chair, and started drawing the lines of their father's hands, gnarled and calloused from years of gardening without gloves. That day, Gregory stood by watching silently, awed by his sister's ability to turn their father's rough edges into something artistic.

With Liv and Carrie gone and nothing to do but make small talk, Gregory adjusted himself in the bedside chair. "How are you doing, Dad?" Gregory asked in a loud, clear voice.

"Good," Bob answered, studying Gregory for a few seconds before his focus dissolved. His head drooped so that his chin sank into his neck, and his eyes closed until Gregory gently shook him by the arm, bringing him back to the conversation. At least once every visit, Gregory wondered if his father had died while sitting there. And in those few seconds, he was never quite sure how he felt about it, for either of them.

"So, let's see," Gregory said. He looked at his dad's face. Should he tell him about Mira? Should he tell him how he had begun to be fully honest with someone for the first time in decades? He didn't dare, even knowing his father wouldn't retain a word of it.

"Liv took Petey up to camp in New Hampshire last Saturday," Gregory said. "He'll be there for six weeks."

"Is that so?" Bob said.

"Happy birthday, Dad!"

Just then, Margaret burst into the room. She was holding a long flat present wrapped in newsprint. Gregory assumed it was one of her paintings. Behind her, Jas, whose real name was Jaslene—but only Margaret ever called her that—strolled in on high heels, her signature footwear that added several inches to her short frame. She was carrying a large aluminum casserole dish.

"Hey, Greg," Jas called out.

"Hi, Jas. Hey, Maggie."

Margaret gave Gregory a quick hug before bending to hug their father in his wheelchair. Unlike Gregory, who fumbled at this simple physical connection, Margaret actually got her arms around Bob's back and held him in a full embrace. When she let him go, he looked jostled but pleased.

Jas set her casserole on the windowsill next to the flowers, then she and Gregory hugged warmly, an acknowledgment that they sincerely liked each other. Jas, who grew up in New Britain and graduated from Central Connecticut State University, was the director of guidance at a high school in Hartford. Gregory imagined that in her thoughtful but take-no-prisoners way, she could earn the trust of both the troublemakers and the students who struggled to open up.

"Happy birthday, Berto," Jas said, and gave her father-in-law a kiss. With a throaty laugh, she thumbed off the bright lipstick mark left behind on his cheek.

Bob seemed to perk up at the attention, and Gregory wondered how he would feel if he could actually comprehend that this curvy Latina woman with red-tinted hair and a nose ring was his daughter's legally wedded wife. Would Margaret's choice in a partner be more tolerable to him than her my-love-is-infinite polyamory phase, when he called her "disgusting" and banned her, for years, from her childhood home? In her twenties and early thirties, Margaret dated whomever she wanted. Multiple men. Multiple women. A combo. Whenever Margaret offered information about one of her relationships, Gregory listened, without asking a lot of questions. Their parents had raised them strictly Catholic, and Gregory had never fully let go of the guilt and shame that came with that. And so he avoided his sister's many romantic entanglements.

Liv had always tried to include Margaret in family events, especially when she and Gregory were first together. But Gregory would find reasons not to in an attempt to deny that part of his life. He was terrified of whom Margaret would bring along; her friends were like strays, eclectic and unpredictable, including a bald scientist named Karl who attended Gregory and Liv's formal wedding in shorts and a bolo tie and lectured to anyone too polite to walk away about how the bacon wrapped around the scallops came from a suffering pig on a factory farm. Although that was a blessedly short-lived relationship for Margaret, people at the club still occasionally brought him up with a chuckle: *Remember that vegan guy at your wedding who couldn't stop talking about slaughterhouses?*

"How do you do it?" Gregory had once asked Margaret when she was still practicing polyamory. "How do you keep all of those different relationships going?" He could still remember her exact reply. The more love you give, the more you get. Her words baffled him. How could one person have that much love to give?

"Where is everyone?" Margaret asked. She was tall and big boned, as their mother used to say, and filled the space at the end of Bob's bed.

"Liv and Carrie are outside setting up," Gregory told her.

Margaret whisked a glass vase from the cabinet beneath the TV and handed it to Jas, who headed to the bathroom to fill it with water.

"How are you doing, Dad?" Margaret asked as she pushed toward his side table, looking for something that needed attention.

"There's cake," Dad said. "Chocolate."

"Carrot," Gregory said.

"Well, of course," Margaret said. "It's your birthday. And Jaslene made the rice-and-bean dish you love. Not too spicy."

Gregory watched, mesmerized as Margaret fixed their father's collar, tugged his cuffs down, and massaged his gnarled knuckles. This man had all but ignored her growing up, thrown her out of the house, and physically abused their mother at least once, and now she fussed over him with an easy devotion.

"Everything good in your world, Greggy?" Margaret asked.

He paused. "Fine. Yeah."

"You don't sound so sure." She sat down next to the bed and pulled an emery board from the narrow drawer of the pressed-wood nightstand. "Time for your man-mani," she said. She lifted one of Bob's hands and filed away at his yellowed nails, her wavy brown hair, threaded with gray, falling into her face as she bent to the task.

How Gregory wished they were closer and he could tell her what was going on with Mira, how he'd found someone who saw through his ugly mistakes and flaws and accepted him as he was, messy and imperfect but trying to be better.

Margaret, judgmental about accumulating unnecessary wealth and social climbing, was completely accepting of unorthodox relationships. If he were to confess to his older sister that a woman he didn't know had appeared in his office two weeks in a row and started doing some sort of talk therapy on him, she'd shrug and say, *I hope you're learning something about yourself.*

Jas returned and arranged the flowers in the swirly green vase. "So pretty," she said, standing back to admire the result. "From your garden, Greg?"

He nodded. "They are."

"So, Dad," Margaret said. She gently replaced his hand on top of the other in his lap. "How about we start this party?" She tucked the emery board back in the drawer, unlocked Bob's wheelchair, and started pushing him toward the door. Jas followed with the casserole, her heels clicking on the vinyl floor.

Watching his sister and her wife move with such purpose made Gregory feel even more incompetent. Could he stay behind for a few minutes? Would he even be missed?

"Grab the present would you, Greggy?" Margaret called over her shoulder. "But careful. It's breakable."

Gregory lifted the package, fingering the thin glass through the wrapping. Everything felt so fragile these days.

9

Out on the patio, Liv offered Margaret and Jas big hugs. Although Liv found certain things about her sister-in-law hard to take—the disheveled apartment and Margaret's relentless talk about her rescue cats—she tried endlessly to be kind and admiring, but she didn't always hit the right notes. *I love the pearly snaps on your flannel shirt, Margaret,* didn't quite ring true coming from Liv in a silk Armani blouse.

It's not you personally, Gregory assured Liv. *My sister just doesn't like rich people.*

While Margaret knew how to play nice in public, she occasionally tested Liv in various ways, but none more obvious than with the artwork she had given them over the years, almost daring Liv to relegate the paintings to the attic. "How can I hang this?" Liv once asked Gregory after Margaret had sent them a large acrylic of a round green-and-brown ball exploding luxury car logos. On the back was the title: *Burst Earth.* The few times that Margaret had visited them in Cambridge, Gregory resorted to temporarily displaying some (but not all) of her art, once even taking down a Dalí lithograph to make room for Margaret's wedding present: an oil painting of a nude man and woman entwined in a daisy chain, flowers concealing their private parts. And yet Margaret, with her keen artist's eye, zeroed in on the telltale wall marks left by the

Dalí, a sign that her own painting had been put up provisionally. "If I'd known color was outlawed in this house," she remarked to Gregory, "I would have done a still life with cotton balls."

Carrie loved Aunt Maggie's bold outspokenness but struggled with her persistent stream of questions about school: *Are you learning legitimate history or the whitewashed version?* Carrie gravitated more easily toward Jas, who, at thirty-nine, was almost ten years younger than Margaret and understood from professional experience that a sixteen-year-old girl didn't want to spend her day talking revisionist history with her aunt.

"How goes it, *mija*?" Jas asked Carrie.

At the table several feet away, but still within hearing distance, Gregory opened a bottle of prosecco and set out a row of short plastic cups.

"Pretty good," Carrie said. "Summer is, like, whatever. I don't know."

"Doing anything fun?" Jas asked.

"I work at our club, so I get to hang out at the pool after I'm done."

"That's cool," Jas said. Her voice dropped to a conspiratorial whisper. "You talking to anyone?"

Without knowing exactly what Jas meant by "talking," Gregory assumed from her guarded tone that she was asking if Carrie had a boyfriend or a crush. Carrie paused, and from the corner of his eye, he saw her pivot her head and check that no one was listening. Gregory began to pour the prosecco, doing his best to seem absorbed in the task.

Carrie leaned in closer to Jas. "Well, there's this girl Jessie who looks mad hot in her purple bikini."

"Ooh, you got a lady!"

"We're just talking. It's so weird. Like, I *think* she's queer. But I don't know." Carrie looked imploringly at Jas and lowered her voice. "But don't say anything, please! I'd die if Princess found out."

Gregory set the bottle down. His most recent fill was bubbling over, but he didn't try to control the puddle spreading across the blue tablecloth. Did he just hear that? Carrie likes girls? Did Liv know? And who was Princess? Liv? Or, God forbid, *him*? Gregory took a breath and tried to steady himself. He would support his kids' sexual preferences whatever they were, but he was surprised to have had no idea about this development. Whom Carrie *liked* didn't matter; it did matter that his daughter couldn't trust him not to judge her. Maybe she'd overheard Liv and him discussing Margaret and thought twice about sharing her crushes with them.

He glanced quickly at Carrie, who was still talking to Jas but in low tones, with their backs now turned to everyone, including him. Was it Jas alone who kept Carrie's secrets, or did Margaret also know more about his daughter than he did? Did Carrie share things with her aunts because he and Liv were too uptight? He picked up the overflowing cup of prosecco and downed it. Acting fast, Gregory refilled his cup, filled two others—one with seltzer—and hurried over to Jas and Carrie.

"Thanks, Dad," Carrie said when he appeared in front of them and handed each a drink. Carrie raised her eyebrows at Jas.

"Sure," Gregory said. He lifted his cup. He wanted the three of them to raise a glass together over something, anything. To create a bond that included him. "A toast to—"

Jas held up a finger to indicate *wait a minute* and said, "Hey, everybody! How about a toast to Bob?" She hurried to the table, picked up two cups, and brought them to Liv and Margaret. They were seated on either side of Bob, chatting across him while each holding one of his hands.

Before Jas returned to the table to get her own, she rubbed a hand across Margaret's back, a gesture so easy and intimate that it filled Gregory with sadness for what he and Liv no longer had. He pictured Mira with her soft, accepting expression. At the end of their last session, she'd gently placed her hand on his shoulder, just as Jas had done for Margaret.

He trained his attention on Carrie, his daughter who was maybe gay, or bi, but wouldn't tell him. She had said something to him that he missed. "What, honey?" he asked.

"Nothing." Carrie enunciated the word like she was stomping on it; then she walked away from her father, who was left standing alone with his second cup of prosecco, which he didn't even like.

Jas raised her cup. "Feliz cumpleaños, Berto!" Everyone toasted and took a sip. With Margaret's help, even Bob guided the rim to his lips. Gregory drained his second cup and went to the table to open the other bottle.

In the post-toast pause, Margaret waved her free hand to hold attention. She announced that she had a present for her father, her tone indicating that she wanted everyone to witness the reveal. She reached for the large, flat parcel next to her chair and carefully balanced it on her father's lap. Bob, looking pleased, started thumbing at the newspaper wrapping, and Margaret patiently let him, without trying to help or finish the job. It took him a few awkward minutes to part all the paper—long enough for Gregory to refill and empty his cup a few more times. He was hungry, but lunch was still under wraps, and since no one had prepared appetizers, there was nothing to absorb the alcohol.

When the newspaper finally drifted to the ground, everyone except Gregory crowded around. Even Carrie was peering over her grandfather's shoulder. Gregory assumed the gift was a painting, but when he stepped closer, he saw that it was one of those oversize frames with a dozen or so openings for photos.

"See, Dad," Margaret said, pointing out the various people. "It's our family. There's your son, Greg, and his wife, Olivia, on their wedding day—"

"Let me see," Liv said, leaning in to inspect the photo.

Gregory took the opportunity to pour a fifth cup of prosecco, which was starting to work on him in the hot sun. He closed his eyes as he drank.

"You guys look like babies!" Carrie said, her tone lighter than usual as she hunched over the frame.

Liv laughed. "We *were* babies!"

Margaret pointed at another photo. "There's you and Mom and Greg and me," she said to their father. "Hey, Greggy," she called. "Do you remember this one, when Mom made us dress up for one of those Sears studio portraits?"

Lifting his chin, trying to rise above the soft, logy feeling that came from drinking in the sun on an empty stomach, Gregory sauntered over and looked down at the photos swimming before him, this constellation of people related by blood but still completely disconnected—at least from him. It was only the darkness, like the black cardboard between the photos, that mortared them together. He made himself concentrate, his eyes landing first on the wedding photo in which he and Liv, smiling brightly, were clinking engraved champagne glasses. With her straight blond hair styled under her veil and her delicate features transformed by makeup, Liv had been almost unrecognizable to him on their wedding day. For a few seconds, as he waited at the altar of First Church on Garden Street in Harvard Square, Gregory thought he was at someone else's wedding and the wrong woman was walking toward him down the aisle.

Next to the photo of Gregory and Liv was a shot from Margaret and Jas's wedding two years ago. With their arms encircling each other's necks—Jas in a low-cut white pantsuit and Margaret in an embroidered red dress that she had made herself—they both wore expressions of glee and maybe disbelief. Although Greg had been disappointed that he and Liv weren't invited to the private ceremony, just the reception afterward at an Airbnb in Winsted, the party turned out to be plenty celebratory, with Jas's extended family up from San Juan and the band that played until three in the morning making it impossible to fall asleep any earlier in his and Liv's assigned bedroom overlooking the lawn.

Finally, he followed Margaret's finger to the Sears photo smack in the center, the focal point of the tableau. He remembered the occasion but not the photo. He had just turned ten and had to change out of his play clothes in a dressing room with a broken lock, terrified that someone would barge in on him in his underwear. Out in the overly lit studio, his parents sat posed on a bench while Margaret, with her well-fluffed eighties hair, stood behind them against the blue paper background. He was positioned next to Margaret and could remember being told, *Move in closer to your sister. She doesn't bite.*

In the portrait, his father looked trim and tall, a different man from the frail one slumped in his wheelchair. But it was Gregory's mother, Carol, who made his heart hurt. The stiff pose, the strained smile. After the shoot, she proudly handed the coupon with the payment to the woman at the register. Nothing like a bargain to lift his father's mood. But then the confusion. She would only receive one small photo for the coupon price. The eight-by-ten would be $19.99 more. *It's in the small print, ma'am. Would you like to upgrade to a better photo package?* Gregory's father stepped in, calling the whole thing a scam, and no they were not going to pay extra for the bigger one. They could take their own pictures at home, thank you very much. This one small photo, like an insult to their cheapness, must have come in the mail, only to be stashed away. He could imagine his mother waiting for it, praying that it didn't arrive on a Saturday, when her husband would likely be the one to bring in the mail.

"Isn't that a hoot?" Margaret was saying. "I found it when I was going through Mom's things. I wonder why she never framed it?"

You wonder why? Gregory wanted to say. With her sketch pad and pens, Margaret was always focused on what she wanted to see, the quirky things that drew her attention, rather than the bitter world of their own family. *You don't remember the strangled smallness of our lives because you were able to look elsewhere,* Gregory thought to himself. But he also knew that he had pulled away, too. He'd abandoned Margaret when she came out to their parents. He hadn't stood up for her when his father kicked her out of the house. Something else to add to his list of regrets.

"What a terrific gift," Gregory said. He turned his back on his family and started walking toward the building.

10

Gregory hadn't been in a church since his mother's funeral nine years earlier, but he felt strangely at home when he entered the nursing home chapel, hidden at the end of the corridor on the second floor. Two rows of brown folding chairs faced a round window that overlooked the slow-moving river that he could never remember the name of. He sat down in one of the chairs and sighed. He knew they'd be starting lunch soon and everyone would wonder where he was.

Closing his eyes, he felt the sun from the window on his face. He just needed a moment, he told himself, before he went back to the party where he would lie to his wife about where he'd been, where Carrie would reveal nothing about herself, where his sister and Jas would protect Carrie and her secrets. And his dad, who had spent much of his adult life making Gregory's mom miserable, would be lauded with attention.

Then Gregory remembered that all of these things that would normally plague him could now be brushed aside. All he had to do was think of Mira, and his worries would cede to a vision of her tucked into his chair, beaming at him. For the first time in his life, he didn't feel alone with his struggle. Mira was there with him, cradling his head to her chest, kissing his hands and then the side of his face, his lips. He could almost taste her, mint and a trace of smoke. They were in his office, but he'd locked the door. No one would disturb them.

He had spent hours Googling her, not even sure what he was looking for: *Mira therapist Indian Boston*, at one point even trying *Indian woman who appears in pink scarf.* He had combed through dozens of LinkedIn and Facebook photos of women named Mira. A few times, he thought he had found her, but no. In the end, all he learned was that the actress Mira Sorvino had a tall husband and four good-looking kids and that *mira*, which means sea or ocean in Sanskrit, was the name of a sixteenth-century Hindu princess who devoted her life to Krishna.

Although he knew he should try to stop thinking about her, he hadn't been fixated on anything so wonderful since falling in love with Liv. It wasn't a crush, or at least it wasn't that simple. Of course he desired her. How could he not? But it was more than that. Mira had pried him open, laying bare the many broken pieces that had been rattling around inside of him for decades.

See, she seemed to say, *all is not lost. We can salvage you.*

Gregory started to pray, "Dear God, please—" But, please what? What did he want? To feel whole again? For Mira to love him? What was love anyway, unconditional acceptance? His life *would* be different with someone with whom he could share his darkest thought. But what about Liv? He couldn't imagine loving anyone the way he had once loved his wife. Even if he struggled to connect with her, he still loved her.

How had he allowed it to go on this long, his slow withdrawal from their marriage? He could never be fully present with Liv as long as he was thinking about that night with Joey. For his marriage to have a chance, he would have to tell her on their weekend away. He thought about confessing everything to Mira first and letting her comforting touch wash away his guilt. He needed to unleash his secret, his pain, his desire.

He felt ashamed for thinking it, but he couldn't stop himself. He said a Hail Mary, but it didn't feel powerful enough in the generic religious room without a cross or icon to be found. He clasped his hands together, pressed his thumbs to his forehead and said, "Dear God, please help me with Mira." He could almost feel the pulse of his longing—just as the door opened.

"Gregory? What on earth!"

He turned quickly to see Liv standing in the doorway, her expression a mix of confusion and annoyance. He stood so quickly he almost knocked the chair over.

"I've been looking for you everywhere," she said.

Gregory approached her, but Liv sidestepped him and let the door shut behind her.

"Liv, I'm sorry. I can explain. I needed a little time to myself. You know how Margaret gets."

"Yes. I know exactly how Margaret gets, but that doesn't mean I run away from a party we're hosting. What is going on with you?"

His thoughts were still slow from the prosecco. He'd come to the chapel to confront the realities of his situation and maybe make some kind of decision. But now that Liv was there, he felt less certain. Did she see him praying? Hear him say Mira's name?

He threw out a distraction he knew his wife would go for. "Did you know that Carrie has a crush on a girl?"

Liv's face got tight, as if he had just said something so preposterous that she couldn't possibly offer a lucid response. "What?"

"I heard her talking to Jas about it."

Liv walked mechanically to the nearest chair and sat down hard. "She's a lesbian?"

"Or queer. I don't know. But she's not straight, apparently. I didn't want to say anything to you at the party."

"What exactly does 'queer' mean?" Liv asked.

"It means not straight," Gregory said, something he knew because one of his queer clients had recently explained the nuances of the terminology.

"So you, what, decided to come here and pray about it?"

Trying to sort out his feelings about Carrie's sexuality certainly wouldn't require him to go to a chapel and ask for God's guidance, and Liv would know that. "It was the only quiet place," Gregory said, his voice apologetic. "And, actually, I was thinking about my mother. I mean, there's Dad getting all this attention, and Mom always baked her own birthday cake."

Liv stared out at the river for a moment, then she turned to Gregory again. "It doesn't matter if Carrie likes girls. Young people get to experiment with their sexuality these days—an option we never really had."

"Absolutely," Gregory said. "And anyway, if it's something she wants us to know, I'm sure we'll find out soon enough." He sat in the chair next to her and lightly slapped his face with both hands. It was a habit he formed after the incident, when the eyes in the windshield haunted him. He would see them coming at him, and he'd try and make the image disappear by bringing himself back into his body. The gesture had become yet another way to avoid the memory.

"Are you all right, Gregory? Honestly, right now, you seem drunk."

"It's that damn prosecco. You know I'm a lightweight."

Would this be the time to tell her? Gregory wondered. *I'm not okay.* If he opened his heart, would she reach out and try to catch him in this free fall?

"I'm worried about you, Gregory. Let's get you in to see a therapist right away."

I've already found one.

"Yes, I should schedule an appointment."

"Will you do it this time? Really?"

"I will," he said, knowing, of course, that he wouldn't. Not the way she thought.

"Good. I think it would help." Liv turned to him with a softness that he seldom saw anymore and reached for his hand. "I'm looking forward to our weekend away. Should I book an inn or an Airbnb? Do you have a preference?"

Gregory stiffened. If he told her at an inn and she fell apart, that could be a loud scene, even if Liv wasn't prone to such displays. But alone with her in a lake house—that didn't feel right, or safe. "I guess an inn," he said, thinking Mira would be proud of him for taking this step.

11

On Wednesday morning, Gregory was able to set aside his thoughts about Mira long enough to stay focused on the needs of his first three clients. At nine o'clock, he helped Jaimie L., a thirty-three-year-old marketing executive with agoraphobia, identify other Boston locations that made him uncomfortable so he could continue with the exposure homework he had been doing successfully for the past several weeks. At ten o'clock, he met with Barry C., who wanted to discuss his eating addiction. Gregory worked with him to challenge disabling cognitions about feeling deprived, and he encouraged him to sit with difficult feelings instead of suppressing them with food. At eleven it was Rita B. with her host of struggles that included a husband who cheated, an alcoholic son who refused rehab, and a lifetime of feeling like she was responsible for everything and worthy of nothing. Together they identified Rita's core values and used them to create a behavioral schedule that prioritized self-care and attending some Al-Anon meetings.

By noon, Gregory had lost his ability to concentrate and could only think about Mira, who would be there in an hour. At 12:45, when Eleanor S. was still complaining about micromanagers above her and insubordinates below her at her biotech start-up, he had to keep from blurting out, *The world isn't here to do everything your way!* Instead, with practiced tolerance, he Socratically questioned the rationale of her narcissistic thought patterns. (*What do you think your boss's priorities are? What would you do in their place?*) But at the end of the session when Eleanor S. was still unable to widen her perspective, he wrapped it up with: "That's our time. We'll continue this next week."

After she left, Gregory experienced ten minutes of what felt like acute ADHD. He sat down in his own chair, thinking he'd wait there and just let Mira come in. Then again, they had already established a routine, and Mira seemed to prefer his chair, so he switched to the wingback, where, in client mode for the past two weeks, he had metaphorically stripped off his professional degree and let Mira lead him into whatever dark quarry of memory and untapped desire he drifted toward. But should he continue to relinquish all power to her even if it felt incredible to be listened to?

He switched chairs again, wondering if he wanted to be in charge or not. Wasn't it more exciting when Mira held the reins? He jumped up, this time circling his office, stopping to glance out the window at the overcast sky and light drizzle. Then he turned his iPhone to selfie mode and checked that he didn't look too frazzled. He didn't, and he impulsively snapped a picture. He studied the photo like Carrie probably did with her selfies, considering his outfit, a royal blue shirt and his favorite tie with an orange design that reminded him of marigolds. He continued to study the image of himself for a few seconds and smiled. How wonderful it was to feel a glimmer of hope, even if his home life was a mess.

Liv sensed something was up. Although the rest of the nursing home birthday party had been uneventful, to the point that Bob had fallen asleep in his wheelchair right after cake, Liv, who had to drive them home, had spent the first ten minutes in the car asking Carrie some carefully phrased questions about her friends.

Eventually, their daughter, having none of it, huffed, "Can we please not talk?" Liv agreed and turned her attention to asking Gregory about his work, only to have him respond with his deliberately brief answers. That night they went to bed barely speaking and still hadn't fully patched things up. How could they, when he'd been spending every evening in the garden to avoid a confrontation or even a conversation? Maybe it would be easier to let the silence keep festering.

Plus, he wanted to be fully present in the experience of seeing Mira for the third time. He was on the brink of testing chairs again when he heard the outside door open. He hadn't realized how worried he'd been that she wouldn't return, until now that he knew she had. He allowed a few seconds for relief to wash through him. She could sit wherever she wanted. All that mattered was that she was here.

When Gregory opened the door to the waiting room, it wasn't Mira. It was Phil Bodkin, who never came in on Wednesdays in the summer. Wednesdays were Phil's day to cycle in the morning and play golf in the afternoon. Even on rainy days like this one, he'd take the afternoon off to have lunch at the club or spend a few hours with his granddaughter in Brookline. Phil's Wednesdays were sacrosanct.

"Phil!" Gregory said, trying to quell the alarm in his voice. "What are you doing here?"

"Nice to see you, too." Phil, casually dressed in khakis and a faded purple polo shirt, unlocked his office, the more spacious of the two, and went in, leaving the door open. "It's about to start raining in earnest, so I figured I'd get a little work done."

"On a Wednesday?" Gregory glanced at his watch, then the outside door. Phil popped his head out. "I only have a few things to catch up on," he said. "Why don't we grab lunch at the diner or bring sandwiches back here? You're free now, right?"

"Um, maybe." Even as the lie came stuttering out, Gregory regretted it, mostly for the trouble it would cause when Mira showed up, which would be any minute.

"Maybe?" Phil peered at Gregory over his wire-frame glasses. Those eyes had seen through hundreds of patients.

Gregory walked mechanically back into his office and collapsed in his chair. Phil lumbered in behind him and sat uninvited in one of the wingbacks, taking up the chair, indeed the room, in a way that infuriated Gregory. He wanted to shout at him to get out, that this was his free time to spend however he wanted. Now it was 1:03, and she was late.

"What's going on, Gregory?" Phil's voice, tuned more to therapist mode than trusted friend, suggested that he was not leaving without an answer.

"Work," Gregory said. "I'm behind on my session notes."

"Hmm," Phil said.

Gregory knew that Phil's uncanny ability to read a room, a person, a situation, was part power play. It was why Phil always made him slightly uneasy, even when they were just catching up over burgers at the club. For that reason, Gregory couldn't let Phil know of Mira's existence, lest he start probing with his deceptively subtle lines of questioning. And Gregory definitely didn't want Phil to witness his reaction when he first saw Mira again. Phil would know instantly that she was something other than a client, and he wouldn't be quiet about it.

"Thanks for the offer," Gregory said, "but I need to take a rain check on lunch and plow through this stuff."

"You seem a little skittish," Phil said. "Not quite yourself."

It was 1:05, and Gregory still hadn't heard the door open. "I'm fine," he said. "Just a lot to do, once I find my files." In anticipation of Mira's arrival, Gregory had almost cleared the surface of his desk so there was no laptop to open, no paperwork to pretend to be engrossed in. He anxiously looked for a place to put his attention in a performance that wouldn't even fool Petey.

Phil, on the other hand, looked supremely relaxed.

Desperate to appear busy, Gregory ripped a piece of tape from the heavy black dispenser but then didn't know what to do with it. When he balled it up in his fingers and tried depositing it in the brown leather wastebasket next to his desk, the tape wouldn't release. Finally, Gregory had to rub it on the rim where it just stuck, refusing to drop in.

Phil leaned back and quietly observed, his fingertips tented together in his signature listening pose.

As Gregory started searching pointlessly through his file drawer, he could sense the sweat seeping through the armpits of his shirt. "Full disclosure, Gregory," Phil said. "Liv reached out to me. She's worried about you. She said that you've been acting strange and even abandoned your father's birthday party."

Gregory turned his gaze on his mentor. Phil had a talent for screwing up his personal life, but his professional ethics were uncompromising. The idea of Phil thinking of him as imbalanced in any way horrified Gregory. He wanted to call Liv and tell her to stay out of his business. But first, he wanted Phil gone from his office.

"I'm fine, Phil," Gregory said. "Liv and I are going through some things. You know how it is with long marriages? But I appreciate your concern. I do."

Phil scrunched up his mouth and shook his head. "Not buying it. Too pat."

Gregory was startled. He knew Phil called people out on their shit—he'd heard about it from shared patients, whose annoyance ultimately converted to esteem. But in a decade of working together, Gregory had never been on the receiving end of his suitemate's scrutiny, not in this way. He couldn't hide from Phil's gaze—an unassailable knowing that he held like a mirror to Gregory's lie. Nor could Gregory stop squirming or glancing over at the clock that now showed Mira was eight minutes late. He stood and crossed the room. Gazing out the window with his back to Phil, he drew a breath and exhaled loudly through his nose. Finally, dropping his voice in case Mira entered the waiting room, Gregory said, "There's this woman. She's coming in now, in fact. So this isn't a good time for us to talk."

Phil's voice betrayed no surprise, no judgment. "A patient?"

"I don't exactly know."

"She's either a patient or she isn't," Phil said. "That's not a gray area."

Gregory wanted to argue that it was now, but he had already said too much. He couldn't afford to lose Phil's professional respect. But he also couldn't lose Mira or shake his unsubstantiated fear—an instinct really—that if he talked about her too much with anyone, she wouldn't come back.

Gregory sighed out what felt like a confession. "She's not a patient. But she's been coming in on Wednesdays at one just to talk."

"Talk?"

"We're becoming friends, I guess you could say."

The air seemed to leave the room, and Gregory found it hard to draw a breath. He had turned off the air-conditioning, knowing Mira didn't like it, but sweat was now dripping down his back. At that point he hoped to God that Mira didn't show up, because that's when Phil, a psychiatric sharpshooter, would really start hunting for Gregory's weak spots.

"Are you sleeping with her?"

"No."

"But you're thinking about it?"

Gregory didn't answer. He didn't know where the boundaries were in his head, and that was a problem. He fell asleep every night and woke up every morning thinking about Mira. She filled the free moments in his day: drinking his morning coffee, walking up the stairs to his fourth-floor office, the breaks between clients, driving home from work. At dinner with Liv and Carrie, he would wonder what Mira was eating and whom she might be with. Standing in his garage at night after putting away his gardening tools, he would stare through the window and summon her, or at least call forth the feeling of having her close: the featheriness of her touch, the electric current that pulsed around her, the way she seemed to emit her own kind of light. When he dressed that morning, he intentionally selected the blue shirt with the marigold tie, knowing it was a unique combination, one that might resonate with her taste for vibrant colors.

Mira had become his spiritual companion, the subject of his dreams, and the embodiment of his longing. He wanted to talk to her, learn from her, and tell her things he had never shared with anyone as they lay curled up in some bed. He needed a reason to alter the course of his life, and she seemed to be offering that. Though Phil might call it countertransference, when a therapist reflects their own unresolved conflicts on the client, Gregory knew it was more nuanced.

"This isn't about sex," Gregory said.

"So, it's a friendship? Or something else?"

"I guess it's something else." Gregory turned away from the window and faced Phil's searing gaze. "I realize this sounds unprofessional, but I need you to trust that I'm figuring it out."

"You told Liv you were going to get help with that."

"I get that she sent you, but this is really between her and me, isn't it?"

Phil leaned forward, and the bulk at his waist bulged over his pants. "Gregory, you know my story. I'm not going to pretend I'm some choirboy here. I have a few relationship demons that you don't even know about, nobody does—and I'm not proud of them. But I want to strongly discourage you from making those same mistakes and burning down your wonderful life with Liv and the kids."

Gregory nodded. While he wanted to argue to Phil that his family life wasn't wonderful at all these days, he simply said, "I get that."

"Can I ask where you met her?"

"She's an old friend," Gregory said. Although it was a flagrant lie, it was starting to feel like the truth. He had spent less than one hundred minutes of his life with Mira, yet she felt like an old soul in a young body, someone he had known for decades.

"A minute ago, you said you were just becoming friends."

"A little of both," Gregory said quickly. "We're getting to know each other again." He went back to his chair and sat down. He wanted Phil to read his face, to see that he was trying to tell the truth, but he didn't know what the full truth was. Only Mira had that information, and she wasn't disclosing it.

"We're all vulnerable to self-sabotage," Phil said, going full-throttle Freudian. "Sometimes you need to negotiate that on a daily basis. Something to consider."

Gregory wanted to protest that this was not about self-sabotage. Quite the opposite. He was starting to believe that if he overcame the darkness in his life, Mira would be the reason.

"Sometimes it's about simpler dynamics," Gregory said, throwing Freud back at him.

"Ha!" Phil chuckled. "If by any chance you're talking about love, I can promise you there's nothing simple about that."

As the two therapists sat there studying each other, their competing theoretical perspectives thickened the air of the stuffy office. Gregory had the feeling that Phil's intrusion was so powerful that it had blown Mira off course, at least for that Wednesday.

Maybe she was skittish and didn't want to barge in while Phil was there; his intensity could be intimidating.

"Well, you're a big boy," Phil finally said, "but take it from someone who has done irrevocable damage in the name of love: these situations seldom turn out the way we expect, and there are always casualties." Phil lowered his head and took a few seconds to compose himself. Then he cleared his throat and looked up again. "It was years before my girls let me back into their lives, and even now Emma still plays it pretty cool. I'm a lucky man day to day, because Beth and I are crazy about each other, but I've hurt people I love, and I'll always have to live with those consequences."

"I understand," Gregory said, thinking how he knew all about hurting people and living with consequences. "But I'm not cheating on Liv. And even if I'm not convinced that we're talking apples to apples here, I appreciate your concern. I really do."

When Phil didn't respond, Gregory thought that maybe they were finally done. 1:16. Would Mira be in the waiting room? Had Phil's voice scared her away? Neither option was good.

"Does she have kids?"

Gregory hesitated. "I don't think so."

"You don't know if this old friend of yours has kids or not?"

"It's complicated. And I'd be grateful if you let me figure it out in my own time."

Phil drew a breath and blew out a slow stream of air. "I'm getting that. I'm also getting that you're pretty anxious for me to leave and for your *friend* to get here. And yet she's not here."

He may as well have put *friend* in air quotes. He clearly didn't trust anything that Gregory had told him. Why should he?

Phil pressed his broad hands to his thighs and pushed himself to standing. With Phil towering over him, Gregory, slumped in his chair, felt diminished.

"I'm going to take off now but promise me you'll think about what I've said."

"I promise."

Before exiting the office, Phil glanced into the waiting room, as if looking for Gregory's friend. He turned back to Gregory and began to say something but stopped himself and walked out, leaving the office door ajar. Gregory sat there, not moving for several interminable minutes while Phil made a phone call in his office. Finally, Phil locked up and left, pulling the door shut a little too hard, the bang reverberating through the suite like a warning. Only then did Gregory unlock the bottom drawer of his desk and withdraw the pink scarf. He folded it into a tidy square like a pillow and held it to his face. He sniffed—mint, smoke, maybe resin, the story deepening with every inhale. Still clutching the scarf, he moved to the wingback. It was almost 1:30 and she wasn't here, but then he heard the chime-like sound of her bracelets. Gregory leapt from his chair and peered into the waiting room.

She was sitting in the same chair.

"Mira!" he cried.

12

As Mira glanced up from her magazine, Gregory realized he was still holding her scarf. He lowered it quickly and stuffed it into his open briefcase he had left by the door that morning.

He was too relieved to be embarrassed, and for a few seconds he just stood there, speechless. "I'm so sorry to keep you waiting," he said. "How long have you been here?"

"Quite a while," she said, her words clipped.

Phil had to have seen her, but why didn't he say anything? That wasn't like Phil, so preternaturally friendly and courteous. Gregory calculated that she must have come in immediately after Phil left, which meant she couldn't have been waiting longer than a few minutes. But how had he not heard her?

When Mira stood, he saw she was wearing flowy red pants and a black sleeveless blouse with a gold chain necklace. To keep himself from reaching out to hug her, he held one arm stiffly by his side and used the other to brace the door open. "After you," he said, ushering her into his office. She walked directly toward his chair and took a seat. He shut the door and lowered himself into one of the wingbacks.

Mira crossed her legs and folded her hands in her lap. They looked at each other, neither of them speaking for a moment, until Gregory said, "I was afraid you weren't going to come today."

Mira's face darkened. "I was here at one o'clock, Greg. That is our appointment time."

He squirmed at the shift in her tone, the crust of anger around her words. "But you weren't. I was here. I was waiting for you, and then my colleague—"

"Phil. I know."

Gregory's breathing quickened. Was she hiding? But where? In the hallway? In one of the restrooms? Across the suite there was that third small office. Phil, the only person with a key, used to sleep there during his divorce, but he always kept it locked. Was she in there watching them?

"I don't understand," Gregory said. "I didn't ask Phil to come in, and I tried to get him to leave."

"But you didn't want him to see me. So now it's"—she glanced at the digital clock that was out of his sight line—"1:32, and our time today is practically up."

Gregory's throat felt tight. His heartbeat sped up. "You're right. I'm sorry. This is your time, our time. But I was expecting you to just come in."

Mira leaned forward. "And what if I had?" she said, her deep brown eyes locking onto his, as if trying to show him something.

When he stared back at her, a dizziness washed through him, the way it had when he dove too deep into Walden Pond one summer day shortly after he and Liv got married. Trying to swim away from his self-hatred, he fought the resistance of the water, diving deeper until the pressure squeezed his lungs, and he was certain his rib cage had cracked open. He was afraid of drowning and afraid of surfacing, knowing that if he survived, he'd have to dry off, get into his car, and drive back home to his life built on a lie. The next day, he woke up with debilitating vertigo, the bed spinning. For three days the dizziness and nausea immobilized him, leading him to believe he was being punished either for trying to die or for the cowardliness of choosing to live. Or both.

Gregory put his hands to his face, his palms cupping his cheekbones and his fingertips touching his forehead as if he could reset his own mind. He felt Mira watching him, similar to the way Phil had watched him, but this was much more penetrating. Phil could see into his mind, but Mira saw everything. He couldn't hide a single lie, a single feeling. When he tried to pull his hands away, he saw a face flying toward the windshield. It was moving so fast he couldn't make out any features other than those scared eyes, just a blur through the glass. He recoiled, covering his own eyes again, but still felt Mira's focused gaze. When the bile started to rise in his throat, he swallowed it down.

"Look at me, Greg," Mira said, her voice gentle but firm.

He shook his head. He was remembering how in that moment in the car, he had made a decision that would change the course of his life and the lives of others. It seemed clear Mira already knew this. He wasn't sure how. Had she been there that night? Was she a bystander, or a relative? Or was she simply a trained psychologist, using what little information he'd fed her to piece together the story? Maybe she was fishing, like a fortune teller or a tarot card reader, using vague suggestions to make him think she knew more than she did. Except something told him that it wasn't a trick. She leaned toward him and encircled his wrists with her fingers. She tried to guide his hands away from his face, but he held them there, straining against her clasp. "No," he told her.

"It's okay," she said, pulling steadily. When he blinked into the rain-darkened room, he saw she was there, her eyes kind, her cool fingers still lightly wrapped around his wrists. Without letting go of him, she slid her slender hands down a few inches until they caught in his.

"I did something terrible, and I hate myself for it," he said, trembling. "And I've never let anyone love me because of it, not even my wife. I—" He tried to cover his face again, but Mira held tight.

"You what?"

"I'm ready to tell Liv everything, because it's time. But I may lose her. I *will* lose her, and the kids." He tipped back his head like he had downed a shot of whiskey and stayed that way, his face hot, his throat burning, staring at the ceiling so he didn't have to look at her. "I sense that you understand what I'm saying."

Mira reached out and placed her hand behind his head. A current of connection passed between them. She danced the pads of her fingers along the base of his skull until he lowered his face to her thin shoulder. This was how he had fallen asleep every night for the past three weeks: pretending she was holding him as he buried his nose in her neck. There he found the source of the scents in her scarf and something else, too, that resinous smell that he now recognized: marigolds, his favorite flower. He inhaled sharply, while the tears, hot and unstoppable, streamed down his face.

"You're not the only one in pain, Greg."

"I know that," he said.

"But do you? Really? Or do you just tell yourself that?"

He pulled back just enough so she could see his eyes. He needed her to understand that he absolutely did know. "It's why I became a psychologist," he said. "To help people with their pain. To make up for what I did."

Mira squeezed his hands. Her face looked so open, so inviting. He leaned forward to kiss her. She drew back, surprised but somehow not angry.

"Oh God, I'm so sorry," Gregory said, hating himself even more. He'd ruined the moment. He just hoped he hadn't ruined everything.

"That's not what we're here for," Mira said. "You have work to do."

"Of course," he said. "It's just—"

"Just?"

"I feel so much less hopeless when you're here. I thought maybe you—"

"You need to face some things," she insisted. "Let's stay focused on that."

Gregory felt the heat of embarrassment creep up the back of his neck. He couldn't answer, but he made himself nod.

"You don't really believe anyone has suffered the way you have," Mira said. "You think you're singular in that way."

After a second of consideration, he shook his head. "No," he said.

"Yes," she said. "You do. And you know you do. I've seen it."

She released him into his chair, letting go of him so gently— the way he used to put down his children in their cribs—that he continued to feel her touch even when they were no longer physically attached. "Never mind that. The only thing that matters right now is that you hold on to a little bit of hope."

"But, Mira, I need to understand. What do you mean by *seen*? Have you been watching me?" He thought of the eyes in the garage window. Were they hers?

"If you've been feeling watched, maybe that's a good thing," she said. "You're becoming more self-reflective and ready to change. A sign of hope."

He sat back carefully. "Hope?" The word, so round and hollow, felt foreign in his mouth. He said it again, "Hope," this time trying to taste the meaning before it escaped like a ring of smoke. "Mira?"

"Yes?"

He wanted to ask, *Who are you?* But he was terrified of the answer.

He opened his hand as if reaching for something, the way he sometimes tried to catch the beacon of light that streamed through the garage window. He closed his hand around the feeling and pulled his fist to his chest.

Mira smiled at his hand, now resting over his heart. "That's right," she mouthed, as if trying not to scare something away. "Hold on to it." She stood quietly and started to steal soundlessly out of the office.

"Wait," Gregory whispered.

She stopped.

"Please don't leave."

"That's not fair to your other clients coming in today. They need you, too."

She said it so firmly, he had to think about it. Did she consider herself a client? He realized in that moment that he had stopped seeing her that way. Before meeting Mira, he had always been able to sit in his office and suppress his own demons. If anything, his shameful past allowed him to recognize the fundamental good in everyone, even his most self-loathing clients. He listened to their pain, helped them understand its roots, and then provided means to sever those connections to their present life. He certainly hadn't been giving Mira that same attention. And he had stopped considering why she had sought him out, even if she claimed he had asked her to come, which he hadn't.

How could he be so selfish?

"Maybe we can schedule another session for later in the week. To focus on you."

Mira hesitated. "That's a kind offer, Greg. But this is all I can find the time and energy for right now. It's challenging enough for me to get here."

"Where do you live? Could I come to you?"

She paused, as if considering the idea. "That wouldn't be appropriate."

He was mad at himself for asking. Of course, it wouldn't be, but the boundaries had gotten so blurry. He didn't physically touch his clients. He didn't unload his problems on them, expose them to his emotional wounds, or try to kiss them. What was this?

"Mira!" he called, just as she was about to shut the door. "Next week let's work on why you're here."

She glanced back in and gave him a slight smile.

"Wednesday at one?" Gregory said.

"Will you be available?" she asked.

"I will," he answered. "I promise."

13

At 5:50, after his last client, Gregory texted Liv: *Going to be late. Don't wait on dinner.* She responded with a thumbs-up emoji, which Gregory interpreted as a truce in their standoff. Maybe Phil had reported back to her "no affair."

A few seconds later she wrote: *Reservation for tomorrow?* This time she added two red heart emojis. He checked the calendar. July 18, their anniversary. Unless they were away on vacation, they always celebrated at the River Club, the setting for their wedding reception twenty-two years ago. That night, their two hundred guests were treated to a cocktail hour with a spare-no-expense raw bar by the pool, followed by a sit-down surf-and-turf dinner and, later, dancing past midnight to a nine-piece R&B band. Gregory thought he would have enjoyed the wedding more if he hadn't been so conscious of his father walking around, shaking his head at the extravagance. *How the hell many mortgage payments did this set you back?* Gregory's mother, Carol, with her gray hair curled and styled on top of her head, laughed and danced with abandon. *This is like a dream*, she whispered as she glided past in her long, lavender dress, champagne flute in hand. And maybe it was her dream, that for one day of her life she could celebrate with joy, fully exempt from her husband's control.

Gregory and Liv always dined at the same private table at the far end of the restaurant, overlooking the golf course. Though he'd never say it to Liv, Gregory wasn't able to fully enjoy the view; it made him think of all the chemicals and excessive use of natural resources needed to achieve the bright green color of the turf. To Liv, the River Club was Stimson family sacred ground. Her father's name was engraved on at least five tournament plaques.

A quick phone call to the club's front desk and Gregory was connected to the dining room.

"I believe this is your twenty-second?" Calvin, the tenured maître d' said after confirming their reservation. Although he pretended to be checking, Calvin knew every birthday and relevant anniversary of all of the longtime club members. He also knew their food tastes, favorite drink, and preferred brand of liquor. Liv and her friends, all legacies who grew up going there, nicknamed him "the club angel" for his ability to make every member feel cared for, even adored.

After hanging up with Calvin, Gregory texted Liv: *All set for 7 tomorrow.* He turned off his phone for the five-mile walk to Cambridge. He had taken the T to work that morning because his car was in the shop, but he couldn't bear the idea of riding public transportation home and enduring the jostle of the rush-hour crowd. He wanted to preserve the feeling of his cheek on Mira's shoulder, the grainy texture of her blouse against his ear, the scent of marigolds, and above all, the rare sense of being understood. When had he last felt so seen but without judgment? *Hope.* He didn't remember what it felt like, but he repeated the word with every step, as if he were teaching himself the possibility. *Hope, hope, hope, hope.*

The rain had cleared, but the sky was still overcast. Mood weather, his sister called it. Once out of the twisted streets of Boston, he walked slowly inside that comforting haze of memory. He barely recognized the landmarks so familiar to him from the evenings in which he changed from his work clothes into running shorts and sneakers and jogged home along the Charles: the Longfellow Bridge, the bustle of Harvard Square, and the expansive lawn at the Kennedy School. Today he was propelled not by the sights but by a sense of feeling awake. Over and again, he relived the moment of Mira holding his hands, then the light press of her fingers to the back of his head before she pulled him to her shoulder.

Who *was* this woman who understood him better than his family did? Better than he understood himself? Three weeks in, he had no idea, but he was determined to find out next Wednesday and give Mira whatever support she needed.

When he arrived home, almost two hours later, Gregory stood at the foot of his driveway and admired the house, as if he were someone passing by. The moss-green shingles blended into the gray sky. When he turned his phone back on, he saw that Phil had called three times and left a voice message. He'd also sent a text: *Got a minute to talk?*

"What the hell?" Gregory muttered, ignoring the text and tucking the phone in his pocket. He was about to head inside when he stopped. Phil's maroon mountain bike was lying in the grass next to the front steps. "Shit." He did an about-face and started speed walking down the driveway toward the garage, when he heard Phil behind him calling, "Gregory! Hold up a minute."

Gregory turned slowly to see Phil coming toward him, his bike helmet perched preposterously on his head. His eyes were wide, and he was out of breath. Had he been in there talking to Liv, waiting for Gregory to come home?

"Hey, Phil," Gregory said, unable to mask his annoyance. "What's going on?"

Phil forced a laugh. "Beth is still baking up a storm, even in this heat. I just brought Liv a loaf of sourdough; it was a nice pretext to swing by."

Gregory stood with his hands on his hips. "You've been lighting up my phone. What is it that couldn't wait?"

Phil drew a breath and countered Gregory's tension with a soft smile. "I started thinking more about our talk this afternoon and wanted to follow up."

"Apparently you already have." Gregory nodded at the house.

Phil shook his head. "I didn't tell Liv anything specific, just that we spoke."

"Okay."

"Did your friend ever show up?"

"Phil, this isn't something I care to discuss right now. And honestly, it's none of your business."

"So she did."

"Jesus, Phil. What is this about?" Gregory knew Phil's modus operandi, how he always had to understand the nuances of any situation. It distinguished him as a therapist. With his mixture of doggedness and empathy, he was able to help the most intractable patients.

"That person you mentioned a few weeks ago—the guy who turned the tables on you in therapy, that's this person isn't it? This woman?"

Gregory drew a long, exasperated breath and looked up at the pewter-colored sky. He just wanted to have a quick dinner then get to work in the garden. "I don't know what to say to that, but right now I'm feeling ambushed. Wasn't our talk at the office enough of a scolding for one day?"

"That's not what this is," Phil said. "I respect your privacy and have known you to make good choices." Phil paused as if choosing his words with care. "We have an excellent working relationship, but that's dependent on us always being honest with each other."

"Really? You've always been honest with me?"

Phil removed his helmet, freeing his hair, damp and matted. Sweat trickled from his brow. "I refer patients to you on a regular basis, so it's my job to make sure your boundaries are rock solid. If there's something untoward going on in your practice, I need to know that."

It was a gut punch. Gregory felt vulnerable enough after his session with Mira, and now this—Phil talking to him with uncharacteristic sternness, demanding information that Gregory wasn't about to share. Yes, they were colleagues, but there was no confusion: Phil was the lead dog.

"I can think of a few times when you haven't been honest with me," Gregory said, taking a risk. "And if you're accusing me of indiscretions, well, isn't that a bit of the pot calling the kettle black?" He gave Phil a warning look.

Phil lifted a finger toward Gregory. "*Never* with a patient."

Gregory looked him hard in the eye, trying not to reveal anything. "Then you'll be happy to know I can say the same."

Phil nodded, still reading Gregory's eyes. "Okay. Okay. Got it. I'm sorry if I overstepped. It's just that I left the office today and had this feeling that you were going to get yourself in trouble, and that would impact my patients, too."

"And you didn't tell any of this to Liv?"

"No."

The men stood in silence for a moment. Phil returned his helmet to his head and looked around the yard. "Garden looks good."

Gregory nodded, his throat felt tight and dry. "All that spring rain."

Phil nodded. "Yeah. And listen, Gregory. I'm not trying to stir something up, but you know I'm protective of Liv. Always have been. She was such a friend to Kathy when—"

"I understand." Gregory didn't want to talk about it anymore. Phil already knew too much. "Can we please shelve this one?"

Phil nodded, but Gregory didn't trust him not to keep pressing the matter.

14

Thursday morning, before Gregory could suggest meeting at the club in separate cars, Liv said, "If you pick me up at six, I can have a glass of wine or two with our anniversary dinner." There was nothing angry or distrustful in the way she said this. It was promising, even. But now he and Liv were riding in his car to Newton with a disconcerting quiet. It was a hot summer night, and the traffic was surprisingly light.

Normally when driving, Gregory would turn on NPR, but that felt too mundane for the occasion, with Liv sitting erect in the passenger seat in a silky white dress and high-heel sandals. Her face was tan, and she was wearing some type of makeup that sharpened the color of her blue eyes. When she shifted in her seat and smoothed her dress, Gregory glanced over and said what the husband of a woman like Liv should say: "You look beautiful."

She smiled and tucked a piece of his hair behind his ear, a gesture so unexpected that at first he pulled his head away before realizing she was just being affectionate. Liv didn't return the compliment, and with good reason. He was still wearing the same gray pants and dress shirt that he'd had on all day. He'd been unable to make any extra effort.

Ever since Mira had come into his life, making him confront his lies, he dreaded returning to the status quo at home, the automated motions of their family life, the disconnect they not only tolerated but had come to accept as normal.

He still loved Liv. How could he not? She had built their whole lives for them. He still vividly remembered the night she took him home to meet her parents—to the rambling Victorian where his family now lived.

He'd been so young and desperate not to fail her or to embarrass himself, but that night, the house on Ashford Street didn't embody repression but rather possibility.

"Mother! Daddy!" Liv shouted as she charged through the front door with Gregory trailing behind, clutching a five-dollar bouquet.

Liv's mother, tall and willowy, appeared from around the corner, smoothing her white chef's apron. She stretched out her hand, and said, "Helen Stimson. How delightful to have you join us, Gregory." She waited for Liv to approach and gave her daughter a cool peck on the cheek. "Hello, Olivia."

Liv had said little about her mother on the car ride over except "She's something. You'll see." Already Gregory was beginning to understand. Helen had the kind of small, elegant features that aged well on women. Although her hair was almost the same pale color as Liv's, Helen's was longer and wavier, caught in a ponytail with loose strands that suggested the effortlessness of her beauty, even for a woman in her late fifties.

Gregory knew that it was the right time to present the flowers, but the "classic bouquet" that had looked pretty at Star Market now felt cheap. Not just for Helen, whose style projected the image of understated wealth, but for an entire house that felt alive with art: oil paintings, vibrant watercolors, and spare, gray sketches—the kind of things Gregory had only ever seen in museums. There was fancy quirkiness, too. A boxy glass frame full of random little things—puzzle pieces, a key, a beach shell—hung at the base of the curved stairway that ended in a wooden orb. On the wall going up the stairs, a collection of black-and-white family photos was artistically mounted rather than framed. Everything had that one-of-a-kind artistry that made Gregory feel like he had landed someplace completely outside of himself. He gripped the bouquet tighter, knowing those red carnations and baby's breath betrayed the world he grew up in, just as he understood Liv's upbringing from the marble end table that held a crystal vase of calla lilies.

But when Gregory handed Helen the plastic sleeve of flowers and said, "Thank you for having me," she received them graciously, sniffing with delight at the peppery scent, tactfully allowing him to believe that he had been wrong and maybe she really did like carnations.

"Where's Daddy?" Liv asked, slipping off her jacket and tossing it on a wrought iron coatrack in the hallway.

"Right here," a deep voice called back. Liv's father, a wiry man, inches shorter than Helen, with a sparse thatch of graying hair and large black glasses, came down the staircase with a brisk gait. "Tom Stimson," he said, extending his hand toward Gregory. "Pleased to meet you."

Liv hugged her father while Helen looked on coolly. With some awkwardness, they moved toward the kitchen, Tom scattering seedlings of conversation—*Finishing up the school year? How did exams go?*—that presumably would take root once they were sitting down. In the meantime, they stood around the granite kitchen island, Helen opening the cabinets, pulling out a succession of vases that were all too large for Gregory's skimpy bouquet. Tom fixed gin and tonics with measured precision.

When Liv asked, "Would you like me to help with dinner, Mother?" Helen waved her off, insisting they should go relax in the sun porch—and she hoped Gregory liked salmon. He didn't but said he did. When he was a child, his family ate Mrs. Paul's fish sticks for dinner on Fridays, and in his estimation, fish was supposed to be a flavorless vehicle for ketchup, not pink and oily. But of course, he would eat whatever he was served, eager to be initiated into a lifestyle he had always thought was beyond his reach.

On the screened-in porch, shaded by a small grove of white pines, Tom asked him about his studies. Gregory answered that he was pursuing a PhD in psychology.

"I did a month of that stuff in med school," Tom said, leaving Gregory unsure of how to respond.

Liv, who was fingering the frost on her glass from the other end of the wicker sofa, explained, "Daddy's an orthopedic trauma surgeon."

"Oh, wow!" Gregory said. "That must be really demanding."

"Yeah, we always envy the shrinks their banker's hours," Tom said. "I never know what time of the night I'm going to be called in to piece together some metacarpals. Must be nice never having to get your hands dirty." He took a sip of his drink, as if to punctuate this declaration of his superior rung on the medical prestige ladder, and Gregory, immediately deflated, was embarrassed by the awkward pause he let happen. But Tom pressed on, "Are you into psychoanalysis? Or what's your thing? Research?"

"Cognitive behavioral therapy. CBT," Gregory said confidently.

"So you listen to people complain all day?"

Gregory cleared his throat and squared his shoulders. "It's a more evidence-based approach than traditional talk therapy. CBT provides cognitive and behavioral coping skills proven to reduce psychiatric symptoms. Studies have even shown it can be a frontline alternative to some psych meds—" Gregory stopped. He wasn't about to start disparaging psychopharmacology and have this guy gobble him up. "Anyway, I'm interested in clinical work."

Helen appeared carrying the vase of calla lilies that she had decided to commingle with the straggling red carnations. No sign of the baby's breath. "Your carnations truly revived this arrangement. Don't you think, Gregory?" It was impossible to tell if she was being kind or arch. Gregory agreed with a murmur. He didn't dare check Liv's expression for a clue. He was shaky enough already.

Helen placed the vase in the center of the coffee table, next to a small dish of olives. Gregory had to sit up straighter to see Tom over the flowers.

"What are we discussing?" Helen arranged herself on the chair across from her husband. She clasped her hands in her narrow lap.

"Gregory's doing doctoral work in clinical psychology," Tom said.

Helen nodded. She turned to her daughter. "Clinical psychology. Isn't that interesting?"

Liv cast an incendiary look at her mother, and Gregory felt something uncomfortable pass between them.

"I was a TA in Liv's class this semester," he offered cheerfully, trying to restore the mood. "She was a great student. She has a natural gift for the subject."

"I'm not surprised," Helen said. She carefully adjusted her hands, showcasing her antique ring, a diamond approaching the size of the olives in the dish. "Olivia is a talented young woman who easily absorbs the information around her. And with all of her exposure to"—she paused—"*psychology*, it makes sense that she would be good at it."

Gregory glanced at Liv who was shaking her head. He volleyed his eyes between the two of them, waiting for someone to clarify. "Mother," Liv said. "What are you trying to say?"

"I'm simply recognizing that you're very intelligent. You take things in. You learn from experience. And this is an area in which you've had a fair amount of experience."

"That's all you're saying? Really?" Liv said sarcastically.

"Is it not okay to be proud of my daughter for being observant?" Tom cut in. "Why don't I help you get dinner, darling?"

"There's nothing left to do," Helen protested. "I'm just letting the fish rest." But Tom was already up and moving across the room toward the kitchen. "C'mon, Hel."

Helen stood slowly and followed her husband out, once looking back at Liv and Gregory, acting as if she didn't know what was happening.

Liv turned to Gregory with a derisive smile. "Ladies and gentlemen, *those* are my parents!"

"They're very nice," Gregory said.

"She's unbearable," Liv said. "She's pretending to compliment me but is actually hinting that I'm messed up." She paused and took a quick sip of her drink. "I have an eating disorder," Liv blurted out. "Anorexia. She can't resist the chance to advertise it in front of my new boyfriend."

"I'm sorry," he said.

"I had three years of therapy, went through four different psychologists and a psychiatrist. I even spent two months at a treatment center in Connecticut. The works." Liv polished off her gin and tonic with a gulp and set the glass down hard on the table.

He'd had some clinical training in eating disorders, but he still didn't know what to say. All he could think about was that she had called him her boyfriend.

"I was all set to start at Middlebury, when she decided that I couldn't be trusted. I was fine at that point. The worst was over in high school. But that's why I go to school down the road. So they—well, *she*—can keep an eye on me."

Gregory slid closer to her. He carefully placed a hand on her bare knee, aware that he was thinking about her weight. She felt so normal, so healthy, but he knew how these things fluctuated. "You didn't want to go to BU?"

She shook her head and squeezed her eyes shut. "I have this unreasonable hope when I come home that *this time* it's going to be different, that my mother will decide not to humiliate me." Liv stared ahead at the table. "I'm sorry. I don't know why I'm telling you these things."

"I'm glad you're telling me."

"I feel like I can tell you anything."

Gregory nodded. He wished she would tell him everything.

"Do you see those olives?" Liv pointed at the coffee table. "My entire adolescence can be explained by that handmade ceramic dish of six olives. Food is supposed to be a still life, untouched. Except for men. Men are allowed to eat, at least in moderation. Women are not. My mother has made that very clear to me."

Gregory studied the dish. In his parents' house, guests—on the rare occasions they had any—would be welcomed with a pile of Ritz crackers and a block of Cracker Barrel. But he never would have guessed that those olives represented an ugly family drama. He turned toward Liv, not unlike the way she had turned to him in the cemetery, eyes pleading. She looked so vulnerable, all curled into herself, knees pulled tightly against her chest.

"Maybe your mother is just worried about you."

"I wish that was it. It's not enough that she's a famous art historian with all her beautiful, valuable, precious things. She has to be a bitch, too." Liv flung her arm in a defeated arc.

Gregory, who had hardly eaten all day because of nerves, was transfixed by the olives, even if they were a work of art like everything else in the house. He looked around the room: a primitive quilt tossed over a chipped blue chair; a carved wooden bowl filled with oranges; the garish red carnations tucked among slender white calla lilies—a flower that would always remind him of Helen Stimson. He looked out at the yard that seemed untended by comparison and wished he and Liv could go outside and wander through that tiny urban forest. He could see down the driveway to an old wooden carriage house covered in a wisteria vine, and even then it called to him more strongly than the perfect sun porch or the foyer filled with art.

Gregory didn't understand how life worked for wealthy people who didn't have to fight about money. Did they just find other things to argue about?

He felt even more affection for Liv *because* of her eating disorder, her controlling mother, and her one-upping father. And before he left the house, he had to show them he was good enough for their daughter, that he deserved her.

"Maybe we should leave?" Liv said. "The only thing that would make this worse is if my brother, Leland, showed up. He's in the middle of his residency at Harvard Med."

"Sounds like an underachiever."

Liv half laughed, and he wrapped an arm around her. She looked away, her eyes so troubled, so anxious, that she seemed like a different person.

"Dinner's ready!" Helen called from the kitchen.

Liv turned to him. "You up for this?"

"I'm going to be a psychologist," Gregory assured her. "You think anorexia and a little family dysfunction can scare me away? Wait until you meet my father."

Liv hugged him quickly, then withdrew. "Where did you come from?"

"A split-level ranch in Connecticut. Where did *you* come from?"

"Here!" She rolled her eyes and looked around the room, and they both laughed and started to stand. Liv said, "One more thing," and pulled him back down again. "After dinner my mother is going to offer dessert in the living room. If you want to get on her good side, say something nice about the hand."

"The hand?"

"You'll get it," Liv said. "You're so much smarter than they are."

Gregory tried to but couldn't repress a smile. Had she really just said that?

During dinner, the conversation stayed neutral enough, covering Liv's summer job at the River Club in Newton, where Tom said he'd like Gregory to join him for golf some Saturday afternoon, and Gregory's trajectory from Connecticut to Boston and how he liked the city—very much, especially the history. Eventually the evening found a congenial balance. A bottle of wine helped. Just one glass in, Gregory started to like these people and felt like he had less to prove. When the bottle was empty, Tom ambled down to the cellar for a second one, and Gregory could see Helen's wineglass was shaking slightly. Liv had told him of her mother's Parkinson's.

After dinner—and the second bottle—Helen moved everyone into the living room, where they seated themselves on a turquoise velvet couch and gold armchairs. On the stone coffee table, Helen set down a small silver tray with four fancy shortbread cookies. As much as Gregory wanted to take one, he couldn't, not after what Liv had told him about the olives.

Helen didn't take one either and glanced at Liv. The cookies felt like a dare. Was Liv supposed to eat one to prove that she wasn't anorexic? Or not eat one so she didn't get fat? He couldn't imagine living with such a script in his head. In the middle of the table, next to the cookies, sat a bronze hand. *The hand.* It was beautiful but disturbing and weirdly lifelike. When Liv nudged him, Gregory cleared his throat and said, "That hand ... is just amazing." No one in his family talked about art except his sister, who was so loud and outspoken, he could only agree with her opinions. But with Liv next to him suppressing a giggle, he didn't give up. "It's so *real* looking. So alive."

Helen sat up straighter. "Isn't it exquisite?" she said. Leaning in, as if imparting a secret, she added, "It's a Rodin."

Gregory thought she had said "Rodin," but that didn't make sense. Wouldn't that make it worth hundreds of thousands of dollars and belong in a museum? People didn't put Rodin hands on their coffee tables, did they? Certainly not people he knew.

"Pardon me?"

"A *Rodin*," Tom piped in. "The French sculptor, Auguste *Rodin*." He leaned over and grabbed a cookie as if to underscore just how ordinary it was to have this priceless work of art displayed in his house, right there next to the shortbread.

"I gave it to Tom for his fortieth," Helen said. She was sitting stiff-backed, her shaking right hand pressed to her lap.

"I think we gave my dad a new toolbox for his fortieth," Gregory said.

Tom gave a solicitous chuckle. "Ever been to the Rodin Museum in Paris, Gregory?" He crossed the room toward one of the built-in bookshelves.

"I haven't," Gregory said. He'd never been out of the country, but he knew of the museum from Laurel Calabrese, a college girlfriend who did her junior year abroad at the Sorbonne. Along with weekly aerograms full of enviable stories about her European adventures, Laurel had sent him a black-and-white postcard of Rodin's statue *The Kiss*. On the back, she'd written, *Getting ideas!* He had pinned the card to his bulletin board above his desk where he didn't just look at it daily but studied the lines, the details, expecting that when Laurel returned, he would try to kiss her like Rodin's white marble lovers. Carved from a single block of stone, they were wrapped around each other, lost to the rest of the world. It was what he wanted: someone to get lost in, or someone who would allow him to lose himself, at least the part he hated. But Laurel stayed on in Paris as a nanny and fell in love with a French guy. At the end of the semester, Gregory took the postcard down and stored it in a shoebox along with the other letters and photos from the girlfriends who didn't stay.

"I'd love to go to the Rodin Museum. I've always wanted to see *Le Baiser*," Gregory said, trying not to botch the pronunciation, while picturing the postcard's French text. "The way the figures are entwined and, you know, the texture and shape of their bodies. It's amazing how Rodin carved those ripples of muscle into marble."

He could feel Liv's quiet approval as she slid even closer to him on the sofa.

"Yes!" Helen said, looking more animated than she had all night. "It's absolutely divine." She closed her eyes as if swooning, and the tremor in her hand became more pronounced. When she opened her eyes, they were watery. Was Helen crying?

"It sounds like you have a true appreciation for art, Gregory?"

"I wish I knew more about it. Liv told me you work in the field."

"I do indeed."

"Leland and I used to put a tennis ball in the hand," Liv said, cutting her mother off. "Remember that, Daddy?"

"Oh, I remember," Tom said, smiling at the memory without looking all that interested. He returned to the sofa with a coffee table book and urged Liv to shift over so he could squeeze in next to Gregory. Tom passed him the book, and there on the cover was *The Kiss*, exactly like Laurel's postcard. Tom reached over and opened to a page of hands. Bronze. Marble. Some grasping. Others curled and gnarled. All were so real looking that Gregory wanted to run his own hand over the glossy page and touch what felt just out of reach.

"The fascinating thing about Rodin's hands is that you can see the deformities," Tom continued. "They're so lifelike, as you astutely said, Gregory. So human." He pointed at the side of the birthday-present hand on the table. "Do you see that pitting? The way the fingers pull down. That's most likely a sign of what's sometimes called Viking disease, because it affects Scandinavian men in midlife. Anyway, I don't want to bore you. But when Helen looks at this hand, she sees art. As a medical doctor I also see the mysterious beauty of science."

Gregory shifted on the cushions. All he could see now were the deformities Tom had pointed out. His own imperfections roiled beneath the surface, invisible but there all the same. Thankfully, Liv broke the spell.

"I see a perfect place to stick a tennis ball," she said. And they all laughed, the way a family is supposed to. Gregory laughed, too, for once feeling like he belonged to something secure and wonderful, something that could hold him. He leaned across the heavy art book and helped himself to two of the cookies. When he offered one to Liv, she took it gratefully.

Later that same night, he brought Liv back to his shabby rental apartment in Brighton. Although he had suggested they go to her place downtown, she pressed to see where he lived. As soon as they were through the door, Gregory wanted to keep the lights off and bring Liv directly to his small bedroom off the kitchen. After the lavishness of her parents' house, his felt stark. But in her resolute way, she asked to look around.

She wandered from the compact kitchen into an equally snug living space that held a double futon, a wobbly coffee table piled with Gregory's textbooks, and a TV set on a slightly rusty bar cart that he and his roommate had found on the curb. Liv studied the space as if trying to solve an intricate puzzle, the conundrum of a twenty-three-year-old graduate student in a top clinical psychology program without a photo or poster on any of the bare walls. As Gregory watched Liv try to find him in the emptiness, he said nothing, just leaned awkwardly against the doorframe with his hands shoved in the pockets of his best khaki pants.

"So spare," Liv said, as if the austerity were a design choice. "Don't you have any pictures? Of family or friends? Something to personalize the space a bit?"

While Gregory tried to justify the blank walls to Liv—*I'm too busy to bother with decorating; the apartment is only temporary*—he thought about the shoebox full of photos under his bed. He couldn't bring himself to throw them out or look at them either. They needed to remain hidden, just like his past.

Liv interrupted finally, saying, "I still haven't seen *your* room."

He took her hand and led her back to the kitchen with its scuffed yellow counters and pungent-smelling gas stove. Before he opened the door to his bedroom, he leaned over and kissed her slowly, trying to convince them both that he was ready for her world of calla lilies and art.

Still kissing her, Gregory started to back into his room with the double mattress on the floor and beige polyester comforter from Sears.

She teasingly bit his bottom lip and ran her fingers through his hair, tugging at it until even his scalp felt charged with desire.

He was careful, afraid of moving too fast. But then she reached down and started to unbuckle his belt. "Is your roommate coming home?" she whispered, her breath hot against his ear.

"No."

"Good." She undid the buckle and lowered her hand, and soon he was moaning deeply.

"Lift me up," she said.

Here? Is that what she meant?

"I thought about this all through dinner, how I just wanted to be alone with you."

Gregory smiled. He couldn't believe this was happening. That someone like Liv could like him this much.

"C'mon," she said. She circled her arms around his neck and pulled herself up toward him.

Gregory got his hands beneath her. He easily lifted her onto the counter that he hoped wasn't covered with crumbs from his roommate's dinner. With his hands still behind her, he let them slide up under her skirt, across her hips, inside her thighs until she was moaning, too.

"Should we—?" Gregory said, nodding at the door. "The bedroom's right here."

She tilted her head and grinned slyly. "I can't wait." She untucked his polo shirt and yanked it over his head then leaned away, inviting him to do the same with her sweater. He pulled it up and off, revealing a sheer white lace bra. He didn't want to drop her sweater on the counter, so he held it for a few seconds, until Liv grabbed it from his hands and tossed it on the floor with a laugh.

He looked at her in the narrow stream of light that seeped between the window frame and the venetian blinds. "God, you're gorgeous."

She trailed the tips of her fingers down his arms, across his chest. "You are, too." She unzipped his khakis, worked them down, along with his boxers.

He reached beneath Liv's short summer skirt and pulled aside her thong, just a damp wisp of lace. She slid forward, and he shuffled closer, his pants now binding his legs. When she wrapped her legs around his waist and gripped the edges of the counter, he managed to lower her onto him, both of them crying out.

Later in his bed, Gregory ran his hands over Liv's body, tracing the narrow contours, lingering on the subtle curve of her waist, studying the lines as if they were the borders of a foreign country that he wanted to learn well enough to live in forever. He'd had girlfriends before, but he'd never made love to one believing they had a future together. Sex had always felt separate from the possibility of love, let alone commitment or marriage. It had been about the physical experience of release, more about losing himself in the act—a brief respite. But with Liv, it felt as if their bodies were speaking to each other.

They fell asleep naked, entwined in each other's arms. When they woke in the night, he began to kiss her again.

"You don't waste much time, do you?" she teased.

He fluttered his lips down the sharp bones of her clavicle, over her small breasts and her muscled stomach, then lower, until she arched her back and clutched the sheets.

For years Gregory replayed that first night with Liv over in his head, remembering a time he gave himself to her completely, their bodies fused and his problems briefly suspended as they made love. Lately, the shelter of sexual healing had declined with her waning libido, his demanding work schedule, and the unpredictable comings and goings of hyperaware teenagers in a creaky Victorian that failed to hide sounds. He wasn't so keen anymore, either. Not with Liv. He feared if he let himself be vulnerable, she'd finally figure him out.

Gregory glanced over at the passenger seat. How he wished she hadn't made such an effort: the outfit, the makeup, the tucking of his too-long hair behind his ear, the careful silence. It made their anniversary dinner charade feel as falsely elegant as Helen Stimson's fussing over his five-dollar carnations.

Yet he knew that wasn't the full truth. It was not about his discomfort with fancy taste or braggy social scenes or even their dwindling sex life and the failings of his marriage. The truth was that he had found Mira, or she had found him.

15

As they headed past the River Club's impeccable row of blush hydrangeas toward the colonial revival building with white clapboard siding and a large cupola where, as Liv once told him, she got caught smoking weed with her high school girlfriends, Liv surprised Gregory by taking his hand in hers. This gesture disoriented him.

Russell Hudson, the club manager, his round belly straining against one of his trademark seersucker jackets, waved at them from behind the long mahogany front desk. "Here's our anniversary couple," he called out, coming around to give Liv a kiss on each cheek and shake Gregory's hand harder than necessary. "You look gorgeous, per usual," he gushed to Liv. "What a bride you have here, huh?" he said to Gregory.

Gregory grasped at Phil's words from the day before. "I'm a lucky man."

"When Calvin mentioned you'd be in to celebrate," Russell said, "we started reminiscing about your wedding. *Best* band ever!"

Liv threw back her head and laughed. If his wife was typically a closed rosebud in the world, she blossomed in this private realm, under the warm light of approving familiarity. Because of her lifelong ties to so many families, she seldom got down the hallway to the dining room without being greeted or stopped over and over. *Is Carrie looking at colleges? Any summer plans? Will Petey play in the Juniors Tournament when he gets back from camp? Haven't seen your dad in a few weeks.* But tonight, it was relatively quiet. Maybe there was an important Sox game at Fenway, something Gregory never followed.

"I'll let you get on with your evening," Russell said, giving Liv's arm a quick squeeze before she and Gregory turned to make their way to the restaurant.

Calvin, the maître d' who had taken the phone reservation, also greeted Liv with a kiss and Gregory with a handshake-back-pat combo, chatting easily as he led them to their table. A silver wine bucket with a chilled split of Moët awaited them.

"You shouldn't have," Liv said, touching the arm of Calvin's fitted suit.

"A little appreciation for our favorite anniversary couple," he said, drawing back Liv's chair so she could slide into the cream-colored seat. He left their menus, promising that Evan would be right with them, and slipped away with the ease of a man whose job was to make members feel as if they were not only uniquely special but being served by a staff that anticipated their every whim.

With Calvin gone, the air of joviality evaporated, and Gregory and Liv were left to face each other across the table set with ivory linens, heavy silver flatware, and a vase of three white magnolia blossoms. "Look," Liv said, sniffing one of the large blooms. "Our wedding flowers! Can you believe Calvin?"

Gregory wished he had brought her a small gift, even just a bouquet of roses from Pemby's. They used to exchange presents, but a few years ago Liv went on a decluttering craze right before one of their anniversaries and announced she didn't need or want any more presents. That first year, she was delighted with the card he wrote her but in subsequent years always seemed a little disappointed when there was nothing to unwrap. He should have remembered.

"So," Liv said. She reached her hands across the table and wiggled her fingers toward him. She was so different from Mira, with her straight blond hair and muted color palette. He looked at Liv's fingers and tried to reignite the spark he used to feel when she touched him.

Gregory drew his hands from his lap and joined them to his wife's. Pressing her lips together, Liv gave him a tight, uncertain smile. A few seconds later, her eyes started to water.

"Are you okay?" Gregory said, afraid of her answer, but impelled to ask. Liv seldom let her feelings spill out, let alone cried. On the rare occasion when she did tear up, she caught herself quickly.

"Actually, no." Liv's voice had a choke in it. "I've been wanting to say a few things. And while this isn't the ideal time—"

Their waiter, Evan, tall with square-jawed good looks, approached the table. Gregory, feeling silly, released Liv's hands and picked up his menu.

"Hello, Mrs. Weber, Dr. Weber. I hear congratulations are in order," Evan said. He popped the cork on the champagne bottle and filled Liv's crystal flute. They all watched as the pale gold bubbles burst to the top, then settled beneath the rim.

When Evan went to fill the second flute, Gregory waved him off. "None for me, thanks." He needed to be clearheaded.

Evan nodded and nestled the bottle back in the ice bucket. "Calvin was just telling me what a great wedding you had."

At this point, even Liv, who cherished her club connections, seemed to wince minutely at the relay of wedding talk, but under no circumstances would she not be fully polite. "It *was* great, Evan," she assured him. "How was your first year at Bowdoin?"

"Fantastic! I can't believe how fast it went. And with the lacrosse season—"

"You know, Evan," Gregory said, cutting him off, "I'm ready to order. Liv, have you decided?"

"Oh, um." She glanced at the menu that she knew by heart. "I guess I'll have the seasonal salad with grilled shrimp."

Gregory ordered the mushroom risotto and a tonic water and made it clear from the directness with which he handed back the menu that there need not be any more conversation about college, lacrosse, or their wedding.

"You didn't have to be so abrupt," Liv said when Evan was out of earshot. "He was just being friendly."

"But you were saying something important."

Liv agreed with a weak smile. Then, with more solemnity than celebration, she lifted her champagne flute and waited for Gregory to do the same with his water glass. It was the moment that he would traditionally propose a toast, to her, to them. *Happy anniversary. To twenty-two years. To the next twenty-two years.* The reliable options ran like a ticker tape through his head as he sat there, both hands gripping his glass. But he couldn't utter a single word for fear the wrong ones would spill out unbidden.

When Liv lightly cleared her throat, Gregory lowered his eyes and caught part of his reflection in the shiny silver butter knife, just the left side of his face, as if he were only partly there. He felt Liv staring at him, but he couldn't lift his eyes from his half reflection.

"Gregory? What's going on?"

He looked up and found his wife studying him. After so many years of putting himself in his clients' shoes, he could easily imagine what it was like to be Liv witnessing her husband in such a nonfunctional state that he couldn't even raise a glass of ice water to their anniversary. He knew his eyes looked heavy and hooded from not having slept the night before, visions of Mira invading his thoughts. At five in the morning, he had finally left the bed and wandered outside to watch the sunrise. Sitting there across from Liv, Gregory felt his shoulders bowing.

Liv, who had been trained by her mother to maintain control under any circumstances, said crisply, "Okay, I'll say something." She raised her chin, giving her voice an atypical haughtiness. "It hasn't been the easiest year, and I'm not even sure what's to blame—"

Gregory felt a click in his chest. He lifted his eyes, hopeful about his circumstances for the first time all evening. Would Liv confess something first?

"I've been struggling to feel connected to you," Liv continued, "and I sense that you may be experiencing something similar."

Gregory didn't dare respond, but he looked at her, his eyes narrowed with gratitude.

Liv drew a deep breath and dropped her voice. "And I want to say I'm sorry for my role in that."

Still holding her champagne in one hand, Liv reached for Gregory's hand with the other. When he didn't reach back, she set down her champagne flute and dabbed her fingertips underneath her eyes to keep from crying. She blinked several times and tried to force a smile.

"It's okay, Liv," Gregory said. "It's going to be okay." His fingers, cold from the glass of ice water, found hers.

She looked at him, her whole face a question. "Is it?"

"Yes. I promise."

Still holding her fingers with one hand, Gregory passed her the cloth napkin from his lap. She clutched it to her cheek. After a moment, she drew a breath and said, "I feel so alone here. I need us to do this together. Respectfully."

He was stunned and relieved. Maybe she was letting him off the hook. Maybe Mira could be his. Maybe he wouldn't have to tell her anything.

"We will," he said. "We will do it respectfully. We'll need to decide when to talk to the kids."

Liv dropped his fingers like they had just caught fire. "What? What does that mean, 'talk to the kids'?"

Evan appeared at the table with Gregory's tonic water and a half dozen oysters. "From Calvin," he said. He set the platter between them with a flourish. "He was just remembering the raw bar at your wedding."

"Enough about our wedding!" Gregory said sharply.

They all froze.

"I'm sorry, Dr. Weber," Evan said in a nervous voice.

"It's fine, Evan," Liv managed to say, although it sounded like she was running out of breath. "We will certainly enjoy the oysters."

Gregory pointed at his glass. "And could you take this back and make it a gin and tonic?"

"Of course, sir," he said, his tone dimmed. "Is there a gin you prefer?"

Gregory couldn't give a crap about liquor, let alone the top-shelf brands always being touted by the club elite. "Whatever's cheapest!"

Evan laughed nervously while Liv kicked Gregory under the table. But he didn't care. He felt like his life had just been pushed further off its axis and was whirling this way and that, and he had no way to stop it. Was Liv saying she did or didn't want to separate? Was it possible that he'd been so caught up in his thoughts of Mira that he'd heard what he wanted to hear? He'd believed she was releasing him, freeing him of his obligations.

After Evan retreated again, Liv leaned over as close as she could get without actually flattening her chest on the table. "Gregory, what are you trying to tell me?"

"I don't know," Gregory admitted. He hadn't eaten since lunch and needed food. Although he would love to slurp down some of those oysters—probably the last oysters of his life—he resisted. "I thought maybe you were saying you didn't want to be married anymore."

"And you'd agree with that? You think we should split up?" Liv's eyes pooled with tears. Gregory looked around and when he did, Larry and Betty Flaven, who were just being seated, spotted him and waved. Terrified that they would come over to say hello, he swiveled his head away. "We should go someplace else."

Liv swallowed visibly and sat up straighter. "We are not leaving. We can talk about whatever we need to right here. May I start?"

"Sure," Gregory said in a defeated voice, just as Evan returned with his gin and tonic. After gently placing it on the table, he retreated without a word. Gregory took a sip, then grimaced at the medicinal taste and set the glass down again.

"What I was trying to say," Liv began, "is that while things between us have felt challenging recently, I'm committed to making our marriage work. But we *both* need to want that. I was not implying anything that would require our talking to the kids. Not at all."

Gregory tried to listen attentively, but it was hard to focus. He rested his face on one hand and adjusted himself in his chair. For a moment, it was true he'd been hoping for a way out, but now he'd only made things worse.

"I feel like I've lost you," Liv continued. "We've been so distant for so long that sometimes I wonder if I ever really had you. Remember how it used to be, when the kids were little? We were a family. It was hard—exhausting even—but we were there for each other, or that's how it seemed. Now you're always hiding from me, in the garage, or in the chapel at your father's party." She settled back in her chair and rearranged her napkin in her lap. "Please say something."

Gregory decided that what he was about to say would sound bad whether or not he ate an oyster first, so he squeezed some lemon and a dab of cocktail sauce on the largest one, lifted it to his mouth, and slurped it down. The salty taste of the sea was so unexpectedly fortifying that he had another while Liv took quick, intermittent sips of champagne. After feeling like he'd regained a modicum of composure, Gregory went to wipe his fingers on his napkin but realized he'd given it to Liv. He used the hem of the white tablecloth.

"It's my turn to apologize," he said, looking up at his wife. "I've failed you in every way, our marriage, too. And I'm not sure we can fix it."

"What?" Liv shut her eyes and shook her head. "Tell me this is not happening."

Gregory knew he sounded callous, but he also felt like he was speaking the truest words he'd ever said to her. And he couldn't stop himself. "It's not fair to you. I can't be the husband you deserve."

Liv leaned in and said with a harsh whisper, "Why don't you let me decide that?"

"Because I have to say what feels right to me. I can't always tell you what you want to hear."

She sat back again and crossed her arms over her chest. "You're having an affair."

"No! I am not. I swear to you, Liv."

"Then tell me what you're saying." She tossed Gregory's napkin onto the table then gave a quick glance around.

Evan sheepishly returned to check on them. He held the silver bar tray in front of his chest. "Is everything okay, Mrs. Weber?"

"She's not feeling well," Gregory explained, starting to push his chair back. "Please give our apologies to the kitchen. And I'm sorry if I was rough on you before, Evan."

"Of course, sir," Evan said. "We all have those kinds of days." *Like you know fuck-all about this kind of bad day,* Gregory thought but said, "Thanks for understanding."

Liv shook back her shoulders and sat up straighter. "I'm actually fine. Anniversaries make me a little emotional, but I'm looking forward to dinner. And, Evan, please tell Calvin the oysters are delicious."

Evan eyed the shells piled only on Gregory's appetizer plate, not hers. "Okay, that's good to hear, Mrs. Weber. So, final answer? Dinner is, um, on?" He looked to Gregory for confirmation.

"Yes," Liv said. "It is."

When Evan walked away again, Liv glared at Gregory. "No!"

"No, what?"

"Just no."

"Are you happy, Liv? With our marriage?"

"You are not breaking up our family."

Gregory reached for his gin and tonic, but as soon as he picked it up, he set it down again and pushed it to the edge of the table, stopping short of sending it crashing to the floor, even though he thought about it. He didn't know what to say or do. He didn't know how to justify his sudden intense desire to split up without telling her everything. The incident. The lies of omission. Mira. He folded his hands on the table in front of him like he was in a business negotiation and he needed to change tack in order not to blow the whole deal.

"Are you sure you're not having an affair? Because I found this in your briefcase." Liv dipped a hand into her purse that was hanging on her chair and slowly withdrew Mira's pink scarf, like a horrible magic trick.

As Liv held up the scarf, Gregory's throat tightened. In his exhaustion before leaving work, he had forgotten to take it out of his briefcase and lock it in his bottom desk drawer.

"It was an anniversary present for you," he said, hearing the low register of deceit in his voice. "But I felt weird giving it to you, because of, well, everything."

Liv looked up through cold eyes. She didn't believe him. She was too smart.

He extended his hand. "If you give it back. I can wrap it up properly." He would go to Saks tomorrow and buy her a new one.

"I don't care about that," Liv said crisply. She unfolded the scarf and draped it over her shoulders where it looked wrong on her, the magenta too vibrant for her skin tone and too bold for her classic white silk dress. It was Mira's color. Why did Liv want the scarf anyway? Was she trying to punish him—or herself? "I'm not letting go of it," she said, decidedly. "And I'm not letting go of our marriage."

Gregory reached for another oyster. He took his time squeezing the lemon, spooning the cocktail sauce, then he closed his eyes as he lifted the jagged edge of the shell to his lips. He tipped the flesh into the back of his mouth, swallowing down everything he wanted to say out loud to his wife, a woman whose only misstep was falling in love with him. He couldn't look at Liv wearing Mira's scarf, likely infusing it with the scent of one of the perfumes she sprayed from cut glass bottles arranged on her dresser.

He finished the oysters, and he sat back and squeezed his hands together. Everything was sliding away, but he didn't know how to catch it and gather it back inside. Just yesterday, he held hope in his hands. Today it was draining out of him, like water through a fist.

Liv emptied the rest of the champagne split into her glass, shaking out the last few drops. As she sipped, they sat in silence until Evan set their entrees down.

When the piquant aroma of parmesan hit his nose, Gregory's hunger surprised him. He tucked his fork into the shallow white bowl. The club chef had sprinkled bits of parsley on the rim like confetti.

Liv lifted her fork, then set it down again. "Do you know why I never wanted to get a vacation home like so many people we know?" she asked. Her tone indicated that it wasn't really a question.

Gregory shook his head and kept eating, feeling more grounded with every bite. He vaguely remembered some conversations about looking at houses on the Vineyard, but nothing ever came of the idea.

"I didn't want to get a vacation home because I didn't know what we'd do there or talk about if it was just us for a week." Liv's voice sounded broken, and Gregory couldn't tell if she was going to yell at him or cry. "Do you know how lonely I feel when I'm with you? Do you have any idea? It's like you're never here anymore. And by *here*, I mean present, with me." She sat back as if trying to duck from the unstoppable flow of her words. "Twenty-two years ago, practically to the hour, you vowed to love me in joy and sorrow for the rest of our days, and now I don't know where you are."

"Liv."

"Let me finish, please." She paused, as if considering how vulnerable she could allow herself to be. "I love you, Gregory. I have done my best to love you despite having been raised by a narcissistic mother who didn't know how to love and a father who loves my brother more than me. I've tried, but I'm not sure you have. We used to be happy. You used to make me so happy. But it's like you've given up on me—on us." She stiffened her jaw, and her throat tightened. "Before you walk away, you owe it to me and Carrie and Petey to try."

Gregory set his fork down. He reached out his hand, and Liv grabbed it like a lifeline, as her words continued to pour out. "I don't think you understand what this club means to me. I know the affluence is obscene, but I'm tired of apologizing to you for that. I grew up here and everyone knows me and my family. They ask me about my work and value my opinion about design. And when my father sees me here like the belle of the ball, I feel—I don't know—like he appreciates me. And I need some validation right now, because I'm starting to feel like a nobody."

Gregory squeezed her hand with a tenderness that felt foreign. "But Liv, you're *not* a nobody. You're a successful editor—"

"I'm a successful editor of art and design books because my mother had dozens upon dozens of them around the house when I was growing up. I read them all without knowing that I was studying for my future. She wanted me to be an artist, and when I had no aptitude for that and decided to write, I couldn't do that either. So, I defaulted to a plan she put in place. And yes, it has worked out, but she was the one with the contacts in the publishing world. Everything I have came from her."

"Not your tutoring work." Gregory insisted. "That's all you, giving to those kids."

Liv considered this.

"And you quit writing to be a mother. You'll go back to it. You're *going* back to it."

"I quit writing because I was mediocre at it. This memoir class I'm in is, I don't know, a distraction. And while I'm throwing myself a big pity party, it's probably worth mentioning that I'm turning out to be a pretty mediocre mother, too."

"That is not true."

"I did fine when the kids were little, but Carrie can't even look at me anymore without scowling. And Petey, well, something isn't there the way it used to be."

"Liv, if I had ten bucks for every one of my clients with a teenage daughter who supposedly hates her, I could retire a lot sooner."

Liv looked hard into his eyes. "My point is that I can't let our marriage fail. I've failed at so many things."

"You haven't failed. This is my fault."

"That's not enough anymore. In my head I've been blaming you for years. Why else do you think I come here all the time? The same reason you probably spend all your free time in that garage or your garden. So we don't have to deal with each other and our problems. I'm at fault, too. We *both* have work to do."

They stared at each other, still gripping hands across the table. Gregory, knowing she was going to cry again, urged her to her feet. Clarity of thought was not on Gregory's side these days, but he was certain they needed to get out of there. She rose compliantly, gathered Mira's crumpled scarf around her shoulders, and let him hurry her through the club restaurant, the opposite of the way they entered on their wedding night when Liv pulled him toward the wildly applauding crowd. This time Gregory focused on escaping as quickly as possible while avoiding eye contact with the Flavens and every other couple hailing their attention. God help him if they ran into Phil and Beth. When they passed Calvin hovering around the host stand, Liv tried to mutter an explanation, but Gregory tugged her down the carpeted corridor past the reception desk where Russell called out to them, but they were already through the sliding glass doors.

Once they were safely enclosed in the car, Gregory hugged Liv, feeling the scarf against his cheek. He put his nose into her shoulder trying to anchor himself with the smell of mint and smoke and marigolds, scents that were losing their strength in battle with Liv's citrusy perfume. He hoped she'd take it off now that they were in the warm car, but instead she held it to her chest.

"Let's go home," he said softly.

"Not yet."

"But, Liv—"

"If we're going to make this work, we need to *do* something."

Gregory stared at the club that now glowed in the muted pastels of sunset. A playground for the rich, blessed with perfect orientation to natural light. He'd married into this kind of extravagance, and at one point it had felt like an accomplishment. A benchmark for all his years of schooling and hard work. But he knew from the beginning that he never really belonged.

He could feel Liv fidgeting next to him, trying to decide what it was they needed to *do* to rise above their misery. He couldn't tell her that it was not going to work. Not ever. She'd never be okay with what he'd done. "I'm exhausted, Liv."

"Head toward Mount Auburn Cemetery," she said, her voice purposeful.

"I don't think that's a good idea."

"For me, Gregory. It's our anniversary, for God's sake. Give me something."

16

"We're almost at the secret gate," Liv said, pressing her face to the passenger side window. "I'll bet it's still there."

The tall chain-link fence and heavily forested cemetery loomed next to them.

"Somewhere around here," Liv said. "Wait! I think that's it. Stop the car!"

Gregory slowed down but kept driving. The shoulder was empty, and he could park anywhere, but he slid by three spaces.

"There," Liv said. "Take that one."

He pulled over and cut the engine.

Liv turned to him, put her hand on his forearm. "Remember our first kiss under that tree? What was it?"

"Willow," he said. "Weeping willow."

She threw open the passenger door. "I want to find it again. That exact tree."

How many times had Gregory revisited the decision he made under that tree? The night Liv remembered as the one they fell in love was the same night Gregory knew he simultaneously loved and failed her. His inability to reveal to Liv what he and Joey Didowski had done when driving home from the Red Sox game began to feel like an additional crime, one he had committed directly against Liv and, eventually, against their marriage.

After the incident, he wanted to blame Margaret. She was the one who had bought the beer and the bottle of Rubinoff 80 proof vodka at Leary's that afternoon. She was dating one of the guys who worked there, and he would sell to her illegally. She would buy for Gregory, too, as long as he promised—*Do you swear, Greg? Swear to God?*—not to drive, which is why he didn't tell her about the Red Sox game.

When Gregory pulled into the Didowskis' driveway that afternoon, Joey, also tall but more thickly built, sat down hard in the passenger seat. He brandished the tickets—a graduation present from his New Hampshire cousins—and slid them into his wallet.

Before Gregory had turned onto West Main Street, Joey was already reaching into the brown paper bag tucked at his feet. "Ready for a brewski?"

Gregory wasn't planning to drink until they got to Boston, but Joey took out two beers, cracked them both open, and handed him one. That was Joey, always pushing the edge in the name of having fun. But that was also Gregory, eager not to offend—afraid to tell his best friend that he wanted to prioritize safety. He reluctantly took the can and began drinking slowly, trying to enjoy every cold swallow as he cruised up I-84, feeling liberated for the first time in his life. He was leaving for college at the end of the summer, and now he had his own car—bought the week before with his savings. This was the freedom he'd been craving, and the beer just sweetened it all. When they passed the sign for UConn, Joey raised his can toward the window.

"Here's to you, man. Full fucking scholarship."

Once in Boston, Gregory drove with caution, following a folding map they'd bought at a service station off the highway. He'd never driven in such a big, confusing city and was relieved when he finally found a parking spot in front of a sports bar near Fenway.

Radio blasting, they sat in the car and each chugged another beer as they watched Sox fans in their jerseys and caps stream past historic brick buildings draped with banners on their way to the ballpark. When their beers were gone, Joey pulled out an engraved pewter flask that had been a graduation gift from his grandfather and carefully filled it with vodka. Before they left the car, they polished off what was left in the bottle.

Happily buzzed, the boys headed into Fenway Park on that perfect summer evening. Two best friends on top of their game.

Their seats were along the first base line, ten rows behind the Red Sox dugout. Almost as thrilling, they were sitting next to three Brazilian high school girls, in town on a summer language program. One of their host families had given them tickets to the game, but the girls kept complaining about how slow it was compared to *fútbol* in their country and how they couldn't even buy beer because the kiosks wouldn't accept their fake IDs. The girls were elated when Gregory bought a couple of lemonades, which they topped off with shots from Joey's flask. Gregory wanted to slow down his drinking, but one of the girls, Candella, who had gray eyes and straight blond hair all the way down her back, seemed to like him. She was eager to hear about his high school baseball team, as if forgetting that she found the sport boring. When the Red Sox finally scored in the eighth inning, she turned to Gregory and hugged him.

"Your arms," she said, "they're like Superman." She squeezed his biceps, and with her hands still clutching him, he flexed as hard as he could. He was feeling good, better than good. He was feeling fucking amazing. He grabbed the flask from Joey and drained it into his empty lemonade cup.

The Sox came back to beat the Rangers 6-3, creating a wildly celebratory mood in the stadium. Staggering down the bleacher stairs with arm around Candella's thin shoulders, Gregory didn't want the night to end.

Joey, reading his mind the way best friends do, said, "Let's find a bar and keep this party going." But the girls had promised their host families they'd be back after the game and needed to get home to Beacon Hill.

"We'll give you a ride," Joey said. He was slurring his words and bumping into people as he navigated the crowded sidewalks around Fenway. Gregory knew he wasn't doing much better, but he also couldn't control himself.

When they finally located the car, Candella and her two friends piled into the back seat, while Joey got into the passenger seat and opened the last two beers. Gregory drank one as he drove, while the girls laughed and shouted directions in Portuguese. At some point, Gregory realized he was completely wasted, with stoplights spinning in his vision and the roads coming at him in a fast, dark blur. How they safely got the girls to Beacon Hill felt like part mystery, part miracle. But they did, and as the three of them slid out of the back seat, shouting their goodbyes, Gregory felt an emptiness at their sudden disappearance. He wanted to get out, too, and hug Candella again, maybe get her number. But when he searched for her out the window, she had already gone inside.

Gregory gripped the wheel and pulled into the street again. Once moving, he didn't know where he was or how to get onto the Mass Pike. "I can't do this," Gregory said. "You drive." He stopped in the middle of a busy intersection, a line of cars behind them honking. Joey opened his door, and they switched places.

Three years after that night, Joey put a bullet through his head.

When Liv got out of the car, Mira's scarf was still wrapped around her shoulders.

"It's pretty hot out. Are you sure you need that?" Gregory asked.

Liv pulled it tighter. "It's perfect," she said, without a hint of sarcasm, as if she had already claimed the scarf as her own. "How did you know I wanted a new pashmina?"

Pashmina. He realized he'd heard that word, but he didn't know that's what the scarf was called. All he wanted was for her to take it off.

Liv led him to the place where the chain-link fence had once been slashed. Gregory hoped that it would be repaired and, therefore, inaccessible. But that wasn't the case. While the fence had been fixed in the old place, Liv found a newer cut and bent it back enough to squeeze through the triangle-shaped opening.

"Damn!" She stopped and pulled at the hem of her dress that had caught on the fence. From inside the cemetery, she held back the makeshift gate and waited while Gregory hesitantly ducked in after her.

"I'm not even sure where I am," he said, straightening up and peering around. The spire of the Bigelow Chapel rose in the distance out of the fading summer light, but he felt turned around under the dark canopy of branches and among the paths of gravestones and crosses snaking in every direction. He thought of Joey, of his funeral that long-ago February morning.

Gregory's father, who had taken the day off from work to attend, walked stoically ahead, past the hearse and up the steps into the entrance of St. Ann's, a red brick monstrosity in the middle of town. Gregory wondered how his father felt about his son's childhood friend lying in a casket in that shiny black car. But Gregory's father's reserve was predictable, even tolerable, compared to his mother in her tired brown coat, hand over her mouth, muttering to herself. Before they entered the church, she grabbed Gregory's sleeve. "Was he on drugs?" she asked in a hushed voice. "Was that the problem?"

Gregory didn't answer. He wasn't about to tell her what Joey's real problem was. And he wanted her to stop asking questions. Facing the reality of what Joey had done, Gregory now had his own question to answer: Should he kill himself, too?

Joey had never said a word about the incident. That was the pact they'd made that night, instigated by Gregory and his fear of his father's wrath. But just over a year later, the boys ran into each other outside of the mall. Joey gave a quick wave and kept walking, but Gregory caught up with him.

"What's up?" Joey asked. He combed his fingers through his shaggy light brown hair and glanced over his shoulder.

"How are you doing?"

Joey looked around nervously. "Good, yeah, good. But I'm running late, you know."

He started to walk away, when Gregory grabbed his arm. "Do you think about it?" Gregory asked in a low whisper.

Joey pinched his nose and twisted his face. His clothes hung loose on his tall frame, and Gregory could tell he'd lost weight. "I got my ways to not think."

Gregory nodded. It had been his idea to keep it a secret, but now he wanted to keep Joey talking. He needed it. Maybe they both did. "I wish I could do that, too," Gregory said. "A day doesn't go by that I don't—"

"You know what?" Joey said, nodding his head at the crowded parking lot. "I gotta run, but if you ever want me to hook you up, you know how to find me."

How many times had Gregory thought about reaching back out to Joey, not for whatever would help him forget but to talk, and maybe get his friend some support? But he didn't. And now they were at Joey's funeral, and Gregory wished he were dead, too. For the past three nights, he had fallen asleep imagining ways he could die. He'd walk himself through the options: pills, gun, hanging, a razor blade to his wrist. Then he'd wake up to another day of life, ashamed of his cowardice. As he lay in bed, he'd replay the accident again in his head, looking for loopholes in his guilt, continually failing to find a single reason to forgive himself. Joey didn't, so why should he?

Sitting in the hard wooden pew between his parents, Gregory was too dazed to cry. Joey was eulogized as a devoted son, brother, cousin, nephew, and friend who found great joy in life, even as he struggled to conquer his personal demons. Next to Gregory, his mother sobbed as if her own son had put a bullet through his head. When it was the time in the Mass to share the sign of peace, his mother, who would normally offer a feeble handshake even to her own children, ignored Gregory's extended hand and pulled him to her chest. He knew at that moment, his body bent into the clutch of her arms, that he would never have the courage to kill himself, not as long as she was alive. He would never inflict the kind of pain that he saw on Mrs. Didowski's face that day, as if her own life had ended with her son's. Something about those few seconds, in his mother's embrace, gave Gregory the strength to sit through the rest of the Mass and drive with his parents to the cemetery, where mourners gathered around the deep, empty grave.

He nodded at Patrick Callahan and his other old friends, and they acknowledged with a tip of their heads that they were connected but had no real understanding of why Gregory stood apart. After the incident, he couldn't pretend to those guys that he was still one of them, carefree except for the rigors of college and the stress of a part-time job. They likely worried about having enough money leftover after paying next semester's tuition to spend spring break in Miami. Gregory worried about whether he deserved to live. He had lost all inclination to see his friends, the ones in his photos—at prom, on their senior class trip to DC, with their arms flung around each other after winning the state basketball championship. The only thing that motivated him to get out of bed that summer was the fear that his father would notice something was wrong and pry into him for answers.

As for his friends, none of them asked why Gregory didn't hang out anymore. They all just stopped calling, the way people set others adrift, because they no longer feel securely moored in each other's lives. And when he saw them in dark suits, their eyes bloodshot from what could have been partying or grief, likely both, Gregory was sure they could read the guilt in his face, see what he had done.

Gregory eyed the chain-link fence, now snapped back into place. "I'm not sure about this," he said to Liv. "They probably have security cameras."

"Don't be so uptight." Her voice wasn't mean but teasing, a less confident, more desperate version of the Liv he fell in love with here on that long-ago spring night. "This way!" She stepped out of her sandals and looped the straps through her fingers. She reached for Gregory with her free hand, unfurled his clenched fist, and wrapped his fingers in hers.

As she pulled him along, trying to wear down his resistance to the spontaneous adventure, Gregory felt the pressure of her effort to rally them back together. But he couldn't bring himself to join in this forced exuberance as she ran, fit from hours on the tennis court, in search of their weeping willow. He felt none of the lightness or laughter she was trying so valiantly to summon. Quite the opposite. He felt as heavy as the death that surrounded him, and he wished they could just return to the car and talk like a normal middle-aged, married couple. He didn't want to find that tree. He didn't want to remember his weakness on their first night together, the romantic levity he managed to conjure, even when he knew he shouldn't.

But he didn't say anything as Liv hurried him along the landscaped paths, running in her bare feet and torn white dress, the pink pashmina billowing around her. Liv was intent and, for a moment, Gregory felt like he was witnessing one of his mood disorder clients having a hypomanic episode when, really, he knew that Liv's MO included the belief that a person could will themselves into fulfilling their own desires or hide what they couldn't bear to see.

But wasn't that what Gregory had always done? Hide? And wasn't Mira trying to unmask him? Maybe Liv could handle what he was finally ready to reveal, or maybe it all ended here, exactly where it began.

"Wait!" Gregory said, letting go of her hand and pausing by a red pine with spindly branches reaching in every direction. It was a steamy July night, and his skin was slick with sweat. He knew that Liv could outrun him, but it seemed clear she was trying to outrun everything that was wrong with their marriage. "I need to tell you something," he said.

She stopped and turned. "What? That you can't keep up?" She was a mature version of young, lighthearted Liv, not the Liv who had grown exasperated with him.

He shook his head. He was going to tell her. Here. Now. He was going to tell her that after Joey took over driving that night, they got themselves completely lost, and soon they were circling around in the Financial District, the one-way Boston streets an inky, ominous maze. Gregory tried to stay focused, but he was too drunk to read the tiny print on the map unfolded in front of him. He was arguing with Joey about which street to take, which is why he didn't see the person on the bike, not until Joey braked hard.

Did Gregory scream? Gasp? He didn't know. But he remembered the horrible *thunk* of the body hitting the hood, and the terrified eyes that flashed at the windshield. He remembered slinking down in the seat and yelling "Drive! Just drive!" until Joey revved the engine and sped the hell out of there, never finding out if the person was dead or alive. And Gregory remembered the feeling that settled into his own body as they merged on the Mass Pike: he was an evil person who didn't deserve to live.

He wanted to finally tell Liv that was why Joey had killed himself and why Gregory had been such a wreck for so long. Liv would either understand or, more likely, release him back into his life, because who would want to be with someone as contemptible as he was? She would realize that she had been married to a stranger disguised as competent psychologist, one who sometimes sat in his office filling out the very worksheets he offered his clients, penciling in answers to questions about his moods and coping style, an exercise in treading emotional water, all to keep himself from drowning in a cesspool of his own making.

"Liv. Please! There's something I need to say."

She didn't hear the urgency in his voice, or she refused to acknowledge it. "You can tell me when we get to the willow," she said. "It's just up there, on the other side of that hill, I think. Catch me."

Without taking his hand again, she spun around quickly, causing the scarf to fly from her shoulders and drift to the ground. Gregory stared at it for a few seconds before dashing several yards to grab it. He clutched the scarf the way he did that first day when Mira left his office. He put his nose into the soft fabric and inhaled—an oxygen mask in a plane that had lost cabin pressure.

When he looked up, he saw Liv had stopped running and had turned around again, one hand on her hip, the other still holding her sandals. With her pale hair and white dress, she looked like an apparition hovering above him in the filtered moonlight.

She laughed and touched her shoulder. "I didn't even notice it was gone," she said. She started toward him, but as she approached, he backed away. When he turned around again, he saw something.

Gregory went cold. At his feet was a small, granite gravestone, newer than its neighbors. He could just about read it in the sparse light of the waning gibbous moon.

Mira.

He rubbed the sweat from his eyes and kept reading.

Mira Patel
March 1, 1960 – June 20, 1989

Gregory dropped to his hands and knees. He was struggling to get air, like he was being choked. Had he really seen that name or just imagined it? Unable to look again, he buried his face in the scarf.

He was seventeen. She was twenty-nine.

Liv's hand was on his back. "Gregory! What's happening? Say something!" Her frantic voice came through the hard thudding of his pulse. "Is it your heart?"

He shook his head no.

She yanked on his shoulders. "Are you okay? What hurts?"

Those determined hands, fighting to pull him up and keep him alive, gave him strength. He drew a breath and lifted his head. He peered at the stone in the uncertain light, staring hard at the name and that date.

He tried to stand with Liv's help, but he couldn't. His legs and arms wobbly, his body trembling, he fell back to the cool ground and lay there, unmoving, his cheek pressed to the grass that blanketed the grave.

17

Friday morning, Gregory's phone jolted him awake. He followed the sound to the concrete floor of the garage, dark except for the first dull wash of morning light through the dusty window. He saw Margaret's name and number flashing on the iPhone screen. If his sister, typically a late sleeper, was calling at that hour, it had to do with their father.

Just as Gregory's hand landed on the phone, it went silent. A few seconds later a text came through, but he didn't look at it. Leaving the phone on the floor, he ran his hands over his face, pushing hard on his eyes, trying to blot away his confusion as to why he was sleeping in the garage in a beach chair. His butt was so low in the webbing that it was scraping the floor, and his back was so tight and stiff, he was afraid his spine would snap if he changed positions too quickly. He slowly flexed his neck forward and discovered Mira's pink scarf haphazardly bunched in his lap. He drew a sharp breath and shuddered at the onslaught of fractured memories from the night before.

"You sure it's not your heart? Where's the pain?" Liv had finally coaxed him from the ground and was leading him along the winding paths. Gregory had stumbled forward, unable to respond to any of her questions, but that didn't stop her from asking more. *Are you okay to walk? Is this too much?* When they arrived at the cut in the fence, Liv yanked it aside so Gregory could squeeze through. Liv followed, the metal clanging behind her. "Give me the car keys. Now!"

Gregory reached into his pocket and was surprised at how easily he could extract the BMW fob and also his wallet, which he held in one hand, wondering at the leathery strangeness as coins fell to the ground. He thought he should pick them up, but he couldn't. He let Liv help him into the car.

"We're going to the hospital," she said, which made no sense because no one was sick, but he couldn't find the words to argue. Every time he tried to speak, only heavy gasps came out. Soon Liv was steering the car toward a brightly lit sign that read Emergency Room, and Gregory, thinking he must have been in an accident, checked his body for blood or broken bones. Nothing. He was intact. But then in his mind, Joey braked hard, and Gregory lurched forward. He saw eyes coming toward him—Mira's eyes—and heard the *thunk* of a body on the hood.

"Oh, God!"

"What?" Liv cried. Gregory didn't answer, but she kept pushing. "Are you able to walk? Do you need a wheelchair?"

Hunkered low in the seat, still clutching Mira's scarf, he shook his head no. "I'm not going in there. I'm fine. I'm fine." As the words came stuttering out, he knew he was saying the wrong thing. But what was he supposed to tell her? That something from his past was coming back to haunt him? Or he was losing his mind? He curled into a ball and buried his head in his hands. When he heard a high-pitched whimpering, he was surprised to realize those sounds were coming from his mouth. But he couldn't make them stop, even as Liv stroked his back and urged him to go with her into the hospital. All he could say was, "Take me home."

Suddenly, Liv's hand was gone. Gregory forced himself to sit upright and put his hand over one of hers. She gripped the wheel so tightly, he couldn't peel her fingers off. He searched for an explanation that would make sense to her, a half-truth he could lean on to rationalize his behavior. "It was my friend Joey, who killed himself," he said. "I started thinking about him, just like on our first date. And it was too much."

After a moment, Liv softened. "I see," she said. She sighed with resignation and turned to him. "I'm not taking you home until you agree to see a doctor tomorrow. I don't care if it's Phil or another therapist. But you have to promise me, Gregory. This is not okay. Do you promise you'll see someone?"

He kneaded the scarf like soft, pliable dough, stretching his fingers around the cloth, trying to gather all of the fabric into his hands. "I will. I promise."

Gregory picked up the phone from the concrete floor and blinked at the text from Margaret. *Call me asap dad had a heart attack.*

Margaret answered after one ring and started spewing details. "He was having chest pains early this morning when Fitz checked on him, so Melissa called the paramedics and—"

"Melissa?"

"Head of nursing. I guess they made it to Hartford Hospital and got him to the ER, but then he had a massive coronary. He probably would have died right away if he'd been at Pleasant Springs, so that's one saving grace. But it's not good. It was called a—wait—I wrote it down. A ventricular fibrillation arrest. V-fib arrest. I don't even know what the fuck that means except they had to do a full cardiac resuscitation, and shit." She drew a harried breath. "So, I guess I'll meet you there in, well, how long before you can get down?"

Gregory suddenly felt like Carrie being dragged to the nursing home against her will. He wanted to ask, *Do I have to go?* Didn't hospitalized people usually survive heart attacks? In the absolute worst-case scenario, if his father did die from this, wasn't the birthday party the weekend before the perfect goodbye, with the whole family gathered to celebrate him? Gregory didn't see any reason to rush to Hartford until he could figure out what had happened the night before, maybe even drive back to the cemetery after work and look at that gravestone again. Could Mira's name and death date be a coincidence? Was he hallucinating? Living in some kind of alternate reality?

"I'm going to the hospital now." Margaret's voice was racing. "Just get there as soon as you can."

How could he tell her he wasn't going? Could he use the excuse of seven mentally unwell clients who needed their sessions that day? Would she understand? If he missed Marion P. at eleven, it would trigger the trauma of her father abandoning the family when she was a little girl. And if he didn't meet with Brandon G.S. at noon, the young man would wander through his week untethered without the reassurance that his government surveillance fear was unfounded. He felt responsible for minimizing these people's suffering, whereas their father was never going to get his full health back and would always suffer from dementia.

Of course, those were his professional excuses. Really, he just wanted to figure out what he'd seen last night.

"You there?"

"Yeah, sorry." He was about to say he wasn't going down, when he remembered his promise to Liv the night before. He had told her he would call a therapist, and he knew that his wife would be nothing if not tenacious about him following through. "I'll grab a quick shower and be there in a few hours," Gregory said, as if he had just gotten his priorities straight and his father's well-being had shot to the top of the list.

After Gregory set the phone down again, he brought the pink scarf to his nose. The scents were still there. She was still there. He let the scarf drop, still wondering who she was. Were his Mira and Mira Patel connected? Were they the same person?

He shook off the idea. *You're being irrational, Gregory*, he told himself. But he couldn't stop turning this puzzle around in his head. How many people named Mira lived in the Boston area in 1989? And how many of them died on the same day that he and Joey killed someone there? Probably not a lot. Probably one.

The death date he saw on that stone would be nothing more than a coincidence if it weren't for the Mira who appeared in his office each week and coaxed him to talk about the incident, unfazed by his revelations, as if she already knew the events of that June night.

He thought of other things he had allowed himself to dismiss, like how she didn't seem to own a cell phone and never carried a purse. Didn't women always have things they wanted to store out of sight? Liv sure did. And how did she get there? Where was her license? Her T pass? Her money? Her keys? He thought of Phil leaving his office without noticing her and Mira saying she'd been waiting "a while." Could she have been sitting there, unseen? He stopped and slowed himself down. Was he trying to talk himself into, or out of, something? He wouldn't know for sure until he went back to the cemetery. But first, he had to get to Hartford.

Gregory stole inside the house. He wasn't sure what time he'd left their bed that morning, but it was hours after they'd arrived home, and sleep still eluded him. He thought about the time Margaret told him and Joey to listen to the end of "Strawberry Fields Forever," and when they heard it—first the build of music like an impending train wreck, then Lennon's distorted voice intoning *I buried Paul*—he and Joey both screamed. They played the ending at least a dozen more times, trying to make sense of those words, so weird and otherworldly. That was how Mira's face kept appearing to Gregory as he lay in bed. It lurched at him through the darkness, over and over again. Was she real? Otherworldly? Was he making connections that weren't actually there? Every time he tossed around in the tangle of sheets, warm with worry, Liv asked if he was okay. What was he supposed to tell her? Finally, he got out of bed, ostensibly to use the bathroom, but instead he wandered downstairs and outside. Inside the garage, the smell of gasoline and an open bag of bone meal settled him the way their white bedroom scented with lavender never could. There in his old beach chair, he must have dozed off for a few hours until Margaret's phone call.

Liv would be getting up soon for work. She'd also be on high alert, listening for him. He showered in the kids' bathroom, letting the hot water beat down hard on his stiff back. He opened their bedroom door, inch by slow inch, hoping to grab some clothes without waking Liv. Too late. She was sitting up in bed, her cell phone screen illuminating her anxious face. She clicked off her phone when she saw him, and the light vanished. "Thank goodness! I was just about to text you. Where have you been?"

Gregory, standing there with a white bath towel wrapped around his waist, realized he'd left his phone on the floor of the garage, but he wasn't about to say that. Liv didn't seem to realize he had slept out there, or else she was being covert about it. "I didn't want to wake you, so I showered in the kids' bathroom."

Liv patted the mattress next to her. "Sit down. Please."

He knew what she was going to say. *What was last night all about?* But he was ready. "Margaret just called," he said. "My dad had a massive coronary. I have to get to Hartford Hospital right away."

"Oh no!" Liv covered her mouth. "Is he going to be okay?"

"That's what I'm going to find out." Gregory went to his closet and started rifling through his clothes.

"Well, you shouldn't be driving that distance until you see a doctor." Her tone, with that motherly mix of worried and patronizing, made him uncomfortable.

"No doctor is answering their phone at this hour unless it's an emergency, so that's off the table."

"Phil will always answer the phone when you call."

"Phil is not the person I need to talk to. He seems to have lost his objectivity." Gregory slid a pair of jeans and a polo shirt from one of the upper shelves and grabbed a pair of boxers and some socks from one of the built-in cedar drawers below. "Plus, I'm absolutely fine now."

"Whatever happened last night, Gregory, was not fine. You were dissociating, or something."

He wanted to correct her and say more likely he was having a PTSD-induced panic attack, but he refrained. "I'm going to see my dad. If I feel strange in any way, I'll pull over and call you." He wanted to get dressed, but not in front of her. He felt exposed enough as she studied him for signs of a breakdown. The last thing he needed was to be standing there naked while she analyzed how he put on his underwear.

"Then I'll drive. We can use the time to continue our conversation from last night. And I can be there to help with your dad."

"Don't you have to work?"

"I have some editing, but I can do that anywhere."

Gregory paused, pretending to consider the idea. "As much as I'd like that, I think Margaret and I need to deal with Dad alone, just the two of us."

When he turned toward the bathroom, Liv hurried over and wrapped her arms around him from behind. He felt her cheek, cool from the air-conditioning, pressed against his still-damp back. "Are you sure? I'm worried about you," she said.

"I'll be fine."

She spun him around until her cheek was on his chest. Holding the clothes in one hand, he lifted the other to the back of her head and scratched absentmindedly, like he would do with their old cat, Leo, when he would curl up in Gregory's lap.

"I meant what I said last night," she murmured into his chest. "I realize you've got to prioritize your dad, but I don't want our conversation to get forgotten or ignored."

"I understand." He stopped rubbing her neck and kissed the top of her head. "I need to get on the road before traffic gets bad."

Liv pulled away brusquely and crossed the room. When she flicked on the overhead light, Gregory had to shut his eyes against the jarring brightness. "Just so you know," she said, "you're breaking my heart."

He paused for a few seconds in front of the bathroom door. He wanted to say something to make it okay, the kind of reassuring things he told his clients when they were feeling like every good thing in their life was being ripped away. He ran through the possibilities: *We'll figure it out. It's going to be okay.* While those things sounded hopeful, they didn't feel true.

So he said something that did. "I'm so sorry I've hurt you, Liv. That was never my intention." Then he walked into the bathroom and shut the door behind him.

18

Gregory stepped out of the elevator into the Coronary Intensive Care Unit and spotted Margaret pacing in front of the nurses' station, an island of activity in the middle of the long white hallway. His sister intermittently glanced at her phone, as if she might have missed a call or text in the five seconds since she last checked it. Gregory headed toward her.

"The doctor is supposed to be in again soon," Margaret said in her rapid-fire way as they exchanged a quick hug. "Dad's getting good care, but when he's ready for rehab, I think we should move him to Spaulding, and maybe I can stay in your guest room for a while. I mean, if that's okay?" She started down the corridor, Gregory hurrying to keep up, before she turned sharply into room 2-CCU, where he didn't expect what he found inside: his father lying in bed with tubes and lines attached everywhere. There was one in his nose, another in his throat; a ventilator tube connected to a machine emitted a droning, rhythmic *siss thump*. There was also an IV in his wrist and an electrocardiogram monitor above the bed—its jolting green line flashing a reminder of life's precariousness.

"Jesus," Gregory said under his breath.

"I know, right?"

He followed Margaret to his father's bedside and stood there staring. He suddenly felt so blessed to be alive in his body that he found it incomprehensible to think one day Petey and Carrie could be hovering over his hospital bed, wondering how long before he drew his last breath. Would they feel disconnected like Gregory did from his father? Would they care whether he pulled through to survive another day? He pictured Petey, his sweet-natured son, standing there, wringing a baseball cap between his hands, wishing Gregory had reached out to him more.

Gregory, though deeply saddened by how vulnerable his father looked, still couldn't bring himself to root for his survival. Rather, he thought the old man needed to go in peace.

How many times had he sifted through his childhood memories, searching for one in which his father wasn't admonishing him for mowing the lawn unevenly—*if you can't do something right, don't do it at all*—or reprimanding his mother for spending too much money on a new pair of shoes when the cheap ones she'd been wearing still had some heel left. Gregory was always on guard when his father was home, often with his bedroom door closed against the shouting. One day he followed the sound down the hallway to the living room. When he peered in, he saw his usually timid mother in a housedress and apron, standing up to his father. Tears streaked her ruddy face as her six-foot-tall husband bellowed down at her. But she kept her head up, for once refusing to back away. Gregory watched, dreading what would come next. No one challenged Bob Weber. When his father opened his palm and struck his mother across the face, Gregory drew back, his breath gone. He would never forgive his father, or himself. Why hadn't he tried to stop him?

Gregory sometimes wished that his father had hit him, if only for the chance to hit him back, to have a place to put his anger. Instead, he held his fury inside as his father punished him in other ways, like the time Gregory skipped school to go fishing with Joey and was grounded for a month. He could still remember his father's words to him that day: *The truth doesn't cost anything, but a lie could cost you everything.*

Gregory winced. Now an adult, he had spent more than half his life concealing the truth. While he still resented his father, he couldn't help but agree with his axiom.

In his childhood years, Gregory struggled to find some version of the father that he longed for in the disappointing one he had. He salvaged those rare moments of connection, however insignificant they seemed at the time, and stored them away for safekeeping. He remembered the time his father gave him a twenty-dollar bill for getting straight As on his report card, almost—but not quite—forgetting that he was instructed to put the money in the bank instead of "squandering" it. Or the year his high school basketball team won the state championship, and he overheard his father boasting at the church coffee klatch that Gregory was the only junior who had played the entire game, start to finish. But why didn't he say anything to Gregory? Why couldn't his father have clapped him on the shoulder and told him he was proud, like Joey's father, who picked up his six-foot-one son with a whoop and carried him around the gym?

Gregory spent years yearning for his father's approval, but after the accident, Gregory's guilt transformed that yearning into resentment. Now it mystified him how Margaret, her face tight with distress, felt so much compassion for this old man who had banned her from her childhood home. While Gregory was still struggling to salvage a few good memories from the wreckage, Margaret had managed to find something that looked like love.

"Is he lucid?" Gregory asked, studying the pale, placid face beneath the wires and tubes.

"No. Too many sedatives. But I swear he recognized me before." Margaret crowded between Gregory and the nightstand, so she was standing directly above her father, where she had probably been keeping vigil for the past three hours.

Gregory had taken his time getting there. Before heading to the hospital, he drove to his office to cancel his clients in peace, or that's what he told himself. His underlying motive was to return Mira's scarf to his desk and out of sight from Liv. His plan had been to lock the scarf in his drawer and be gone before Phil rushed in, Starbucks in hand, at 8:55 for his nine o'clock patient. They hadn't spoken since Phil's last bread delivery, and Gregory was happy to let things settle down a bit more. But Phil was already there, attending to the ficus plant in the waiting room.

"You're slacking a bit here, Gardener Greg," Phil had said. His voice was upbeat, which relieved Gregory. Phil was gathering the dead leaves scattered at the base of the large potted plant, the care of which fell into Gregory's purview. "You know my reputation for killing green things."

"Sorry about that," Gregory said. The goal was to duck into his office without Phil noticing the scarf in his hand, but his lock was acting up.

"Any replacement plant goes on your tab." Phil glanced up with a smile just as Gregory managed to get his door open. After taking a quick step inside, Gregory was about to shut the door when Phil appeared in front of him, watering can in one hand, crumpled brown leaves in the other. "What's that?" Phil asked, pointing his fist of leaves at the scarf.

"This?" Gregory asked, casually lifting the balled-up pashmina like he'd forgotten he was holding it. "Oh, um, a client left it in the waiting room the other day, so I tossed it in my briefcase. I'm just leaving it in my office, making sure it gets back to her."

"Which one?" Phil's voice was urgent, pushy even.

"Which one what?"

"Which client?" Phil pressed. "Who left it?"

Gregory was not going to speak Mira's name out loud to anyone, or give Phil anything else to be suspicious about. Thinking fast, he said, "Susan C. You know how she loves her bright colors when she's coming out of a depression."

Phil didn't respond. He kept staring at the scarf, transfixed.

"You okay, Phil?"

Phil closed his eyes and shook his head as if trying to loosen a memory. "Right," he said. "Susan C." He walked away, carrying the watering can into his office instead of returning it to the corner cabinet. On another day, Gregory would have popped into Phil's office to tell him about his father's heart attack, but he wasn't about to extend their conversation. Phil, in his perceptive way, must have known that Gregory was lying about the scarf and deduced that it belonged to the "friend" he had been waiting for on Wednesday. Without delay, he carefully folded and locked Mira's pashmina in the bottom drawer of his desk and left, calling goodbye to Phil on his way out. When Phil didn't answer, Gregory gently pulled the door shut behind him.

"Hey, Dad! It's Maggie again. Can you hear me? Greg is here, too." Margaret was now standing shoulder to shoulder with Gregory beside the hospital bed, and he realized that he didn't know anyone—even his hypersexual manic clients—with more porous personal boundaries than his sister. Gregory was uncomfortable with her closeness, after so many years of trying to distance himself from her—and everyone else who cared about him.

Their father's pallor was ashen, and the only acknowledgment of recognition was a brief fluttering of his eyelashes that seemed like nothing more than a reflex to Gregory.

"There! Did you see that?" Margaret said, pointing. She plopped down in a chair by the side of the bed, stroking their father's hand and muttering encouraging words, while Gregory stood to the side, overwhelmed by his sister's compassion. After a minute, Margaret jumped up and said, "Oh, sorry, Greggy. You should take a turn. Dad's been listening to me yammer all morning."

She stepped aside and Gregory sat down hesitantly, mindful of the tubes keeping his father tethered to life. With Margaret hovering over him, Gregory made himself touch his father's limp hand, the skin so paper-thin he felt like it might tear. What was he supposed to say? In the nursing home on a Sunday afternoon, it was easy enough to fill his father in on the ordinary stuff of life. The kids. Liv. Work. He often prattled on with the impassive tone of someone reading from the phone book. But right now, all he could think about was the night of June 20, 1989, when Gregory made the snap decision to tell Joey to drive away from the accident and never mention it again. He did it because he was scared. But once Joey was driving and shaking and crying as he frantically tried to navigate the labyrinth of one-way streets, Gregory's feelings of terror switched to prayers—that they'd get away with it, that the police wouldn't catch them, that no one had seen his license plate or how they had hit that person. Person. He hadn't known if it was a man or a woman, the body hurling at their windshield so fast that any features were indistinct. He didn't know that it might have been Mira Patel, age twenty-nine, innocently riding her bicycle on a summer night through the streets of Boston.

Why? Why did he leave the scene of a hit-and-run? Why didn't he force Joey to stop? Yes, it would have been a legal nightmare to get arrested, although they were minors and Gregory wasn't driving. But there was something else. Whatever punishment the court of law inflicted—maybe time in juvey and hundreds of hours of community service—would have been tolerable. What he could not abide was his father knowing what he had done. Bob Weber, an uncompromising, God-fearing man, made his judgments in black and white. He saw good and bad, right and wrong. He didn't acknowledge shades of gray—the color of most mistakes, even his own. So there on the Mass Pike, paralyzed with fear as they drove back home, he made Joey swear to never say anything to anyone. *Never. No one. Swear? Do you swear on your life?* They would not read the paper or watch the news. They would learn nothing about what they'd done. Once Joey had his mechanic friend remove a dent on the hood where the body had landed, they would never speak of it again, erasing that one fateful moment from their minds and memories, disassociating themselves from the life they took.

True to their pact, Gregory never found out what happened or whom they had hit, but he had always believed, without official confirmation, that the person on the ground was dead. Joey must have known, too. But neither of them ever said that word out loud. *Dead.* Instead, the acknowledgment of their guilt passed between them like a shadow. Gregory assumed that's how it would be whenever they ran into each other, until they were old forgetful men with a fading recollection of their horrible shared secret.

Leaving the cemetery after Joey's burial, Gregory's family drove home in silence. Gregory felt both anger and grief. If only he could tell his dad. As a psychologist, Gregory had helped dozens of men with their father issues, but he had never been able to help himself. He had never managed to forgive his own father for making him so fearful, so gut-wrenchingly terrified of getting caught in a lie or admitting a mistake, any mistake, let alone a life-destroying one.

Margaret put her hand, heavy and warm, on Gregory's shoulder. "Just tell him you love him," she said. "I'm sure he'll hear you in his own way."

Gregory tried to steady his voice. "Hey, Maggie. I didn't have breakfast. Could we maybe find the cafeteria and grab a bite?" At first, Gregory thought he wanted to be alone, because he always wanted to be alone. But he had barely slept, and with last night's revelations in the cemetery, he didn't trust himself. He was starting to fear that Liv was right, and he was losing touch with reality, or worse, he already had.

Margaret left her cell phone number with Erin, a young red-haired nurse who promised to text the second the doctor arrived. She directed them to the cafeteria, adding, "The fruit salad is really fresh. My humble opinion."

Margaret got a large coffee and a raspberry Danish, while Gregory grabbed coffee, a bagel sandwich, and the fruit salad. They sat at a table overlooking a cherry tree and a bench, now occupied by an elderly woman tethered to an oxygen tank. At her side, a younger woman, possibly her daughter, attended to the woman with solicitous attention.

Margaret ripped off a piece of her Danish and dipped it into her coffee. Damp crumbs fell into her cup as she hovered over it, chewing with her mouth open. A few years back, Gregory and Liv had treated Margaret and Jas to dinner in Boston when they were in town for the Women's March. He was glad they weren't at the club, where everyone knew them, because he was embarrassed by his sister's table manners. They'd grown up under the same roof, yet she'd avoided becoming a people pleaser—unlike him, who always worried about being judged. Margaret didn't care what anyone thought of her, something he now appreciated.

"You okay, Greggy?" she asked.

Gregory took a sip of his coffee, scalding but thin on flavor, and set it back on his tray. He kept his eyes down, afraid of anything that might trigger him. "Honestly? No."

"I feel you. This whole thing with Dad, huh?"

"It's not that. I mean, it's not *just* that. Things have been a little rough with Liv. More than a little, actually."

Margaret put her Danish down and studied his face. Gregory always forgot how pretty she was. With her hair pulled back, her green eyes shone.

"You're not splitting up, are you?"

"Liv doesn't want to, but I don't know."

"Is there someone else?"

"Not really."

Margaret snorted. "In my world, 'not really' means *yes.*"

"There's someone I can't be with, technically speaking. But it's more than that."

"Married?"

"Just complicated beyond anything I can explain." Gregory wrangled the plastic wrap off his bagel sandwich to reveal a rubbery egg flopping out the side. He pushed it to the back of his tray and opened his fruit salad. With some effort, he managed to spear a grape with one tine of his white plastic fork.

"Well, I expect there'll be a shit show if Liv finds out about another woman." Margaret paused. "I assume a woman?"

Gregory rolled his eyes. "Yes. A woman." He chewed his grape slowly, trying to figure out how much he could reveal to his sister. "I know you've never been a fan of Liv, but she's a really good person."

Margaret popped the last coffee-soaked piece of the Danish in her mouth and dusted her hands together. "She is a good person. It's her money I can't stand."

"That's not fair. That mostly came from her mother, who treated her like shit by the way."

Margaret cocked her head to the side in thought. "I guess my real problem isn't with Liv. It's the way *you* changed when you met her."

"What are you talking about?"

"Where do I start, *Gregory*?" She drew out his name like it was an insult. "You were this sweet, uber-smart kid with your full ride to UConn *and* graduate school. Then you met Liv and got all swept up in her country club set, and, I don't know, it was like you were too good for the rest of us. Suddenly you're off to Paris for this anniversary and Tahiti for that one, and whenever I wanted to get together, you always had something going on at the *club*."

"I've never been to Tahiti."

"You know what I mean." Margaret nodded at Gregory's abandoned egg sandwich. "Are you going to eat that?"

Gregory picked up the anemic-looking bagel and set it on Margaret's tray. He continued to work his way through the fruit salad. After a minute, he asked, "That's what you think? That I thought I was too good for you?"

Margaret shrugged. "You acted like you were ashamed of me, us. Always distancing yourself."

"Who's us?"

"Me. Mom. Dad. Anybody I was involved with."

Gregory put down his fork. "I distanced myself from you because"—he almost said it—*because of something I did.*

"I'm listening."

"Because I didn't want to deal with Dad, and I guess you and Mom were casualties of that decision." Even as he said it, he knew it was a lie, and worse than that, he knew Margaret knew it, too. Did she also know he used the excuse of her lifestyle to push her away?

"Well at some point it felt like none of us met your social standards. A gay hippie chick like me was never exactly warmly welcomed into that crowd. Not that I give a flying fuck about any of them. Jesus Christ, Liv's brother with his yacht and her father with his Jaguar." She looked at him. "But I didn't expect you to hold yourself apart, too."

Gregory folded his arms onto the table and lowered his head. On a daily basis, he helped people heal their deepest emotional wounds, but right now he could feel his own wounds festering, like an infection seeping into his bones. Of course, he wanted to separate himself from all of them, not just his father. Not only were they reminders of what he'd done, but if anyone could see through his lie, his family could. So, he went off to college and tried not to look back. When Liv appeared, showing him the path to a different kind of future, one that involved money and privilege, he was so grateful for the chance to turn away from everything that came before. And, yes, that included Margaret who, on a good day, could make him crazy with her know-it-all attitude and proselytizing. Of course he loved her, but she was still a lot.

"I'm sorry, Maggie. I never wanted to hurt you, or Mom. I just—" He shook his head as the exhaustion of two sleepless nights walloped him. He wished he could put his head on the gray laminate cafeteria table and go to sleep. He shut his eyes and struggled to open them again, until he heard his sister's worried voice through a haze.

"Greg? What's happening?"

He shook himself awake and sat up straighter. "Sorry. Liv and I had our anniversary dinner last night. I barely slept."

"What's this, like your nineteenth?"

"Twenty-second."

"Wow! I remember that wedding like it was yesterday. That raw bar alone probably cost more than my apartment."

"The Stimsons like their parties."

"It was ridiculous. That whole day."

"Lay off, Maggie, okay?"

Margaret sat back hard in her orange chair and stretched her long legs out in front of her. She polished off half of the bagel sandwich, extracted the other half from the plastic wrap, and bit down hard. "I'm not trying to guilt you into something, but this has been weighing on me for a long time."

"Our wedding?"

"How marginalized I feel." Margaret's cell phone buzzed, and her hand shot across the table to grab it. "Hey Jazzy!" Margaret said, her mouth full of food. "I'm here with Greg. They don't know anything. Okay. I'll tell him. Yep. That would be great. Dunkin still wasn't himself this morning. I don't want to leave Dad until we know something." In the next moment, Margaret slipped seamlessly into Spanish, her words fast and fluent. From the drop in her voice, Gregory could tell they were talking about something serious. When he checked his own phone, he found two missed calls and a text from Liv that read: *You there? I'm worried sick. PLEASE BE IN TOUCH!* She'd added a red heart emoji.

He texted back: *Here and safe* with a smiley face.

As Margaret finished up her call, even Gregory with his long-forgotten high school Spanish understood *te amo, vida.*

"How's Jas?" he asked as Margaret set the phone down and shoved the last piece of bagel in her mouth.

"We have stuff going on, too."

"Anything you want to talk about?"

Margaret shook her head. "Not really."

Gregory nodded, pretending not to feel hurt that his sister couldn't share things with him. But of course, she couldn't. That's not who they were, and it was his fault for always shutting down her efforts to connect.

"You know that Jas really likes you?" Margaret said.

"I really like her, too. And you're great together. You had a few significant others that, well, didn't seem like the best fit."

When he raised an eyebrow, Margaret failed to suppress a wry chuckle. Soon they were both laughing. That's when Gregory realized something about her. Because his sister had always seemed so sure of herself and unoffendable, he didn't know how badly he had been hurting her all these years, even when she came at him with nothing but her annoyingly fierce brand of love. He thought of what he might say to a client who was feeling shunned by her brother, but everything that came to him sounded too clinical, so he gathered his courage and decided to say something simple and honest.

"You know what's so impressive about you, Maggie?"

This time she raised an eyebrow at him, and he saw the mannerisms they both possessed, the shared traits that brothers and sisters aren't always inclined to notice. "How *yourself* you are."

She shrugged. "Is there anyone else I could be?" She took a long sip of her coffee.

"You know, I envy that in you."

Margaret set the coffee down hard. "You envy me? With your zillion-dollar Victorian and beautiful kids?"

"You're a good person," he said. He pointed his finger up, in the direction of their father's room. "And I still don't understand how you can be so nice to him."

"It's pretty simple," she said, pausing for effect. "Therapy."

Gregory rolled his eyes and snickered. "I've heard of it."

"At some point, after I'd worked out a bunch of my issues— thank you, Dr. Lis—I realized Dad wasn't that bad."

"But our childhoods, Maggie, every day was something to dread. The anger. The constant shouting. The judgment about any purchase, however small. I still can't buy a dress shirt for myself without hearing him tell me to put that money in the bank instead." Gregory dropped his voice to imitate his father. "*Don't you already have some perfectly good white shirts?*"

Margaret folded her arms across her chest and studied him. "He didn't torture me the way he did you. He mostly ignored me, so I ignored him for years, as if that would punish him. But after a while, it just seemed stupid to spend so much energy being pissed at a broken man who was losing his marbles." She shrugged. "I don't think he knew any better or ever learned how to be a father."

Gregory felt disembodied, like he was standing outside of himself watching two people, one of them him, talking about his life but with all of the wrong details.

Margaret leaned across the table and put her broad, paint-speckled hand on top of his. "You don't have to forgive him for whatever you think he did to you—"

"And to Mom," Gregory cut in.

"Sure. And to Mom," Margaret said. "But you definitely have to work on your own stuff."

Gregory pulled his hand away. "Please don't tell me how to manage my life."

"Fine." Margaret said, sitting up again. She held herself as far from him as she could get while still sharing the table. "You do what you want. And, truthfully, I don't care if you work on your issues or not, but I'll tell you one lesson I learned the wrong way from Dad." She looked at him, her eyes pinched. "Don't ignore your daughter."

Gregory polished off the rest of the fruit salad, barely taking time to chew.

"Carrie's a great kid, but she needs a father who sees her," Margaret continued. "And if you don't like how Dad treated us, don't do the same thing to her."

Gregory glared at her. "I don't."

"Oh really? When was the last time you hung out with Carrie? Or had an actual conversation with her?"

"She pushes me away no matter what I try."

Margaret threw up her arms. "She's sixteen! Pushing you away is her fucking job. I'm sorry, but isn't this what you do for a living?"

Gregory stared past Margaret's shoulder and took a swallow of his coffee.

"You know," Margaret said, her voice softening, "Jas works with some kids whose childhoods make ours look like a sitcom. She tells me stories that are devastating. But she says the parents who decide not to give up on their kids, well, they're the ones who turn things around."

"I haven't given up on Carrie. Not even close."

"But are you fighting for her? When she pushes you away, you can't just back down and slink off."

Gregory looked at her, saying nothing. When did he last fight for anything? His father scared the fight out of him years ago.

Margaret checked her phone. "We should get back upstairs."

Gregory gathered the garbage from their table and returned their trays to the counter. He and Margaret walked in silence toward the elevator. "Hey, Maggie," he said, trying to sound casual. "Do you believe in ghosts?"

"Of course!" She said it without hesitation, the way he would have answered *of course not* if someone had asked him. "How else would we explain Pinky?"

"Pinky?"

"Mom used to swear there was a ghost in our house. She'd see her drinking tea in the kitchen."

Gregory stopped walking and scanned back through time. He had the vaguest memory of this, but it's something he would have dismissed back then. His mother would always talk about angels coming to help her with various tasks. St. Anthony was called when something was lost. St. Jude for hopeless cases.

"She did, didn't she?" Gregory said, though he wasn't convinced he actually remembered.

"I'm not making it up," Margaret said.

"Why Pinky? I mean why did she call her that?" He couldn't help but think about the pink scarf.

"I don't know. But if you want to talk ghosts with someone, ask Jas. She loves that shit."

19

With his father stable, Gregory left the hospital in the late afternoon. His mind was racing throughout the drive home. Mira. How did she come into his life? His analytical nature forced his brain to try and reason out the possibilities about his unusual client. His first idea was highly unlikely, but he couldn't rule it out: perhaps they did kill a woman named Mira Patel in the hit-and-run thirty years ago, and the Mira who appeared in his office was her daughter or niece or a relative who had been able to make some connection to him. He didn't know how she would have done that, but it always amazed him the way people could figure things out these days.

As much as he loathed to admit it, he next had to consider the possibility that he was losing his mind as a result of exhaustion and mounting stress. He'd listened to his clients create complete fictions about seeing figures that didn't exist, but when someone is slipping away from reality, it tends to permeate everything in their life. Yes, he wasn't sleeping well. Yes, his synapses weren't firing with their usual conviction. But his experience with Mira was too focused to suggest an emerging psychosis, so he put a pin in that one.

The most improbable option was that he'd seen *his* Mira's grave. As a psychologist for whom a large part of his practice was getting people to step away from irrational thoughts and focus on a more reasonable evaluation of the data, he was trying his best to bury this idea. The problem was that some of the data defied explanation.

At one point, Gregory pulled into a gas station off the Mass Pike and began to Google *Mira Patel hit-and-run*, but he shut off his phone before the search results popped up. He was terrified that they would confirm what he always believed about that night. He never once denied that they'd hit someone, but he knew that ever since the accident he'd been engaging in a willful—and mostly effective—suppression of his worst fear. If he made that change too abruptly, from wondering what had happened to knowing for sure that the person had died, he didn't think he could handle it. He was overwhelmed enough by guilt and self-loathing, and if it got any worse, he might end up like Joey.

The theory that made the most sense was that it was all a big coincidence, or he had read the gravestone wrong. It had to be that. When he and Liv sneaked into the cemetery, he was still in a fog from their argument. He needed to see for himself.

Gregory arrived at Mount Auburn Cemetery a half hour before closing. He could have gone in through the main entrance, but he wasn't sure he'd be able to find the grave again unless he retraced his steps from the night before. He also didn't want to risk having his car trapped inside when the gates were locked at seven.

He parked on the same side street and stole in through the broken fence, a now weirdly familiar portal for him. At least this time, he stepped into the cemetery in the glow of sunset. It was less terrifying than being there in the dark, but the shifting shadows of the trees made the gravestones appear animated, alive.

Gregory walked slowly for several more minutes, trying, with his disoriented sleep-deprived brain, to remember where Liv had turned to lead him up the hill. There were so many slopes and twisted walkways. While every intersection was marked with a quaintly lettered black-and-white sign named for local flora and fauna—Violet Path, Nightingale Way—those names meant nothing to him when he didn't have his bearings. Following instinct, Gregory kept walking and scanning the names on every stone that he passed, stones that all began to look alike despite the nuances of artistry and design. After several moments, he started to think he was going in the wrong direction, when he stopped abruptly. An orange border of marigolds lined the path directly ahead. He now knew where he was. He inhaled deeply and began to walk again, quickening his pace, until he was standing on Marigold Path. It was a sweltering evening, the third in a heat wave that threatened to last for several more days. Gregory's polo shirt was spotted with dark patches of sweat, but his chest cavity felt cold, chilled with fear.

"Marigolds," he said in a disbelieving whisper, then looked around quickly to make sure no one had heard. But there was no one there. "She smelled like marigolds."

He clenched his fists and closed his eyes until he had the courage to stand in front of the gravestone. He wanted to find out if he had seen it correctly: her first name and her death date. He wanted confirmation that this was all a strange coincidence or that he'd been delusional last night, unable to distinguish between reality and an imagined world. It's not that he wished he had a psychotic disorder, but at least psychosis was treatable with medications.

But he knew. Even before he drew another breath of that resinous-smelling air and opened his eyes to look at the stone. He knew that in the light of day, the engraving would read exactly as it had the night before.

As his eyes traced the letters of her name, *MIRA*, he noticed something else: the crabgrass and carpetweed had been cleared away, ripped out by the roots, and a bouquet of pink stargazer lilies rested on the grave. Gregory wiped the sweat from his brow, his hand trembling. Someone had been here recently. He glanced around, but the cemetery was empty. Who had visited Mira? And did they know what he'd done? As he bent to finger a petal on one of the lilies, imagining what the mourner must have felt, his stomach lurched. He had no idea what was happening.

20

Gregory drove straight from the cemetery to Mattress Firm in Fresh Pond Mall, arriving ten minutes before closing. He told Ray, the solicitous sixty-something salesman in a navy suit with too-big shoulders, that he needed a cheap twin mattress.

"Divorce apartment or dorm room?" Ray asked, chuckling. When Gregory glared at him through eyes that hadn't been properly shut for two days, Ray said, "Got it. One twin. I'm guessing no box spring?"

Ray helped tie the clumsy purchase to the roof of the BMW, and Gregory gave him fifty bucks as a tip. Sweating profusely into his shirt collar, Ray thanked him with a handshake, adding, "I hope you get to keep the bimmer."

A few minutes later, Gregory pulled into his driveway and stopped the car in front of his garage. When he couldn't manage to untie the knots in the twine, he got his garden snips and slid the mattress off the roof, the way he and Liv wrangled the family Christmas tree every year from car to foyer to living room. If he weren't so tired, he would be sad thinking about what might not be this year, but he was barely functional and had to focus on getting the mattress into the garage. After shoving it through the door, he released it and watched it smack down in the space that once accommodated Liv's father's Jaguar convertible. He hated to do this to Liv, but he was trying to protect her from whatever was happening to him.

Approaching the house, Gregory caught a glimpse of Liv through the kitchen window. She was perched on a stool at the white marble island, her laptop screen throwing an ominous glow on her face, a wineglass within reach. He wondered if she was working on something for her memoir class and what exactly she might be writing about.

When Gregory stumbled into the doorway of the kitchen, Liv took her time looking up at him. He had filled her in by text after he and Margaret had talked to the doctor in the late morning. The heart attack had affected his father's ability to have a regular heartbeat. He was on high doses of antiarrhythmic drugs, but it didn't look promising, not with his dementia. Margaret would visit tomorrow, and Gregory would return on Sunday. Liv had tried to call several times, but he never answered.

Gregory lingered in the doorway, afraid to fully enter the room, anticipating the conversation that he simply didn't have the stamina for. He was worn to the point of brokenness. But when he looked in Liv's eyes, beyond the judgment, he saw the dim flicker of sadness.

"Any changes with your dad?" Her voice was flattened, and he could feel her distancing herself. It was self-preservation, clearly, trying to give him nothing else that he could hurt or reject.

Gregory shook his head. "He's alive because of machines. But he's in rough shape."

Liv nodded. "And the long-term prognosis?"

Gregory ran a hand through his hair, scratching his head vigorously, trying to keep his own body from shutting down. The only thing he wanted to do was collapse on his new mattress, but first he had to surreptitiously extricate sheets and a blanket from the linen closet. "Not good. They'll know more if they can wean him off the ventilator."

"Well, please keep me updated." Liv's gaze returned to the screen, as if signaling that she was done talking to him in an official capacity, but the coolness would continue. "Carrie and I got takeout from Punjab," she said, nodding toward the fridge. "There's some Tandoori chicken and other things. I don't know if you've had dinner or not."

"Why Punjab?" Gregory asked.

Liv gave a quick shake of her head. "What do you mean?"

"Since when does Carrie like Indian food?"

Liv looked at him, her head cocked, and he realized how diminished she seemed, perched on a stool in this high-ceiling kitchen, redone to her dream specifications when her father moved into a condo in downtown Boston with his new wife, Toby, and deeded them the house. Gone were the dark, custom quarter-sawn oak cabinets, French enamel stove, and oversize rack of vintage copper saucepans. Liv had replaced it all with sleek, minimalist cabinets, disappearing appliances, and that generous Carrara marble island with counter seating for six. Three pendants now cast symmetrical pools of light, reminding Gregory of that cup game in which you had to pick the one concealing the coin but no one ever got it right. He felt like he had never stopped to look at the kitchen in quite this way, how the expansive room seemed to swallow Liv in its whiteness.

"Am I missing something?" she said, her tone tilting toward accusation. "Carrie wanted to try *malai kofta*, so we ordered from Punjab. Meanwhile, you're barely communicating with me, plus you look like something the cat dragged in. Your father just had a massive heart attack, and I don't know what the state of our marriage is. So I guess I'm not exactly sure why you're acting like Indian takeout is the fucking problem."

Liv almost never swore, and the word seemed to surprise her. Her eyes widened for a few seconds before she reached for her glass and, realizing it was empty, moved robotically to the island's integrated wine fridge to grab the bottle.

"I'm just drained," he said, still cautious about going any farther into the room, feeling like he'd be entering her combat arena and wouldn't make it out unharmed.

"Well, if you're tired, maybe you should go to bed."

Gregory nodded but didn't move. They were in a standoff, neither of them anxious to prolong the conversation or ready to declare it over.

With her lips pursed and chin lifted like she was trying not to cry for the second night in a row, Liv refilled her glass and set the nearly empty bottle down harder than necessary. "And if you plan on sleeping in the garage, well, here's to that." She raised her glass and took a big gulp.

When Gregory looked at her blankly, she said, "I heard your car pull up and saw you dragging that mattress across the driveway."

"It's temporary."

"It's ridiculous. What are we supposed to tell the kids when they ask why you're sleeping out there?"

"How about that my snoring is bothering you?"

"We have a guest room," she said, snidely. "Two, actually."

"I just need some space to figure out what I should do."

"What *you should do*?" Liv slapped her palm on the cold stone. "You should see a doctor, like you agreed to last night. How is it that I've been in therapy for thirty years, and you act like it's going to kill you to do some work on yourself? Why is that, Gregory? Why do therapists suck at getting help? If my best friend killed himself, a therapist is probably one of the first people I'd call. If that's even what's going on here."

Liv turned her back on him and stood at the counter. In her white ribbed tank top and short, blue skirt, her arms and legs looked lean and strong. He remembered that May night years ago when he stood in this kitchen falling crazy in love with her. He had imagined a future of sharing meals with her parents, the four of them gathered casually at this island, which at that time was a dark veiny granite, her mother marinating vegetables with fancy balsamic from Formaggio, her dad fixing his beloved gin and tonics while rhapsodizing about some surgical conundrum that had kept him in the OR for eight hours. There was some of that gathering and meal sharing over the years—plenty, actually—but it never felt as good as Gregory hoped it would. The incessant thrum of guilt—the backbeat of his life—ruined every sweet moment. And his inability to do anything about it, to share the truth with Liv, pushed him further and further away from her.

Standing there, wishing he could relieve Liv of some of her confusion and pain, he let himself taste the words in his mouth. *There's this thing that happened. I should have told you years ago. And, yes, it's about Joey, but it's more than that, too. It's everything. And now it's taken over my life.* What if he just cleaved away the decades of lies with the sharp blade of honesty? Would it hurt her more or less to know the truth? Because in that kitchen, feeling unfiltered and close to the edge of his own destruction, he wanted to tell her.

"Please stop staring at me and say something!" Liv was gripping the edge of the counter.

Gregory paused. He drew a deep breath until it filled his lungs with something akin to courage.

"Oh, and FYI," Liv said, before he could speak, "I'm going to Visiting Day at Petey's camp tomorrow—by myself."

Gregory's head dropped as he remembered the plan. He hadn't seen Petey in three weeks and suddenly missed him fiercely.

"I still want to go," Gregory said. "In fact, I'm planning on it. I mean, I'm going."

"Well, *I* don't want you to go. I want you to see a doctor before you do anything else. I can't be with you when you're like this."

"You don't get to tell me I can't see my son," Gregory said, struggling to measure his tone, anger spilling right over the edge of his exhaustion.

"Maybe not now," she hit back, "but the way you've been acting, at some point I might." It was a gut punch that presumed a lot of things, a causal chain that he couldn't bear to follow to where Liv had landed—because he kept pushing her there. Separation. A custody battle. He knew Massachusetts law favored mothers. He'd seen clients who were devoted fathers have their hearts crushed, their connections to their kids shattered.

Liv bit her lip. Gregory was about to go to her, put his arms around her, when she straightened up and walked brusquely away from him. Even in anger, Liv moved with a dancer's grace. She left through the side door into the living room, where the turquoise couch had been replaced long ago by a cream-colored one. Liv returned seconds later with her arms full. "If you want to sleep in the garage, then go." She tossed a decorative pillow and nubby white throw at his feet.

"Liv! Please! Don't make this more dramatic than it is. I just need some space. My head is spinning with work issues and stuff with my dad."

"Really? *Your* head is spinning? Well, by all means do whatever you need to sort that out. I'm just your wife, so definitely don't talk to me!"

She started to walk away toward the main stairs but stopped and turned toward him again. "By the way, what happened to the pashmina?"

Her tone contained both hurt and a challenge.

Should he keep up the lie? *Oh, I think it's upstairs. Hmm. Not sure. Did you check the back seat of my car?* He swallowed down his fear of the truth. "It wasn't meant for you. I wanted to tell you that night, but I—"

Liv turned around. "Who is she? Someone from the club?"

"What? No. It actually belongs to one of my clients."

His wife stepped toward him, cautiously, as if he were a slightly dodgy stranger. "You really *are* having an affair," she said, moving in close enough to read the lies on his face.

Too tired to respond, he said nothing for a few seconds, while she stood there, her body rigid with accusation. He remembered their first date in the cemetery. Liv's teasing question posed with anticipation of his denial. *Do you have a girlfriend?* They had both laughed off the idea. And now, twenty-four years later, she was ready to find him guilty.

"It's not an affair. I promise you, Liv. A client left it in my office. I'm not sleeping with her or anyone else."

"But you *want* to sleep with her?" Liv tipped her head back and raked her fingers through her hair. "What is happening, Gregory?"

"I just need some rest. It's been a hell of a few weeks."

She lowered her face and turned her eyes to his. "Do you love her?"

Gregory almost collapsed. How could he ever begin to explain the complexity that was Mira? He couldn't. "I love *you*, Liv."

Liv looked neither relieved nor convinced. "But last night you all but asked for a divorce. Why?"

They needed to talk, but not when he was this overwrought, and not in response to her rage. He hesitated. "Please let me go with you to see Petey tomorrow?"

"Do you, Gregory?"

"Do I what?"

"Love her?"

"No."

Liv lifted her palm like she wanted to slap him, and he wished she would. It might give her some small sense of release. And he certainly deserved it—a slap and a whole lot more. But instead of striking his cheek, she turned her palm to her own mouth and shook her head. "I don't believe you." After a few seconds, she lowered her hand and stood up straighter, her narrowed eyes conveying judgment worse than any slap. Then she spun around and stormed out of the kitchen.

Gregory waited until he could hear her upstairs opening and slamming doors, louder than normal, but probably not as loudly as she wanted to. He thought of how her mother used to infuriate her, and how Liv had learned to repress that anger.

It was quiet again after several minutes. Gregory collected the pillow and blanket from the floor and headed down the driveway toward the garage. Once inside, he tossed the pillow onto the mattress and collapsed.

21

Click. Slam. Click. Slam. Gregory woke to the sound of Liv opening and shutting the car door several times. Fighting to stay awake, he could picture her with the bags of snacks she'd brought for Petey, going back into the house again as she remembered one more thing she had forgotten to pack. He didn't want to get up, not yet. He'd been having a dream about Mira, and he was trying to lie very still so his memory of it wouldn't vanish before he could mine it for clues. In his dream, Maggie, Phil, and Liv were visiting him at the hospital. He was the one lying in bed full of tubes, not his father, and Mira, it seemed, was the doctor. He kept trying to tell everyone that Mira wasn't real, but he couldn't speak because of the tubes in his throat.

When Gregory heard Liv start her Audi, he crawled out of bed—his single mattress still sheathed in plastic—and searched the concrete floor for his jeans. He was zipping them up as he hurried outside to flag her down. By the time he got to the end of the driveway, she had turned the corner and was gone from sight. He staggered back to the garage.

When Gregory woke up the second time that day, his cell phone read 1:22. He put on his smelly shirt from the night before, pushed open the side door, and stepped barefoot into the afternoon sunshine. He could have kept sleeping for another few hours, but he needed to use the bathroom. As he headed into the house, he realized Carrie was likely just waking up, too, and decided to suggest they have lunch together, even if he didn't see her agreeing to it.

He remembered the old days when he and Liv had full control of the kids' Saturdays. For years they took Carrie to dance classes—ballet, tap, modern, jazz—until she lost interest in all of them, disappointing Liv, who was eager to see her daughter embrace the arts while simultaneously getting exercise. Petey was a different animal. Athletic and easygoing, he played soccer from the time he was in kindergarten and now started on a Cambridge travel team. As the kids approached tweenhood, gone were summer Saturdays spent as a family at the club pool or in a rental cottage on the Vineyard, and Gregory now understood why Liv was always inviting friends or her brother and his family to join them for a few days here and there. Only after speaking with his sister yesterday did he realize—horribly—that they had never invited her. When Liv would suggest it, Gregory always resisted, claiming that he and Margaret had different ideas about how to spend a vacation or suggesting that her plus-one would likely be insufferable or, worse, a plus-two.

He could add *never including his sister* to his running tab of fuckups.

Gregory pushed the front door open quietly, thinking if Carrie was still asleep, waking her up wouldn't improve his chances with her. But as soon as he was inside the air-conditioned house, he heard loud laughter over a driving pulse of music. He followed the female voices through to the kitchen, where he found an empty orange juice carton tipped over in the dish drain. Nearby on the marble counter was a half-empty bottle of Grey Goose. Liv would never have a screwdriver for breakfast, not even on the brink of separation.

"Hello?" he called out. "Carrie?" The music shut off abruptly, leaving the house ominously silent.

When he heard a noise, almost a scuffle, Gregory walked quickly through the dining room into the sun porch. Carrie was sitting thigh to thigh on the white wicker sofa with another girl. His daughter's eyes had been transformed by thick makeup that made the shock on her face more pronounced. She jumped to her feet and took a step away from her friend, a young woman with ink-black hair and a row of piercings in each ear.

"Jesus Christ, Dad! I thought you guys went to see Petey." When she looked at the glass-topped coffee table, as if to assess the damage, Gregory followed her gaze. There were two tall plastic Mickey Mouse tumblers, souvenirs from a long-ago family trip to Disneyworld, and what looked to be a vape pen. Her friend, meanwhile, quickly tucked a bag of weed into the backpack at her feet.

Carrie looked up at her father—her eyes wide.

This wasn't the day Gregory was preparing for, and he needed to adapt. But as he stood there trying to formulate a response, he thought his bladder might burst. "I'll be right back," he said, his eyes trained hard on Carrie, indicating that she was not to disappear.

In the bathroom mirror, he studied his shaggy hair and heavy eyes ringed with dark circles. He splashed cold water on his face then reached for the white guest towel inscribed with a chunky black *W*. He dug in the medicine cabinet and excavated a small comb and a sample-size mouthwash. As for what to do about Carrie, he was flying blind and wingless. He knew what his father would have done to him in this situation, and while he would have hated it, it might have taught him a lesson that saved him from a life of misery.

Then he thought about what Margaret had said: *She needs a father who sees her.*

Back on the sun porch, the friend had vanished. Carrie was gathering the Mickey Mouse cups and other detritus of what was clearly an aborted weekend party for two, courtesy of her parents' well-stocked liquor cabinet.

Gregory sat down in one of the two wicker chairs, a move that made Carrie rush to clean up even faster. But just as she was about to duck into the kitchen away from his scrutiny, Gregory pointed at the table. "Put those back down, please."

Carrie froze before slowly setting the cups and crumpled cocktail napkins on the table. She worked her hands into the pockets of her tight jean shorts. She folded in her shoulders, as if there were a possibility of actually vanishing from her father's sight. Still not meeting his gaze, Carrie stared at the floor.

"What's your friend's name?" Gregory asked.

"Jess. Jessie." Her voice was more sullen than scared.

Gregory remembered the *mad hot in a purple bikini* line and felt glad for his daughter, who at almost seventeen was possibly venturing into her first summer crush. Or maybe she'd been doing this kind of thing for years, although he didn't think so. "Did she leave?"

"Yes."

"She's not driving, is she?"

"She took the T."

Gregory nodded. "Sit down."

Carrie sighed heavily and plopped down on the sofa. She sandwiched her hands between her knees and fixed her eyes on the glossy coffee table book entitled *Summer Light*, a Liv project about how to host casual, seasonally inspired summer parties.

"I'm going to give you two options," Gregory said in the same voice he used when he told a client with addiction issues that they had to make changes or they'd blow their recovery. "Your choice. Okay?"

Carrie shifted her eyes to the side in something between assent and an eye roll.

Gregory leaned in and reached for one of the capped Mickey Mouse cups. He shook it, mostly trying to determine how much she'd had to drink, before setting it back down. After doing the same with the second one, he hazarded that they were just getting started. Plus, she was obviously coherent.

"Option one: I can tell Mom about this, and the three of us can have a conversation when she gets home tomorrow. She'll probably want to ground you, and I would support that. In the meantime, you can use the weekend to start your summer reading."

Carrie squeezed her eyes shut, trying not to cry. As a little girl, she had always cried easily, but he didn't know if that was true anymore. He saw so much hostility in her that he never knew what was really going on beneath the low simmer of anger. "Great," she muttered.

"The other option is—well, wait, do you have to work later?"

"No."

"Then option two is that you hang out with me for the rest of the day, and Mom never finds out about any of this." He didn't feel terrific about bribing his daughter into spending time with him, but he'd do whatever it took to start rebuilding what they'd lost. He wouldn't be like his father.

Carrie looked directly at him for what felt like the first time in months. Her eyes crinkled with uncertainty. "Wait, what? You're not going to tell Mom? All I have to do is hang out with you today?"

As soon as Gregory saw how easily he could leverage this, he realized he should have set a few more ground rules up front. He shook his head. "Not a word. Except there's one other thing."

She huffed. "What?"

"No phone the whole time we're together. Starting right now."

Carrie paused. She probably hadn't been away from her phone for five minutes all summer, let alone several hours. She withdrew it from her back pocket and reluctantly set it upside down on the table.

"And I want to say one more thing."

Carrie sighed.

"When you get your license, don't you ever, and I mean ever, drink and drive. If you or your friends needed me to pick you up, or—"

"Oh my God, Dad! It's so not an issue. We call an Uber, or there's a DD. We're not stupid. Plus, I'm never going to get my license because you never take me driving."

He nodded. "You're right. Let's get you out there practicing. If it weren't for Mickey there"—he nodded at her drink—"I'd say we could go today. But definitely next week."

"Whatever."

Gregory drew a breath and clasped his hands together. "Thanks for the reminder. I've been slacking on that."

After a few seconds, Carrie looked at him sternly. "Why are you being all nice to me?"

Gregory snorted and answered truthfully. "Because it's about time I was nicer."

"No, seriously," Carrie continued. "When I saw you standing there, I was like, I am so dead. Aren't you supposed to be in New Hampshire or something?"

"I have to stick around in case anything happens with Grandpa."

"He's getting better though, right?"

"I hope so, but let's not talk about that now. This is our day together. What are you up for?"

Carrie tilted her head. "What? Don't we have to garden and stuff? I thought this was you making me do chores."

Gregory waved that idea away. "I was thinking more like lunch in Harvard Square."

"Oh shit!" Carrie cried out, then quickly covered her mouth. "Sorry."

That's when he noticed them: three silver bracelets on Carrie's left wrist.

When he tried to speak, his jaw trembled, and he struggled not to sound accusatory, or terrified. "Where did you get those?" He nodded at her arm.

Carrie lowered her hand, and the bracelets made a chiming sound. "These?" She spun them around on her wrist, the same way Mira had done when she was wearing them at their first session. "Mom left them for me. I think."

"You think?"

"I don't know. They were just in my room. She's always leaving me clothes and jewelry and stuff. Usually I hate it."

Despite the coolness of the shaded sun porch, Gregory could feel the sweat on his neck. He ran his fingers through his hair. Is this what Mira meant by "seeing"? Was she lurking around their house, watching them?

Carrie shrank back into the sofa. "You're freaking me out, Dad. What's the big deal? I'm sure it was Mom."

Gregory wasn't sure. But if Carrie found out that those bracelets just appeared in her room, left by someone other than Liv, his problem was going to get even bigger. He tried to sit back and look relaxed. "Sorry. Sorry. Of course it was Mom."

Carrie shrugged her shoulders and lifted her arms defensively. "What? They're just stupid bangles. Do you want me to take them off? I don't even like them that much. I only put them on because they were there." Carrie had to squeeze her hand to get the bracelets over her knuckles, but she managed to slide them off and drop them onto the side table.

One rolled and clattered onto the stone tile floor. "There," she said. "Happy?"

Before either of them spoke again, the doorbell rang.

Gregory sat up, hyperalert. "Who's that?"

Carrie exhaled with exasperation. "That's what I was about to tell you. Jessie—well, we—ordered some stuff from The Cheesecake Factory."

Gregory stood and reached for his wallet in his back pocket. As he headed through the house to the front door, he automatically went into diaphragmatic breathing and began the type of internal dialogue he recommended to clients who were losing touch with reality: *Likely, it was just a coincidence*, he told himself. *Who's to say they're the same bracelets?* He reminded himself of the Occam's razor principle that helped with cognitive reframing: the simplest explanation was most likely the true one.

Liv left the bracelets. Put it out of your head and have a good day with your daughter.

He took four more calming breaths, vowed to let it go until he was alone again, and opened the front door.

Gregory returned to the sun porch with a large, striped plastic bag. Carrie waited sheepishly on the couch. "Ninety-eight dollars before the tip? How the hell many cheesecakes did you get?" he asked.

"I'll pay you back."

Gregory cocked his head. "Wait a minute? Did you order alcohol?"

Carrie lowered her face.

"So, what were you going to do if he wanted to see your ID?" When Carrie didn't answer, Gregory said, "I can always run this by Mom."

"No!" She waved her hands in protest. "Just don't get all freaked out."

Gregory's voice hardened. "Tell me."

"Jessie has a fake."

"How old is she?"

"Seventeen?"

"Is she your," he hesitated, "girlfriend?"

"Jesus, Dad! Don't be weird. If I don't answer, are you going to tell Mom? Like is that how the whole day is going to go?"

"Hmm. I wish I'd thought of that earlier," he said, teasing, "but I guess not." Letting the Jessie thing drop, he hoisted the bag on the table with exaggerated effort and started unpacking the variety of plastic containers, asking Carrie what each thing was. Mac 'n' cheese balls. Loaded tater tots. A bacon glamburger.

"A glamburger? Huh," he said, and moved on to two slabs of cheesecake, one chocolate, one dotted with bright red strawberries. When he got to the drinks, tall lidded plastic cups, he shifted them aside. Then he paused. He still couldn't completely let go of his worries about the bracelets, and a little alcohol might help calm his nerves. And since he was here supervising, maybe he could show his daughter that she didn't have to be devious about alcohol and abuse it the way he used to. What if his father had sat down with him over beers when he was still a teenager and told him he was there for him? Might things have gone differently?

Gregory nodded at the drinks. "Which one is yours?"

"I guess that one," Carrie said, her voice a mortified whisper as she pointed at a frothy, peach-colored concoction.

He slid it toward her with a straw. "What are you drinking?" he asked. "Rum punch?"

Carrie shook her head at him. "Are you on something?" She indicated her father cheerfully sitting across from her, offering alcohol. "Or is this some kind of trap?"

"Trap?"

"I don't know. You're acting crazy."

He thought about that for a beat. Was it so obvious that he might be losing his mind?

"It's not a trap, honey. I'd rather teach you about drinking in moderation. I know what happens when there are no limits." Gregory drifted off, then took a small sip of the sweet drink in front of him. He found it surprisingly refreshing and had to resist gulping it down. Guys at the club were so hung up on their extra-dry martinis and Manhattans, but those never held any appeal for him. Maybe he needed to try more fruity beverages. He reached for one of the mac 'n' cheese balls and leaned back, trying to relax.

In the meantime, Carrie turned sullen as she sat across from him, sipping her own drink, probably hoping to lose herself in the alcohol. Gregory realized that however preferable it was to chill with her father instead of being grounded, this was still not the afternoon of debauchery she had planned for.

"Okay if I amend the plan a bit?" he asked.

Carrie shrugged her defeat. "You're the one in charge."

"If our day together goes well—and I don't see why it shouldn't—you can hang out with your friends tonight. But that's later. Right now, you're with me."

Carrie's lips released the straw. The smallest hint of a smile played at the corners of her mouth. Gregory smiled, too, wishing he had finagled a day like this years ago when she was starting high school and began to drift away. Her eyes darted around. "Who are you, and what did you do with my father?"

Gregory studied his daughter's features, her overly made-up eyes. People would say she looked like Liv because of her big round eyes, but he saw himself in her face—the doubt and longing that were never far from the surface. She would turn seventeen in October, and he wanted to weep at the idea of all the years he'd lost with his family, with his daughter. "I've been a crappy dad lately, Carrie. I haven't been here for you."

"That's not true!" She picked up a tater tot and bit delicately. Well trained by Liv, she finished chewing before speaking. "You're busy. You work really hard to take care of people so we can have nice stuff. I get it."

Gregory polished off his mac 'n' cheese ball. When he asked if he could have part of the glamburger, Carrie pushed it toward him. "It's Jessie's. I'm trying to not eat meat."

"I didn't know that," Gregory said. "What else?"

"What else what?"

"What else don't I know about you because I've supposedly been so busy?"

Carrie shrugged and reached for the fries. "I don't know. Nothing really." She opened a package of ketchup and made a viscous red puddle in the top of the container. "Can I put the music back on?"

Gregory slid her phone across the table so she could sync to the stereo. When she was done, she miraculously set the phone down again instead of responding to any new texts that might have popped up. The pulsing drumbeat now reverberating through the speakers felt like his heart when he was nervous. Fast, hard, racing. Then a high, dreamy sounding female voice cut in.

"Who's this?"

"Billie Eilish. You like it?"

"Yeah. A lot." Gregory made a mental note to pay more attention to his daughter's music. "But you were saying about nothing going on—"

Carrie sighed. "I don't know."

"What don't you know?"

"Like, all of my friends have a thing, the way Petey has soccer and, you know, Sammi plays the piano. She's practically professional. But I don't have a thing."

"That's because you're a renaissance woman. You do a lot of things well. You're really good at baking."

"Seriously, Dad? All of my friends are good at baking."

"You play field hockey."

"Right, the sport for girls who don't play real sports. Plus, I suck."

"How can you suck if you made the team?"

Carrie raised an eyebrow. "Everyone makes the team."

"Then what are you saying? Do you want to have a 'thing,' or do you think you should have one because other people do?"

Carrie groaned and flopped back against the couch. "Everyone is so into the college thing. Mom has me signed up for some stupid SAT class, and I'm supposed to start with a math tutor next week. But I don't give a shit about math!"

"Mom just wants you to do well. That way you'll have options."

"Well, it's a waste of money, because I'll never do well in math."

Gregory doctored his glamburger with ketchup and took a big bite. It tasted good and fatty with all that bacon, plus grease and condiments dripping out onto the waxy paper. For the first time, he really understood why his client, Barry C., a compulsive eater, loved this kind of stuff. It was delicious. "Do you want me to talk to Mom?" he asked.

Carrie stiffened. "It's not just Mom. Everyone in my class is so focused on getting into college. But I don't even know what to focus on."

"Forget about everyone else. Let's start with what you *like* to do."

Carrie tightened her lips. "I guess I like to write. But it's kind of Mom's thing. So that's taken."

"Mom doesn't get to own writing. And she'd be thrilled to know you were interested in it."

Carrie shrugged away the thought and grabbed a fry. "Did you have a 'thing'?"

"We didn't have to have 'things' in those days. I was a good student, good SATs, played basketball and baseball. That was it."

"And you got a full scholarship to UConn?"

"That's right. But my parents also didn't have much money."

"That sounds pretty sweet. I mean the scholarship and stuff."

It was sweet. Gregory spent most of his senior year with his escape to college wrapped up, blissfully unaware that he would soon do something that would bring decades of misery. He glanced at Mira's bracelets on the table. He wanted to tell his daughter, so riddled with confusion, that she had no idea how life could blindside you. He also wanted to give her a hug, but he was not going to push his luck. He took another bite of glamburger and hoped she'd keep talking.

"Everything is so intense now," Carrie said. "It's not enough to have a thing, but you have to have a style, too."

"A style?"

"Like how you dress. Arty or vintage or sporty."

"What's yours?"

Carrie squirmed in her chair. "I don't really have one."

"Well, how do you get one? Do you just decide?"

Carrie studied Gregory, as if assessing if she could trust him, so he busied himself with one of the tater tots, trying to appear as nonthreatening as possible. "It's just that when my friends go shopping, I'm not into it. They're all so skinny, like Sammi who weighs about ninety pounds, and she's taller than me."

"What about Mom? She'd love to take you shopping."

"No, thank you." Carrie put down the fry she was about to eat and sat back with her drink. "I don't need Mom with her yoga bod staring at my flab in the dressing room."

"Stop with the flab. You are perfect *and* gorgeous."

"You have to say that. You're my father."

"It doesn't mean it's not true."

"The point is I can't go shopping with my friends, because they're extra-small and I'm medium."

"Medium, huh?"

"That's me."

"So let's go shopping."

"What do you mean?"

"Us. Now. We could walk over to Harvard Square."

Carrie furiously shook her head *no*. "I'll run into half my class."

Gregory knew he had pushed his luck. But after a few seconds of consideration, Carrie said, "Could we go to the Natick Mall?"

"Is that the one where I used to buy you all the American Girl doll stuff?"

Carrie nodded.

"Let's go."

An hour later they were wandering through the cavernous mall with its sleek white walls and natural wood accents. With high-end stores and a Tesla dealership, the mall catered to the well-to-do residents of Boston's tony western suburbs. It was relatively empty on a summer Saturday afternoon, when would-be shoppers were likely at their vacation homes.

Whenever Carrie lingered in front of a store, Gregory urged her inside to look. He ended up buying her a black sundress, a pair of navy-blue sandals, two cotton sweaters, and a pair of mom jeans, as she called them. When they were standing in front of a display of oversized button-down shirts, Carrie told him that her friend Nells got one from her older brother, because it was the kind of thing you should get from somebody, not buy new. Gregory quietly decided that later he'd look through his old shirts and try to find a faded Oxford that might be what she had in mind.

When they approached the American Girl store, they exchanged a smile and picked up the pace. As soon as they were inside, Carrie handed Gregory her shopping bags and started lifting up various dolls, exclaiming over the accessories that were once—not many years ago—all she dreamed about. "Do you know how much I wanted Julie *and* Kit?" Carrie asked, cradling a doll in her arms. "But you guys said I had to pick one."

As Gregory watched her search the aisles, he remembered how fun it had been to spend time with Carrie when she was little, before she had to have a *thing*. Back then it was enough that your doll had her distinct thing and style, and the pressure was otherwise off. If only he could repeat some of those years with her, a do-over. This time, he wouldn't take those easy, innocent moments for granted.

Gregory suggested they stop for ice cream on the way home, but Carrie said she wanted to have her cheesecake. When they got home, they sat at the kitchen island, scraping forkfuls from the two thick slices.

"That's something I like about Jessie," Carrie said casually. "She's not afraid to eat."

Gregory didn't look up or respond to this. He felt his daughter handing him a small piece of herself, and he wanted to treat it like the fragile thing it was. After some time, he asked, "Does she live around here?"

"Beacon Hill."

Gregory raised his eyebrows, imagining an elegant brownstone overlooking the Public Garden—some of Boston's best real estate in a city full of expensive old homes.

"Friend from the club?"

"Uh-huh."

They ate for another moment in silence. "Hey, Dad?"

"Yes, honey."

"Today didn't suck." Without meeting his gaze, she scooped up the last piece of cheesecake with her fork and brought it to her mouth.

22

With Carrie at the club for the next several hours, Gregory ascended the narrow staircase that led from the back of the second floor to the attic. He paused on the top stair before drawing a breath and stepping into the low, angular room, oppressively hot on this July night. He peered around cautiously, his heart thudding.

Was Mira there?

He waited, his whole being alert to the possibility. When he didn't hear or see anything unusual, he didn't know if he was relieved or disappointed. He didn't even know why he thought she'd be in the attic. If she were a ghost—the bangles had made that a more serious consideration for him—then maybe she was haunting his house, too. Watching them. Him. Gregory's knowledge of ghosts—mostly limited to what he had learned from watching *Scooby-Doo* with the kids when they were little— seemed to suggest that attics were a likely place for them to linger.

He inhaled deeply several times to see if he could detect one of her scents. Nothing. Just stale air and mothballs.

"Mira?" Gregory called in a shaky whisper. He was answered by the hollow silence of the attic and the droning chirp of crickets in the trees outside.

Gregory was soon sweltering in the airless heat of the attic. Sweat trickled down his face and blurred his eyes, yet he resisted the urge to flee back down the stairs into the air-conditioned house. He made himself stay put and listen for another moment, until he felt overcome with self-consciousness. Of course, no ghost was going to appear in his attic. Or his house. Or his office. He really was slipping. Even Carrie noticed.

He switched on the light to mitigate the effect of any strange shadows and assured himself that his imagination was in overdrive. "I'm okay," he said out loud.

Gregory looked around at the dozens of boxes lying about, shoved under the rafters and left scattershot around the floor from all the times Liv had gone up to look for something. Gregory sometimes thought that while Liv kept the house in her own image—tidy, organized, stylish—the attic was the hidden chaos inside her brain.

Scanning the space, he noticed three of his sister's framed paintings leaning against the back wall. He ducked under the low ceiling, gathered the paintings, and placed them in a pile by the door. Then he stood with his hands on his hips, wondering about all of the other mystery boxes. He knew they held stories of their family's past—the ones Liv maybe wrote about in her memoir class. When his eyes landed on the cedar chest that had once belonged to Liv's mother, he couldn't resist lifting the heavy wooden lid and peering inside at the random assortment of blankets, linens, clothes. There on top was Petey's silk christening gown. Gregory took it out and let the small ivory-colored garment unfurl in his hands. He remembered that late spring day so well: With Liv and Carrie beside him, he held Petey in his arms as the minister blessed his son with holy water. They hosted a luncheon at their house afterward, and when it was time for Petey's nap, Gregory insisted that Liv stay and enjoy the guests. He said he would put Petey down. But instead of laying him in his crib, he sat with him in the antique maple rocker until he fell asleep, his head heavy and warm, on Gregory's shoulder. While Petey slept, Gregory whispered promises to his baby boy: He would always be there for him; he would always have a father to rely on. But here was Gregory, rifling around in the attic, looking for God knows what, while Liv went alone to Petey's Visiting Day.

Gregory tucked the gown back into the trunk and noticed another familiar item. He excavated the brown-and-orange zig-zag-patterned afghan that had covered his mother's legs as she rested on the living room couch in her final years after her stroke. Gregory had always hoped she would outlive her husband and enjoy a few peaceful years without him, but a blood infection abruptly ended her life at age seventy-four. Gregory yanked out the afghan and shut the lid on so many other memories buried inside: Liv's lace wedding gown, his black tuxedo jacket. Relics from another life.

After a last cautious look around, he wrapped his sister's paintings in the afghan and headed downstairs.

Back on the air-conditioned second floor, Gregory grabbed a set of sheets from the linen closet in the hallway then darted into the master bedroom to get his pillow. He stopped to look around, and when he did, he saw that Carrie had returned the bracelets to Liv's dresser. He picked up the three thin silver bangles and tapped them together. They clinked dully. He tried to put them over his wrist, but they were too small and strangled his fingers. He took them off and carefully returned them to the dresser.

Gregory shut the bedroom door behind him and lugged everything in one clumsy armload down to the garage. Using nails and a hammer from the tool bench, he began hanging Margaret's paintings on the bare wood walls. One looked like the sun bursting into a bright red color—an image that could be cheerful or depressing, depending on the observer's mood. The watercolor of a crowded boat full of brown people on a stormy sea was less ambiguous. When he lifted up a black-and-white painting of a feather, he hesitated. It had been a birthday present to Liv, when she was still trying to be a writer. It was simple with clean, spare brushstrokes. On the back in his sister's coiling script, he saw the one-word title: *Quill.*

He set it aside for Carrie.

Then he sat down on his mattress and let out a deep breath. His gaze drifted to the window. And there they were. The piercing brown eyes staring at him.

He turned away quickly, his chest tightening. When he found the courage to look again, no one was there, just glassy darkness. He moved carefully to the window and peered out into the night. The nearest neighbor's house was through a grove of trees, twenty yards away. Had he seen their lights flick on?

No. He'd seen eyes.

"Mira?" he called.

No one answered.

Gregory walked in small circles around the cluttered garage, navigating the tool bench and the whiskey barrel. He bumped into his beach chair but kept moving, trying to outpace his fear. What was Mira up to? Did she want him to pay for what he'd done to her?

With his hand over his chest, Gregory stopped walking and tried to take a deep breath. The air wouldn't go in.

He sat down and tried to control his breathing—slow breaths in, slow breaths out—but it only made him more tense. He was having another panic attack. He felt like he was going to suffocate.

He knew what he needed. To talk to Liv. A familiar voice that would ground him. He dialed her number, but the phone went straight to voice mail. She'd had a long day and was probably asleep with her phone on silent.

His chest felt like there was a boulder on it. He was gasping now. Phil.

He didn't pick up right away, but Phil finally answered, clearing his throat before he spoke. "Kath? Is that you?" he said, his words slow and sloppy. "I had a little bit too much. I'll be home when I feel okay. Nothing to worry about. Okay? You okay?"

"Mmm-hmm," Gregory murmured.

He waited. He wanted Phil to keep talking. The sound of his voice, even drunk and disoriented, was calming to him.

"Good, good," Phil said. "See you tomorrow. Love you."

Gregory put the phone down and collapsed on the mattress. For the first time in several minutes, he felt like he could draw a breath.

23

Gregory unlocked his bottom desk drawer at eight o'clock on Monday morning, one hour before Jason V. was scheduled, and knew immediately that Mira's scarf had been moved. He remembered exactly how he had placed it there on Friday: folded in a square, flat on the bottom of the drawer with the Ziploc bag of pill bottles concealing it. He was rushed, but careful, and would have sworn on his children's lives that none of the material was showing around the edges. But now the scarf was askew, with pink cloth visible under the bag, as if someone had taken it out and carelessly shoved it back in.

Gregory returned the brass key to its place beside the fluorescent orange ruler in his top drawer and studied the desk for other clues. Hiding a key in the same desk that one was trying to safeguard was a pretty feeble security system, but he had never had a reason to suspect that someone would want to break into his bottom drawer. It had only ever held that bag of mostly expired benzodiazepines from Dr. Harris, his primary care physician, who willingly wrote Gregory any scripts he asked for. No psychiatrist required. Gregory no longer took anxiolytics regularly, but there were still days that he popped half an Ativan to keep himself from going into a panicked frenzy.

If someone did want to get into the drawer, they had to breach the locked door to the waiting room and then his office door, also locked. As mentally unwell as some of Gregory's clients were, none had ever shown signs of wanting to steal from him. If anything, his desk seemed so safe that he usually felt ridiculous locking it. But what started years ago as a precaution against anyone finding his pills had morphed into habit. And he liked that plastic bag being inaccessible to everyone. Or so he had thought.

As Gregory opened all four drawers and searched for other suspicious signs, he knew that someone had gone through his desk. Nothing looked wildly out of place, but the tape dispenser was tucked too far back in the corner, and his yellow notepad wasn't fully flush to the right.

Phil was the only other person with a key to his office. There was one time in ten years that Phil had used his own key to get in; Gregory, away on the Cape for the weekend, feared that he'd accidentally left the window open and asked Phil to close it when a thunderstorm was heading toward Boston. Otherwise, they'd always had a tacit agreement to respect the other's space, which is why Gregory felt nauseated when he considered the implications of someone breaking in and taking out the scarf. Had Liv convinced Phil to lend her the key—perhaps claiming that Gregory needed something—and then trawled through his desk for clues? Did the awkward discussions about Gregory's "woman friend" lead Phil to do some detective work of his own?

Then Gregory had to consider the strangest possibility of all: Was it Mira?

Had Mira moved from trying to heal him to haunting him— and his daughter? Maybe he'd upset her last time when he'd tried to kiss her. She'd brushed it off in the moment, but perhaps he'd read that wrong.

The back of his neck stiffened. He needed to lock that idea away until he could see her again on Wednesday at one. That was not for two days.

With less than an hour left before Jason V. arrived, Gregory knew he could get some notes done or take a walk outside to clear his head. But he sat there motionless, and in that short time decided that no one—mortal or immortal—had broken into his desk. He must have imagined that he had covered the scarf with the bag. After all, by Friday morning, he had been on day two of almost no sleep; in addition, he had just learned about his father's heart attack and had been moving quickly in case Phil barged in.

Nobody had touched the scarf.

Gregory sat for a while longer. He began a slow inhale of four counts, followed by an eight-count exhale. But then he stopped in the middle of a long exhale, pulled out his phone, and started a text to Phil: *Any chance you popped into my office to check on something over the weekend? No worries if you did. Just wondering.*

His thumb hovered over the send arrow for a moment, but then he stopped and reread what he'd written. It sounded too accusatory. He deleted the text and started again: *It looks like some things might have been moved in my office over the weekend. Nothing's been taken that I can tell. Could also be my imagination. Wondering if anything looks amiss in yours?*

Again, he was ready to press send, when he hesitated. This one made Gregory sound like a lunatic. *Some things might have been moved, or it could be my imagination?* Yeah, no. He deleted it.

He opened his drawer and fingered the scarf.

He could no longer hold back. Drawing a deep breath, Gregory removed his laptop from his briefcase and set it on his desk. He murmured a hasty apology to Joey for breaking their pact and opened the screen before he had time to change his mind.

It was distressingly easy to find the Mount Auburn Cemetery

website. It was harder to type *Mira Patel* into the Burial Search box. As soon as he pressed enter, her name appeared. Beneath her name was the same birth date and death date as he had seen on her gravestone. There was even a square on a map indicating where she was buried. When Gregory enlarged the screen, he saw: 8111 Space 4 Marigold Path.

He opened a new tab for the *Boston Globe.* Gregory navigated to the archives and typed *hit-and-run* and *Mira Patel.* An article came up from 1989: "Harvard Medical School Resident Is Victim in Fatal Hit-and-Run."

He scrolled down—his hands shaking so badly he struggled to control the arrow key—until a small black-and-white photo appeared. A smiling woman with long dark hair and dark eyes. Peering closely into those eyes, he *thought* it was his Mira, but the photo was so grainy he couldn't know for sure. When he enlarged it, the resolution only degraded.

Gregory's rib cage tightened. He rubbed his face over and over trying to scrub away his confusion, his fear. He started to shut his laptop, but he stopped and forced himself to read:

Mira Patel, 29, of Brighton, was hit and killed by a car on Bosworth Street in Boston while riding her bicycle late Tuesday night. The Harvard Medical School resident was believed to be biking home from a concert when she was struck head-on by a driver who fled the scene. The victim was taken by ambulance to Brigham and Women's Hospital, where she was pronounced dead on arrival. Anyone with information connected to this incident is encouraged to call the Boston police at—

Gregory's body grew clammy. He pushed away from his desk and lowered his head between his legs. He stayed that way for several minutes, until he thought he could safely sit up without fainting or vomiting. He reached for one of the bottles of water that he kept on hand for clients, unscrewed the cap, and chugged it. When he finished, he twisted the empty bottle between his hands, transforming it into a stiff rope of plastic.

At nine o'clock, Jason V. spent his time bemoaning the fact that his girlfriend was always so frustrated with him that she never wanted to have sex anymore. Gregory was barely able to concentrate with the distraction of Mira-as-ghost literally haunting his thoughts. Was she eavesdropping now—attempting to help him? When he suggested that Jason should try showing more interest in his girlfriend's art classes and new puppy, he reminded Gregory that he had tried that already. At which point Gregory looked at his client blankly and said, "Well then, let's see. How about we both come in next week with three new ideas?"

At ten o'clock, Gregory saw Barry C., who had switched his Wednesday appointment to Monday and seemed uncharacteristically pleased with himself. He was down eight pounds (160 to go) and was happy to use the time to enthuse about the wonders of being in ketosis. He raised his travel coffee mug, explaining that there were two tablespoons of butter melted into his dark roast, and credited Gregory with helping him find the strength to try a restricted carb diet. Gregory managed some words of encouragement before sending him on his way.

At eleven he met with Marina K., who had become depressed after menopause. Gregory spent a half hour listening with whatever attention he could muster to something that had happened over the weekend with her grown daughter. When she finished her story, he offered no insight or guidance beyond recommending that she take a walk in the woods. "Why should I do that?" she asked. When he didn't have an answer, Marina said, in her most motherly voice, "I should let you have a little extra time to get a coffee or something to eat." Then she stood abruptly and headed for the door. He smiled weakly and didn't try to stop her.

In those twenty extra minutes before his noon client, Gregory decided to run downstairs to Starbucks and grab a sandwich. With his routines disrupted, he hadn't had time to prepare lunch at home.

All weekend, Gregory had worried about Mira leaving another sign for his family to find. On Saturday night, he had considered sleeping in the garage, but once he'd seen those eyes in the window, he knew he couldn't leave Carrie alone in the house. So after picking her up from the club, they hung out in the family room, eating popcorn and binge watching *Schitt's Creek* until one in the morning.

On Sunday, Gregory went back to Hartford Hospital, where nothing with his father had changed for better or worse, then returned home just as Liv was pulling in from her trip to New Hampshire. After unpacking the car in silence, they stood awkwardly in the kitchen while Liv filled Gregory in on her visit with Petey, mentioning at least three times what a wonderful time they'd had and how it was fine that Gregory wasn't there, a detail that slid sharply into his gut like one of the well-honed Henckels in the knife block on the counter next to him.

When Liv went upstairs, Gregory grabbed a yellow legal pad and an envelope from the office and headed to the garage. He sat in his beach chair and wrote a letter to Petey, recounting the many things that felt special about his son's childhood. Gregory wrote five single-spaced pages about standing on the soccer field on chilly Saturday mornings in the fall and spring, watching him play his heart out; about their weekend walks to Pemby's for muffins; and about the forts they used to build in the yard. He wrote how lucky he felt to have a son and that he was brokenhearted he couldn't see him on Visiting Day—but that Mom had said he was doing great. When Gregory finished, his fingers cramping, it had become so dark outside that he needed his cell phone flashlight to address the envelope. He thought about not sending it, wondering if Petey would even want to read five pages of his father's sentimental ramblings. But Gregory ultimately decided he would mail it, suddenly desperate to be in communication with his son.

Now, as he stood in the waiting room, locking his office before he grabbed food, Gregory noticed a band of light streaming from under the door of the third office. Phil's share of the rent included that small, extra room, but Gregory hadn't seen him use it in several years. He had never been inside, and only Phil had a key to what briefly became a makeshift studio apartment when he was going through his divorce. Gregory suspected that this was the site of some indiscretions, too, although he never again wanted to discuss such a thing with Phil. Mostly the office sat mysteriously empty, but Gregory knew someone was in there now. He quietly crossed the room and opened the door from the waiting room into the hallway; if he had to yell for help, others on the floor would come to his rescue. With one finger on his phone's keypad, poised to call the police, Gregory stood in front of the door and listened. He heard some shuffling around and throat clearing. He was about to knock, when the door swung open.

Phil, looking groggy and disheveled, took a step back. "Gregory! You scared the bejeezus out of me."

"Sorry, Phil! I saw the light on and—"

Phil backed up into the room and sat down hard on a green pullout sofa bed that had not been restored to its daytime form. A rumpled sheet had freed itself from one corner of the mattress, and a gray fleece blanket hung over the side, pooling on a red, Oriental-style throw rug. Otherwise, the room contained a small wooden table with two matching chairs. On the table were three white takeout containers plus an empty bottle of wine. The tangy smell of unrefrigerated Chinese food hung in the air. Gregory tried not to let his eyes wander too much, but he couldn't help himself, riveted by his first glimpse of Phil's hidden world. He had no idea why Phil kept it like this when the office space, however small, could fetch at least $2,000 a month in Boston's real estate market. For some reason, Phil wouldn't give it up.

"Are you all right?" Gregory asked.

"I'm fine."

But Gregory knew something was wrong. Was Phil having another affair?

"What about you?" Phil said, his voice uncharacteristically flat. "You doing okay?"

Gregory hesitated. "Yeah. I'm okay." How could he say he was having a quasi-therapeutic relationship with the ghost of a woman he had killed thirty years earlier in a hit-and-run? And that she was possibly haunting him for it. *Oh, and by the way, I'm starting to wonder if you had something to do with moving her scarf around in my bottom drawer?*

Gregory continued gripping the door handle. He studied Phil, who looked like he wanted to collapse onto the mattress and go back to sleep, a feeling Gregory knew well.

"Can I do anything for you?" Gregory asked. "Get you a latte?"

Phil combed his fingers through his thinning mane. "I'm good," he said, still not looking at Gregory. He held up his beefy arm and squinted down at his gold chronograph watch. "But I have to get to Mass General for a meeting." When he made no effort to move, Gregory knew Phil had something to tell him.

After a few more seconds of silence, Gregory nodded at the sofa bed. "Not to pry, but is everything okay with you and Beth?"

Phil chuckled. "Beth and I are great. Just great." Phil's red eyes, with dark fleshy pouches beneath them, betrayed a different truth.

Gregory indicated the chair. "May I?"

Phil nodded and checked his watch again.

The inside of Gregory's mouth felt like baked parchment paper. "This is going to sound crazy, but by any chance did you go into my office over the weekend?"

Phil looked up quickly, his eyebrows raised, his jaw slack.

Gregory held up his palms. "No big deal if you did. I'm just wondering."

After a few seconds in which Phil seemed unsure if he had gone in or not, he drew a deep breath and exhaled slowly. "I did," he said. "I did go in."

"Well, that's fine. I thought that maybe things looked a little moved around."

Phil didn't respond. He just sat there, his fingertips pressed together to form an orb. After a long silence, Phil said. "I ran out of scotch and thought maybe you had a bottle in your desk. Sorry, I should never have done that without asking."

Gregory nodded, giving Phil a pass on what felt like a teenager's risible lie. Phil knew better than anyone that Gregory, who could go months without drinking, would never have scotch in his desk.

"That's fine," Gregory said, forcing a laugh. "Sorry I couldn't help you out in your moment of need."

Phil's mouth turned up in a quick, insincere smile.

"Another thing," Gregory said, his voice hesitant. "Do you remember getting a call from me on Saturday night?"

Phil squeezed his eyes shut then popped them open again. "I'm embarrassed to admit I don't. Was it important?"

"Just checking in."

"On a Saturday night?"

Gregory paused. "Yeah."

"Anything I can still help with?"

"All set."

They sat there staring at each other, letting the strangeness of the conversation settle, each knowing the other was concealing something. Finally, Phil stood with a groan and held up his hand to usher Gregory out of the office. In that moment, Gregory decided to skip Starbucks to avoid a walk down four flights of stairs with Phil. He stepped inside his office thinking he should say something—*See you later, Phil. See you tomorrow. Have a good day*—but no words came out.

Gregory quickly locked the door and took the scarf from his bottom drawer. He also removed the Ziploc bag of pill bottles and emptied it into the drawer, shaking out any crushed residue from the sharp corners. He folded the scarf and slid the square of magenta cloth into the bag. He sealed it and buried the bag beneath some files at the bottom of his briefcase.

24

On Tuesday evening, with the air charged from a late afternoon thunderstorm, Gregory was out in the yard mindlessly fertilizing the strawberries, only able to think about one thing: how he had to get through the night and three morning clients (it would have been four, but Eleanor S. was on vacation), before he could see Mira again. When his cell phone rang, he plucked it from his back pocket with two dirt-covered fingers and glanced at the caller ID. *Margaret.* Gregory slid the phone back into his pocket and measured another scoopful of fish bone fertilizer into the green plastic watering can. He ignored the voice mail alert, but the text pings were too much. He went into the garage and dropped the phone onto the tool bench. His sister had been calling hourly, sometimes to report another eye flutter. Gregory needed a break.

He was back in the garden when Liv, talking on her cell phone, came out of the house. She carefully picked her way across the wet grass toward Gregory. "Of course, Margaret. Yes, I understand," Liv said. "Here's Gregory. If there's anything I can do. Of course. You, too."

Liv handed her phone to him without a word, but her eyes were wide with warning. She folded her arms across her narrow chest and pretended to be looking at the strawberries, while staying within hearing distance.

Margaret's voice sounded broken, like she'd been crying. "The EEG results came in. Dad's brain-dead."

Gregory gripped the watering can tighter. He knew that brain-dead meant *dead*. There was no recovering from brain-dead.

"The priest will be here any minute for last rites."

Gregory let the watering can fall from his hand. "Shit."

"I know."

He drew a breath, tried to steady himself. "What happens now?"

"Dr. Lee takes Dad off the ventilator tomorrow, and that's the end of the road—his anyway."

"Tomorrow?"

"First thing in the morning."

Gregory didn't know what to say. He thought this heart attack would be just another example of his father not backing down and Gregory would have several more years of ambivalent Sunday visits to room 109 at Pleasant Springs. Now Margaret was saying that their father was almost gone.

"I see." Gregory kicked at an anthill, trying to dissolve the tiny brown volcano into a patch of grass. "So what should I do?"

"You should get your butt down here is what you should do. It's our last night with Dad, and we have to sign some things, take care of paperwork, stuff like that."

Gregory let out a long sigh. Liv was listening, so he spoke in low tones. "Is the timing up to the doctors? Can they wait until tomorrow afternoon?"

"What? Why?"

"Well, the thing is, I have another eight-hour day of clients tomorrow, and I already missed last Friday. If you're okay with handling this tonight. I'll be there—"

"Jesus! I'm sorry Dad's death is such an inconvenience for your income stream."

"It's not that, Maggie—"

"So what the fuck is more pressing than your father's last hours?"

As her words hung there between them, Gregory pretended to notice something around the other side of the house and walked quickly toward the blue spruce, away from Liv.

"Here's the problem," he said, hoping his sister would understand if he told the blunt truth. "It is *crucial* that I see my one o'clock client tomorrow. I obviously can't say why for confidentiality reasons, but you need to trust me. This session is also a matter of life and death."

"Is this the person you were telling me about? The love interest?"

"No!" he said in a firm whisper. "I mean it's that person, but it's not what you just said."

"But it is her? That woman?"

He glanced back across the yard at Liv who was now inspecting the tomato vines. "I'm not discussing this with you. But if it's possible to wait until tomorrow afternoon, I can be there by four."

"Can you even hear yourself Gregory? 'I can be there by four.' Do you know how heartless you sound?"

"I know I do, but I can't explain it right now. Either way, I've made my peace with Dad. I don't need any more goodbyes. That's your stuff to resolve."

Margaret was silent for a long moment in which Gregory stood perfectly still, hoping that his sister would finally accept what he had been trying to tell her: she couldn't force him to care about their father.

When Margaret began speaking again, her voice was low and graveled. "Well, I'm glad you've resolved everything with Dad. Congratulations. But you are absolutely right that I haven't. I never felt like I was part of our family growing up, and it took me years to even have a relationship with Mom and Dad. Now I don't have any close family except Jas and Dad and your kids. But not you. I've *never* had you. And even if you can't be there for Dad tonight, I had this crazy idea that maybe—oh gosh, I don't know—maybe you could be there for me. Or for us. As a family."

She let out a deep guttural sound worse than crying. Gregory paused, wavered for a minute, but he knew he had to see Mira again if he was going to able to be there for *anyone*. How could he be a more present brother and father, with his thoughts consumed by another? How could he be honest with Liv until he'd achieved some clarity around this surreal situation?

Margaret stopped. Gregory waited. Soon she would say a snarky goodbye, and their phone call would be over. But she started speaking again, this time in a querulous whisper. "Do you know that for years I've wanted a brother? And now I'm asking you to be there while we help our father die, but you can't do it. Not for yourself, or for me. So, fine. Stay there and fuck your patient's brains out, or whatever it is you do with her. And if you need me, I'll be at Dad's deathbed with my wife, who cares way more about our father than you do."

The phone clicked off and Gregory stood there holding it to his ear. He leaned his head back, looking beyond the pines at the fast-moving clouds. Everything was leaving him, and he couldn't seem to stop it from happening. He had one moment in time to find out why Mira was coming to his office and to beg her for forgiveness. She had been so annoyed that time he delayed their session fending off Phil. If Gregory wasn't in the office tomorrow at one, he doubted she would ever come back. If she had ever even been there to begin with. After thirty years of praying for this chance, he was going to miss it. And then what? A broken marriage and another thirty years of sending prayers into a void? Or worse, giving up.

He was about to slip the phone into his pocket when he realized it was Liv's. But he couldn't turn to face her, even when he heard the pad of her feet in the wet grass behind him. When his shoulders started to heave, she put a hand on his back, and he wanted to fall into her arms and tell her how he had ruined everything, every relationship. He'd been a shitty brother, a distant son, a useless husband, an incompetent father. He had destroyed his friendships and damaged his marriage because he couldn't be truthful with anyone. He had not lived an honest day since that date engraved on Mira's tombstone: June 20, 1989. As much as he had hoped their marriage would save him, it didn't, and it wouldn't. And he certainly couldn't tell Liv that his one chance left for absolution—the thing he'd been waiting for since he was seventeen—was Mira. But now he had to choose between his dying father and his own redemption.

Gregory rubbed a filthy palm over his face. The dirt felt like sandpaper, rough against his skin. He wished he could rub his life away, make it vanish. Joey spared himself decades of misery. If only Gregory had that kind of courage, he'd gather every pill from his bottom desk drawer and swallow them all down with a bottle of 80 proof vodka.

"So this is it?" Liv asked, her voice tender. "For your dad?" She touched the hand covering his eyes.

Gregory lowered it; why not let her see him cry? Maybe she wouldn't remember him as cold and heartless. "I'm heading down to Hartford now." He handed her phone back. Liv didn't even frown at the mud he'd left on the case.

"I want to go with you."

Gregory shook his head. "Thank you, though." He wiped at the tears now flowing down his face, mixing with the dirt in his eyes.

"I'm so sorry, Liv. I am." He tried to blink out the dirt, but it only got worse, and soon he couldn't see anything.

"Why don't you let me come? I want to be there for you and Margaret. For your dad, too."

Gregory shook his head again. "I have to get through this in my own way," he said, not quite a lie. The part he omitted was that he *had* to see Mira tomorrow. He couldn't go on with his life without learning of her intention. Was she mad at him? Trying to punish him? Was there room to make amends?

With one eye squinted at the ground, he found his way back across the yard to where he had left the hose. Beside it lay a single marigold blossom, broken off from one of the plants almost twenty feet away. He reached down for the flower and pressed it to his nose, almost rubbing it into his skin. That smell of resin, of musk. That was her. He stuffed the blossom into his pocket. Then he picked up the sprayer handle and blasted water at his forehead until his vision cleared. He was about to let the hose drop when he hesitated and pointed it at himself again. Holding the sprayer above his head like a shower, he drenched his entire body with water until he couldn't feel anything but the wet, numbing cold.

When Gregory went inside the house to pack for Connecticut, he ran into Carrie on the stairs. Despite having stripped down to his boxers, he was still dripping wet. "What's going on?" Carrie asked, looking at her father standing there in his underwear, eyes rubbed red. He closed his fist around the marigold blossom. "Did Grandpa die?"

"Not exactly, honey, but soon. I'm heading down now to say goodbye to him."

"Oh no! Is Mom going, too?"

Gregory shook his head. "No. Aunt Maggie is there, so she and I are going to handle this."

"What about Jas?"

"Jas will be there, too, I think."

"So why isn't Mom going?"

Liv, who had been listening from the living room, came to the foot of the stairs. "I'll probably have to pick up your brother at camp, sweetie. It's better if I stay here."

Gregory turned to Liv. He wanted to show his gratitude for this quick, elegant save, but she wouldn't look at him.

Carrie's eyes darted back and forth between them, "Can I come?"

Gregory hesitated. "You want to come to the hospital? We're going to be there all night. It could be longer." He looked at the ceiling, wondering how he would make the trip back to Boston if Carrie came along. "And—"

"And what?"

"And Grandpa is, well ..." What a strange thing to say out loud, he thought. "Do you want to be there when he passes?"

He felt Carrie weighing her thoughts. After a minute she said, "Yeah. I think I do. He *is* my grandpa."

This made the whole trip more complicated.

25

Gregory told Carrie he had to swing by his office for some papers and that she could wait in the car. At his desk, after canceling his clients by text, Gregory hovered over a piece of cream-colored letterhead stationery. He thought about what to say should he not be back by one o'clock. He wrote:

Dearest Mira, Because of extraordinary circumstances, I can't keep our session. You have no idea how devastating this is to me, but—

But as he was writing, he realized that in some extreme situation, Phil might read the note, and Gregory didn't need him to see Mira's name.

He touched the outside of his pocket, checking for the marigold, and started again on a fresh sheet of paper. No name.

I'm terribly sorry to miss our session. My father is at the end of his life, and I need to be there. My hope is that we can meet next Wednesday at 1 p.m., if not sooner. Please be in touch about an earlier appointment. I'm happy to accommodate.

He read it through twice to ensure the note was both vague and specific. After adding his cell phone number at the bottom, he tucked the letter into an envelope with *Wednesday 1 p.m. client* written on the outside. He sealed the flap and taped the envelope to the waiting room door, desperately hoping he'd be able to remove it before Mira arrived.

Gregory and Carrie stopped to grab sandwiches at Archie's Deli before driving down the Mass Pike with her playing deejay, queuing up songs, singing along in her soft alto voice. Gregory knew he should ask her things, pick up where they left off on Saturday, but he was too distracted. All he could think about was Mira and her reaction if he didn't make it back in time. He knew Phil would likely be there in the morning and hopefully would ignore the note. But in his Phil way, he might also start putting things together, something that had Gregory concerned. When he had brought the scarf home in the Ziploc bag, he tucked it into his father's old toolbox in the garage, something no one else would ever consider opening. He couldn't risk losing the scarf. It was a physical manifestation that proved Mira existed, and he was desperate for her to exist. After closing the toolbox, Gregory found an old padlock that he used to secure the scratched silver shackle. He dropped the tiny key in a mason jar that he buried inside a ten-pound sack of bone meal.

"You okay, Dad?" Carrie asked after he'd barely spoken for the first half hour of the ride.

Gregory forced a smile. "There's just a lot of stuff in my head right now."

"I guess it's weird to know your father is going to die any minute."

"Really weird."

"But Grandpa was kind of a jerk to you growing up, right?"

"He was. Yes. But I'm trying not to think about that now."

Carrie scrolled through her phone. "So what *are* you thinking about?"

"Nothing really."

"Yeah, you are."

Gregory glanced at her. Over her tank top, she was wearing the faded blue Oxford shirt he had pulled from his closet and left in her room on Sunday morning. "You and your sixth sense."

"My friends always say that."

"Yeah?"

"I'll say something, and they're always like, *How did you even know that?*"

"Give me an example."

Carrie hesitated. "I don't know. I guess I always know who likes who and which friends have hooked up before it's public knowledge." She jacked up the volume, creating a protective wall of music between them, and started singing along. After a moment, she stopped and said, "Dad, why were you so weird about those bracelets?"

Gregory swallowed. He was grateful for the music, for Carrie pretending to be lost in the lyrics. What was he supposed to say? He thought about Carrie's question as they rode in silence for another mile; he'd have to say something, or she'd know something was off. "I just hadn't noticed them on you before."

She laughed. "Really? That's the best you can do?"

"You'd make a great therapist," he said. "Maybe helping people is your thing."

"No, thanks. That's *your* thing."

"You can always tell me stuff, if you ever want to talk."

"I'm good." Carrie started the song from the beginning again, even though it wasn't over.

Gregory tried to keep his face relaxed. He didn't want Carrie to see how painful it felt that his daughter wouldn't come to him with her problems. Of course, it was also normal. Teenage girls didn't typically open up to their fathers, but he still wished he were a different kind of father. His lie of omission had infected not just his marriage but his whole family, and he had spawned a legacy of disconnect and silence with his children.

"So who do you talk to about stuff?" he asked.

Carrie paused, as if deciding how much to disclose. He'd seen this calculation hundreds of times in sessions, clients weighing the emotional risk of revealing themselves. "Sammi. Sometimes Jas."

"Not Aunt Maggie?"

"Sometimes. But mostly Jas."

"What about your friend Jessie?"

"What about her?"

"Can you talk to her about stuff?"

"Don't try to swerve by making this about me. I'm not one of your patients."

Gregory tightened his grip on the wheel. He felt so seen by his daughter, and to feel this exposed to Carrie made him realize that his cracks—the ones he tried so hard to conceal—were showing.

Gregory took a deep breath and, before he could stop himself, said, "You know my childhood friend Joey?"

"The one who killed himself?"

"Did I tell you that part?"

"I found a newspaper article at Grandma's. Is it true he shot himself in the head?"

Gregory swallowed hard. "Sadly, yes."

"O ... kay," Carrie said, slowly. "So why are you telling me about him now?"

Gregory licked his lips. "I guess driving through Connecticut reminds me of him. And with Grandpa about to die—"

"Got it. So what was he like? Your friend?"

Gregory couldn't help but smile slightly as he remembered Saturday afternoons in the summer with Joey and their other best friend, Patrick Callahan, always itching for something fun to do in a place where not much seemed to happen. "Sometimes we'd go down to the brook near Joey's house," he said. "At one end, there was this cement tunnel that smelled like garbage. We would dare each other to go as far as possible into the tunnel, trying to see what was around the bend. This was before Google Maps, when the world was still a mystery. We had no idea where it led. Patrick and I would always turn back before the first bend. We were terrified, but Joey would keep going, and if we didn't stop him, he probably would have gone clear through to the other side, wherever that was. He wasn't afraid of anything."

"What else?"

Gregory sighed. "I don't know how well you remember Grandma and Grandpa's house, but—"

"I remember it. With the dinged-up aluminum siding that made it look like an old can? And Grandpa had that huge garden with the beehouse in the back."

"Exactly. That was Forest Road, and a lot of times we'd play in the woods across the street. Again, Patrick and I were pretty cautious, but Joey convinced us to make a fire circle out there, and when we were kids, we'd walk about a half mile into the woods and just burn things, anything—sticks, paper, old birch bark. Sometimes Joey would steal his mother's cigarettes, and we'd sit around the fire, trying to smoke without coughing. We were so desperate to be cool. Once Joey took a bottle of brandy from his parents' liquor cabinet, and we all got so drunk we threw up. Just three teenage boys puking our guts out in the middle of the woods on a Saturday afternoon."

"Wow!" Carrie said, her tone gently mocking. "You were such a badass."

Gregory laughed. "Joey could convince us to do anything. He used to try and get me to shoplift candy."

"Jesus, Dad!"

"I never had the courage to actually steal anything," Gregory said. "Not with all of my father's lectures about honesty. But Joey was fearless. Sometimes it was like he wanted to get caught." Which is why Gregory made Joey drive that night. He'd put his daring friend behind the wheel, because if they got caught, Joey would take the blame.

"What was Joey's family like?"

Gregory sighed, trying to think of something that he could tell her. "Well," he began, "I was always a little jealous of the Didowskis, because there was this restaurant on West Main Street called the Roost. It was one of those folksy places with weathered shingles that made it look like an old farmhouse. I can still picture the sign with the red-and-gold rooster. Joey's family ate there almost every Friday night.

"In seventh and eighth grade, Patrick and I would try to make plans on a Friday afternoon, but Joey could never meet us until later. He'd always say, 'I have to go to the Roost.'"

Gregory told Carrie how he wished that just once his family could eat there, too, and he could finally know what it felt like to sit in those red vinyl booths and try the same exotic dishes Joey talked about: baked stuffed shrimp and Southern fried chicken. He always wondered what made it Southern.

Gregory's father, unwilling to squander money at a restaurant, expected a home-cooked meal on the table each night. Gregory's mother would rotate through her standards—meat loaf, spaghetti, pork chops—that she prepared according to recipe cards kept in a green plastic file box stored at the back of the counter. Gregory used to riffle through the cards, looking for the dishes his mother never cooked—chicken divan, shepherd's pie—delicacies she would only talk about making, while relying on the same ten or so cards, smeared with red sauce or drops of oil, each meal tasting exactly like itself, with little variation from week to week. The Roost was Gregory's Holy Grail, an experience he longed for but never imagined having.

Then one day when Gregory was thirteen, his mother went to the hospital for stomach surgery. For the five nights she was away, he and Margaret and their father ate the meals his mother had left in green Tupperware containers in the fridge, each labeled with a night of the week. The last night she was gone, Friday, his father was supposed to cook spaghetti, but he didn't follow the instructions properly and overcooked the pasta into starchy clumps. It was one of a handful of times he heard his father swear. Margaret and Gregory were still expected to eat every bland bite that couldn't be masked by red sauce and meatballs, poured cold from the container because his father hadn't bothered to heat them up. That night, their father never asked, *How did I do making dinner?* as he had every other night. It was obvious. When it was time to clean up, his father dumped what was left into the garbage, hitting the pot hard against the side of the plastic garbage can, trying to dislodge the unpalatable mess, startling Gregory with every loud bang.

The next afternoon, after bringing Gregory's mother home from the hospital, his father announced that they would be going to the Roost for dinner. It came out more like a concession than a treat, but Gregory didn't care. He was finally going to experience the place he'd wondered about for so long.

At six o'clock that evening, he and Margaret trailed their parents through the barn-red door into the foyer, his mother taking small, careful steps, sometimes pausing to grip her abdomen and draw a sharp breath. Once inside, he felt a strange reverence, not unlike when he walked into church each week where the vaulted ceilings and stained-glass windows transported him. But this was so much better, livelier and more colorful. He felt drawn in by the dim lights and loud, friendly warmth of the Saturday night crowd filling the booths and shiny maple tables, many pushed together to accommodate large celebratory groups.

The big open room smelled like steak, and something about being there made Gregory stand up straighter. He felt older somehow, and when he peered into the bar area that adjoined the dining room, he could see there was a TV with the Red Sox playing, but for once he didn't care about watching the game. This night was too important.

When the waitress, an older woman with tan wrinkled arms and a pencil stuck in her hair, brought them menus, his father was quick to point out the $3.99 children's menu to Margaret and Gregory. Hamburger, spaghetti with meatballs, hot dog. His father shook his head. "Four bucks for a lousy hot dog. Could have made a whole package at home for that price."

When Gregory read through the rest of the offerings, he saw baked stuffed shrimp, prime rib, and the Southern fried chicken he'd always wondered about. Those meals came with two side dishes, including something called rice pilaf. And while he didn't just want to order a hot dog, he knew better than to ask for a big meal, some costing $12.99.

"I'm not terribly hungry," his mother said and briskly closed her menu as if to prove it. "I'll just have a grilled cheese sandwich."

His father ordered a beer, while his mother asked for a ginger ale. Maggie and Gregory were allowed to order sodas with their kids' platters, and he got a Coke that came in a tall puckered cup with a straw.

His mother, whose face was even paler and thinner than when she'd gone into the hospital, tried to make cheerful conversation. "Well, isn't this a treat!"

Gregory's hot dog came on a heavy oval plate with a small pile of fries, and he liked that the roll was warm and buttery. But as hard as he tried to make it last, he ate everything too quickly and still felt hungry, maybe even hungrier than before he started eating. His father said his steak was tough for the price they were charging, but he still devoured every bite.

"It's funny," Gregory said to Carrie. "The thing I remember most is how I thought eating at the Roost was going to change me. But it turned out to be kind of, I don't know, dull. Lonely, even."

"So what did?"

Gregory shook his head. "What did what?"

"Change you?"

Gregory knew exactly what had changed him, but he was not going to tell her. After some reflection, he said, "I don't know that anything *changed* me."

Carrie said nothing. She didn't even touch her phone when the song ended. She just waited for him to fill the silence she'd left open.

Gregory was grateful for the darkness and the whirr of passing cars. "I guess I wanted to be old enough to drive away," he said slowly, as if just figuring it out himself. "I saved my money and bought the Supra. I took your mother out on our first date in that car."

Carrie seemed satisfied with that answer. Or maybe she didn't want to think about her parents and how tenuous everything felt. She slumped down in her seat and sighed. "I wish I could have a car."

"Yeah," Gregory said under his breath, his face tightening. He thought of Mira's life that never was. And his own, equally unlived. "That car changed everything."

26

Jas jumped up from her chair by Bob's bedside and rushed over to hug Carrie. She rocked her back and forth. "Hey, *mija*. So glad you're here."

"How's Grandpa doing?" Carrie asked when Jas released her.

Jas, who was wearing a short jean jacket over a yellow sundress, pressed her lips together and shook her head. "Not so good."

Carrie moved closer to the bed to hug Margaret. Jas hesitantly opened her arms to Gregory. Grateful for her embrace, however reluctant, he wanted to linger inside it to delay facing his sister. When Jas let go and that inevitable moment happened, Margaret stared at him, her tired eyes glaring.

"I'm really sorry about the phone call," he whispered. "It's been a brutal couple of weeks."

After checking to see that Carrie wasn't listening, Margaret leaned in. "And I'm sorry my brother can be such an asshole."

Gregory brushed past her to join Carrie by the bedside, and together they studied his father, no longer the same withered but distinct man he was just days ago. The tubes and pumps were keeping his body alive, but his brain was inert.

"This is a lot," Carrie said.

"Apparently his heart was a ticking time bomb," Margaret said, coming up beside her.

"What happens now?" Gregory asked.

"Dr. Lee is coming back first thing in the morning," Margaret said.

His sister's muted response to the same question he'd already asked her on the phone felt like an olive branch. Gregory vowed to honor it by keeping things peaceful, which meant letting her direct the proceedings, and putting Mira out of his mind until his father passed.

His sister touched a hand to their father's forehead and smoothed back a few white hairs over his mostly bare scalp, speckled slightly with rust-colored age spots. It was his father's face, but it didn't react to Margaret's touch in any way.

"The doctor expects he'll survive the night, but there's no guarantee. And in the morning," Margaret paused, drew a breath, "they turn off the machines."

"That's so wild," Carrie said softly. "To know the exact day that someone is going to die."

"I know," Margaret said, still stroking their father's head. "Jas always says you never know what's coming next, so you have to love like crazy."

"*Ama como loco*," Jas chimed in.

"You can have all the money in the world, all the stuff," Margaret continued, "but if you don't have love, what's the point?"

Gregory twisted his hands, grateful for the *siss thump* of the ventilator that masked a loud swallow. Margaret's words, as surely intended, went straight to his heart, like the drugs being pumped into their father. Gregory remembered a time many years ago, when he and Liv loved like crazy, as crazy as two people could love. But they couldn't sustain it. Well, he couldn't.

All the money in the world. All the stuff. Margaret made it sound like a crime, while she and Jas lived close to the bone in their funky second-floor apartment, wrapped up in some simple, crazy brand of love he'd give anything to experience again. And there was his father alone in the hospital bed, about to die, and Gregory couldn't remember a moment when he loved him in a pure, honest way, let alone like crazy. He reached back to his boyhood, searching for something—a walk they had taken, a Christmas morning when his father didn't shake his head in judgment after calculating how much money their hand-wringing mother had dared to spend on a few practical presents: clothes for school, some new winter boots, maybe a board game.

Didn't he have any untainted memories to store away for when his father was gone? Gregory squeezed his eyes shut, anxious to find something worth rescuing from the rubble of his childhood. He thought of the beautiful gardens his father created and how hard he tried to be a good provider. Maybe that was enough.

An older nurse sauntered into the room, clicking the pen on her lanyard to discreetly announce that a non–family member was among them. Gregory felt relieved by the distraction.

"I'm Robin," she said in a raspy voice, like something in her throat needed clearing. "I'll be looking after your dad tonight."

"Nice to meet you, Robin," Margaret said. "I'm Margaret, and this is my wife Jaslene, my niece Carrie, and my brother"—she paused as if she didn't want his name in her mouth—"Gregory."

"How are you all doing?" Robin asked no one in particular, her tone not quite inviting an answer.

"Okay, thanks," Jas said. "Considering."

Robin, who had cropped gray hair, nodded her understanding. "It's a hard thing." She turned back to check the monitor and the line to Gregory's father's wrist. She tweaked the ventilator and inspected the catheter that led to a plastic bag of urine dangling from a hook on the side of the bed. "We'll keep him comfortable until the doctor comes in tomorrow morning,"

Robin said. She adjusted the blanket around their father's chest with the tenderness of a mother tucking in a child.

Gregory put his arm around Carrie's shoulder and pulled her to his side. "Any idea what time that will be?"

"Dr. Lee? Seven or so," Robin answered, her back still turned as she studied his father. "He has an early surgery, so it could be later. But we'll take good care of your dad tonight. That I promise." Robin continued studying her patient with such compassion, this nurse who knew Robert James Weber only by the remaining functions of his body. It made Gregory furious that he had never figured out how to set aside his own pain and find a way to care for this man. What kind of mental health provider was he, if he couldn't generate any compassion for his dying father?

No matter how hard Gregory reached for dutiful love in this time-suspended hospital room, panic about missing Mira tomorrow kept wrenching him away. Gregory could not shake the sense that Wednesday at one was the only time he and Mira could meet, nor his fear that if he broke their linkage of sessions, he would end up destroying his only remaining path to redemption. If that was even her intention for him. In recent days, he'd been forced to consider other possibilities: namely that Mira was not a benign presence and he would find that out when she had a chance to talk. Or another that he still hadn't let go of: she was all in his head.

He was only certain that he needed to leave Hartford tomorrow by eleven at the latest, although ten would allow him to drop Carrie at home before shooting into the city.

"Is there something else we need to do?" Gregory said to Robin, thinking it best to take care of all the logistics as soon as possible. "I think I have to sign something?"

He looked at Margaret who, pretending not to hear, shuffled to the other side of the bed. With her head still bowed, she tucked the edge of the pale blue blanket under their father's arm.

"I'll check for you," Robin said. She slid the Lucite clipboard from its holder by the door and flipped through the pages. "The DNR order is signed. Looks like everything is in place as far as advanced directives go."

"What's a DNR order?" Carrie said.

"It's short for 'do not resuscitate,'" Jas quietly explained. "It's so the staff knows they can let the person die—peacefully."

"Oh," Carrie said.

"It's all taken care of," Margaret said.

"Your grandpa is lucky to have his beautiful family here," Robin said. "But I'm afraid you can't all stay overnight."

Gregory leaned across their father's chest to bring his face closer to Margaret's. "Don't *I* need to sign something?" he whispered. "Isn't that what you said on the phone?"

Margaret shook her head again. "All set."

All set? The only thing that was "all set" was that Margaret had manipulated him. He understood her motivation—he *had* been planning to skip his father's passing, but he was angry. He was desperate to see Mira; couldn't Margaret understand that? Since their last meeting six days ago, Gregory felt like his grasp on reality was slipping. He needed answers; he needed them in order to move. In what direction, he was unaware, but it was clear Mira was the key to changing his life. After his one o'clock appointment with Mira things would be different.

The door handle clicked under Robin's hand. "Can I get anyone anything before I go to my next patient?" Robin said, her voice flat, as if discouraging any big asks.

"Thank you, Robin. I'm going to stay here with my father tonight," Margaret said, her chin suddenly high, her tone superior. "So if there's an extra blanket?"

"I'll get you a pillow, too."

"That would be great."

Gregory glanced at the black vinyl recliner under the window. There wasn't enough space for a second one. But even if there were room for him to stay, he'd never be able to sleep with the incessant beeping and whirring. Still, he felt like he was supposed to want to be with his father on his last night, or at least show Margaret and Jas that he wasn't completely callous.

"Is it okay if I stay, too?" he asked, hoping Robin would say he couldn't.

Robin looked over her shoulder into the hall. "The rule is one overnight visitor per room, but we make an exception for comfort care. If you can get by with a regular chair, you're welcome to stay." She placed her free hand over her heart. "I wouldn't want someone to send me away under these circumstances, so I sure won't do that to you."

"Thank you," Gregory said, touched by this tired nurse's kindness toward him, a feeling that chilled into loneliness the moment she left. There was Jas, shoulder to shoulder with Carrie. And Margaret, standing in the only space close to the bed that wasn't blocked by IV poles and machines, stroking their father's arm. If Liv were here, would she be standing by him or with Margaret? At home, she was likely making plans to pick up Petey from camp, relieved that she didn't have to spend any of those long road hours in her sullen husband's company.

Gregory wasn't sure what to do or say next, when he noticed Margaret trying to catch Jas's eye and signal something.

"You don't need to stay, too," his sister said to him, not meanly but firmly.

"You and Carrie can sleep at our place," Jas said, adding warmth to her voice so it sounded like a real welcome. "We'll come back first thing in the morning. Or if anything happens, we'll rush over tonight, yeah?"

Carrie looked at him imploringly. "Can we, Dad?"

"Sure," he said, forcing a smile. But he was mad. He was mad at Margaret for trying to control the situation and making him come here only to lock him out.

Before they left for Jas and Margaret's apartment, Gregory inserted himself close to the bed. When he sensed Margaret was watching him, he rested his fingers lightly on the blanket covering his father's arm and said, "Hang in there, Dad. I'll see you in the morning."

27

Carrie rode in Jas's car, which left Gregory to drive alone to the apartment, a second-floor walk-up in the part of New Britain known as Little Poland. Gregory was a few streets away from Jas and Margaret's apartment when he made a quick detour onto Broad Street, then turned onto Travis Road. He drove for a few more minutes and slowed the car in front of what was once the Didowskis' tan colonial, now painted gray with white trim and a new picket fence. Joey's father died years ago from a heart attack, and his mother passed about five years later from cancer. That's when Joey's younger sister, Debbie, whom Gregory would flirt with in high school, sold the house and moved to Florida.

The house was dark, its inhabitants likely out or asleep. Gregory looked up into the second-floor window that was once Joey's bedroom, hoping to see something he hadn't seen before. He was starting to believe in signs. Could Joey send him one from the other side? Eyes in the window? A flashing light? He watched for several quiet minutes before pulling away.

As Jas opened the door to let Gregory in, the smell of kitty litter wafted into his face. Gregory thought Jas was going to turn and head up the stairs, but she lingered next to him on the dark landing. The bare bulb overhead made her dyed burgundy hair look eerily purple.

"Sorry about you and Mags," Jas said. "She's having a hard time with some stuff, you know?"

"A hard time?" Gregory said in his restrained psychologist's voice. The stairway smelled not only like cat urine but also of dust and strong spices absorbed by the cracked plaster walls. Gregory also got a whiff of the stuffed-cabbage odor that Margaret would sometimes unleash from plastic containers at the nursing home, telling her father that the downstairs neighbor, Mrs. Janicki, had made *galumpki* for him. He loved the strong smell of Polish food and how it reminded him of the Didowskis' house, always loud and lively.

Jas sighed heavily, and Gregory wasn't sure if it was the hard time itself, or the burden of smoothing things over between him and Margaret that was weighing her down.

"I don't know how much Mags has told you, but we've been trying to get pregnant, and it's not really happening. You know how she's always wanted a baby?"

"Margaret? A baby?"

"She tried a bunch of fertility stuff that didn't work, so this is—was—kind of our last hope." Jas pointed at her belly. "She wanted to be able to tell your dad he was going to have another grandchild, even if he didn't totally get it." She looked up at the ceiling and squeezed her eyes shut. "Now she can't."

"I had no idea."

When Jas looked down again and tried to smile, the shadows deepened the lines of her usually youthful face. Her eyes were teary. "Losing Berto is hitting both of us real hard."

Gregory knew he should hug Jas, but his arms didn't obey his intention. At least the pragmatic side of his brain, always a safer arena for him, still functioned.

"I would love to help somehow. There's a great clinic in Boston where friends of ours—"

Jas held up her palm. "Thanks, but let's just get through the next few days."

He nodded, feeling stupid. Jas—who was, of course, on Team Margaret—also must consider him an asshole for not prioritizing Bob in his last hours. At least she was better at hiding her disgust behind compassion.

Jas turned and hurried back up the steep staircase. Gregory followed, gripping the wobbly banister. When they reached the second-floor landing, the door was open into the kitchen, a steamy room with a scuffed vinyl floor, yellow counters crowded with mason jars full of paintbrushes, and empty beer cans stacked against the wall like a bumpy aluminum backsplash. Gregory hadn't been there in several years, not since he and Liv and Margaret had moved Dad into the nursing home and his sister wanted help transferring some of their mom's old stuff to her apartment. Margaret's apartment had been bohemian then, and a little messier than you'd expect for someone in their forties, but certainly not this bad. Gregory curbed his judgment, considering that the stress of trying to have a baby and taking care of his aging father had left them with little time for themselves, let alone household duties.

"Excuse the mess," Jas said casually. She extended her arm around the kitchen, like he wouldn't have noticed it. "Do you want something to eat? Or drink? We have some nice mango juice."

Jas opened the fridge and Gregory immediately recognized a green Tupperware bowl from his childhood.

"I'm good," he said, quietly, trying to work his way past her. "I really just need sleep."

"The office is all set up for you. Carrie's snuggling in with me."

In the living room, two cats were curled on an olive-green

sofa, but Gregory felt the presence of other felines lurking else-where. Opposite the couch were two matching floral chairs that used to be in his parents' house and, to the side, the plaid wing-back that he and Maggie were forbidden from ever climbing into, its seat now piled with *Mother Jones* magazines. The early American–style brown china cabinet Mom had been so proud of stood in the corner, crammed with her old Royal Doulton figu-rines and a hodgepodge of teacups and dishes. Every Saturday, his mother would take a special cloth and buff the honey-colored maple to a high shine. Gregory stopped himself from gasping at what felt like a sudden immersion in his past. His only family keepsakes were his father's old gardening tools in the garage, too solid and useful to discard.

Gregory was relieved when Jas led him into the office, a small room off the living room with windows overlooking Bond Street. It was barely big enough for the pullout sofa and a cluttered com-puter desk on which a giant monitor rose above piles of books and papers. The glow of the streetlight penetrated the vinyl shades, filling the room with a dull yellow light. When Jas said goodnight and pulled the door shut, Gregory set his bag on the desk chair and inspected what he assumed was his sister's work-space. Amid the dozens of small drawings tacked to a corkboard above the desk, he noticed a black-and-white sketch of his father's hands. He remembered Margaret starting the drawing in the nursing home one afternoon while their father slept, but he had never seen the finished result. As he studied the sketch, he was surprised by the fine details and how the hands almost looked alive. Gregory carefully traced the outline of his father's thick, knotted thumb, when Carrie walked in.

"What's going on with you and Aunt Maggie?"

Gregory wanted to collapse on the pullout sofa bed that Jas had thoughtfully made up with pale blue sheets and two pillows, but he forced himself to remain standing. "It's just the stress of Grandpa dying. You don't have to worry about it, honey." But he knew she was worried. Her outer toughness only worked when all of her people were getting along.

"Just tell me what's going on."

He held a finger to his lips. "Aunt Maggie's dealing with some hard things."

"What things?"

Gregory, whose work had trained him to be meticulous about boundaries, paused. "I'm sorry sweetie, but it's not for me to share that."

When he reached to hug Carrie, she spun away and headed out the door. "I'll ask Jas. She'll tell me."

With the compressor on the air conditioner clunking every twenty minutes, waking him from whatever shallow sleep he'd fallen into, Gregory staggered into the bathroom at two in the morning in search of drugs. In the narrow medicine cabinet, he found several prescriptions for Jaslene Rodriguez, mostly fertility hormones, but nothing that would help him sleep. Under the counter, next to a bottle of Drano and a box of tampons, he found an almost-empty bottle of Children's Benadryl. He put it to his lips and downed the last of the cloying, cherry-flavored liquid like a shot. Several hours later he woke to the sounds of cats prowling around outside his door. Gray morning light flooded the small room, and as he lay there on the sofa bed, he thought how strange it was that his father, whom Gregory had spent his life trying to separate from, would soon be gone.

28

They arrived at the hospital just before seven. Margaret was stretched out in the recliner, a white blanket bunched in her arms like a baby. She blinked her eyes open at the sound of them entering and looked around drowsily. "What's happening?"

"Just us, *mi amor*," Jas said. She crossed the room and handed Margaret an iced coffee from Dunkin'.

"Thanks, *vida*," Margaret said and pulled Jas to her for a kiss.

"How is he?" Gregory asked.

"Still with us." Margaret struggled to sit up in the chair while holding her drink. She looked at Carrie, who was yawning conspicuously, and asked, "Did you get some sleep, hon?"

"A little," Carrie said. "What about you, Aunt Maggie?"

"Not much, but I'm fine."

Margaret set the coffee on the windowsill and got up to hug her niece. The affectionate gesture read differently to Gregory, knowing now how badly she wanted to be a mother. "Here, you sit down. I need to stretch," Margaret told Carrie.

Carrie plopped down into the blanket nest with her iced mocha. After a minute, she pulled out a small journal and pen from her backpack.

"What have you got there?" Margaret asked.

Carrie held up a book with a polka-dot cover. "Jas gave it to me."

Margaret smiled at Jas, who had taken a seat in a chair against the far wall.

"She likes writing," Jas said. "And I remembered I got that from one of my students."

Gregory tried not to look at his phone, his watch, or the clock on the wall that told him just how fast the minutes were ticking away. He sat waiting for Dr. Lee.

Erin, the red-haired nurse from the other morning, entered quietly and asked if anyone needed anything. Gregory wanted to say *just the doctor*, but he knew that Margaret was policing his words. Jas finally spoke up. "Any sign of Dr. Lee?"

"He's still in surgery. But he should be here super soon." Erin went through the same checks as Robin had the night before but with none of her older colleague's professional calm. Her movements were halting and uncertain, and after she adjusted the ventilator a bit, she waited and adjusted it again, then a third time, at which point she left it, even though she didn't look fully confident with the final result.

As Erin checked the monitor, the urine bag, and the IV, Margaret and Jas locked eyes, but only Gregory spoke. "When you say super soon, what does that likely mean? Ten minutes? An hour?"

Erin turned to face them, striving for cheerfulness. "There were some complications in his surgery, but he'll be here as soon as he can. So probably somewhere between ten minutes and an hour, but closer to an hour. I think." She smiled uncomfortably and asked again if she could get anyone anything. Or would they like her to try and call a chaplain in?

"I think we're good," Jas told her.

When Erin left, Carrie looked up from her journal. "What's going on?"

"It could be a while," Jas said. She pulled her chair to the foot of the bed and rested a hand on the blanket covering Bob's feet.

"Sorry, Dad," Margaret said, looking down at him. "We're doing our best."

Trying not to sound frustrated, Gregory said, "I'm a little confused. Isn't it just a matter of shutting off the ventilator? Why can't another doctor do that?"

"Why do you ask?" Margaret said. "You in a rush or something?"

Gregory cast her a look, then shifted his gaze to Carrie, who peered up again from her journal.

"I mean how many times have you checked your watch this morning?" Margaret said.

"Can we please talk outside?" Gregory asked.

As Margaret followed him into the hallway, Gregory could feel Carrie's stare like a knife in his back. They walked in silence past the nurse's station and into a small, empty room marked Family Waiting Area.

He sat down hard on one of the two brown leather love seats while Margaret perched carefully on the other. "Please stop making me feel worse than I do right now," he said, "especially in front of my daughter."

"Well, please stop acting like Dad's dying is an inconvenience and we're keeping you from your whatever-she-is?"

"What I do with my life is my business." He rocked forward, setting his elbows on his knees. "You get to behave however you want, and I don't say anything about that."

"Well, these are exceptional circumstances," Margaret bit back. "I'm trying to create a serene environment for Dad. That's my goal here. And if there's nothing else you have to say, I'm going back in there to be with him." She stood and started to leave.

"Maggie! Please!" he called before she could get out the door. She turned around and he saw the pain in her face. The pale skin. The sunken eyes. All this time he had thought she was so happy with her life, unburdened by kids and able to devote endless energy to her save-the-world projects. He had no idea she was longing for a baby that she couldn't carry or that she wasn't as fulfilled as he'd always believed.

"What do you want?" Margaret said. "For me to tell you it's okay to hate Dad? Hate away! There's my blessing on that. Now, excuse me, but I've got bigger things to worry about than your fucked-up priorities."

They looked at each other for a few seconds. Gregory said, "I'm sorry about everything you're going through. I really am."

Margaret's mouth stiffened. She shook her head as if clearing her thoughts, and turned sharply down the hallway.

He took out his phone and started to call Liv. He just wanted to hear her voice. But then she would start to ask questions, or want to drive down, and that couldn't happen. He returned the phone to his pocket and thought about Mira. Would he be late, and would she find his note? And would it scare her off, or break the spell? He couldn't imagine not seeing her again.

On the way back to his father's room, Gregory lingered around the nurse's station, where he waited for Erin. When she finally came toward him with her bouncing red ponytail and swaying walk, he signaled her over. "Since Dr. Lee is taking so long, I'm wondering if there's another doctor who could step in and help us out? This waiting is so stressful. And I really want my father out of his misery as soon as possible."

Erin looked toward the room, her eyes uncertain. "I totally understand! But the thing is, your father's not in misery because he can't feel anything. He's not conscious."

"I see," Gregory said in a low voice, fearing Margaret would come out in the hallway and catch him in this act of subterfuge. "But if there's another doctor available, I just thought, maybe." He sighed heavily. "We're just anxious to, well, move forward."

Erin's eyes shifted to the nurse's station, empty except for a man that made Gregory think of Fitz from Pleasant Springs. Boy, did he wish Fitz were the one helping with this. "I think it's better to wait for Dr. Lee, since he's been in charge of your father's care. I'll try and get him here ASAP."

When she bolted away, Gregory remembered being a young postdoc at McGrath Psychiatric Hospital and often having no idea how to respond to a needy client, always worrying that he could ruin someone's life with one wrong therapeutic suggestion.

At 10:26 a.m., Dr. Lee arrived with Erin behind him talking nervously. He was thin with a stooped back that Gregory recognized as the surgeon's hump; his father-in-law had one from long hours bent over the operating table. He strode into the room with a nod and a brisk hello and went straight to Bob's bedside. Margaret jumped up and stood beside him. Gregory did, too. Jas and Carrie popped out of the recliner, where they had been curled up together.

"It's time," Dr. Lee said after a glance at the monitor. "I assume you've all said your goodbyes?"

"We have," Margaret said and rushed to the other side of the bed to be with Carrie and Jas.

"Would anyone prefer to wait outside while I turn off the machines?" Dr. Lee asked. "I don't expect any unpleasant reactions. It's just a personal choice."

"I'm staying," Margaret said.

"I'm good, too," Jas said.

Gregory looked at Carrie. "Should we wait outside, honey? What do you think?"

Carrie looked at him, then at her aunts. She drew a breath and shook her head. "I'm okay."

Gregory stood alone next to Dr. Lee, watching as he reached above the bed to shut off the IV. He then withdrew the needle from his father's neck and waited a few seconds before shutting off another switch.

Without the incessant *siss thump* of the ventilator, the room was blessedly more peaceful. Gregory could hear the slow beeping of the EKG that, as he understood it, would now stop. But it didn't. The green line slowed, but it didn't flatten.

Margaret held one of her father's hands, while Jas and Carrie rested their hands on the blanket covering him. As soon as Dr. Lee excused himself and stepped out of the room, Gregory took his place next to the bed, his eyes flickering back and forth between the monitor and his father's placid face. He could hear Erin and Dr. Lee talking in the hallway.

"What's happening?" Carrie whispered.

"No clue," Jas said. Her voice was weak and choked with tears.

Dr. Lee came back in and studied the monitor for several seconds. He put a stethoscope to his father's chest. "He's starting to breathe on his own," he said. "This happens sometimes with the fighters. It just means it's going to take a little longer than anticipated."

The clock on the wall showed 10:40, and Gregory knew he had five more minutes. The EKG screen slowed a bit but mostly held steady. He could see the slight rise and fall of his father's chest with each shallow breath.

"It's okay, Dad," Margaret said. "You can let go. It's time now."

For the next several minutes, Gregory silently offered similar words of encouragement, while trying not to think about the distance to Boston. His mind drifted to the note on his door. What if Phil removed the envelope in some misguided effort to protect him from ambiguous doctor-client territory? Or worse, replaced it with some other meddlesome note to protect Gregory and Liv's marriage?

At 10:45, when Gregory knew he couldn't wait another minute, he mustered his courage and crossed to the other side of the room. As Margaret glanced over, her eyes red from wiping tears, Gregory reached for Jas's elbow and pulled her aside. In a whisper, he asked if Carrie could stay with them until he could get back later that evening to pick her up.

Jas squinted with confusion. "You're leaving? Now?"

Gregory blinked, saying nothing. Jas finally consented with a slight nod of her head.

He signaled Carrie over. He leaned down and said he'd be back to pick her up in about five hours.

"Where are you going?"

"I have to see a client in Boston. It's an emergency."

"But Grandpa's about to die."

Gregory headed toward the door with Carrie trailing him. "What is going on?" she called.

"Go back in there and be with Grandpa. For me. Please?"

When they stopped in front of the elevator, Carrie glared at him. "What the fuck, Dad? He's *your* father."

Gregory tried to hug her, but she pulled away and started running back down the hallway. When the elevator dinged and the doors opened, Gregory lunged in.

29

Stuck at one of Hartford's ridiculously sedate intersections, Gregory snapped his ticket from the hospital garage against the dash. He couldn't risk the radio. He needed to focus all of his attention on getting to 22 Blesdow Street by one o'clock. In the hospital elevator, the Waze app had given him an ETA of 12:51. Now it said 12:54. That meant no traffic jams, no getting stopped for speeding, and no damn delays on the Mass Pike. When he passed the exit for UConn on I-84, he thought about his college days, his desperation to do something good with his life after Joey was gone. Although straight As and making the Dean's List every semester never brought him real relief, excelling in school gave him a distraction, a reason to stay alive. He'd never seen his mother happier than the day he graduated summa cum laude.

And wasn't that his excuse for surviving the last thirty years? To stay alive and make other people feel better?

Waze now predicted an arrival of 1:00, and Gregory hoped no one but Mira would be there waiting. It was a perfect day for golf, and he prayed Phil would think so, too.

At noon, with only an hour left to drive, Gregory fixated on the impending session. He hated not knowing anything about where Mira was physically when she wasn't with him. Would he be lucky enough to glimpse her going from the street into the lobby, or might she arrive early, read his note, and vanish? Had she ever been there at all?

Gregory tried to calm the spin of thoughts as he merged onto the Mass Pike, but he couldn't stop wondering if he had really just fled his father's deathbed for an appointment with a ghost. Was he running to his own rescue, or would this be an overdue reckoning for his crime? Or was he simply blowing up his family?

Boston traffic was thick. Out-of-state cars jammed the streets, and clusters of camp groups and tourists crowded the crosswalks. When the arrival time jumped to 1:01, Gregory darted around a Prius stopped at a yellow light and gained the minute back.

At exactly one o'clock, Gregory parked his car illegally in front of his office building. Inside the lobby, he considered the elevator, but it was lingering on the eighth floor, so he threw open the heavy stairwell door and took two steps at a time until he was standing on the fourth-floor landing. He tore down the hallway and around the corner and arrived panting at the door of his suite. The envelope was gone. When he tried the handle, it was locked. His watch said it was 1:01. He struggled with the key but finally heaved open the door and staggered into the waiting room.

Empty. Exactly as he had left it the day before.

His arms dropped to his sides, and he threw back his head. Maybe he was going off the rails. How would he ever face Carrie's questions and Margaret's judgment? How would he explain his decision to Liv?

He stared at the plaque on his door. *Dr. Gregory Weber*. Maybe this was the message he was supposed to get from the elusive Mira: You're a doctor now. You have responsibilities. Drive to Hartford and beg forgiveness from your family for leaving your dying father. Then go back to being the Gregory who was a good psychologist; a decent, loyal husband; a loving, if often clueless, father; an imperfect, but caring, brother; and a semi-shitty son. Because there is nothing else.

Gregory unlocked his office and stumbled inside.

She was sitting in his chair—one foot tucked under her thigh, hands folded in her lap.

He drew a breath of relief that seemed to come up from his knees. He braced a hand against the doorframe. "You're here," he whispered, closing his eyes. "You're here."

After a moment, he opened his eyes. Mira remained still and silent. Her dark hair fell loosely over her shoulders. Her ivory linen dress almost covered her legs. She was barefoot.

"Mira," he said, her name came out like a plea. He took a step toward her. He had never wanted to embrace her more or felt more prohibited from doing so. "My father is dying, but I had to see you today."

Mira nodded and pressed her lips together knowingly, her soft, amorphous gaze trained on him.

Gregory staggered forward a few more steps and dropped into the closest wing chair. "Tell me. Please. Tell me everything."

Mira laughed lightly. "But you were right there, Greg. There is nothing to tell you that you don't already know."

"So then?" He stared at her folded hands for strength. He raised his eyes to Mira's unbelievably lovely—and deeply scarred—face. He had to hear her say it. "You're the person—"

"Yes."

As Gregory sank in his chair, the sweat of nausea erupted from his neck and forehead. He reached for the wastebasket and put it between his knees. He retched over it, but nothing came out.

"I'm sorry," he said. He made himself look up at her. "I'm so sorry."

"I know," Mira answered softly. "I've never doubted that."

"Really?" He studied her, the slightness of her body compared to her strong voice, her dress, luminous against the black chair. She was beaming at him like the shaft of light that poured into his dark garage. "But how did you know?"

"We know things, at least the things we need to know or have the patience to find out."

He hesitated, unsure of the correct terminology, fearful of offending. "So, are you a ghost?"

She recoiled the way his clients did when he named their disorders, and for a horrific moment he sensed her desire to flee his clumsiness. But she straightened her torso, and without flinching from his full gaze, Mira said, "What do you think?"

Gregory slumped back. He gripped the chair arms so tightly he felt the upholstery shifting under his fingers.

When Mira put her hand on his arm to calm him, her skin felt cool. Had it been that way before, too? Had he only imagined her warmth when she touched him?

"You are a ghost," Gregory whispered. He released his clutch on the chair.

"I prefer 'spirit,' but as you like."

"Why are you here?"

"Almost every day since the accident you've prayed for forgiveness. As I told you in our first session, you asked me to come."

Gregory scanned the years, remembering all of the places he had prayed. His blue bedroom on Forest Road. His dorm room at UConn. His graduate school apartment in Brighton where he was living when he met Liv. Nightly in his dark garage.

"You didn't call for me directly, of course, but I knew I was the one who could help you."

"You mean, you're still around because I kept you here?"

Mira slid into the wing chair next to him, so they were inches apart, face-to-face. When he searched for her scents, he got the faintest whiff of smoke.

"You don't have that power over me. No one does." She clasped her pale hands together. "I didn't cross over because of something *I* did."

Cross over. Gregory, thinking he might faint, leaned as close as he could to her face. He saw the thin scar that ran from her nostril to the corner of her mouth. Another fuller one cut across her forehead, and a third wound down the left side of her face, hooking under her chin. "But you didn't do anything wrong."

She put her forefinger to her lips. "We all have our secrets, Gregory. Please don't make assumptions about mine."

That voice. It was so confident but also heavy with regret. He wished he could go back to that first Wednesday and maintain enough control to help Mira make peace with whatever was oppressing her.

"You have carried your burden through three decades of life, and I have carried my burden three decades past my death," she said. "We are separate beings with separate pain and guilt, but we are also linked by what happened that night."

"What burden have *you* carried?" Gregory asked. "Joey and I hit you with my car. We were driving drunk, first me, then Joey. We could have hurt anyone. You were just riding your bike—"

Mira shook her head dismissively. "There you go again, as if you are the only one who has ever suffered the guilt of a horrific mistake."

"Right. Okay." Gregory nodded, finding his psychologist's voice. "What is it that keeps you here?"

"What keeps me here?" Mira drew a breath that sounded hollow, like air being blown across the mouth of a bottle. "My inability to forgive myself for being reckless when I knew better. My eagerness to live out my desires without stopping to consider how my choices would impact others. Typical and narcissistic twenty-nine-year-old selfishness."

"That's what twenty-nine-year-olds—or people of any age—are like sometimes, Mira. There's no reason to hold yourself to overly precious standards of behavior."

"Precious? Please don't lower the bar for me when you don't lower it for yourself. You need to accept my responsibility in what happened, Greg," she said firmly. "Otherwise, we're both still lost."

Gregory shook his head. "That seems a thousand times too harsh. I was drunk inside a vehicle. You were on a bike, riding home from a concert. I read the article."

"I should not have been riding my bike in Boston that night. And if I hadn't been there, you wouldn't have killed me."

"That doesn't make any sense."

She leaned back. "What doesn't, exactly?"

Gregory retreated, pressing his back against the chair. "Well, of course, I know that everyone has regrets and pain," he said after a moment. He tried to find the right language, but he was grasping. "And your pain must be worse because you're, well, dead." As soon as he spoke the words out loud, he realized how absurd they sounded.

"That's quite an assumption, Greg. In the belief system in which I was raised, life and death are part of a cycle. One is not necessarily better than the other. They both simply *are*."

"So is this—you being here—a religious thing?" Although he chose his words carefully, he felt like everything he said was going to annoy her.

"It's how the afterlife works," she said flatly. "We're of every background and faith. But if you die and can't cross over, belief alone won't get you to the other side."

"Then what does it take? To cross over?"

"One thing only." She paused. "Facing the reasons why we're still here. Not pretending to, and not bypassing the real work under the guise of ritual."

"So every spirit who doesn't cross over is just sort of"—he hesitated—"in limbo?"

"We're all in a perpetual state of waiting, each with our unresolved issues." Her lips tightened and she turned toward the window. "I think I know what yours are." Her dress looked more gray than ivory and seemed looser on her body.

Gregory lowered his eyes, struggling to accept not only what Mira was telling him so matter-of-factly but that he was even having a conversation with a spirit. He looked down at his watch. It was only 1:05.

"And, yes, my parents did believe in ghosts," Mira continued. "In the beginning I'd linger around my mother. But they—my parents—both died quite young. Not long after I did." She let her gaze drift back to him. "My death broke their hearts. And that's my fault."

Gregory tried to neutralize his tone. "Mira, *I* took your life away. *I* broke their hearts. I also took away your chance to practice medicine. You would have been an incredible doctor."

A wistful smile played at the corners of her mouth. "A psychiatrist."

He squeezed his eyes shut at the unfairness. Her death was a waste not just of Mira's life but of what she would have done with that life and the lives she would have helped as a doctor.

"I wanted this, a clinical practice." When she indicated the room, her arm looked weak. "I wanted to help people understand themselves and heal their pain. Just like you."

Gregory shook his head. "Why are you being so forgiving when I took that away from you? I took *everything* away."

Mira sighed and readjusted herself in the chair. "For such a good psychologist, you're doing a terrible job with me. I need you to keep your own guilt out of this and stop invalidating mine."

"But—"

"It's my turn to be the patient!" She was insistent, but her voice sounded muffled. "Allow me that, please."

"Okay," Gregory said. "You've always been in control here. I need to change that." He got up and walked to his own chair, reassured by the steadiness of his legs underneath him. Once he was seated inside the familiar convexity, with his elbows on the perfectly curved armrests, he felt more alert and composed. Out of the range of her coolness, his body warmed.

Mira's shoulders were trembling, her hands, the translucent white of sea glass, were covering her face. He sat quietly and let her cry for as long as she needed, the same as he would do for any flesh-and-blood client. Minutes passed before she spoke again, her voice even softer. "I hurt many people by being out there that night."

Gregory leaned forward. "Tell me more," he said.

When Mira shook her head, her dark hair brushed against her face.

"You can trust me," Gregory said.

She half smiled, and he knew she was remembering back to their first session. "Why do you think I kept coming back?" she said.

"Tell me how I can help you."

Mira shut her eyes against his question. "I'm angry, too. Angry that I never got to practice medicine or have a family. I know I'm better off than many. At least that's what I'm always telling myself. Maybe I'm one of the lucky ones. I made it to twenty-nine, went to college and medical school. I even fell in love once, as I told you before."

"You get to be angry, Mira. For what you didn't have."

Mira looked at him as if she wasn't sure he was right. But after a minute she assented. "Well, then I'm not just angry." She smiled wryly. "I'm thoroughly pissed off."

Gregory nodded.

"And I'm tired of stagnation," she admitted.

That word: stagnation. Gregory sat up straighter, slightly terrified of what she might ask him to do. Because that had to be part of it—why she came back and why she wanted him to come here on this day, of all days. After thirty years of failing to find absolution, he owed her whatever she asked of him.

"How can I help with the stagnation?"

Mira's voice was deliberate. "If *you* can find your way to forgiveness, *I* can, too. We can both move on."

She had reclaimed the therapist role. Or maybe they were sharing it.

"I'm not sure I understand."

"I think my words were clear," she said perfunctorily. "But let me simplify it. I'm asking you to forgive yourself."

"I have to forgive myself for killing you?" Gregory said.

"Yes." Mira pursed her lips.

"But how?" Gregory could hear the pleading in his voice, but he couldn't help it. "I've tried for decades. If anything, I feel worse after hearing about your parents and your unfinished career. Your unfinished life. I'm starting to think I should have died, too."

"No!" Mira's voice was firm. "There was a moment—my moment—when I had a choice, and I made the wrong one. You did the same in your moment. We both have to go back and release ourselves from those moments while also taking full responsibility for their outcomes. Because endlessly wishing we could go back and undo them, or hiding with busy activity and performative atonement, won't resolve anything. In case you haven't noticed, I'm not the only one who's in limbo."

They studied each other in the afternoon light: two therapists, two stubborn patients—both unyielding in their attachment to the pain they had caused. Mira blinked and Gregory saw something: a flicker in her brown eyes, as familiar as his own. He leaned toward her. The eyes he had seen in the windshield were hers, but they were his eyes, too. Compassionate, but sad, and also terrified. A reflection of the fear he had felt when her body thudded toward him, then flew away to die.

For thirty years, Gregory had been so afraid of the person he killed. Of the repercussions if he or Joey ever confessed their crime. But he could see now that the fact of Mira's death was not what kept him from doing the right thing. It was the fear of facing himself outside the shelter of his private penance.

It was his job as a therapist to show her possibility. Didn't she come to him for help?

After a moment, Gregory inhaled deeply and took a chance. He lowered himself to his knees beside Mira. All he had to go on was his instinct.

"I'm not sure how this works," he said and carefully opened his arms.

Mira hesitated before moving toward him. Her body was as light as breath, boundaryless. When Gregory hugged her, he felt no limitations of flesh and bone. It was like he was being held in his own embrace. He wanted to stay that way and not move, because it was the closest thing to self-love he had ever felt. But he had to finish the process that Mira had started; he had to carry out her request. After he figured out how.

He breathed slowly, rhythmically—always a good start, but soon he felt her guiding him without speaking. She took his hand, and he felt the coolness of her palm as she led him back to the memory. When he saw where she was taking him, he shut his eyes and flinched, but he did not resist. This was where he had to go. This was where he had never left. He landed hard in the car when he was yelling at Joey to take the wheel, and Joey said,

"Sure, Weber, I'll get us home safe." It was a moment Gregory had revisited and regretted almost every night since it happened. If he had only pulled over and stopped driving, thrown the keys down a drain if he had to.

Gregory paused and realized something. That was not the moment he was looking for. That was not where his regret began. He wound back through the night: dropping the foreign exchange students in Beacon Hill, drinking spiked lemonade at the baseball game, then earlier in the car, raising a beer with Joey. No. The moment he was looking for happened before that, before the car ride and the drinking. His regret began when he was still at home with his family, when Margaret handed him the paper bag from the liquor store and made him swear he wouldn't drink and drive. He lied to his big sister and said he'd be hanging out at Joey's all night.

Gregory shuddered and drew his arms tighter around Mira, around himself.

"What is it?" Mira whispered.

He was looking at his seventeen-year-old self—lanky and baby-faced with scared brown eyes. Gregory was back there, watching Greg.

"I was so young," he said, "and angry. I can see that now. I wanted to get away from them, or really from him, from my father and his moralizing. I wanted to find out what freedom felt like."

"And how did it feel?" Mira asked, her voice pushing for something. "That freedom?"

Gregory was standing in the yard on Forest Road, car keys in hand. He had already stashed the paper bag in his car—all gassed up for the trip to Boston.

"I'm leaving, Dad," he called to his father, who was across the yard digging another garden bed. Gregory was grateful for the distance.

His father turned toward him, gripping the shovel. "Where are you going?"

Gregory's jaw tightened. "To Joey's. I'm sleeping over."

His father nodded and, as always, reminded him to be respectful to Mr. and Mrs. Didowski.

"It felt terrible," Gregory said to Mira. "As strict as he was, I hated lying to him and using the Didowskis that way. I knew in my gut that it was wrong. But I ignored it. I guess because lying was the only way I thought I could be a normal teenager. I wasn't brave enough to challenge him."

"Go on."

Gregory opened the car door and looked down at the paper bag on the floor of the passenger side. He glanced up at his father who slowly lifted his work-worn hand to wave goodbye. Then Gregory got in the car, shut the door hard, and, without looking back, pulled out of the driveway.

"I just wanted a night with Joey at the game, but my father wouldn't have let me drive all the way to Boston." He hesitated to make sure he was catching everything. "I never meant to hurt you," he said.

"Then see the boy you were who made that mistake," Mira said. "And forgive him."

"I don't know if I can."

"If you can't forgive him," she said, "then I can't forgive the person I was. I need you to do this, or you'll keep holding me back."

Gregory thought of all the people who needed him to forgive himself—Liv and Carrie and Petey and Margaret—and how he'd always found an excuse not to. Because of the person he killed. Mira. Gregory closed his eyes. He pushed himself into the pain he felt, until he was no longer just watching that teenage boy but *was* that boy before the accident, scared and angry and longing to be free. He could feel his father's judgment, a hot hand pressed to his chest.

"Can you do it?" Mira whispered. "For both of us?"

Gregory didn't know what he was supposed to do. No psychology text had prepared him for this. Part of him wished he could keep Mira there forever. But that's not what she wanted.

Still holding Mira, Gregory drew a breath and released it. Then another. He sensed Mira's impatience, but he had to take his time, trust in what he was doing.

After a few moments of breathing steadily, Gregory called back the teenage boy again. This time the boy looked right at him, his stricken brown eyes pleading, his shoulders folded in with the burden of his shame. Gregory knew it was after the accident.

Gregory looked at his younger self, riddled with guilt for the life he had taken.

"It's okay," Gregory whispered. "It's going to be okay."

The boy blinked at him, as if trying to understand. He shook his head. He didn't believe him. He needed more.

"It's okay," Gregory said again and swallowed back any last reluctance. "I forgive you."

The boy didn't look sure. Gregory said it again, this time with certainty. His voice, gentle but clear. "It's okay, Greg. I forgive you."

He was so astounded, he said it again. "I forgive you." And again. "I forgive you, Gregory." He felt something shift in his chest. The heaviness lifted. He drew a hand from behind Mira's back and placed it over his heart to make sure the feeling was real. He smiled and let out a deep, guttural sob of relief.

After a moment Gregory drew back and looked at Mira. Her eyes were shut, and her face had a troubled tightness. She had found her moment, but if he tried to comfort her, he would only impede the pain she needed to experience and process. He stayed as close to her as he could, and after a while she began to cry softly. He recalled the first day Mira walked into his office and instigated her unconventional agreement to heal them both. Their tears of forgiveness dissolved that pact; they were freeing themselves.

Which meant Mira would leave.

And Gregory would finally live.

When Gregory realized the room was silent again, he didn't know if minutes or hours had elapsed. He glanced at his watch. It was just after three o'clock.

"How do you feel?" Mira asked him, her voice still only a whisper as she withdrew from his embrace. She looked older to him, or maybe he imagined it; certainly no less beautiful.

Gregory glanced around, surprised by the solidity of his office, the familiarity of his surroundings. "Different," he said. "Lighter."

"Me too." Mira moved into a wing chair. "But don't your clients usually feel better when they end a session?"

"That's often what they say. Sometimes not."

"You know," she added, "the real work happens in the real world."

"I know, I hope I'm not too late," he said. "I'm just grateful that you waited for me, that I had this chance. That *we* did."

Mira's smile flickered. "I have always appreciated your heart, Gregory, and that you never stopped asking for forgiveness. That gave me the courage I needed to do this."

He heard a door slam down the hall.

"I've stayed close to my family, but also yours. I was always looking for guidance. After the accident, I would visit your parents' house. Your mother called me Pinky. It was the way I lifted my little finger when I'd drink my mint tea."

Gregory shifted his body enough to reach in his pocket and pull out the crushed marigold from the yard. He held it up.

Mira smiled shyly. "A little reminder that I needed you here today."

"The bracelets, too?"

She nodded. "They were a present from my mother."

He felt a pang as he realized her scents were gone.

"Many never cross over," Mira continued, "because they can't resolve the thing that keeps them earthbound. Fortunately for me—and you—I needed to heal. I'm only sorry it took so long, for your sake. For me, well, time matters less."

"Why did you come to me now and not years ago when it happened?"

Mira's frown hurt him, but he didn't want or need to look away. "I wasn't ready. I was too full of self-pity to understand my own role in the events. And also—"

"Also?"

"Your daughter."

"Carrie?"

"I saw that you were losing her. And I didn't want that to happen to you, not after what losing me did to my parents."

"Is Carrie in some kind of danger?" His temples throbbed, and for the first time since leaving the hospital, he desperately wanted to be back in Hartford with his family.

"No. Carrie is smart, and she knows herself better than I did at that age. But she was drifting away, and no teenage girl wants a father who is either hiding in his garage or awkwardly lunging at her for a hug."

"Have you been watching us?"

"Only from the outside. It was a benevolent impulse, while waiting for you. I didn't want another child to grow up without her father."

Gregory hesitated. "And my father?"

"He passed."

"I don't suppose he needed any forgiveness."

"How do you feel about that?"

"I feel like I loved him. I was confused and, like you, angry. But I loved him." Gregory stopped talking, overwhelmed by a moment so long ago it felt like it happened in another lifetime. He was a little boy, maybe five or six, kicking a ball around in the backyard on Forest Road when his father came over holding a trowel, the very one Gregory still used. At first, little Greg was afraid. He was always afraid, but his father took his hand, opened his small palm and poured in a few tiny brown seeds. Next, he led him to the garden and kneeled with him in the dirt. He showed Gregory how to poke holes in the loose soil, place a seed in each, and lightly tamp.

He blinked hard and looked at Mira again. "I suppose I feel grateful."

Mira nodded and glanced at the clock. "Well, Gregory, that's our time."

"A few more minutes?"

"Our work is done. And I don't want you to waste any more of your"—she paused and smiled—"life."

He reached for her hand one last time to thank her, but when he heard the words—*thank you*—they weren't coming from his mouth. The words, like the ringing of a far-off bell, sounded in the distance. By the time he realized it was Mira who was thanking *him*, the chair was empty, and she was gone.

30

Gregory dashed into the garage. It was nearly five o'clock. He couldn't wait to get up to the house and tell Liv everything—well, almost everything—but first he wanted to cut a few flowers to bring her and stopped in the garage for his garden shears.

He had heard back from Margaret. In a single text, she said Bob died at 11:02. Carrie wanted to stay with her and Jas for the next few days, until the funeral. Maggie's terseness was as loud as a howl, one Gregory knew he deserved. He would beg her forgiveness later, but Liv was his priority now. With Petey still at camp, they had a rare night of privacy. That would leave time for a long talk, twenty-four years overdue. Freed by his own forgiveness, Gregory was finally going to be honest about the accident. Beyond that, he was ready to be the husband she had always deserved.

He was heading to the side door when he saw Liv marching down the driveway, her arms pumping furiously. She was moving like a small, sturdy tank.

"Liv!" he called, waving to her. She didn't wave back. As soon as she was closer, he saw that her teeth were clenched, and her eyes, red and glaring, were almost unrecognizable.

"How dare you!" she shouted. She raised her fists and started pounding on his forearms.

"What is going on? Gregory reached for her wrists, but she evaded his grasp and pushed behind him into the garage. Gregory followed, watching as she pivoted this way and that, scanning the detritus of the past days—glasses, dirty dishes, the crumpled blankets, his laptop cord.

"You're pathetic! You are so pathetic!"

She continued to survey the room, as if looking for something specific, and for a moment he thought she wanted the scarf. But her eyes landed on the whiskey barrel, and she lurched to grab his father's longest shovel. She yanked it out by the wooden handle, drew a quick breath, and chopped at the wall, smashing the steel blade against the old wood.

Gregory felt a flush of panic as his heart rate spiked, his body flooding with adrenaline. He wanted to stop her but couldn't be sure she wouldn't turn the tool on him.

As she lifted the shovel again, he took a step back, stumbling on his mattress. She took another swing, this time scraping the shovel across his workbench, sending nails and screws and tools clattering to the floor.

"Stop!" he yelled. "Please, Liv! I don't understand!"

She walked toward him, dragging the shovel behind her. Her face, blotchy. "How long have you been fucking her?"

"What?"

"Don't insult my intelligence." She banged the shovel blade on the floor, then made her voice high and pleading to simper in his face. "*I'm just grateful you waited for me! That we had this chance.*" She shook her head. "Seriously?"

When he realized that Liv had overheard his last exchange with Mira, he almost vomited. She must have been standing there, outside his office, the door ajar.

"I can explain! Liv, please. But put that down before something terrible happens. I'll tell you everything. It's not at all what you think."

"That's laughable, Gregory. You are going to explain leaving your dying father to be with your girlfriend, or whatever she is?"

"Oh God! No! That's not what happened!"

"When Margaret told me that you had to meet a client, I knew right away. But I sure didn't expect what I heard. Who else have you done this to? How many women have you seduced?"

"She's not a client, and she's definitely not my girlfriend. I don't have a girlfriend."

Liv's eyes looked pinched. "Then who is she?" she asked, punching every word. "Who is that woman you were talking to?"

"She's a therapist."

"Ha!" Liv's voice was thick with sarcasm. "A therapist? Really? You've resisted therapy for as long as I've known you, and now, when you need an excuse for why you ran out on your father's last minutes, you have a therapist?"

"Liv, you have to let me explain. It's so complicated."

"You have had a hundred—a thousand—chances to explain. You're out of chances."

"I just need one more, Liv. Can we please just go up to the house and talk?"

"Talk? That's what you want to do? Well then you know who you should talk to? A lawyer. You are going to need a good fucking lawyer, Dr. Gregory fucking Weber!" She lifted the shovel and banged it down hard. When the metal clanged on the concrete floor, he felt the reverberations in his body.

Gregory's heart was racing so fast it felt ready to burst out of his chest. He also knew he could lunge forward, restrain Liv's arms, and put a stop to this. Should he? He didn't think she would actually lift the shovel and slam it into him. But he didn't recognize this person. He didn't know what she was capable of.

What if she did it? What if she ended his life before he could start to live it again? God, the irony. For the first time in decades, he didn't want to die. He felt whole. He wanted to make up for lost time. He wanted to be a husband to Liv and a real father to Carrie and Petey.

And there was his wife, determined to break him, and with good reason.

"Please!" Gregory lowered his voice, this time trying to soothe her. He reached his hand out, hoping he could make his way over to her, pry the shovel from her, and defuse her resolve. "Please give me a chance, Liv." His voice was calm. "I'll talk, I'll tell you everything."

But Liv pulled away, drawing the tool handle closer to her body.

"Liv, please," he whispered. "Give me five minutes."

"It's too late," she said, her eyes locked to his. "It's over."

She brought her left palm to the smooth wooden handle. She gripped it with both hands, testing the weight and leverage. Then with the strength of a thousand tennis matches, she lifted the shovel to her shoulder and hurled it through the garage window.

31

Gregory lay on the mattress in the cool garage, scratching at the bites on his arms from the mosquitos that flew in and out of the broken window. It was the morning of his father's service, and he needed to get himself up the hill and into the house to shower and dress, avoiding any significant interaction with Liv, but he was reluctant to leave his last minutes of refuge. The way things had been going since Wednesday, he expected to be shunned at the ceremony.

Margaret had made all the arrangements without consulting him, deciding to forgo a full Catholic Mass and instead have Father Joseph do a small memorial service at DeLuca's Funeral Home at eleven that morning. Gregory had received this logistical information via a short, impersonal, unsigned email from Liv.

He understood her anger and, at first, even took some hope from it. He clung to the idea that if Liv, who had never so much as elbowed or slapped him in twenty-four years, cared enough about this supposed adultery to nearly threaten him with a shovel, then there was still some passion left in their marriage. After their blowout, he perched with his cell phone on the step of the garage and sent Liv a series of texts that alternated between acknowledgment of her anger and entreaty for her to give him a chance to explain. Liv blocked him at 10 p.m. after his seventh unanswered text, but there was still a light on in the bedroom when he went outside to relieve himself at midnight.

The next day Gregory picked a single white daisy from his garden and left it on the doorstep with a note that said, *Can I please have ten minutes of your time?* He later watched furtively from the yard when Liv came across his offering on her way out of the house. She hurled the flower toward the compost pile in the far corner of the yard and conspicuously tore up the note. She refused to look at him on her way to the trash barrel next to the garage, where she released the shredded pieces like they were burning her palm. As she was heading back to the house, Gregory called, "Liv, please?"

She kept walking.

Gregory returned to the garage and started writing down the details of his story on the yellow legal pad, hoping Liv might be more open to reading an actual letter, penitent and respectful. But when he read over the first two pages, he realized he sounded like someone suffering from delusions. Assert in writing that the ghost of a hit-and-run victim had come to him for therapy? And for "the good of his family" he met with the spirit client four times and let her show him how to release decades of psychic pain? That would be his undoing in court, professionally and paternally. He'd only be allowed to see Carrie and Petey during supervised visits in grim family lounges of a psychiatric hospital.

Mira's forgiveness therapy might have worked for her, but Gregory's earthbound relief had been short-lived, and Mira's stated objective to keep him connected to Carrie wasn't working out at all. His daughter's only response to his multiple phone calls and texts was a single text on Wednesday night: *RIP Grandpa.* No emojis and no reply to Gregory's much sweated-over follow-up text of a red broken-heart emoji.

Thursday afternoon, soon after Liv had left to pick up Petey at camp, Gregory snuck into the house, where he took a shower, microwaved two frozen burritos, and hunted around for some decent stationery. Back in his garage, he tried the last thing he could think of: he wrote Liv a short, simple note, saying how sorry he was and how much he loved her. He left it in the mailbox, which she would check when she and Petey returned home from New Hampshire. The entire six hours she was gone, Gregory held on to the possibility that his son might arrive home happy to see him. Petey, always sweet and guileless, and allergic to emotional drama, might not hold out the same judgment as Carrie and Liv. When Gregory heard Liv's car pull into the driveway, he dashed outside. Petey's bright blue eyes stared at him blankly through the passenger window, and as soon as he was out of the car, he bypassed Gregory on his way to retrieving his duffel bag from the trunk.

Gregory understood: no hug, which was age appropriate. So he attempted to engage Petey with questions about camp: "Was it fun? How were your counselors? Did you play some soccer?" But Petey's clipped one-word answers showed none of his usual warmth.

Liv, walking back up the drive from the mailbox, left as much distance between them as she could without trampling the lawn and disappeared briskly into the house without so much as a nod. Gregory didn't see his note among the bills and circulars in her hand, but unless she had left it in the box, it had to be there.

Petey continued giving short answers, but he looked so unsure about whether to fold or unfold his arms and was so skittish about eye contact that Gregory wondered if he was doing more harm than good by trying to have a whole reunion conversation during his son's first few minutes home.

"Well, you sound like you're pretty tired from that long drive. I bet you'd like to go inside and chill."

"Yeah." Petey heaved his duffel bag onto his newly broad shoulders and walked toward the house.

That's fine, Gregory thought. Petey was probably starved for electronics and a decent shower after a month in the woods. They could always talk later, maybe try the new gourmet burger place on Huron.

Gregory watched his son lope up the steps. At the top, Petey halted, then turned and looked straight down at him. "Carrie said you left when Grandpa was dying."

Gregory wanted to fall on his knees and beg for forgiveness. "Petey. I know it's hard to understand. It's also hard to explain. I'm—"

But Gregory couldn't finish the sentence. There was no way to explain to his thirteen-year-old son what had happened. Petey was kindhearted but he was also naive and rigid: he divided human behavior, especially adult behavior, into categories of good or bad. No mixed behavior allowed, and no imaginable third category.

But he didn't have to finish the sentence, because Petey, with an expression of righteous disgust, had turned his back and disappeared into the house.

Gregory still couldn't move. Since meeting Liv, he had never felt so alone. Lying there on the twin mattress in the garage, immobilized with fear, he wished Liv had slammed that shovel into him instead of the window, because that would feel less painful. After he survived today, he could slink away and leave them free of his disappointing existence. But how would he get off this mattress, let alone endure hours of grieving for his father in the company of a family that despised him?

For the hundredth time, Gregory reached for his phone and started to text Phil. If anybody could get him on his feet it was Phil, Boston's top pharma guru.

He brushed past the stream of condolence messages from his canceled clients to get back to Phil's text: *Sorry about everything. Let me know how I can help. P.*

He hovered his finger over the text box, but once again Gregory stopped himself. His career was all he had left in the world, and if Phil continued to question Gregory's stability and ethics, then his livelihood could vanish, too. Over the years Gregory had seen Phil put patient safety and sanctity before everything else. Not once had Gregory seen him waver on that.

He could never tell Phil what he'd done without forcing Phil to write him up.

Gregory dropped the phone and stared through the empty window at the dull morning sky. No wood, no glass, no dust, and no eyes. Only relentless gray clouds. Just two days ago, he felt better about life than he had in thirty years. He couldn't wait to leave the garage and move back into the house again, restart his life with Liv, and forge connections with Carrie and Petey strong enough to survive any teenage mistake or misfortune. Gregory tightened his jaw. This day was going to be awful. He practiced the advice he gave clients, telling himself, *Just get through it. Just get through today.*

He slowly rose, slipped on his work boots, and shuffled over to the broken window. He stood in the shattered glass and felt the cool dampness inside the gray light. He inhaled the soft smell of cedar and exhaled slowly. Then he clasped his hands in prayer and said, "Help me, Mira. Please help me."

Ten minutes later, lingering on the bedroom threshold, Gregory heard Liv showering behind the closed door of their bathroom. He walked briskly to his bedroom closet and grabbed his dark gray suit, a blue shirt, his marigold tie, and black brogues. He was about to slip away unseen, when he paused, unable to resist scanning the room. The white duvet was heaped at the foot of their king-size bed, and the top sheet, pulled completely over to Liv's side, was twisted loosely around itself. Gregory dropped his funeral clothes on the upholstered bench and took the time to untangle the sheet and shake it into place. He yanked up the duvet and smoothed it over the bed, pausing several times to feel the cool cloth under the brush of his calloused palms. He was about to pull the duvet over Liv's pillow, when he noticed the indent her head had made. He had to stop and steady himself.

He turned toward the bathroom door and listened— the shower was still running. Swiftly he lowered his nose into the pillow and buried his face in the softness. There she was in the layers of scents: lavender oil and the floral fragrance of her white cotton nightgown. What else? When he thought more about Liv, he could conjure the smell of chlorine and sweat on her skin and the coffee she sipped as she stood at the kitchen island gazing out at the yard. He kept inhaling until he was dizzy, trying to find his wife's complexity and store it inside him, in case.

In case.

He buried his head deeper in the pillow and closed his mind on the unthinkable.

He heard the shower turn off from far away. He couldn't waste another minute.

Gregory hurried to the bathroom door and tapped lightly. The door swung open in a whoosh of rose-scented steam, and Liv was standing there with one towel wrapped around her hair and another tucked in above her chest. He ached to run a finger along the tan lines left by her bathing suit.

"Oh. I thought it was Petey," she said and shut the door in his face.

Gregory knocked a second time and called her name. Liv's response was the sharp click of the lock. Then she turned on the radio.

He pressed his forehead against the glossy painted wood. "Five minutes, Liv? That's all I need to explain. You don't even have to open the door."

"There is nothing to say that can't be handled by our lawyers."

"Liv, it's my dad's service today."

"And I'm glad you've decided to set a good example for the children by attending. Now please get dressed and leave the house."

He paused and placed his palms on the door. "What happened on Wednesday has to do with something I did when I was seventeen. A horrible, horrible mistake I made."

Liv scoffed derisively. "Seventeen? Really? You're blaming an affair with a patient on a mistake you made as a teenager? Congratulations, Dr. Weber. You've switched categories, from pathetic and unethical to sociopathic."

Just as Gregory blurted out his worst sin, the hair dryer blasted on and engulfed his words. He tried again, this time shouting what he'd been afraid to say to another living soul. "I killed someone, but I couldn't tell you. I was too scared. But I'm ready to tell you everything now. Please, Liv!"

He waited.

Liv turned up the radio so loudly the door vibrated under his fingers and forehead.

32

Gregory sat in his car outside of the funeral home, parked as far as possible from Margaret and Jas. He didn't want any part of the sympathetic milling about and paying of respects. He could probably endure Maggie's hostility and Jas's pity and Liv's cold indifference, but he couldn't face Carrie's and Petey's rejection. He couldn't stand them watching him accept teary hugs and long handclasps while thinking him a monster for leaving his own father's deathbed.

He would take his place in the ceremony, but if he went in too soon, he'd have to look his father's mourners in the eye and say, *Thank you for coming; he had a good life, was a hardworking man and an excellent father*, while knowing his own family life would crumble as soon as he left the service. While Liv and the kids might feel even more united with Margaret and Jas, the solidity of their connection would also serve to wall him out.

Gregory had settled his numb gaze on the sickly privet hedge that bordered the parking lot, when a large black Mercedes turned in too fast and parked one space away.

Gregory stiffened; his tolerable blankness driven out by a flush of panic.

The email from Liv said the service was going to be small, mostly family. But to Liv, Phil practically was family, so of course she would want him there. Who else from his life was going to witness the spectacle of Gregory being shunned at his own father's memorial service?

Phil chirped his car lock and limped over, one hand gripping his arthritic left hip. Gregory shoved open the door and stood with his hands by his side, lost.

Without saying a word, Phil wrapped his huge arms around him in a bear hug. Gregory let out a sob against Phil's shoulder, marveling at how fortifying Phil's hug felt, at how he could transfer his acknowledgment of pain with the strong muscles of his arms and chest.

"I'm sorry about everything," Phil said, after he released him. "So sorry."

"Did Liv tell you about—?"

"She did," Phil said. "And all I can say is, I've been there. It's brutal, but you'll get through it."

"It's not what she thinks. What happened is too strange to explain."

Phil cocked his head as if he wasn't convinced. "Whatever it is, or was, all I can tell you is that it's going to get worse before it gets better. Take it from an expert at screwing up relationships."

"And the kids," Gregory looked up at the cloudy sky. His stomach hurt, and his head ached, and all he wanted to do was hold Liv in his arms. He couldn't get that wish—as futile as it was—out of his mind. He didn't know how much he could miss her, the vastness of it.

"One thing at a time, my friend. One thing at a time." Phil put a hand on Gregory's back and gently guided him toward the canopy-covered entrance.

They walked together down the maroon-carpeted hallway and turned into the room with the name Robert James Weber printed on a small gold wall plaque. There was an open memorial book for signing names and a basket of prayer cards with a familiar black-and-white photo of his father when he was a handsome, thick-haired man in his forties. Gregory took one of the cards and studied the picture closely. For the first time, he saw his own eyes in his father's. The sadness. The resignation. On the back there was a poem that Margaret must have chosen. He slipped the card into his jacket pocket without reading it.

Inside the windowless room, three rows of wooden folding chairs faced an open casket upholstered in ivory-colored satin. He averted his gaze. Off to the right, Margaret and Jas were speaking with the funeral director. In the front row, Father Joseph, who used to bring communion to Gregory's father in the nursing home, sat in his black vestments, a Bible open on his lap.

When Jas caught Gregory's eye, he looked at her pleadingly, believing she was his one chance to be heard. But she sniffed the air and swiveled her head away. With a last encouraging pat on Gregory's shoulder, Phil took a seat in the back row. Gregory forced himself to walk to the front of the room and kneel on the low padded bench beside the casket. As he studied his father's pallid skin, stuffed with cotton and preserved by formaldehyde, he was surprised by Margaret's choice of presentation. He was expecting a more environmentally friendly option, but there was his father embalmed and enlivened with lipstick and rouge, lying in repose in a shiny maple casket. Bob's hands, which gripped a strand of silver rosary beads, looked bigger and healthier than they had when he was alive—the age spots erased. Gregory wanted to put his own hands over them to experience the last touch of his father's skin, but he stopped himself, knowing he was being not just watched but scrutinized.

Gregory murmured the Lord's Prayer to himself as best as he could remember it, but the *trespass against us* part always tripped him up, so he trailed off without finishing, except for a hasty *deliver us from evil. Amen.* When he stood again, he saw that Liv's father and his second wife were standing behind him, waiting to pay their respects. He nodded carefully at them, but Tom and Toby looked right past, notifying their errant son-in-law that his trespasses had not been set aside for this event. Gregory took a seat in the middle of the front row—it was his father's funeral, after all—and within minutes the chairs around him began to fill. Liv's brother, Leland, arrived with his six-foot-tall wife, Ingrid. Then came Gregory's two older cousins, Paul and Eric, the only children of Bob's eldest brother, who had passed away from cancer years ago. There was also a woman who was a neighbor on Forest Road but whose name Gregory couldn't remember and didn't care to.

Liv entered in a gray silk dress, followed by Carrie, in the black sundress Gregory had bought her at the mall the weekend before, and Petey, who was wearing a navy-blue suit, slightly strained on a body that looked like it had grown another few inches at camp. They sat in the front row next to Margaret and Jas, while the two seats to Gregory's left remained empty.

Through the quiet of the room, Gregory heard the chiming sound of Mira's bracelets. He looked over, expecting to see her sitting in the chair next to him. But it was Liv. She was wearing the bracelets. Maybe it was a sign—that Mira was still there, watching over him.

Just after eleven, Father Joseph stood and went to the raised podium beside the casket. He welcomed everyone to the service for "our dearly departed brother Robert James, a man who lived and died with Christ." Gregory tried to listen, but he could feel the eyes on his back, the judgment. There he was, Dr. Gregory Weber, a respected psychologist, the son of the departed who, as most people in that room believed, had fled his own father's deathbed to have sex with one of his clients.

The elderly priest droned on about how Robert, who lived a life blessed by God, would be dearly missed by his beloved children, Margaret and Gregory. When Father Joseph said his name, Gregory thought he heard Margaret snort. There were several generic platitudes about Bob's Catholic faith, culminating in the right to rest in eternal life with God. *Amen.*

Wearing a dark-green pantsuit, Margaret stood up to press Father Joseph's hands and bow her head, adorned with a piece of black lace. At the podium, after thanking everyone for taking the time to join her family, Margaret carried on as if all were normal. She began what was essentially a review of their father's life, explaining how Bob was born in 1935, in the middle of the Great Depression, and grew up on a farm in Connecticut with his two now-deceased older brothers, Emil and Albert. She talked about how Bob's parents, who emigrated from Germany and had worked hard to build a middle-class life, lost everything in the Depression, creating a legacy of extreme financial caution. As a result, their father knew how to pinch his pennies, but he also learned to value the small things, like the joy he took from gardening, always producing a yard bursting with vegetables to feed his family. She talked about her beloved mother—Bob's devoted wife, Carol—who had died nine years earlier, and how her father never fully recovered from that loss. She added that his last few years in Pleasant Springs Nursing Home were lovely and comfortable, thanks to his caregivers, who looked after Bob with such kindness.

With her biography of their father concluded, Margaret continued to ramble. Always better visually than verbally, she never seemed to find the point of her stream-of-consciousness eulogizing, yet she managed to excise Gregory from every burnished memory, not once mentioning his name and acting as if she were an only child. Finally, after what felt like an eternity, she turned to the casket, blew a kiss, and said, "I love you, Dad."

Before Margaret sat down, she nodded at Carrie who rose to her feet clutching the cloth-covered journal Jas had given her.

Carrie walked to the podium where she stood awkwardly, one hip jutting out. In a shaky voice, she said, "This is a poem I wrote for my grandpa. It's called 'Taste This Sweetness.'" She cleared her throat and began reading from the open book.

> *The flickering line goes flat, and all that you knew and forgot*
> *is stored inside and can't be shared.*
> *What is locked in the safe box of your soul?*
> *A secret you can never tell?*
> *You will remember the beehouse you showed me.*
> *You broke off a wonder of waxy cells dripping gold*
> *and said, "See how God provides."*

Carrie lowered her head and walked shyly back to her seat. Gregory wanted to catch his daughter's eyes—his now filled with tears—to tell her how beautiful her poem was. And he wanted to ask her about that line. What was it she had said about secrets? The safe box of the soul? Liv gave Carrie a squeeze, while Petey leaned over to poke her knee. Watching his daughter try to suppress a smile, Gregory ached with a fatherly pride.

He started to panic. If he didn't find a bridge back to his family, he would never be able to tell his daughter how proud he was of her in that moment. Nor would he ever be able to help Petey—prone, like Gregory, to keeping his feelings inside—with the specific paternal challenge of how to be a good man. He thought of Petey's harsh, judging look on the stairs the day before and feared that his son might be lost to him. Carrie, too, might never talk to him again, and all Gregory would have with her was that last drive to Connecticut. He couldn't help but wonder if that line in her poem was a message to him.

He reached into his jacket pocket for the tissues that he had tucked in there earlier. With the clump of tissues, he also withdrew the memorial card. He saw that it was Carrie's poem printed on the back. He scanned it for the lines she seemed to speak straight to him: *What is locked in the safe box of your soul? A secret you can never tell?*

Gregory sat back, clutching the card. Maybe Carrie had left a window cracked for him to share his truth someday. But how long would it stay open? Liv was ready for divorce court, where the false story of his affair would get distorted and used against him. He'd lose his professional license and his ability to practice the career he loved. Far worse—the only thing that mattered anymore—he'd spend the rest of his life without Carrie, or Petey, or Liv. He tried to wipe the tears away, but he couldn't keep up, and soon the room was a dark blur.

Carrie's voice kept coming back to him: *A secret you can never tell?*

Margaret returned to the podium again, and Gregory knew the service was nearly finished.

He slowly rose to his feet and began walking toward his sister. With his back to the room, Gregory whispered to Margaret, his voice softly modulated, "I'm going to say a few words."

She glared at him.

Gregory stared back.

After seeming to weigh the risk of letting him speak versus the spectacle of a sibling brawl beside their father's casket, Margaret took a single step back and ceded him the podium. Before retreating to her chair, she squared her shoulders and leaned close enough to put her mouth to his ear. "If you say one bad thing about Dad," she whispered, "I will come up here and shove a Bible up your ass."

Gregory could feel the heat coming off her even in the overly air-conditioned room. From the corner of his eye, he saw Liv adjusting Petey's shirt collar, refusing to look up at him. He was sure she wanted to grab the kids and flee, but she was too polite to add to the tension that he had already caused.

Gregory straightened his tie and smoothed down his lapels. He reached into his pocket and fingered the now dry marigold blossom he had tucked there that morning. Then he began.

"The first thing I want to say is thank you to my sister, Margaret, for arranging this service and to all of you for coming here to honor my father, Robert James Weber. I know we are here today to remember Bob, but in order to speak honestly about my father, I need to tell you something that I did when I was seventeen, something that has informed *my* life. Although it's too late to tell my dad, I am hoping that if he could hear me, he'd know I was finally trying to do the right thing. This is something I have never said aloud to any human being."

Gregory gripped the podium and faced the mourners. He spoke slowly, tasting the bitter novelty of every word. "It was June 20, 1989, and the Sox were playing the Rangers in Boston. My best friend, Joey, had two tickets to the game, one of which he gave to me. I'd just bought a car and was going to drive us to Fenway Park.

"On the way, I drank a beer. We had more to drink at the game, and even more on our way out of Boston late that night."

He didn't dare look at Margaret to see if she remembered going to the liquor store for him that afternoon or the lie he had told her as she handed him the bag.

"At about eleven o'clock, when I said I was too drunk to drive, I made Joey take over. I was afraid of what my father would say if we came home after curfew."

The room grew more still, uncomfortable. Gregory looked up at the low, bland ceiling and caught his breath before continuing.

"The next thing I knew, Joey and I were arguing over which road to take." Reflexively, he began to wince at the memory, but for the first time he was not afraid. He felt heavy with remorse but not afraid.

Gregory did his best to keep his voice from shaking. "There was a woman coming toward us on a bicycle. We didn't know she was there until we saw her body thud against the hood of the car. It was the worst moment of my life and close to the last moment of hers."

He was crying, but he didn't wipe away the tears.

"I realize I could say that Joey hit her, but it was my car. I was too drunk to drive, and I made Joey get behind the wheel. *We* hit her. *We* killed her. I am just as guilty as the driver."

No one moved. Two undertakers in black suits stood motionless in the doorway.

"After we hit her, we panicked. Like the little cowards we were, we drove away, because we didn't want to get caught. It was our lowest moment, and we failed the most basic test of human compassion: stopping to help."

When he gazed out at the room full of people, everyone sat perfectly still, watching him. Liv was perched on the edge of her chair with her hands twisted in her lap, her face blanched. Carrie and Petey sat upright, their eyes wide. In the back row, Phil's expression was inscrutable, not his usual all-knowing-doctor face.

"Later, I convinced Joey to make a pact to never tell anyone, to never find out anything about the accident," Gregory continued. "That way we could sound oblivious if anyone tried to question us. And strangely, we didn't get questioned. There weren't surveillance cameras back then. No photos of my license plate. No one ever traced my car. We kept our secret, but Joey couldn't stand the pain of what we had done. He died by suicide three years later."

Gregory paused to say a silent prayer for Joey's family.

"Suicide was not the solution—it never is—but neither was living with my sin, my secret. It prevented me from being able to function in relationships in a normal way, which hurt the people I tried so hard to love."

Gregory looked at Jas and Margaret, now clutching each other's forearms, and Liv, who had one hand pressed to her mouth. When he saw Petey's face and Carrie's wet eyes, he swallowed back his fear and continued.

"This is the part where Bob Weber comes in. If I had been more like Bob Weber, I would have had the strength to keep the keys out of the ignition until we sobered up, and a brilliant young woman would not have died that day. Or if I had had Bob's honesty, I would have told someone, no matter how hard it was. I would have paid for my crime and atoned openly. But that's not what I did.

"When we lost Joey, I thought about telling the truth. But I didn't, for fear of hurting his parents, who had already suffered so much. As a parent now, I think it would have been better for them to know. They may have attributed his suicide to something they had said or done, and that kind of doubt will torture you far longer than even the most painful truth. But I recoiled from all my chances."

Gregory risked another glance at his family, three strong and distinct, yet interconnected, people. How much had his lie stopped him from perceiving their openness to him all these years?

"I also regret to admit that when I was young, I thought I had gotten away with it. But of course, I hadn't. There is no getting away with that kind of crime. Not in your heart, or your conscience. I have been punished every day of my life since that night. And everyone who is here today out of love for my father, and who has known me since, has also been punished by my lie."

He looked at Margaret. "My sister has borne the brunt of my concealment longer than anyone. In addition to coping with my lack of emotional availability, she has shown an endless amount of love to our parents without the support of her brother by her side. And I am deeply sorry that was put on you, Maggie. That wasn't fair. Despite my behavior, you and Jas have been the most wonderful aunts to Petey and Carrie, something I can't thank you enough for."

Margaret lifted a hand to her chest and shut her eyes. Jas remained closed off, with her body turned away from him.

"Because this ceremony might be my last opportunity, I also need to apologize to my wife and children, whom I have loved more than anything in my life. I was in graduate school when I met Olivia Stimson. She was unlike anyone I had ever known: strong and smart and beautiful, and unconditionally loyal. I knew instantly she was the love of my life. She still is. But I made the devastating mistake of never telling her what I had done. Instead, I carried my lie of omission into our marriage, and it poisoned our family. Liv, who has been a loving and devoted partner in every way, has endured unnecessary pain because of my cowardice, and she has been deprived of having the husband she deserves.

"As a father, I've been inconsistently attentive to Carrie and Petey, relying too much on them to intuit the profound love and admiration I have for them, without showing it in everyday moments. My secret has built a wall around me and made me wary of talking to my kids openly, honestly, the way a father needs to, especially as they become young adults, for fear of somehow contaminating them with my self-loathing. Carrie and Petey believe I'm absent because I'm a workaholic, heroically dedicated to my clients, when really, I've just been hiding."

He looked at his family. Liv's face was pale, her mouth slightly parted. Petey's head was bent into his lap, while Carrie was now leaning forward, listening hard. He knew that he was co-opting his father's funeral, making the day about him and his mistakes, but he didn't know if he'd get another chance to tell everyone, all at once, what he'd done. It was his father's voice that encouraged him to keep going.

"And that's how I lived for almost thirty years, until something happened a few weeks ago when someone—a psychiatrist, a woman—came into my office and claimed the last open appointment. Quickly and uncannily, she alerted me to what I was losing by living so furtively and how my coping mechanism wasn't viable. Despite being blessed with a wonderful family, I had hobbled them, and also myself, by allowing my festering wound to control me.

"And in all the wrong ways, I blamed my father for that. I told myself, *If he hadn't been so strict, if he hadn't been so judgmental, so black and white, I would have come forward.* But that's not true. The truth is that my father died a broken, but honest, man, and I know if he had been conscious on his deathbed and I had said to him, *I have a choice, Dad, I can stay here in your final hour, or I can go correct my lie*, he would have ordered me to go. So that's what I tried to do on Wednesday. I met with the psychiatrist, named Dr. Patel, who came to my office and helped me work through my fear and shame. Then she left me with these words: *The real work happens in the real world.* Which is why I'm telling you this.

"I regret that through my choices, I've deprived Margaret of a supportive brother and Liv, Carrie, and Petey of a functioning family. But I have another regret, and that is how I treated my father. He was stern and overly strict at times, and he made plenty of his own mistakes, as we all do. But I didn't have to blame him for mine. I somehow thought that if I weren't afraid of my father, I would have told somebody what I'd done. But the truth is, I wouldn't have, and only now that he's gone can I see that.

"Bob Weber was a tough man who was raised in tough times, as Maggie just shared. That is true. But he was determined to be a husband and a father who provided for his family and made their lives comfortable, and he hated that he never quite achieved the peak of that goal. Money was always a worry in our house. I think he felt ashamed about that, because he was working so hard for such a modest reward, and his guilt sometimes made him act irrationally, even cruelly. I mistakenly thought he resented me because I cost money and I wanted things that cost money. But it wasn't about me, which is something I tell my clients all the time, too, so you'd think I would have caught on sooner."

Gregory looked over at his father's casket and lowered his head. He paused to consider precisely what he wanted to say. After a moment, he began slowly. "It's too late for me to tell my dad how much better I understand him and the lessons he tried to teach me now, and it's too late for me to give back the years I failed to be the man I should have been. But it's not too late for me to embrace and embody the best parts of Bob Weber's legacy. I feel lucky to have this chance."

Gregory turned forward again. He tried to look around the room, but he couldn't see clearly through his tears. He spoke anyway. "From now on, I'm going to do my best to live with strength and honesty, in all ways, with everyone—the way my father would have wanted me to. I thank you for coming here today to honor and remember Bob. And thank you—all of you—for helping me, by bearing witness to my promise."

Gregory left the podium and began to make his way down the aisle, trembling as he navigated past the rows of chairs. His plan was to flee before he had to face anyone, but he heard footsteps behind him. Someone grabbed him by the arm. At first he didn't recognize Fitz, who was wearing a suit instead of scrubs. But Fitz pulled him in with strong, comforting arms, until Gregory found the strength to hug back.

When Fitz released him, he said, "Mr. Bob lives on in you and Maggie and in those great kids."

Gregory nodded and thanked him for making his father's last years so good and safe.

On his dash to the hallway, Gregory noticed Phil bent over his thighs in the back row, his head in his hands. Phil had never met Bob, but sometimes grief waits for proxy outlets. Gregory didn't stop to talk to Phil to find out. He didn't want Liv or the kids to feel obliged to comfort him or ask questions that he'd have to answer honestly but was too emotionally depleted to handle.

Gregory gained the privacy of his car and turned on the ignition. He wanted to drive without thinking. He wanted to be this new Gregory, whoever he was. But just as he put the car into drive, a text came in, and he had to look, in case it was from a client.

We need to talk.

It was from Phil.

33

Phil lumbered into the garage, his face stricken, his eyes unable to focus. He was wearing his funeral trousers and capped shoes, but he'd left his tie and jacket in the car. His sleeves were rolled up above his strong hairy forearms, the left one cinched by his gold watch.

"Thanks for letting me come now," Phil said.

"Of course," Gregory said. What else could he have done? When he tried to demur, Phil insisted it was urgent.

Phil scanned the jumble of broken glass and tools still scattered across the floor, but he said nothing. When he didn't see another beach chair, he carefully sat down on the edge of Gregory's mattress and tried to make himself comfortable, holding one leg bent in at the knee and letting the other stick out straight.

"Here! Take the chair," Gregory said. He started to stand even though he wasn't sure the cheap aluminum frame would support Phil's weight.

But Phil waved him off and flopped back on the mattress, splaying his polished wood heels on the concrete floor. He closed his eyes and ran his fingers through his unkempt hair. It was an odd posture, but Phil didn't seem to care. After exhaling loudly, he said, "You ready for this?"

Gregory steeled himself. Maybe all he had to do was listen. "Sure."

"It was the spring semester of '89, and I was asked to guest lecture about drug trials to a class of residents at Harvard Med. I had just given my usual spiel and was getting ready to head out, when this young resident comes up to the front of the room." He paused, as if the words were stuck. "Mira Patel."

Gregory's whole body stiffened. His Mira?

"She was gorgeous. That dark hair. Those smart brown eyes that seemed to know more about you than you were ever going to tell. One look and I was besotted, head-over-heels crazy about this woman I didn't even know. I still can't explain it. Kathy and I had only been married about a year, and we had Grace on the way. I thought I was happy in my marriage, but then I met Mira. That's a pretty lousy thing to say, but I'm being truthful here about something I've never told anyone." Phil looked across the garage at Gregory. "You set the truth bar pretty damn high today."

Gregory squirmed and tried to settle himself, thinking about how Mira had the same effect on him. He tried to slow his breathing. He couldn't have another panic attack. Not now.

Phil didn't even notice.

"Anyway," Phil continued, "Mira asked some nuanced question about my lecture, but I can't remember exactly what it was, something about MAO inhibitors. She was so assertive, so intelligent. Just in that short exchange, I could see the mind at work behind those eyes. After I answered her question, she thanked me, gave me a big gracious smile, and turned away. But before she could go, I asked her to have lunch.

"There's my pregnant wife at home, and here I am setting out to seduce this young woman, a student no less, who was on her way to becoming a brilliant doctor. But she said yes, so that's how I justified it, which is its own brand of disgusting.

"Over lunch she told me about her parents. According to the doctor, her mother couldn't have children, so her first husband divorced her. But she remarried, and the Patels moved to the States and miraculously got pregnant with Mira. She was their only child, raised with enormous love. And she turned out to be a science whiz. When she went to med school and then got accepted to Harvard's residency program, they were proud beyond words."

Phil paused; maybe he was crying. Gregory was struggling to control his own responses. He tried to keep himself from going over to Phil, looking him in the eye, and asking him to swear on his life that he wasn't making it up. Instead, he sat in his chair and took one belly breath after another, while Phil continued, oblivious.

"At that lunch I didn't want to tell Mira I was married and had a baby on the way, but she kept probing for my story, getting me to open up. She was so damn good at finding the thing you were trying to blunt, then sharpening it and handing it back to you. It was brutal but also a thing of beauty.

"After our lunch, I walked her across Harvard Yard to where she had parked her bike, an old blue Raleigh racer. Before we said goodbye, I asked if I could see her again. She tilted her head at me, and I thought she was going to say no. I saw her struggling to answer. So when she said yes, I knew she felt what I felt—guilt mixed with attraction."

"Wait, I need a minute, Phil." Gregory leapt from the chair and walked over to his broken window. He shoved his hands in his pockets to try and keep them from trembling. Could he be making this up? He turned to Phil who was staring at the ceiling so intently that Gregory followed his gaze to the cedar beams. Phil could be a prankster in the office, but he wasn't callous. Which meant Phil knew Mira. Phil knew the woman Gregory had killed.

Gregory would have preferred to stand, but he sat back down in his chair. He rocked his torso back and forth, rubbing his slick palms on his thighs, over and over. Between the recent Boston heat wave and his physical reaction to Phil's story, Gregory thought he might dissolve in sweat.

"You okay?" Phil asked.

Gregory made himself sit back. He wiped his palms on his suit trousers one last time and clasped his hands together. "I don't know."

Phil drew a breath and exhaled in a low moan, then began again, his voice more vigorous, as if he were determined to get the whole story out before the retelling destroyed him. "Mira was entrenched in a tough residency and doing extra lab work at the Brigham, but we always made time to see each other. That went on for a couple of months, me feeling more guilty by the day, but not enough to stop myself. Kathy was having the kind of pregnancy that makes a woman less interested in sex, not more, so it was easy for me to compartmentalize the physical stuff. Then there was this one Tuesday night that Mira was performing in a solstice concert at the Tremont Temple downtown, and I wanted to go. Kathy wasn't feeling well, and as I kissed her goodbye, I promised myself I would end it with Mira that night. I had to. Grace was due in five weeks.

"I hopped on my mountain bike and rode to the concert. I don't know how anyone could have noticed any other performer. Everyone was dressed in these bright colors, but there was Mira, radiant beyond words in an orange dress. After the concert, Mira promised to meet her friends at the Parker House for drinks, but she found me in the back row, and we left together. No one saw us. As we walked over to where she had locked her bike, she said she was chilly." He smiled at the memory. "She was always chilly but never seemed to have a coat. If I had one, I would have given it to her, but I didn't. So I told her to wait a minute and ran to where I saw the lights still on in this little boutique across the park. When I knocked on the door, the owner signaled they were closed, but I did some funny dance to plead my case, and she let me in. I saw a pile of oversized scarves, mostly dull colors except for, well, you know.

"When I returned to Mira, I draped the scarf around her shoulders. She pulled me against her and wrapped me in it, too. It was the first time I told her I loved her, and she said it back to me. I can still hear the sadness in her voice.

"I told her that I had to go home, and she nodded. She understood. But then she asked for a little more time to say goodbye. Despite every instinct that told me to say no, to just ride my bike home, I agreed."

Gregory shook his head, even as Phil kept talking. Gregory wanted to stop him, as if in doing so he could also stop time, stop Mira from dying. But Phil carried on, speaking words he had likely never said out loud to anyone.

Gregory understood that need.

"We got on our bikes and started riding to my office, which back then was the third room in our suite on Blesdow Street. Mira started pedaling fast, the pink scarf blowing behind her like a superhero cape. It became a game where she disappeared around one corner after another, and I tried to catch up with her. I was laughing and fumbling with the gears on my bike, falling farther behind when I heard the screech of tires, then a thud. The most sickening feeling came over me. It took forever to reach her, and I didn't even realize when the car—your car—had sped past me that I should pay attention to it. When I finally got there, she was lying in the street, her head thrown back and her eyes—God help me, those eyes." Phil paused and put his hand on his chest. "I looked down the street for the car, but it was gone. As much as I wanted to find that driver and murder him with my bare hands, I had to stay with Mira."

Gregory tried not to shift in his chair. It wouldn't be inconceivable that Phil was still looking for revenge. But then he kept talking. And it became clear that this confession wasn't about revenge. It was a purging. Gregory steadied himself and listened, just as Mira had listened to him.

"Somebody called 911, and I waited until the ambulance came, at which point the paramedics pushed me away. They put Mira on a stretcher and loaded her body into the ambulance, and I never saw her again. I collected the scarf that had flown into the street, but I never said goodbye. I never came forward to say what had happened, because I knew it would blow up my family life and destroy my career. I was torn between seeking justice and my own self-interest. And to what end? I didn't think Mira would even want me to. She certainly didn't want me telling her parents she was having an affair with a married doctor. So I did nothing except write them a condolence letter extolling her brilliance.

"But I held on to that scarf, the only thing I have left of Mira. I've kept it in a drawer in the extra office since that night. At first, I hoped—prayed, actually, which is a lot for an agnostic—for the person who hit her to be caught and punished. For a while, I fantasized about doing that myself. I was overcome with rage that slowly transmuted into shame. But at some point, I realized I was just as guilty. And, over the years, I began to wonder about what part her identity played in all of this. Did the fact that she was a woman—an Indian woman at that—have something to do with a lack of interest in bringing the person who killed her to justice? Or maybe, like you said, there was just simply nothing that could be done."

Phil rolled onto his side and faced the wall. "It's all my fault. If I hadn't betrayed my own damn ethics, Mira never would have died."

Gregory sat still, his chest pounding. He was so dizzy he could barely see. Then the dizziness gave way to nausea. He gripped his stomach until the feeling passed, then he sat up again and looked around for something to wipe the sweat away. He found a dirty cotton sock on the floor and drew it across his eyes, his forehead, the back of his neck. He blinked at Phil whose chin was pressed against his chest.

Gregory took a moment to collect his thoughts, then chose his words cautiously. "Why did you come to my house that Wednesday, after we'd talked in the office—"

"I thought that you were up to something," Phil said, "because I felt like Mira was there, in the office. I went out to the waiting room and had this sense of her. I could hear the jingle of these bracelets she always wore. It was like I'd seen a ghost." Phil drew in his legs and curled into a bulky ball.

Gregory paused, unsure if he should say it. But couldn't Phil handle anything? And didn't he need to know the full story, too? "You did," Gregory said, after a moment. "See a ghost."

Phil exhaled loudly and looked up at Gregory. His eyes narrowed. His shook his head back and forth. "No. No."

"That night you went into my office? What were you looking for?"

Phil rubbed his eyes. "This is—no. This doesn't make sense."

"Just tell me why you went in."

"When I saw you with the scarf, I knew it was hers," Phil answered slowly, as if systematically walking himself through the sequence of events. "Then I went to my old office and realized it was gone. I started to get paranoid, wondering if you knew something. But I'm the only one with a key, so it didn't make sense. But I didn't know who else could have taken it out, or why you would have."

Phil licked his lips and swallowed. "After she died, I could never let go of that office. It was the only place we ever made love. For months afterward, I'd go in there and write her letters, begging her to forgive me. As if."

"And that Saturday night when you slept there?"

"I had just been to her grave. I hadn't gone in years, but something compelled me. I brought flowers. I couldn't go home, so I went to the office for the weekend and hit the bottle pretty hard. I got so obsessed with getting the scarf back that I finally went into your office and found it in the bottom drawer. I thought about saying something to you—I don't even know what—but when I heard from Liv about your dad, I just couldn't give you any more trouble. At the same time, I didn't know what the hell kind of tricks you were up to with that scarf."

"It wasn't a trick, Phil. Mira took the scarf from your locked office and left it in mine."

Phil shuddered and sank deeper into the mattress. "No. No, Gregory."

After several minutes in which neither man spoke, Gregory staggered to his feet. It was all too much for him to process, so he did what he had become an expert at in his twenty years as a psychologist. He sublimated his own feelings and focused on the client.

He walked over to the bag of bone meal and dug down to the bottom where he found the mason jar he had stashed there the week before. With some fumbling, he managed to remove the key and unlock the padlock on the toolbox. He opened the lid and took out the sealed bag with the scarf. He went to Phil and squatted on the floor beside him. He gently slid the scarf from the bag and tucked it into Phil's large hands. Phil clutched it to his face.

"Before today," Gregory said, "I thought I'd be able to convince Liv of what really happened in my office on Wednesday. Redeem myself. But I'm not sure I should ever have hoped for that. I want to believe Mira's spirit stayed here so we could all forgive ourselves. Me, Mira, and now you. I want you to believe that, too. That's what she would want: forgive yourself, live your life, do your work, and love your family. If you can't do it for yourself, then you've got to do it in honor of Mira's memory."

Phil turned to Gregory, his bloodshot eyes imploring. "If what you're saying is the truth, then why didn't she come to me, too?"

Gregory took a moment. He'd been wondering the same thing as Phil had been talking, but now he understood. "Probably because the work had to be done with me," he said. "It was my actions that killed her. She needed me to forgive myself before she could forgive herself. I don't think she could have moved on if I'd remained stuck." Gregory paused. "She would have been a great clinician."

"You're right about that," Phil said.

"Or maybe it's because she never stopped being in love with you. Just as you're still a little bit in love with her. And we both know you can't be an effective therapist when your head is clouded with that kind of love. Who knows how you would have reacted. You might have tried to take ownership of her pain."

Gregory sat back on the floor. The concrete was cool beneath him. "She was so smart. She knew what she had to do. For all of us."

Phil's mouth twisted as he considered this. He managed the slightest nod. "Have you been able to forgive yourself?"

Gregory sat still and let himself be in his body, a test. He half laughed, still unable to believe that the guilt had lifted. The electric cable of fear had been unplugged from his chest. "I believe I have, Phil. I think I'll be able to move on." He paused. "Now only one thing matters. But I'm going to need your help."

34

Liv and Gregory met in the driveway by his car. They rode the five minutes to Mount Auburn Cemetery in silence, Liv beside him in the passenger seat in a floral skirt and a yellow tank top, the bright color highlighting her fatigue. Her blue eyes were rimmed with red. Her hair was pulled back in a ponytail, a style she seldom wore anymore. She kept tucking stray hairs behind her ears, only to have them come loose again. When he glanced over to thank her for being open to this, he saw her left hand was bare. No rings.

Gregory turned back to the road and said nothing. With his eyes trained straight ahead, he now had to consider the worst possibility: that it was already too late.

Instead of parking on the side street and crawling through the broken fence, Gregory pulled into the grand Egyptian revival entrance gate and slipped into an open spot in the small asphalt strip.

They had only had three conversations since the memorial service. There was a brief exchange on Saturday evening after Gregory summoned the courage to call her and ask if they could meet in person to talk. Liv spoke kindly to him, but also cautiously, her voice strained. She said she was exhausted and wanted more time to process everything that had happened. The words *I need a few days* made him nervous.

The second time was at ten o'clock that same night. She called back to say she had just talked with Phil for almost two hours. "A spirit?" she said. "Are you out of your mind? What is going on with you two?"

The third conversation was five minutes after that. She called again and agreed to the outing.

It was a hot Sunday afternoon at the end of July. Except for a few walkers and some birders with wide-brimmed hats and binoculars earnestly dangling from their necks, the cemetery was mostly empty, giving off that expansive feeling of time drifting backward and forward.

As soon as Gregory stepped out of the car, his face beaded with sweat. The air was so thick, he almost suggested they sit in the air-conditioned car to have their conversation, but they weren't there just to talk. He had to show her, too.

As Gregory struggled to get his bearings from a map on the side of the Visitor's Center, Liv wandered to the edge of the parking lot and stood in front of a large bush in full summer bloom. Gregory watched as she cupped one of the fragrant white flowers, as delicate as a teacup, and brought it to her nose. She looked different to him. Fragile but not broken. This had changed her, too. But had she outgrown him?

The combined effort of the task in front of him, plus walking forty feet across the parking lot in that humidity, made him sweat profusely. He sidled up beside Liv and straightened himself in an effort to appear composed, despite the fact that he could wring out his polo shirt. The truth was that underneath the sweat, the shock of Phil's story, and a week of wretched sleep, he felt more like himself than he had in thirty years. The world was different when you didn't have to hide. Everything looked so damn beautiful, especially

Liv with her messy hair and tired face. He wanted to hug her, to promise her, to beg her. He wanted to drop to his knees and vow to be a different man with her. He wanted to grovel and pledge his heart, but he didn't, for fear it might scare her. He was still learning how to be this new person, himself.

"That's a rose of Sharon," he said, nodding at the bush. He stopped short of suggesting he could plant one by the garage. He didn't know if, after today, they would still be sharing an address.

The air had that unsettling quiet of hot days when the only noise was the buzzing from the power lines. He tried to find comfort in the summer lushness of this vast botanical garden, but that was the old Gregory who could be so easily consoled by nature alone. This Gregory needed people. He needed Liv and Carrie and Petey.

"Ready?" he said.

Liv nodded.

More now than ever, he wanted to reach for her hand, but he couldn't subject himself to the possibility of rejection. He had no idea where he stood. Instead, he did what he had come there to do. He asked her to follow him. They walked for several minutes, side by side, in muggy silence.

Once Gregory had located the right general area, he could almost follow his nose to Marigold Path, that small border of musky orange and yellow flowers that would always remind him of Mira.

Was she watching over him?

He found her gravestone easily this time, even though it looked different to him: less ominous and more ordinary—a rounded granite marker that in some ways seemed too simple for a woman of Mira's complexity. But there she was among the marigolds. Gregory stood in front of the stone, hands on his hips, appreciating her. One day soon he'd come back with flowers from his garden.

Liv stood beside him, reading what he now had memorized. He was desperate to pour out his explanation but had vowed to proceed with restraint. So he followed the plan he had created in his head that morning. He sat down in front of Mira's grave and patted the grass beside him.

Liv lowered herself to the ground several feet away and carefully adjusted her skirt around her thighs.

As they sat together in the sultry quiet of the afternoon, two flesh-bound humans among the grave markers, Gregory began to tell Liv everything, starting with his prayer to the beam of light in the garage and Mira appearing in his office the next day.

"Who did you think she was?" Liv said, speaking for the first time since they'd arrived. She was leaning in, her palms open in front of her like a plea. "I mean, Gregory, you're asking me to accept an explanation that is so far-fetched, so beyond the realm of our normal reality. You do know that, don't you?"

"I do, Liv. I do know that. But anything else wouldn't be the truth."

"Whose truth?

"*The* truth."

"Did you think she was a client?"

Gregory shrugged his confusion. "At some point I knew she was there to save my life."

Liv sat back again, and Gregory watched her try to make sense of what he would have rolled his eyes at just a month ago. "Go on," she said.

He told her every detail he could remember of his four Wednesday sessions with Mira, trying to answer thoughtfully whenever Liv interrupted with a question: *Could this all be some elaborate prank?* "I swear to you it is not." *Could you be having PTSD from the accident?* He shrugged at that.

He told her how, on their anniversary date at the club, he was disoriented by what had been happening with Mira. He felt understood by her, even forgiven. It made him think that he wanted to leave their marriage for Mira's acceptance. "But really, Liv," he said, his eyes searching hers, "I just wanted to leave the lie. And she seemed to be offering me a way to do that." He left out the part about being attracted to Mira and trying to kiss her. Liv didn't need to suffer any more for his sins.

When Liv ran her hands over her face, he didn't know if she was wiping away tears or sweat or both. "You could have told me, Gregory. At any point, you could have just told me what you'd done."

"But I couldn't have."

She drew her hands from her face and stared hard into his eyes. "Yes, you could have. On our first date here, you should have said something. I was so in love with you already, you could have told me anything."

"Anything? That I had murdered a person in a hit-and-run? Vehicular manslaughter? And that my best friend killed himself because of it? You wouldn't have let me drive you home."

"Then after we were married and had to make it work for the kids. Why not then?"

"When? As I was spooning out pasta on a Tuesday night?"

"We also had a private life."

"You know how you used to talk about the shame you felt growing up with your overachieving brother? How you just wanted to hide from your family, because they always made you feel less than?"

Liv's pursed lips and unwavering gaze were her assent.

"I was rotten with shame, Liv. And I would have lost you."

"And just like that, she"—Liv nodded at the grave—"she healed you?"

"She showed me how to heal myself."

Liv paused. "Were you in love with her?"

"I loved her because she helped me, but no." Gregory tracked Liv's eyes until they met his again. "I have only ever been in love with you."

Liv closed her eyes and shook her head. Gregory eased himself a foot closer. "I screwed up, Liv. I screwed up everything. I lied to you, to everyone. But mostly to you. I get that you can't trust me. I don't blame you. I don't know if I'd trust me either. But this is all I have left. I'm no longer that person, and I never will be again."

When Liv didn't fight back, Gregory tentatively reached out and put his hand on top of hers. That she let it stay gave him his first bit of hope. He ran a finger over the white band of flesh where her rings had been. "I won't ask you to forgive me," he said, struggling to sound calm, "but I'll take whatever you have. And if you say you can't do it, that it's over, well then"—he paused and squeezed his eyes shut—"well then, I'll have to accept that. But I'm not ready to give up on you." He looked out at the sea of gravestones and the waves of heat rising from the black asphalt paths. "Mira didn't save my life, Liv. You did. Every day for twenty-four years, you gave me a reason to live. I'm here because of you."

Liv brushed back the tears from her eyes and stared at Mira's gravestone, like a puzzle that she couldn't solve. After a moment, she tucked her hair back again and stood with conviction. "I'm sorry. I need some time."

Gregory started to get up, but she waved him back. Then she left, just walked off down the path without another word.

As he watched her go, he had to physically stop himself from chasing after her. All he could do was wait. If she didn't take him back, he would have to accept that. He thought his punishment for killing Mira was lugging around a sack of guilt for thirty years, but nothing could be more punishing than Liv leaving him now. The person who loved him so deeply, so unconditionally that she stayed with him, enduring his darkness, never giving up on their marriage, refusing to believe they weren't supposed to be together. He saw now that he'd let her down, not only by lying to her but by failing to support her passions and dreams. If she wanted to be a writer, then he'd tell her to quit her job and be a writer. If she wanted to tutor students after school or get another degree, he'd encourage her to do it. He would no longer let his past hold her back.

Her figure was getting more and more distant as she walked away from him beneath two-hundred-year-old trees. No matter what happened, he had kept his promise to tell her the truth.

Liv was far away, just a bright shape walking deeper into the shadows. Gregory felt like someone had inserted a sharp blade into his abdomen. He lay on the grass and shut his eyes. He was exhausted. And the heat. He widened his eyes in an effort to stay awake. There was Mira's name carved in dove-gray granite.

How did her parents choose this spot?

How did he find her here?

The letters and dates on the stone faded. "Mira," he whispered. "Please bring her back."

He shut his eyes and saw himself running through his house, each room unfolding in front of him like an empty box. He was calling out to her. *Liv. Liv.* He even shouted *Olivia*, as if he could reach back in time and find the college student who once trusted him. But no one answered. He was in his waiting room on Blesdow Street. It was empty, but someone was in the small office. *Liv? Is that you?* He pushed open the door to see Mira sitting at the table drinking tea and reading the letters Phil had written. *Can I help you?* she said. She drew her scarf from around her shoulders and handed it to him.

Gregory heard someone calling his name. He blinked his eyes open to find Liv standing above him. Her hair, released from its ponytail, hung over her face, and she looked just as she had on their first date. He wanted to reach out and touch her cheek. He didn't dare.

She leaned over and pressed her fingers on the top of his shoulder. "Come."

Gregory scrambled to his feet so fast he tripped and caught himself on Mira's headstone.

Liv took his hand, and he gripped back so tightly, she had to wriggle her fingers to loosen them. Then, in her determined way, she led him up the hill and down a smaller path. She walked with such sureness, Gregory realized she'd been there in the intervening years without him, searching for a way back into their marriage.

The weeping willow, more than two decades older than when they last sat beneath it, was solid and thick with long waxy strips of summer growth. Liv pulled Gregory inside the pale green sanctuary, where they stood together, cool and sheltered from the rays of the late-afternoon sun.

Liv blinked hard and began haltingly. "I tried to talk myself out of this, of us, but I couldn't. I'm not sure I can accept what you've told me, but I'm also not sure it matters. I love you. And I don't want to lose you."

Gregory put his hands on her shoulders. He could feel her strength beneath the softness. "You won't lose me. I'm here."

She looked at him, her gaze unwavering. "Are you?"

Gregory nodded with uncertainty. "Yes, I finally am. And if you give me the chance, I'll love you differently. Without shame. The way I've always wanted to love you."

"What if you can't? What if nothing changes between us?"

She started to look away, but he took her face in his hands and turned her head so their eyes were locked. "It already has."

After a moment, her tired eyes softened, and she nodded slowly.

Gregory pulled her to his chest. He pressed his lips into her hair. He was crying so hard he almost choked. "I'm going to make it up to you, Liv. I promise."

Her voice broke, but he could tell she was smiling. "And I'm going to hold you to it."

They stayed there for several minutes, reluctant to let each other go, but they finally did, without a word. Hand in hand they started back toward the car, just as the sun was beginning to set, coloring the sky pink, the lower edges deepening into magenta. As they walked down the hill, Gregory felt light, as though his feet weren't touching the ground. But then Liv stopped midstep and pulled him from his stride. She held herself still, listening closely, the way people do when they sense a shift in the weather.

ACKNOWLEDGMENTS

Publishing my novel has been the realization of a longtime dream. But the reality of working with Zibby Owens, Anne Messitte, Kathleen Harris, and the entire Zibby Books team has been better than a dream. I am deeply grateful to be part of a publishing family that not only values stories as the connective tissue of humanity, but also supports and nourishes authors, body and soul. Thank you to everyone at Zibby Books for making this process collaborative, rewarding, and joyful.

One of the best parts of this experience has been the friendships I've developed with my fellow ZB authors. I am grateful to have a posse of whip-smart writers who are with me on this wild ride.

Thank you to Jeanne McCulloch for your gentle manner and superb edits on my first rewrite. And to Christine Utz for thoughtfully shepherding me through the final one.

I wrote *Wednesdays at One* in isolation in the summer of 2020, but it took the following village of patient readers and insightful professionals to help turn that draft into a book. Each one of you has had an impact on these pages: Sara Backer, Alison Price Becker, Susan Keane, Olivia Kate Cerrone, Susan Curtin, Fae

ACKNOWLEDGMENTS

Engstrom, Christine Foster, Tim Grace, Paul Januszewski, Elizabeth Junod, Pete Lackey, Ellen Beth Lande, Marjorie Leary, Steve Maas, Margaret Moody, Connie Mooney, Steve Morgan, Helen Phillips, Edie Ravenelle, Victoria Redel, Laura Registrato, Katie Rimer, Emily Sharp, Emma Westwater, Lis Zimmerman.

Much gratitude to the Magnolia Park Writers who are always there with encouragement and deviled eggs: Catherine Carney, Elissa Jacobs, Alicia Jones, Eileen Kenneally, Sue McGovern, Denise Ouellette, Ann Wynne.

Thank you to my pod of cherished writer friends who, over shared meals, frantic phone calls, and back porch meetings under electric blankets, have provided edits, advice, love, and the inspiration I needed to keep going: Lynette Benton, Jane Delury, Erica Ferencik, Margaret Muirhead, Maureen Stanton.

Lisa Carey, you are that friend who knows how to help my heart *and* fix my words.

Holloway McCandless, wise friend, word sorceress, and fairy godmother to this book, I will always be grateful for the way you swooped in and worked your magic.

Thank you to my beloved girls, Diana Costello and Marilyn Osowiski. You keep me sane, honest, and connected to my past, where all my stories begin.

Betsy Miller, sister extraordinaire and fearless first reader, when I sent you those ridiculously rough pages each morning in the summer of 2020, you said exactly what I needed to hear: "I like it. Keep going."

Phineas and Adeline, thank you for understanding what this means to me and cheering all the way. I am bursting with love as I watch you put your own creative voices into the world. This one's for you.

Mark Santello, your experience and insights, your attention to therapeutic nuances, and the hours you spent poring over my pages helped make these characters real to me. You are a brilliant psychologist and an exacting editor, and I could not have written this book without you. Thank you for your support, your belief, your unwavering love. There's no one else I'd want to make this journey with.

ABOUT THE AUTHOR

Sandra A. Miller is the author of the award-winning memoir *Trove: A Woman's Search for Truth and Buried Treasure*. She has written about relationships and self-discovery for the *Boston Globe*, the *Christian Science Monitor*, the *Washington Post*, and many other publications. Her essay about her unconventional love story with her husband was made into the short film *Wait*, directed by Trudie Styler and starring Kerry Washington. She teaches writing at the University of Massachusetts, Lowell, and lives outside of Boston with her husband, with whom she has two grown children.

○ @sandra.a.miller

www.sandraamiller.com

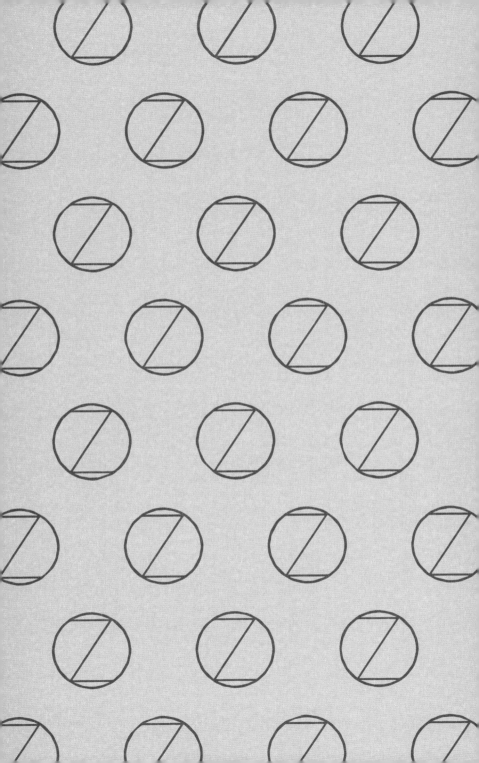

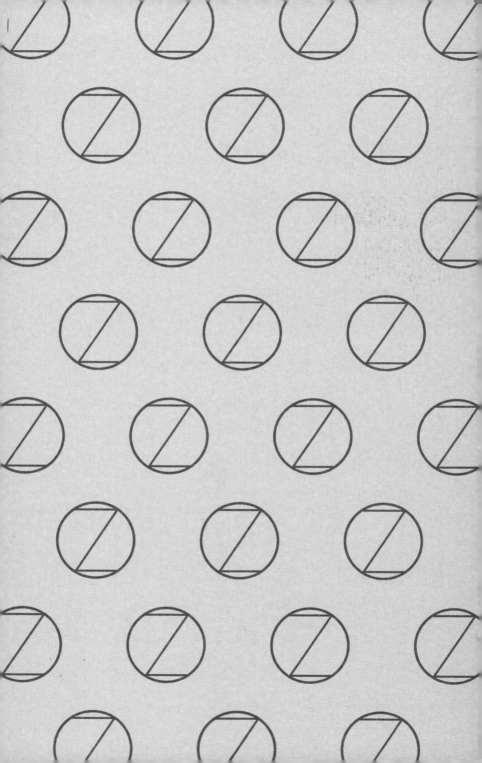